Footprints on the Horizon

**Also by Stephanie Grace Whitson
in Large Print:**

Secrets on the Wind
Watchers on the Hill
Valley of the Shadow
Edge of the Wilderness
Heart of the Sandhills

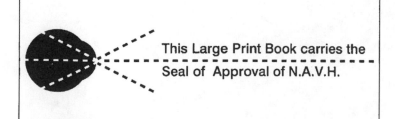

This Large Print Book carries the
Seal of Approval of N.A.V.H.

= 281 CR 1 DM

Footprints on the Horizon

Stephanie Grace Whitson

Thorndike Press • Waterville, Maine

Copyright © 2005 Stephanie Grace Whitson

Pine Ridge Portraits #3.

All rights reserved.

Published in 2005 by arrangement with
Bethany House Publishers.

Thorndike Press® Large Print Christian Historical Fiction.

The tree indicium is a trademark of Thorndike Press.

The text of this Large Print edition is unabridged.
Other aspects of the book may vary from the original edition.

Set in 16 pt. Plantin.

Printed in the United States on permanent paper.

Library of Congress Cataloging-in-Publication Data

Whitson, Stephanie Grace.
    Footprints on the horizon / by Stephanie Grace Whitson.
       p. cm. — (Pine Ridge portraits ; 3)
    ISBN 0-7862-8203-7 (lg. print : hc : alk. paper)
    1. World War, 1939–1945 — Nebraska — Fiction.
  2. Fort Robinson (Neb.) — Fiction.   3. Ex-prisoners of war
— Fiction.   4. Soldiers — Fiction.   5. Widows — Fiction.
6. Large type books.   I. Title.
PS3573.H555F66 2005b
813'.54—dc22   2005024590

For Daniel

As the Founder/CEO of NAVH, the only national health agency solely devoted to those who, although not totally blind, have an eye disease which could lead to serious visual impairment, I am pleased to recognize Thorndike Press* as one of the leading publishers in the large print field.

Founded in 1954 in San Francisco to prepare large print textbooks for partially seeing children, NAVH became the pioneer and standard setting agency in the preparation of large type.

Today, those publishers who meet our standards carry the prestigious "Seal of Approval" indicating high quality large print. We are delighted that Thorndike Press is one of the publishers whose titles meet these standards. We are also pleased to recognize the significant contribution Thorndike Press is making in this important and growing field.

Lorraine H. Marchi, L.H.D.
Founder/CEO
NAVH

* Thorndike Press encompasses the following imprints: Thorndike, Wheeler, Walker and Large Print Press.

A Word from the Author

Of the dozen novels I have in print, *Footprints on the Horizon* is my first historical novel set in the twentieth century. I never expected to be interested enough in events beyond 1900 to want to read the dozens of books and newspaper articles I usually ingest before tackling a new project. That changed a few years ago when I encountered the WWII exhibit at the Fort Robinson Museum in western Nebraska.

My overactive imagination had already been at work during my stay at the fort as I learned about Dull Knife and the Cheyenne Outbreak and stood, weeping, on the spot where Crazy Horse was killed. But then, on the second floor of the museum, I came around a corner and was startled by the figure of a man asleep on an army cot. Of course it was only a museum exhibit, but it was a realistic one, and it immediately drew me in (this was back in the day before museums had to shield exhibits behind Plexiglas boxes and barriers).

When I returned home I began reading

about German PWs in America. (The term was PW then . . . not POW.) Preliminary research raised the "what if " questions I have come to recognize as the seeds of a story I want to tell. What was it like, I wondered, for the very people whose sons were fighting against Germans in Europe to have Nazis working on their farms and ranches? How was it, I wondered, that these people interacted in such a way that more than a few of the prisoners returned to Nebraska after the war and became American citizens? How could lifelong friendships be forged between former enemies?

The book you hold in your hands is the result of my personal journey into the not-so-long-ago past in search of answers to these and a hundred other questions. But because it is a work of fiction, it combines experiences and accounts from many places in the United States where German prisoners were interred. For example, according to Tom Buecker, author of *Fort Robinson and the American Century*, a personnel shortage at Fort Robinson prevented the prisoners held there from working on the farms and ranches in the surrounding community. But in his book *Prisoners on the Plains*, Glenn Thompson tells of prisoners from other camps throughout Nebraska being transported — sometimes by farm wives — to jobs in their respective communities where they did everything from working in town bakeries to harvesting apples and sugar beets. Therefore, your author's disclaimer is this: While documented precedent does exist for the events in my story, details regarding exact locale have been adjusted to accommodate the fictional lives of my imaginary friends.

Prologue

March 1945
Four Pines Ranch

People who make a point of "wanting the plain truth" fall into two categories: liars and fools. And that *is* the truth or my name isn't Clara Joy Jackson — which, of course, it is, even if most of Dawes County, Nebraska, doesn't know it. I've been called CJ for over half a century, so most of my neighbors don't even know what that C and that J stand for, which is fine with me. I never liked the name Clara and it's been sixty-six years since I was what my mama — may the good Lord rest her soul — called her "little bundle of joy."

But back to the topic at hand, that being "the truth." The main truth that controls my every waking moment these days is this: America is at war. The impact of that bit of truth didn't really hit me personally until Johnny showed up at the ranch-house door in a United States Army uniform. Before that moment, calving and foaling and gentling yearlings and mending fence and

11

putting up hay and the thousand other things on my rancher's chore list kept the war literally "over there."

Before Johnny enlisted, I did what I could to avoid thinking about the war. The good Lord said to "be anxious for nothing," and I seem to have the ability to do that. If I can fix it, I do. If I can't, I don't worry over it. I may wear out my knees talking to the good Lord about a thing or two, but once I've done that, I'm usually able to leave it where it belongs — with Him. And that's how I had handled the war up until Johnny enlisted. Every Sunday in church I prayed right along with everyone else for an Allied victory. I contributed old machinery to the iron drive and used kitchen cookware to the tin drive. I saved grease after reading a formula in the *Crawford Tribune* that told us how many tablespoons of fat yielded how many pounds of dynamite and such. Who would have ever thought that draining the grease off bacon could be patriotic? Shoot, I even sacrificed my ration card to my niece, Jo, so she could get herself some of those nylons she likes so much. Oops . . . there I go . . . talking about "the truth" and bending it in the same speech. The truth is, giving Jo my ration card didn't take a bit of sacrifice on my part because one thing this old girl does not have a need for is nylon stockings. I only own one dress, and when I put on my dress boots with it I don't show any leg at all. No, I don't need any nylons — that's for sure.

As I was saying, until Johnny showed up in that uniform, I was doing my best to let the Lord handle the big picture while I continued to breed the best horses I knew how and raise the best beef possible — which is no different from what we've done here at the Four Pines since my daddy, the late Caleb Jackson, bought the place. As far as I was concerned, God and the army could take care of Hitler and Mussolini and company. But then Johnny signed on — along with his best friends, Paul Hunter and Delmer Clark — and that brought the war off the front page of the newspaper and right to my front door in the panhandle of Nebraska.

John Boone Bishop is the kind of boy every woman dreams about when she day-dreams about her grown son. He's good-looking and respectable, strong and loyal. Shoot, I'm making him sound like one of those dogs over in the K-9 corps at Fort Robinson. Don't think that. Johnny's about half full of mischief and trouble. But he's not at all meanspirited. Just spirited.

13

Which, I suppose, is why he aimed for the air corps. He wanted to be a pilot, but instead he's part of the crew. On a B-17.

I shouldn't be surprised at his wanting to fly. I can remember way back to when he had to climb up on a tree stump to get aboard his horse. Before we'd go riding up into the bluffs, Johnny would look into the distance — a person can see halfway to heaven from atop one of our bluffs out here in the Pine Ridge area — and he'd watch the eagles riding the wind and then hold out his arms and pretend to do the same. He thought it was fun to get right to the edge of a cliff and look down on where the mountain goats had made a path along the rim of a drop-off. It scared me to death the way he always wanted to climb up to the highest point and go to the edge. That's because years ago his daddy, Will, darn near got killed when he and I climbed higher than a human ought to climb. But Johnny never got hurt. He always has loved the heights, and now he has his wings. Will and I are proud and scared to death all at the same time.

I fell in love with Johnny the day he came to live at the Four Pines. Will stepped down from his pickup with a bundle in his arms and limped up onto the porch. Will always limps when he's burdened down — whether it's bone-weariness or heart-weariness, doesn't matter. Anyway, Will limped up onto the porch and pulled the corner of the blanket back so I could see that baby boy's face, and that was it for me. You see, Johnny looks just like his daddy, and it's no secret that I've loved Will Bishop all my life, so there was nothing to do but love Johnny, too.

"Well," Will said slowly, like he always talks when he's got a lot to say. "Here we are, CJ."

"Welcome home, Will," I said. My eyes still fill up with tears just thinking about it, even though that was nearly twenty years ago. I had a huge lump in my throat, and I couldn't say anything else right then, but I patted Will's shoulder and led him inside. We had coffee — strong and black, just like Will likes it — and then we headed down to the cabin my old foreman, Ted Cramer, had just vacated, and both Will and Johnny have been here at the Four Pines ever since.

Now the liars in Dawes County would have all kind of things to tell you about Will Bishop and CJ Jackson if you were to ask to "hear the truth." They would say I kicked Will off the ranch when he took a liking to a little slip of a woman up the line in Whitney.

Or they would say that Will and Mamie were never really married and they only stayed together because there was a baby coming, and they'd probably say that I took Will back because it was the only way I could have a child to raise.

The fools of Dawes County have a different version of "the truth," which is much more entertaining than the liars' version, but no less foolishness.

So I will tell you the real truth about Will and Johnny Bishop and CJ Jackson. As I said, I have loved Will Bishop for as long as I can remember. I loved him so much that when he asked me to marry him I said "no." Because I knew that the one sure way to kill our friendship was for us to get married. The Good Book says that wives are supposed to submit to their husbands, and I am here to tell you that the man who has what it takes to make CJ Jackson submit to male foolishness has yet to be found on God's green earth. I am as good a rancher as ever owned land in Nebraska, and I don't need a man telling me what pasture to use or which stallion to breed to my mares or how to negotiate a better price for the hay I sell to the remount at Fort Robinson. I just don't need the interference — even from a man as good as Will Bishop.

So when Will proposed marriage, I looked him square in the eye and said, "Will, I love you with all the heart God gave me to love a man. But I won't marry you. Now don't bring it up again." And, to his credit, Will didn't. He didn't moon about, either. It did surprise me a little when, a few months later, he married Mamie. But Will is neither a fool nor a liar, and he knew he'd heard the truth when he proposed to me the first time, so there was no need to make a big fuss.

Just about the greatest heartbreak of my life is the knowledge that Mamie Parsons never had one whit of appreciation for what a wonderful man she had. Mamie was one of the fools who wanted a truth of her own making. Will told her he wanted to ranch. Mamie heard, "Just give me a few more years to save up and we'll move to town." Will told her that sometimes he was slow and tired because of the accident. Mamie heard, "I'll only be able to dance two or three dances at parties." Will told her she'd have to be careful with money. Mamie heard, "We'll have to buy last year's model instead of a brand-new car."

Right from the start, Mamie's foolishness rearranged Will's truthful words. No one realized how bad it was. Mamie got pregnant right away. Now don't be shocked because I said that word. I know there are some women who just don't think it's polite. But for heaven's sake, I breed horses. Pregnant is a *good* word. Usually. But Mamie Bishop's reaction to pregnancy made me worry for Will. She said all the right words when people congratulated her, but I could tell something wasn't right about it.

Johnny was barely weaned when Mamie disappeared. Will took it bad. I stayed away, not wanting people to gossip. Of course, that didn't do a bit of good. It only hurt Will, and the gossip didn't stop. But not everyone in Dawes County is a fool or a liar, and thankfully, someone did the right thing. My phone rang one night and a voice said, "Will Bishop and that baby need you." *Click.* That was it. I don't know who called, but I'm glad they did because the next morning, when I went to Will's place, I saw how right they were.

Johnny was screaming with a combination of hunger and hurt. He had the worst case of diaper rash I'd ever seen. Well, all right. I'd never really seen all that much diaper rash, but Johnny's was bad. Will took one look at me and burst into tears. He was so low he didn't even try to talk, just handed me Mamie's note.

I cannot live the way you want me to live.

Do not try to find me.

That was it. Not even a word about her own child.

"I've lost the ranch, CJ," Will said. Blubbered, really. "I've lost my wife and my ranch."

I didn't believe the last part, but it turned out to be true. Will was mortgaged to the hilt — and trying to please Mamie did him in.

"Plenty of people have lost ranches, Will Bishop," I snapped back. "You get yourself straightened up and get this baby into town to see Doc Whitlow. And when you've got whatever it takes to fix that boy's raw bottom, you get packed up and come home. Rachel's as old as dirt, but she's spry as they come and she will love having a baby to tend." Rachel Greyfoot, may God rest her soul, was Lakota Sioux, and she came to the Four Pines with my parents and never left. "I'll have Ted moved out in an hour and the place will be ready for you. He's worthless and I need you."

I need you. When Will heard those words, his shoulders heaved and his whole body shuddered. Then he raised his chin and stood tall. He didn't look me in the eye, but he said, "I told you Ted didn't have what it takes."

Of course I was tempted to throw those words right back at him because that was exactly what I had said to him when he told me about Mamie. *"She doesn't have what it takes to be a rancher's wife, Will. And you'd know it if you could see past that tiny little waist and those big blue eyes and look into her soul. That girl's all fluff and no substance."*

I could tell Will was remembering the very same thing, because he literally took a step back and his jaw began to work like he was clenching his teeth to prepare for a blow.

My friendship with Will probably turns on three moments in our lives. The first was when Will, who was an officer's child and therefore from a world I had no part in, chose to do a kindness for "the ranch girl" who was the school outcast. The second was when I said no to his proposal of marriage. And this was the third. It took everything in me to do what I did next, which was to nod my head and say as softly as I could — softness just doesn't come naturally to me, you know — "Yes. You did. I should have listened."

Will blinked a few times when he heard me say that. Tears welled up in his eyes again, and for a minute I thought I was

20

going to have to snap him out of it — again. But he gave a little shake of his head and swallowed hard. "If we don't drive in tonight, don't worry." He looked around him, and I think maybe he had the feeling of waking from a bad dream. He put his hand on the edge of the table that was piled high with dirty — and I do mean dirty — dishes and said, "I want to clean this place up. It won't do for Chase to see it this way when he comes out to look it over for the bank sale."

"I'll do it while you're in town at the doctor's." Of course it was only natural for me to offer, but the minute I said it I wished I hadn't. Sometimes a man needs to clean up his own mess, and I realized this was one of those times.

Will just shook his head. "I'll see to it." He looked around some more. "May take a while." And then Will Bishop surprised me — which isn't easy for a friend to do when you've known each other nearly your whole lives. He laughed. "May take a long while."

"You don't know the first thing about cleaning a house or doing up laundry," I protested.

"Sure I do," he said. "Learned how to do it all since I got married."

Apparently Miss Mamie was even less of a

ranch wife than I had thought.

He went to Johnny then, and as soon as that baby saw his daddy, he smiled all over himself. Will reached out his finger, and Johnny latched on to it with his little hand. And so, the next morning the Bishop men came home to the Four Pines ranch. And Johnny took possession of the corners of my heart that hadn't already been given over to Will.

The fools and the liars of Dawes County are right about one thing: The bond between Will Bishop and CJ Jackson is enduring. They just don't know the details, which is fine with me. If there's one thing I can't stand, it's people putting their nose into business that isn't theirs to be in. Which is exactly what I said to Will the other day when he told me he thought I was little better than a traitor to my country and our Johnny if I did what I planned to do.

One

Yea, mine own familiar friend,
in whom I trusted,
which did eat of my bread,
hath lifted up his heel against me.

PSALM 41:9

The fact that Will Bishop had loved Clara Joy Jackson for over half a century made raising his rifle and taking aim at her kitchen window harder than he expected it to be. His hand shook as he peered around the cab of his truck. He'd argued with himself half the morning about it. Even after he saw CJ leave for town, he hesitated. But he couldn't come up with anything better to get the bullheaded woman's attention. So here he was, crouching down, resting the rifle barrel atop the truck bed siding and closing his eyes, wishing he could think of another way.

He'd argued until he was blue in the face all through the winter — which was something, considering he rarely said more than three or four words at a time. He'd even called her Clara Joy just like her mother used to when CJ was in real trouble. But no amount of arguing could make the foolish old woman change her mind.

Their biggest blowout had occurred a few days ago. "I don't care if they're blue-skinned orangutans from the North Pole," CJ had said. "The remount depot has a few thousand hungry horses and mules depending on Four Pines hay, and there's a long line of neighbors just waiting for me to give up so they can put their name on the dotted line." CJ slammed her coffee mug down and went to the window — the very window Will was now planning to shoot out. With her back to him, she said, "Last fall I had to ask *Clarissa and Ben* to come out and lend a hand with the haying, Will. I was that desperate. And it's only going to be worse this year. The war just keeps going and more local boys keep leaving. There's no other way." She nodded toward the southeast, where, little more than a dozen miles from the ranch, a prisoner of war compound had been added to the Fort Robinson remount depot operation. "If the Germans will work, I'll be glad to have 'em."

Will brought up what he thought was his

best argument yet. "Our own United States War Department says the Nazis are fanatics who would rather kill themselves than be captured. Now, I know that's likely a touch of propaganda, but, CJ, we just can't have them roaming the farms and ranches out here. It's too far from one place to the next — too far from help if there's trouble."

"They won't be roaming. And there won't be trouble. It's not forced labor. The Geneva Convention wouldn't allow that. They'll be paid for their work."

"And you feel all right about that?" Will argued. "Paying the enemy?"

CJ snorted. "You were at the meeting when they explained how it works. They don't earn cash. It's just coupons to spend at the post exchange."

"Don't matter," Will said a little louder than he was wont to talk. "It still ain't right."

She turned around and faced him. "You stuck by me through the dirty '30s, Will. You were there when we had to slaughter cattle because we couldn't feed 'em, when the oats didn't grow and corn was little more than a dried ear with no kernels. Nature is finally beginning to smile on the Sandhills again, and I can't believe you want me to lose out because I don't have

25

the manpower to manage nature's bless-
ings."

"Folks won't stand for it, CJ. You can't
expect them to forget what they've been
told. You can't expect them to have forgotten the last war, either. It wasn't that
long ago."

"Abel Wilson from Phelps County was up
here at the last remount sale, and he's already been using PW labor from Camp At-
lanta. Hasn't had a bit of trouble. His own
wife picks the prisoners up and drives them
back at the end of the day. They eat at the
same table with the Wilson family for lunch.
Shoot, Will, half the people around here
have roots in Germany. People know better
than to think every PW is a Nazi." CJ ran
her fingers through her short gray hair and
adjusted her glasses. She always adjusted
her glasses when she was being stubborn —
almost like she appeared to be considering
another person's viewpoint when what she
was really doing was waiting for them to see
things her way. Will could almost imagine a
stubborn teenager inside her. "It's my decision," she said. "I'm turning in the request
forms Monday."

"I won't stand for it," Will said, raising
his voice just a little to make his point.

CJ's blue eyes were cold. "You don't have

to agree. But you do have to be civil and work alongside 'em. Or . . . or else." She snatched her hat off the hook by the back door and left.

After the door slammed behind her, Will had watched out the kitchen window. She headed across the road to the old barn. He could picture her storming around in there, jerking up buckets of oats for the horses, mucking out stalls, muttering to the memory of her father who had built the barn with his bare hands . . . and giving a thousand reasons why she was right and "that old fool Will Bishop" was addled. The more he thought about CJ and that "or else" she'd tossed out, the angrier he got. He could take a lot from CJ Jackson. Most of the time he liked her spit and fire. But when she drew *that* line in the Sandhills, a man had to do what a man had to do. Love the woman or not, love the land or not, he was not going to stand around while some Nazi cut hay in the very field where his Johnny had learned to ride. Times might be tough and help might be scarce, but hiring Nazi prisoners was *not* the right answer. It just couldn't be.

So Will followed her out to the barn.

"What are you going to say to Johnny?" he blurted out just inside the door. "He's over

27

there right now in the line of fire. What are you going to say when he comes home and finds out you hired the very men who might have killed his friends?"

For a moment, Will thought he'd finally gotten through to her. She tossed a pitchfork full of hay into the corner of the empty stall, and when she looked at him she had tears in her eyes. She swallowed. But then she took a deep breath and said in that quiet voice that was worse than shouting, "I'm gonna throw my arms around him and say welcome home. I'm gonna tell him I did what I had to do so that he'd have a home to come back *to*." Anger flickered in the blue eyes. "And I'll thank you not to try to use the blood of my friends and neighbors to coerce me."

Now as Will crouched behind his rusting blue pickup and replayed the scene over in his mind, he couldn't help feeling bad. The old woman was right about one thing. Bringing Johnny and the other boys from Dawes County into it probably wasn't fair. And while Vernon Clark had said he'd shoot his herd and burn his fields before he'd let one "Kraut" set foot on his place, there were other people just as firm in their beliefs that it was only practical to use the labor that was available, no matter what language it spoke. But Will agreed with Vernon Clark, and it was Clark's blustering that gave Will the idea to fake a little vandalism on the Four Pines.

Maybe, he reasoned, if CJ understood how strong some folks felt about things, just maybe she would reconsider. So he'd waited for her to head into Crawford with her paper work requesting prison labor, and then he whitewashed *Nazi Lover* across the front porch. At the last minute he decided that maybe shooting out a window — which he would fix before nightfall — would put some muscle into the protest. He knew it was a desperate thing, and he felt bad about it, but he was compelled to convince CJ that the boots that had clicked together to the sound of "Heil Hitler" should never be allowed to touch Four Pines soil.

Grunting softly, Will raised his rifle and took aim. He'd been squatting for a while, arguing with himself about whether or not he was going too far, and his weak leg pained him. Just as he was about to squeeze the trigger, his leg went out from under him. His chin hit the edge of the truck bed so hard he saw stars. As he slid to the ground the rifle went off, harmlessly aimed toward the sky. His ears were still ringing when he realized someone was coming up the road.

He saw a flash of red top the hill on the horizon. Scrambling to his feet, he limped the two steps to the cab of his truck, but he was too slow.

CJ had barely skidded to a stop when she hollered out the passenger side window of the red pickup she called Sadie, "What's going on?"

As both his vision and his hearing cleared, Will slapped the dust off his backside and stepped to the front of his truck. Staring across the hood of his own truck, he stammered, "I tho-tho-thought you went to town."

"Left one of the forms on my desk," CJ grumbled as she started to climb out of the truck. Then she paused halfway out, holding the door, staring in the direction of the house . . . and the whitewashed lettering just to the right of the front door. Her mouth fell open. Closing her door, she walked toward Will's truck and peered in the bed of his truck . . . at the can of whitewash and the paintbrush. She stared at Will, then at the rifle still in his hand. Turning around to face the house again, she ran her fingers through her hair. She adjusted her glasses before turning her head to glare at Will.

In that moment, Will would have given

everything he'd ever owned to make up for what he had done, which, he could see in CJ's eyes, was to hurt her to the very core. "You've just got to listen to me, CJ," he begged. "You cannot do this. You will alienate neighbors for miles around, and no matter what you think, you will never be able to explain it to Johnny in a way he'll understand. We can't have Nazis on the place, girl. Why can't you understand that?"

CJ just stood there. She, who was never one to mince words, didn't say anything. After too many moments of brittle silence, she set her mouth, lifted her chin, straightened her shoulders, and headed for the old barn. She emerged with a bucket in one hand and a rag in the other.

"I'll do it," Will said, and reached for the bucket. CJ ignored him. She walked across the road to the cistern, filled the bucket with water, stepped up on the porch, and began to scrub at the whitewash. As the lettering melted into milky streaks, Will turned away and, rifle in hand, headed along the well-worn path to the only place in the world he had ever felt at home. Inside his cabin, he sat down at the table and put his head in his hands, trying to muster up the energy to pack.

If my heart hadn't already been broken into a thousand pieces by that whitewash on the house, it would have broken the next morning when Will knocked on the back door. He *knocked,* mind you. Like some stranger. As if I hadn't been sitting at the kitchen table watching him walk up the path from his cabin, knowing something was on his mind because his bad leg was dragging a little. As if I hadn't been there since 5:30 a.m., like I've been every morning since I was a young girl waiting to tag alongside my papa when he made his way down to the barn or out to the herd.

Will knocked like he was a visitor, and after that there just wasn't much to say. I went to the door and stood there hating how awkward things felt between us and wishing Will would cross over the divide and end it. Shoot, I don't even know if I needed to hear an apology. I hadn't delivered the papers yet, and I was beginning to think maybe I wouldn't. The truth is, if he would have just come in and poured himself coffee like always, I probably would have buried the whitewash issue and thrown out the papers requesting PW help, and never brought it up again.

But Will knocked. So I went to the door and stood there and waited for him to say what was on his mind.

"C-called up Bill Harker over at the remount," he said. "They've got trainloads of horses coming in for resale. Said he'd be happy to have me."

I think he was waiting for me to ask him not to go. To say I'd been wrong. I didn't.

He cleared his throat. "So I'll be headed out come Monday."

"No need to wait," I said. "Might as well get yourself settled before you start work."

We stood there staring at each other for a minute, like two old boxers waiting to see who was going to start the next round, and finally Will turned and headed for his cabin. I went back inside and sat down at the kitchen table. I couldn't quite get my mind around the idea that Will and Johnny's cabin was going to be empty come Monday morning. I suspected Will would probably leave while I was at church Sunday. All of a sudden I wondered where he'd be leaving *for.* From what I'd seen down at Fort Robinson the last time I checked in with the head of the breeding program, they were hard-pressed to keep roofs over the heads of the soldiers coming in, let alone add a civilian to the mix. Things had really changed in recent years. Back in the '30s, it wasn't unusual for a married man and his wife to end up with a six- or seven-room officer's house all to themselves. But that had changed since Fort Robinson was named the central remount station for the cavalry. Horses by the thousands were being cycled in and back out again as the army switched over from hayburners to gas hogs. As if the Remount Division wasn't enough, the army decided to train its war dogs out here, too. That meant a whole new compound full of buildings, kennels for over a thousand dogs, and the staff to run it all.

And with the addition of a prisoner of war camp, Fort Robinson just plain ran out of beds. Men were taking rooms in towns as far away as Chadron — and that is twenty-eight long miles away, especially in the winter, when snow can drift over the two-lane highway in less than an hour. I wondered just where the animal superintendent thought he was going to put a civilian employee.

I got up and went to the kitchen door and opened it. "Will," I called. He was halfway down the path by then. When he stopped he cupped his left ear with his hand so he could hear me better. "There's no need for you to move out. The Four Pines has been your home all this time. You can drive the forty-five minutes to work. We've got the gas allowance to do it, even with the rationing."

He seemed to consider the idea, but then he shook his head. "Bill's assigning me to training and conditioning. Says he needs a good hand with a couple of the stallions they want put out to civilians in the breeding program. He said there's one for sure that needs some sense worked into his head. I'll probably set up camp in one of the barns so's I can keep an eye on things." He shrugged. "It's for the best."

To hear Will Bishop say he preferred a barn to his own home on the Four Pines hurt so much it made me mad. "All right, Will," I said, "whatever you think." And I slammed the door as soon as I said it. I didn't even watch Will walk away. Instead, I tore out the front door and headed off up the road, walking as fast as I could while I told God exactly what I thought of Will Bishop and Vernon Clark and all the other idiots in Dawes County who couldn't see beyond their own prejudice against Germans to notice God's own answer to our concerns about the manpower shortage on our ranches and farms.

"They're like that fool on the roof in the flood, Lord," I said out loud. I tend to talk

35

out loud to the Lord when things are really churning inside me. "You know the story I mean. Those folks are on the roof watching the water swirl around them and praying for help. And a man comes by in a leaky boat and they turn him away because God is going to answer their prayer. And then they drown and go to heaven and ask you why you didn't answer the prayer and you say, 'I sent you a boat! Why didn't you get in it?' That is not me, Lord. I've got the faith to ask you for help and the sense to see when you send it and I don't *care* how it's dressed. Whether it says *PW* on their shirts or not, they are young and strong and I need 'em. Now why can't Will see that?"

And there I was, walking my Sandhills, talking to God, crying. I cry when I get mad. And I was *mad.* Finally, I said, "Well, Lord, I guess I can thank you I had the sense to stay single, because you surely know I would never have submitted to this foolishness about not using German manpower on the Four Pines." I turned around then and looked back down the hill toward where my ranch lay, nestled beside a spring-fed pond in the low spot of a thousand hills of sand.

Now a lot of folks from the city come out here and think all they see is nothing. "It's so empty," they say. But it's not empty. Not to someone who has the eyes to see. A person can see nearly all the way to heaven from the top of the ridge that looks down on my ranch. There's not a tree or another house in sight. Just miles and miles of rolling hills where the soil is mostly sand and only the toughest grasses stick. It's that tough grass that makes the best grazing in the world. And it's the fact you can see where you are that makes me love it so.

The sun was high in a bright blue sky, and the pond was glowing like one of them sapphires you see in the fancy jewelry shops. I closed my eyes and took a deep breath, inhaling the sweet aroma of warm earth that promised prairie blossoms in the near future. Then I looked toward the old barn my papa built right across the road from the house, remembering how I held some of the boards in place while he nailed them up. The house is the work of his hands, too — at least most of it. There was a little two-room cabin made of cedar logs when Papa and Mama moved onto the place with their new baby, Clara Joy, but Papa added a big open loft. He always wanted a "passel of boys" to fill up that loft, but the Good Lord only gave Laina and Caleb Jackson two children, and both girls at that. It frustrated Mama somewhat that I was more interested in being

Pa's right-hand "man" than I was in learning to cook, but sixteen years after I was born, she finally had another little girl who was exactly what Mama thought a lady should be. That's Clarissa, and never were two girls more different than my sister and me. I won ribbons at the county fair for my calves while Clarissa won ribbons for her fancy work.

When Clarissa started to date, she never gave the local ranchers' sons a glance. She went for town boys all the way, and she finally landed one — and a preacher at that. My ma and pa took their religion very seriously, so they were thrilled when Ben Hale proposed to Clarissa. And I must say that, while I don't have the fancy words Ben has, I know in my heart what's right and what's not, and I look forward to Sundays and Ben's sermons. He has a way of saying things that brings a little bit of heaven itself right into the church. There have been times I have gone to church more out of duty than anything else — and to avoid Clarissa's Monday morning phone call wondering where I was — and right when I expect it the least, God speaks to me the most.

Anyway, I stood up on the hill looking down at my ranch and the work of my father's hands — and mine, too, because I've added a bigger barn and more corrals by the south spring — and a new head wrangler's cabin. For Will and Johnny. But Will was leaving the Four Pines. Maybe for good. I felt like I had just been kicked by a yearling foal — which, if you have ever experienced such a thing, you will understand is a powerful kind of hurt. All of a sudden, I wasn't mad anymore. I was just hurt, with a deep-down kind of hurt that only a man can give a woman when she loves him. Now, I remind you — I know I love Will. So that wasn't the thing that made me cry. It was just the whole business that we couldn't come to agree — or at least to agree to disagree — and get on with the business of ranching together.

As I stood there, looking down on my ranch, a kind of loneliness settled over me such as I hadn't felt since Will married Mamie Parsons. *"What will you say to Johnny?"* Will had asked. And right now I wanted to ask him the same thing. What would he say when Johnny came home and found his papa had moved out of the only real home they had ever had?

Being all emotional about things and talking about feelings and such has never been my cup of tea. But I can tell you that right then, standing up on the hill and looking down on the only part of the world that had ever mattered to me, I blubbered like a baby. It just seemed like I was caught between two impossible things. Not having enough help might mean losing the Four Pines. But not having Will and Johnny on the place . . .

So I told God I would delay delivering the papers requesting PW help until tomorrow, and I asked Him to change my mind — if it needed changing — and to give me wisdom to know what to do and the courage to admit I was wrong — if I was, which I doubted. And then I made myself stop crying and headed toward the old barn. I told myself I just wouldn't think about it anymore, and for most of that afternoon I managed to keep my mind on the ranch and off Will. And it worked — mostly — until supper, which I ate alone because Will just didn't show up.

I was standing at the kitchen window washing my plate when I saw the light come on in Will's cabin, and in spite of all the pep talks I'd given myself that day, I considered walking down there and begging him to stay. I considered tearing up the request forms I was set to deliver to the county agent the next morning. I lay awake most of the night, asking God over and over again about what I should do. Part of me wanted God to convince me I'd been wrong. Part of me wanted to walk down to Will's place and knock on the door and say I was wrong. But then it was dawn, and as much as I had tried to think of a way around it, I could not think I had done anything wrong in accepting the help I felt God had provided in answer to my prayers.

And so, when morning came, I climbed into my old Chevy pickup and headed into the county agent's office in Crawford and filed my request for German PW help. I didn't stop by Clarissa and Ben's. I had had enough arguing and just did not need any more advice, which Clarissa would feel obligated to give. When I got back to the ranch, Will was gone. He had left a note on the table. All it said was *You can reach me at the remount if you need anything. Will you please make sure I get Johnny's letters?*

It rankled me that Will felt he had to ask me to bring him his own son's letters. As if I wouldn't. I sat and stared at the note for a long while before walking down to Will's cabin and going in. I had already decided I would leave Johnny's things in his room so that when he finally came home he could pick right up with ranch life. Maybe he would want to be my head wrangler. Maybe by then Will would have come to his senses and moved home.

I headed into Johnny's room, thinking I'd use his bedding to drape the sofa and such — to sort of close things up temporarily, like families do to their summer lake houses and what not. But I never went into Johnny's room. I just stood at the doorway and stared at the empty walls and the empty place under Johnny's bed where he had kept an old footlocker full of treasures. Empty. Empty. Empty. Will had emptied the place of any trace of himself and Johnny, save for the faint aroma of Old Spice aftershave.

It made me so mad I cried.

Two

*The angel of the Lord encampeth
about them that fear him,
and delivereth them.*

PSALM 34:7

"I won't have it!" Clarissa Hale slammed both palms down on the kitchen tabletop and leaped out of her chair.

"Now, Mother —"

"I am *not* your mother, Benjamin Hale!" She glared, first at her husband and then at Jo. "Do you *hear* what your daughter is saying?" She reached up and swept a once-blond curl off her once-smooth forehead. "She doesn't see a problem with her going to the ranch? She doesn't see a reason for us to worry?!" Touching her own graying hair brought Clarissa's attention to Jo's golden tresses. The unruly tumble of curls that made Clarissa feel slovenly transformed her daughter's face into a gilt-framed Renaissance portrait, which irritated Clarissa even more.

43

"How many times do I have to ask you not to come to the table looking like Tarzan's Jane?!" Clarissa motioned toward the doorway that led first into the living room, and from there into a small back hall and two bedrooms. "Go fix your hair and calm down. We'll talk later."

The girl frowned. "*I'm* not the one who needs to calm down," she said beneath her breath — just loud enough for her father to hear.

Benjamin Hale suddenly seemed to have trouble with his pipe. He withdrew it from his mouth, inspected the bowl, and then tapped it gently on the edge of the table.

"Don't you dare take her side against me," Clarissa said. "And stop fussing with that pipe." She reached for the pipe, then thought better of it and sat back down. "It's just not right for you to smoke, and you know it. What would the congregation think if they knew their pastor was a secret smoker?"

The Reverend Benjamin Hale took a maddeningly long time to fiddle with his pipe. When he finally spoke, he didn't address the smoking issue. "I can't say as I see any reason Jo shouldn't spend her summer out on the ranch, same as she has every summer of her life."

Clarissa's cheeks blazed red. "You can't be serious."

"Oh," Benjamin said, leaning back and smiling at his daughter, who had just returned from combing her hair and was standing in the kitchen doorway fluttering her eyelashes at him, "but I am."

"You two," Clarissa said. Jumping up from the table again, she went to the stove and, lifting a lid, took a taste, made a face, and added salt before replacing the lid. "I never could do a thing with either of you."

"Don't cry, Mama," Jo said, and settled back at the table.

"I'm not crying!" Clarissa opened the oven door, retrieved a pie, and straightened back up. She glared at her husband. "I suppose you'll spend our gas ration taking her out there, too."

"No need," Ben said. "CJ can take her home with her some Sunday after church."

Clarissa plunked the pie onto the hand-crocheted hot pad in the middle of the table.

"Mmmm," Ben said, inhaling deeply. "Smells wonderful."

"Humph," was all Clarissa could say.

"You make the best apple pie in the county, Clarissa Jackson." Ben got up from his chair and wrapped his arms around his wife.

Clarissa pretended to struggle. "Just because that line got you a date when I was single doesn't mean it will work now. And this isn't apple pie, anyway. It's soda crackers and spices."

"That's my girl," Ben said, nuzzling her hair. "Doing her part to conserve and still winning blue ribbons at the fair."

"Where are you going now?" Clarissa said to her daughter, who was headed for the back door.

"Out to do *my* part — plant the victory garden."

The door slammed shut before either parent could respond.

"That girl," Clarissa said, sitting back down at the table, "is out of control. Entertaining at the Servicemen's Club, coming in late, running around with Delores Black. Last week Josephine wanted to go over to the Sioux Theatre and see a matinee. On *Sunday*."

Ben offered up his plate for a slice of cracker pie. "It was Ronald Reagan and Ann Sheridan." He grinned up at his wife. "Even *you* like Ronald Reagan. And I don't see how singing 'America the Beautiful' at the Servicemen's Club on a Saturday evening is going to lead Jo down a wrong path. There's nothing wrong with giving the boys from Fort Robinson a wholesome way to spend their free time. Crawford doesn't have much to offer in comparison to New York City, and according to Tom Hanson, a lot of the new recruits are from big cities. He said they step off the train out at the fort and look around like they've just landed in the wilderness. Which, I guess, if you are used to Manhattan, it is."

"All the more reason to keep Josephine away from them," Clarissa said, "and probably the reason Delores is so interested. That girl is trouble waiting to happen."

Ben shrugged. "High-spirited, maybe. A trifle under-disciplined, probably. But Mrs. Black has not had an easy time raising a daughter alone. Tom seems to think she's done a good job of it."

"Tom Hanson's judgment about Stella Black has been blinded by a twenty-two-inch waistline and a permanent wave."

"Now, Clarissa —"

Clarissa returned to her original subject. "Josephine has no business being out at the ranch this summer, Ben. Not with my sister insisting she's going to hire prison labor." She shivered. "Will Bishop certainly had a thing or two to say about it, and Josephine is not even his child. I cannot begin to understand how her own father can just glibly

47

wave good-bye and let his little girl go."

"Will's thinking is colored because of Johnny. I can't fault him for that, but Tom has been working at Fort Robinson since the first load of prisoners arrived nearly two years ago. He knows Jo goes out to the ranch every summer. He'd say something if he thought we should change that."

"Have you asked him?"

"Well, not directly . . . but he's been my deacon for years, and I know he'd say something. And as far as CJ's decision goes, for her to risk losing her hay contract won't do a thing to help John or the war effort. In fact, the argument could be made that Four Pines is essential to *winning* the war."

Clarissa snorted. "Right. So for my sister to dine with Nazis is patriotic."

"She won't be dining with Nazis. She's hiring some prisoners to do chores. Don't be so dramatic. And as for Jo, she's eighteen years old, and the more we try to tether her to a hitching post, the more she is going to struggle to break free. We've got to loosen the reins. Let her take the bit in her mouth and run a little."

"She's not a horse, Benjamin. She's a young woman."

"The analogy fits," Ben said. "If we try to keep her here in Crawford all summer, she just might hop a train and head out some morning with Delores for WAAC training at Fort Des Moines."

"I *want* her to hop a train," Clarissa said. "For Lincoln and the university this fall. But until then, I don't see anything wrong with a mother wanting her only child to spend her last summer at home."

"The ranch *is* home to Jo," Ben said. "She's got her own room out there, CJ adores her . . . and we're going to let her go. Word has it they may not have enough guards to let any of the prisoners work off the military reservation anyway. But even if they figure a way around that, CJ told me herself she wants them mostly for cutting hay. That's far enough away from the house and the barns that Jo won't so much as see the *PW* painted on their shirts."

Clarissa glowered at him. "They are *Nazi war criminals.*"

"Maybe some are," Ben said. "But a lot of them — according to Tom — are just young boys who got drafted and did what they were told. Tom says most are pretty much model prisoners. They aren't at all what he expected. He almost likes one or two of them. Goodness, honey-lamb, one of them got off the train and recognized a guard. The two of them lived next door to each other in Brooklyn."

"Well then," Clarissa sniffed. "If you and Tom think they are so wonderful, let's just invite a few up for Sunday dinner after church next week. I'll make sauerkraut and sausage."

"That's not my point, and you know it," Ben said. "Everything in Jo's world has changed in the last year. No high school girl expects her friends to be in danger for their lives. But not a day goes by that she doesn't worry over John Bishop. No high school girl expects her friends to die. But Delmer Clark and Ron Hanover did. The war has changed what we eat and where we go and what we pray about. There's one thing it doesn't have to change, and that's Jo's time at the ranch. She loves it. And I want her to have it — not just on the weekends she sometimes spends out there now. I want her to have her summer."

Her husband didn't lay down the law very often, but Clarissa recognized this as one of those times. "If she loves that ranch so much," she mumbled, "maybe she should just move there. Then she wouldn't have to even talk to me. Ever."

"Now, Clarissa, you don't mean that."

Clarissa got up and headed to the sink with her pie plate. She hadn't wanted to play dirty, but a mother had to do what a mother had to do. Without turning around she asked quietly, "And what about Mia? What's her summer going to be like with Josephine gone?" Through the window she could see her daughter as she bent over in last year's shorts to cover the row of seeds she had just scattered. "Josephine Hale!" Clarissa called through the torn screen. "You get in here and put on some slacks. The entire neighborhood doesn't need a girlie show!"

Josephine stood up, arched her back, and raised her hands to the spring sun, then minced to the next row and began to thin out seedlings.

Ben brought their coffee cups to the sink and stood just behind his wife. "She didn't hear you," he said.

"Oh, she heard me," Clarissa muttered, yanking the hot water faucet on. "She likes knowing half the neighborhood is watching those long legs strut around the garden." She slid the pie plates into hot water and grabbed the dishrag, scrubbing as she said, "I don't know where I went wrong, but somewhere along the way I forgot to teach my daughter modesty. I *told* her she'd outgrown those shorts when she dragged them out a few weeks ago."

"She's young," Ben said. "Don't be so hard on her." He tugged on one of his wife's errant curls. "Wasn't all that long ago I was watching your legs while you —"

"Stop that!" Clarissa said, blushing as her husband ran his hands over her hips.

"This evening when Jo's helping out at the Servicemen's Club, we'll have the house to ourselves — mm-hmm." Ben reached around her waist.

"Reverend Hale, you behave yourself!" Clarissa pretended to struggle, but she leaned back against her husband and kissed his cheek before grabbing his hands. "You have a sermon to polish."

"All right," the preacher said and backed away. "I'll behave. Until Jo's gone." He twitched his eyebrows at her. "But my sermon is just about as polished as it is going to get." He winked at her from the doorway.

"You," Clarissa scolded, "are a naughty boy." Snatching the teakettle off the stove, she poured herself a cup of hot water and called after him, "And you didn't answer my question. What about Mia Frey?"

Crouching over the seedling garden, Jo pretended she didn't hear her mother telling her to put on pants. The vague murmur of her dad's voice from inside made her smile.

She stood up. Arching her back she stretched, brought both hands up to her eyes, and pushed her hair back as she lifted her face to the sun. It had been such a long winter. She could not wait to be finished with school and head for the ranch. She was sick of indoor life, and very soon now it would be over.

Another door somewhere up the block slammed. At the sound of two angry voices, Jo pursed her lips. The neighbors must be at it again. Just as she stepped over a row of seedling snow peas, a child emerged from behind the garage and, nestling her chin in the niche created at the top of the picket fence, stood mutely watching her.

"Hello, Mia," Jo said, glancing up at the girl's unnaturally pale face and equally pale, mournful eyes.

The child didn't answer.

"You want to help thin out a row?" Jo asked. She looked back over her shoulder toward her mother's kitchen. "I bet there's a cookie left in the cookie jar."

Mia unlatched the gate. Slipping inside the yard, she went to the row next to Jo and stooped down. The two worked their way up and down the garden rows side by side. Once in a while Jo would make a comment or ask a question. Mia's one-word answers told Jo more than tears or childish tales could have, for Mia Frey had once been a talkative child — before her daddy returned from the war. Henry Frey had volunteered the minute war was declared on Germany and been badly burned in a crash on one of his first missions. After a little over a year in a foreign hospital, he came home. As far as Jo knew, almost no one in Crawford had actually *seen* Hank Frey since his discharge. Rumors abounded, but being the preacher's daughter and thus a frequent topic of rumor herself, Jo was disinclined to believe anything she'd heard — except what came out of little Mia's rosebud mouth. Hank Frey had a hook instead of a right hand and a disfigured face that frightened his daughter.

When the weeding was done and Mrs. Frey still had not come to fetch Mia, the girls set to folding the laundry hanging on the clothesline positioned between the rickety garage and the back of the house. Finally Jo said, "Why don't you stay the rest of the afternoon? You can have supper with us."

Mia glanced at the Hales' back door with such longing Jo had to swallow to keep the tears from her eyes. "I'll have to ask Mother. She might want me to stay home."

Mother. The Frey family was one of the reasons Jo found herself questioning her father's insistence that God's angels kept track of everything and everyone in Crawford, Nebraska. If that had ever been true, Jo was positive some angel had forgotten to transfer *Frey* to the next page of his — or her — book of Families to Watch Over. As far as she could tell, things had gone steadily downhill for that family since Mia's father came home and practically barricaded himself inside the house. Not long after that, Mia started referring to the woman who had been *Mommy* as *Mother.* Beyond mentioning the hook and the scarred face, she never talked about her father, and whenever Jo spent any time at all in the Hales' backyard, Mia appeared, pretending to busy herself in the alley, scratching in the dirt, singing to herself, pulling the earliest dandelion bloom, waiting, hoping for a chance to come into the Hales' yard. Only when Jo's father stepped out on the back porch and called "Hello, Sprite," did Mia's face light up. Even Mama, who was not given to hospitality, had a soft spot for Mia.

And on this Saturday afternoon in early spring, with only a little encouragement from Jo, Mia slipped out of the Hales' yard and up the alley and was back in record time, her pale cheeks flushed and her eyes sparkling with happiness. "Yes," she panted, leaning against the fence. "Mother said I can stay. Long as I want." She pointed to the laundry. "I'll fold the rest if you'll take them down. I can't quite reach the clothespins yet."

Promised supper at the Hales, the real Mia Frey emerged, and Jo realized once again how fitting was her father's nickname for the child. Like a sprite, Mia flitted across the yard, infused with such energy she couldn't stand still. Running to the clothes-line pole, she grabbed it and spun around it until she collapsed on the grass laughing, "I'm dizzy!"

"Are you hungry, too?" Clarissa called from the back porch. She nodded to the girls. "Come have some milk and a cookie while it's still warm." She set a plate at the edge of the porch and went back inside.

Mia ran to the porch ahead of Jo and had devoured her cookie and drunk half the glass of milk before Jo arrived. Jo grunted, "I'm too full from lunch," she said, and looked down at Mia. "Any chance you can eat another cookie?"

Mia took the cookie. "We're out of our sugar ration for this month," she said. "A prisoner that works in the office gave Mother some — Mother said they don't have rationing up at the fort. But Father found out where it came from. He was mad. He threw it out."

"Well," Jo replied, "we've still got sugar. And all the milk and butter we want, thanks to Ella."

"Ella's a good old cow," Mia said as milk dribbled down her chin. She swiped it away with the back of her hand, then burped loudly.

"Mia Frey!" Clarissa scolded from just inside the back door.

"Sorry, ma'am," Mia said, stifling a grin when Jo pursed her lips and puffed out her own cheeks pretending to burp soundlessly.

"You girls get the laundry folded and come on in. You can set the table while I start dinner."

"Yes, ma'am," Jo said. Together, they headed back to the clothesline. When they were finished, Mia grabbed one handle of the overflowing wicker laundry basket and Jo took the other. Once inside the back door, they set the clean laundry atop the table on the back porch. They washed up and set the dinner table, and by the time the Reverend Hale got home from making his hospital visits, Mia Frey was no longer the pale, frightened child who lived two doors up. She was Ben Hale's "little sprite."

Three

*Hath God forgotten to be gracious?
hath he in anger
shut up his tender mercies?*

PSALM 77:9

As she turned sideways to see if her slip was showing from beneath her polka-dot dress, Helen Frey thought she heard the floorboards in the hallway creak. Relieved that it was Friday and Mia had already left for school, she stepped away from the mirror and reached for the gray felt hat perched at the foot of the bed. Bowing her head, she settled the hat in place and worked at the pin with her eyes closed, hoping that if Hank flung the door open he wouldn't notice that she'd moved the dressing mirror so he wouldn't see himself if he came in.

When no one came to the bedroom door, she sat down on the foot of the bed and spun to the side so she could see herself. It surprised her when she really looked at the woman in the mirror these days. How could someone so worn out on the inside still appear somewhat . . . attractive . . . on the outside? How could someone about to burst with sorrow look so trim? How could she possibly still look like the girl who had kissed her high school sweetheart good-bye and stood waving as his train pulled out? But she did, and that proved that you really could not judge a book by its cover.

Her gaze drifted away from the mirror to the window and a view of Mia's tire swing.

"She's too little to use it," Helen had said when Hank decided to hang an old tire from a limb of the giant hackberry tree in the backyard. "She'll fall off."

"Come here, Spridget," Hank had said, sweeping his six-year-old daughter into his arms and showing her how to balance inside the tire. "By the time Daddy gets back home, you'll be so good at swinging you'll be wanting to try out the trapeze when the circus comes to town!"

Was it really only two years ago, Helen thought this March morning — only two years since Mia giggled and screeched with pleasure while her Daddy swung her on the old tire? She'd grown so much since Hank left that now she preferred draping her gangly legs over the top of the old tire while she spun around and around and around, hanging on to the rope with one hand while, with the other, she leaned down and traced circles in the grass. Helen closed her eyes, thinking how much her own life had become a blur, just like Mia's view of the world from her spinning tire swing.

She looked back at the woman in the mirror. She and Hank had had such plans. How naïve she had been, Helen thought, crying and begging him not to volunteer to go to war. She was so afraid he would be killed. How childish she had been. She had never suspected that worse things could happen than a man getting killed in battle.

Stop it, stop it, stop it, stop it. Helen jumped up off the bed. *Her* bed now. That, at least, was not her fault. She hadn't done a thing when Hank came home but smile and throw her arms around him. She'd kissed the side of his face that was nothing but scars and cried and whispered *"I love you, darling."* For a fleeting minute she'd thought maybe it would be all right. But then Hank turned to Mia.

Helen had tried so hard to prepare their little girl. "Daddy's been hurt, honey. He may not look the same. But underneath the blanket he's still your daddy." She had thought herself creative to come up with that analogy. Underneath a blanket was a soft mattress, and underneath the scars was the same daddy who loved them.

If only Mia could have playacted. Just a little. But she was too young to understand. "Take that off," she demanded, pointing to the right side of her father's face. "Take that blanket off. I don't like it."

Just as Helen had tried to explain, Hank tried to understand. He smiled down at his daughter. "It's not that kind of blanket, sweetheart," he said. "I can't take it off." When he reached for Mia, she slunk behind her mother.

Helen took Mia's hand, and looped her other arm through Hank's. "It'll be all right, darling," she whispered, "just give her a little time."

Hank nodded. Then he shook her off. "Haven't learned to manage this hook yet. Need to pick up my duffel."

He had forbidden her to tell anyone he was coming home. As she saw the looks people at the train station cast their way, she was grateful. They walked home in silence with Hank leading the way. When Helen joked that he'd forgotten his hometown and tried to lead him toward Main Street, he shook his head. "Don't want to see anyone." Then he snorted, "And they sure don't want to see me." The walk home stretched before them like a marathon to a weary runner. Even though it was unseasonably warm, Helen had shivered beneath her wool coat.

At home, Mia exchanged her coat for a thick wool sweater and went to her tire swing in the backyard. Hank dropped his duffel inside the front door and then walked through the house to the back. From just inside the screen door he called to her. "Be careful, Spridget."

Helen smiled at him as she set the table for supper. Surely it would help for Mia to hear the special nickname. What happened next broke Helen's heart. Mia lost her balance and fell to the ground with a thud. Instinct sent Hank out the door and across the yard to help the daughter who had always wanted her daddy when she was hurt.

But Mia screeched. "Get away! Don't . . . don't —"

Helen went to the door just in time to see the last remnants of the man she had loved torn away. Mia was sitting with her back pressed against the hackberry tree trunk, her face hidden in her hands.

Hank must have been trying to reassure her. He must have said "It's Daddy," because Mia shouted, "I want a new daddy! I don't want this *ugly* daddy!"

Helen saw his broad shoulders slump as he turned back toward the house. When he came in the door, she reached out to put her hand on his shoulder, but he pulled away and stumbled toward the stairs. She heard his feet landing on each one with a thud as his heavy footsteps retreated.

Holding back her own tears, Helen went outside to calm Mia. By the time Mia felt better and brave enough to see if that really *was* her daddy inside the wounded body, Hank had locked the bedroom door.

Helen and Mia had dined alone. Through the door, Hank told Helen he needed to rest awhile. She should go on to Wednesday evening services and choir practice.

"Take Spridget with you," he said through the door.

Helen went. Mia joined Jo Hale in the Sunday school rooms, helping keep track of the choir members' children while their parents practiced. Helen plastered on a big smile and said yes, Hank was home and no, they didn't want visitors yet because he was just bone-weary and needed to rest. The young women seemed to believe her. Only old Mrs. Koch didn't. She nodded and squeezed Helen's arm.

"I have prayed for you every day, Helen. I won't stop." She blinked a few times and then leaned close. "The women at home have to be heroes, too." She gave Helen a quick hug and hurried away.

At home Helen discovered that while she and Mia were at church, Hank had moved out of their bedroom and up the rickety stairs to the attic. Late that night, she heard him descend.

"Sweetheart," she said, and headed into his arms.

"Don't," he said, his voice hollow.

"But —"

"I said," he repeated, "don't. Don't call me sweetheart. Don't pretend you're happy. Just . . . don't. Now go back to bed. I won't bother you and I don't want you bothering me. You'll need to keep your job out at the fort. This hook they gave me . . . I don't know what I'm still going to be able to do at the garage." He paused. "I doubt folks are going to want to come to a freak show every time they need their oil changed."

Feeling as though she'd been punched in the midsection, Helen stammered, "All right, dear." She retreated to her bed and lay wide-awake for the rest of the night.

That had been weeks ago. For the next few days, Helen didn't know whether Hank was alive or dead. She worried about the cold up in the unfinished attic. She told Mia her daddy was sick and that he didn't want them to "catch it," but at night, when she heard him on the stairs, she lay listening . . . longing . . . wishing he would open her door and whisper her name and take them both to places in the dark where they could forget. One time he did. Helen's spirits soared. Finally, she thought, they were finding each other again. Lying in his arms, she thought that maybe things were going to be all right. But early the next morning Hank pushed himself out of bed into the cold room . . . and *apologized.*

Helen wanted to scream. What had she done? Didn't she welcome him completely? Hadn't their love been sweet? For Mia's sake, she had pretended to be asleep. Best to say nothing, she told herself as her husband crept back up to the garret.

And now both Helen and Mia had accepted the fact that Hank lived in the attic. Helen learned to lie. She made up stories about things Hank said or did at home. She made excuses. She warned Mia not to talk about Daddy, and after a few weeks, people stopped asking. She avoided Mrs. Koch, who, as far as Helen Frey knew, was the only woman in Crawford who suspected that the army had been wrong when they said Hank Frey survived the crash of his B-17.

Thank God for the Hale family. Helen had never really liked her pastor's wife. But since Hank's return, Clarissa and Ben and their daughter, Jo, had become a lifeline for Helen and Mia. If it hadn't been for the Hales and old Mrs. Koch, Helen didn't know what she would have done these past weeks. She wondered what she would do when school was out and Mia was supposed to be at home all day. She'd thought she would be able to quit her job out at the fort as soon as Hank came home. She'd expected life to be normal. She'd been such a fool.

The sound of a car honking jolted her back to the present, and she hurried out into the hallway and, with a glance up the stairs at the closed attic door, made her way downstairs and out onto the front porch just in time to see Tom Hanson across the street holding his car door open for Stella Black. She felt a pang of jealousy as Stella minced down her sidewalk toward the car. Before sliding into the seat, she called to Helen.

"I'll miss you today, honey."

"Thank you," Helen replied. "I'll be back tomorrow."

Helen waited for the car to head out before descending the porch steps and going down the sidewalk toward the street.

She couldn't risk Stella Black noticing that Helen Frey, who had said she was taking the day off to be room mother at Mia's school, was walking in the opposite direction of the school. While she waited for Stella's ride to round the corner and head for Fort Robinson, she glanced up at the garret window centered above the porch. Was it her imagination, or had there been a flicker of movement just then? Her heart pounded. It wouldn't do for Hank to be asking questions. Not today. Inhaling deeply, she headed downtown. By the time she arrived at the cottage Doctor Whitlow used for his office, Helen Frey was herself again — the hardworking wife of a war hero.

Shortly after lunch on Saturday, Jo crossed the street and headed for Stella Black's front porch, where Delores waited, ensconced on the porch swing reading a magazine. At her approach, Delores turned the magazine around so Jo could see a full-color photograph of Betty Grable. "Looks like you," she said.

Jo plopped down on the porch swing with a sigh.

Delores closed the magazine. "So?"

"So I can't go," Jo said. "I already knew I couldn't. I should have told you. Asking

67

only made my mom angrier."

"Why not? What could be wrong with Charlie McCarthy and Edgar Bergen?" Delores asked.

"It's not the movie. It's the day. Remember? No movies on Sunday." She looked sideways at her friend. "I could have gone to the matinee today. But now it's too late."

"Of all the dumb things," Delores Black said. She closed the magazine and dropped it on the concrete.

"You go ahead," Jo said. "I heard it's really good."

"Naw," Delores said, shaking her head. "I'll wait for you. We can go next week." She hopped up. "Let's go downtown and get an ice cream, anyway." She jangled the change in her pocket. "Before this burns a hole." Touching Jo's arm, she whispered, "We don't have to walk straight home. The sooner we get back, the more chores they'll have lined up for us."

Jo grinned. "That's what I like about you, Delores. You're always thinking." With a laugh, she headed off toward the park with her friend.

"Why'd you have to go and be a *Baptist,* anyway?" Delores asked as they walked along. "They *never* have any fun. You should just tell your parents you're going to be Methodist or Episcopalian — or Catholic. Why not Catholic? We can do whatever we want." Thunder pealed from the clouds that had been gathering all day. "Come on," Delores said, looking up at the sky.

"You can *not* do whatever you want," Jo retorted. "Not and be on good terms with God." She pointed toward the thunderclouds swirling in from the west. "We're gonna get drenched."

"Not if you hurry," Delores said. She turned around and called over her shoulder, "And I'm on *great* terms with God, thank you very much. I go to confession and do my penance and attend mass. If that doesn't get me points with God, what would?"

Jo picked up the pace. Lightning crackled out of the clouds. "It's not what you *do* that makes the difference." She pointed to her heart. "It's what's in here." She hurried up the steps to the park shelter. Together the girls leaned on the railing along the edge of the shelter and watched the storm approach.

"Is that you talking or the Reverend Mr. Hale?"

Jo frowned. "It's me. Why?"

Delores tossed her head. "Well, if it's not

what you *do* that makes the difference with God, how come you have that long list of things you can't do?"

Jo looked down at her petite friend. She expected to see the now-familiar grin that said Delores was only teasing, but the girl's dark eyes were serious. *I should have an answer,* Jo thought, feeling a little ashamed, for if the preacher's daughter didn't have the answer to a basic question like that, there was something wrong. "I don't know," Jo finally said. Her face brightened, "But if you really want to talk about it, we could go over to my dad's office and ask him."

"Oh right," Delores rolled her eyes and made a face. "That's *just* what I need to do. Can't you just hear my mom after someone tells her that her only daughter has been checking out the Baptist church?" She perched atop the railing that bordered the shelter. "She'd have a heart attack. And besides, there's going to be a downpour any minute."

"I thought your mother liked me," Jo said, pretending to pout.

"She does. But I don't think her enthusiasm quite extends to the rest of your clan. Call it cautious acceptance. And don't push it." Delores swept her straight black hair

70

back off her shoulders and pretended to make a ponytail. "So. You can't go to the movies tomorrow. Can you work in the club kitchen with me tonight?"

Jo sighed. "I want to — *so* much. But Mother had a fit the last two times I helped out."

Delores dropped her ponytail. "You sang 'America the Beautiful' to cheer up the soldiers," she said. "What could possibly be wrong with that?"

Jo shrugged. "I don't get it, either. I was going to ask Dad to work on her, but he already stood up for me when she objected to my spending the summer out at the ranch. I don't think we'd better push her about anything else just now."

"My gosh, Jo, is there anything your mother *isn't* upset about right now? You always spend your summers out there."

Jo shrugged. "And every summer she hopes I won't."

"You can't help it if you take after your Aunt CJ instead of her," Delores said.

"I know," Jo murmured. "But she just doesn't think it's ladylike to work a ranch. She doesn't think men find it attractive."

"You're ladylike enough to have one of the cutest boys from our class writing you practically every day," Delores said. "It's

71

not like you aren't already practically engaged."

Jo sighed and shook her head. Sometimes
it bothered her the way everyone assumed
things about her and Johnny Bishop. But
that was not information she could trust to
Delores, as much as she liked her. "I can't
help it if I hate sewing and cooking. I've
loved horses ever since I knew what one
was. Daddy says horses are in my blood on
both sides. His grandpa raised racehorses
back in Kentucky."

"It's fate," Delores said.

"Maybe you're right," Jo agreed. "I just
wish Mother wouldn't take it so personally
that I'd rather go out to the ranch and work
for Aunt CJ than stay in town this summer."
She bit her lower lip and stared into the distance. "Sometimes in the winter when the
sky's been gray and we're all snowed in —
sometimes I feel like I can't breathe. Like if I
don't get out into the wide open spaces I'm
going to suffocate." She tossed her head and
inhaled. "I feel *alive* when I'm at the Four
Pines. Honestly, just about everything else I
do is filling time until I get to go back there.
I'd move right now if I could."

"Well, I'd agree with your mom that you
should graduate first, but then — why can't
you? Move right after graduation. Make it

permanent. Everyone knows you're going to end up out there after Johnny gets back."

Jo sighed. There it was again. As if her future was already mapped out for her. "I promised I'd go to the university in Lincoln," she said.

"What for?"

"Mother's got her heart set on me getting an education," Jo said. "That's all she talks about. How women are going to have all kinds of opportunities once the war is over. How the world isn't going to be the same now that people have seen what women can do." She raised her left arm and struck a Rosie the Riveter pose, flexing her bicep.

"Now let me get this straight." Delores paced around the bandstand gesturing while she talked. "Your mother is all excited about opportunities for women — she wants you to go to school so you have more than the usual choices women have . . . but she's counting on Johnny to see to it that you make the usual choice and get married?"

Jo laughed. "Exactly."

"So she wants you to choose . . . to make the choice she would have made . . . if she had had a choice . . . when she chose."

"All right, all right," Jo said, waving at Delores to be quiet. "I get the point. It doesn't make sense to us. But it does to my mom." Jo frowned, "She likes Johnny a lot. But I think sometimes she wishes she hadn't gotten married so young."

"You're not your mother," Delores interjected.

"You can say that again."

"Maybe *she* should go to the university," Delores said. "And let you be what you want to be."

"I don't mind the idea of going to college," Jo said. "Aunt CJ says there's nothing wrong with a woman rancher being educated." She looked off into the distance. "And Mother means well. It just seems like it's going to take so long to get back here." She hopped down and smoothed her skirt. "And Aunt CJ isn't getting any younger. There's a lot I've got to learn from her. Stuff you can't find in books. Things Aunt CJ just seems to have a sixth sense about."

"Like what?" Delores blew a bubble and popped it.

"Like how to tell if a mare's going to have it easy or tough when she foals. And how to calm down a nervous mama. And breeding. Aunt CJ's always had an uncanny talent for pairing up the right stallion with the right mare."

Delores's face turned bright red, and she

laughed nervously. "Josephine Hale, shame on you!"

Jo, whose face was almost as red as her friend's shook her head. "Well, gee, Delores. It's part of the job."

When huge raindrops began to fall on the shelter roof, Delores looked at her watch. "Shoot!" she shouted. "I've got to get going. I promised Mom I'd clean house today. She's working overtime."

"I'll help," Jo said, just as the heavens opened. "Come on!" she said, "nobody ever died of a good soaking!" She started down the steps. The spring rain was cold. With a shriek, Jo skittered back under the leaky metal roof of the park shelter. Tiny hailstones began to fall amidst the raindrops. Lightning cracked and both girls squealed and jumped.

"That hit nearby," Delores yelled.

Jo nodded. The girls huddled together. While they waited, a train approached from the east. Delores's eyes grew wide. "Prisoners!" she said, and nodded toward the train. Its windows had been adjusted from the outside so they could only be opened a couple of inches.

Delores leaned closer. "Nazis!" she whispered.

As the rain diminished, the sound of

squealing brakes joined the receding thunder. Slowly, the train came to a stop within shouting distance of the park shelter.

A guard stepped out on the platform between the two cars nearest the shelter. Lighting a cigarette, he looked to his right and to his left, and then descended to the opposite side of the tracks.

"Come on," Delores said, grabbing Jo by the elbow. "Let's go take a look. That guard was cute."

"Don't be ridiculous," Jo said sharply. She drew back. "My mother would have a cow if — Delores!"

Delores was already down the shelter steps. At the edge of the park, she crouched down behind a row of bushes from where she looked back toward the park shelter, motioning for Jo to join her.

Jo looked from Delores to the train car and back again. She shook her head. Delores waved, then made a gesture as if she were praying. Jo scuttled across the grass. "What on earth do you think you are *doing?*"

Together they stared. A dozen faces were looking in their direction. Jo grabbed her friend's arm. "Let's go. We shouldn't be here. I don't know why the train's stopped, but that guard is gone and —"

76

Delores pulled away. "Don't be silly. They aren't going anywhere. Look!" She nodded toward the train. "They're waving hello."

It was true. A couple of the men held up their hands in greeting.

Delores waved back.

"What are you *doing?!*" Jo said between clenched teeth.

"Diplomacy," Delores said. She smiled toward the train. "Wouldn't you want people to be nice to Johnny if he was on his way to a PW camp somewhere?"

"Don't even *think* about that!"

"Well?" Delores shrugged. "You know you would." She nodded toward the train. "Look at that one. He can't be a soldier. He looks like someone's little brother."

If Jo hadn't known better, she would have thought the round-faced soldier with the big eyes was frightened. Another face leaned closer. It was not so young. And not friendly. "The one with the short hair looks mean," Jo muttered.

"Yeah," Delores agreed. "But look at the one next to him. Wow."

Delores's "wow" was just that. Blond hair, square jaw. Jo couldn't see his eyes too well, but she imagined them as being a gorgeous blue.

"Beautiful American girls . . . can you please tell us where we are?"

The handsome blond was being shouldered away from the window by someone with dark hair and a moustache. He repeated the question. "Please, dear ladies. Have the kindness of the angels that you resemble."

"That does it," Jo said. "We're leaving."

"Nebraska," Delores called out. "You're in Nebraska."

A rumble of voices erupted on the train car.

"My uncle lives in Boston," one of the German prisoners called out.

"We have cousins in New York," another said.

"Do you have any cigarettes?"

Suddenly the guard who had jumped down on the opposite side of the train reappeared. He stomped out his cigarette and scrambled up the stairs, across to the park side, and down the steps.

"You! Girls!" He came charging toward Delores and Jo. "What do you think you're doing?"

"What do you think *you're* doing?" Delores said, lifting her chin. "You're the one who was supposed to be guarding them. I saw you jump down to have a cigarette, so

78

don't act all high and mighty."

The soldier stopped. When he spoke again, it was with less anger. "Hey, it's all right. I just don't want you to get hurt, that's all."

Delores made a face. "That would be kind of hard, wouldn't it? Since the windows are nailed practically shut?" She nodded toward the train. "And what's wrong, anyway? They never stop in Crawford."

The guard shrugged. "Something on the tracks up ahead. We'll get moving before long." He looked at the sky, then gazed toward the buttes in the distance. "You know how much farther Fort Robinson is from here?"

"My mom works there," Delores said. "It's about ten miles."

"Finally," the soldier said, shaking his head. "Never thought we'd get here." He nodded toward the train. "Some of those men have been accusing us of running the train through a maze. They don't believe we could be going in a straight line. Sometimes I wonder if they're right." He smiled down at Delores.

"Where you from?" Delores asked.

"Brooklyn." He looked in the direction of the buttes again. "I thought Nebraska was all flat."

"You probably thought we still have fights between the cowboys and Indians, too," Delores said, nudging Jo.

"Don't you?" the soldier grinned, and Jo couldn't tell if he was teasing them or not.

"Not very often," Jo said.

"What does anyone ever do around here, anyway?" the soldier asked. "I mean, it's so . . . empty."

"There's a movie house," Jo said. "And some churches. And a Servicemen's Club on Main Street."

Delores spoke up. "Jo here sings for the variety show out at the fort sometimes."

Jo glowered at her. Voices up the line caught the soldier's attention.

"So . . . if I come to the Servicemen's Club some night, any chance you'll be there?" He was looking at Jo.

Delores linked her arm through Jo's and spoke up. "You never can tell," she said.

The train began to move. The private jogged back to the car full of German prisoners, grabbed a handrail, and hauled himself aboard. As the train picked up speed, he leaned out and yelled, "Franco Romani."

Inside the train car, hands were raised as if to say good-bye. Jo saw the older short-haired soldier sit down. The youngest prisoner stood staring at them. Jo barely noticed him. She could not take her eyes off the tall blond, who did not look back but sat with his profile to the window and his nose in the air. Now there was a Nazi a girl could hate.

As the train receded into the distance, Delores nudged Jo. "So, Mrs. Four Pines Ranch, you gonna sing in the variety show again or not?" She leaned against Jo's shoulder. "Private Romani from New York might be there."

Jo shook her head. "Mother would throw a fit." She paused and looked down at her friend. "And Private Romani is *not* my type."

"Oh, right. And what, pray tell, is your type?"

"Hmm," Jo said, and turned to walk toward Main Street. "More Cary Grant, less Eddie Bracken." She giggled. "And no Fred Astaire."

Delores rolled her eyes, "Do the 'no-dancing' Baptists have a rule against pouring punch?"

"Of course not, silly."

"Well then, come and pour punch." Delores leaned toward her. "That Private Romani was real cute. And he liked you." Delores nudged her. "Come on, Jo. Mrs. Blair is going to be the chaperone. She's as upright a citizen as could ever be."

"Maybe," Jo said. "But Mother and Mrs. Blair had words at the county fair last year, and Mother's not too keen on her."

"Honestly!" Delores exclaimed. "It was only jelly for goodness' sake."

"*Only* is not a word my mother uses when it comes to whether she brings home a blue ribbon or not."

"She got blues for pie and pickles," Delores said. "It's not like she had a baby in the 'Beautiful Baby' contest and Mrs. Blair said the little thing was ugly."

Jo laughed. "All right, all right. I'll ask. That's all I can say. But I don't think I'll mention Mrs. Blair as chaperone. Deacon Jones's wife is going, too."

Delores laced her arm through Jo's. "Good plan. Everyone knows Mrs. Jones can't bake her way out of a paper bag. So maybe your mother will approve of her."

"Absolutely not!" Clarissa exclaimed over supper. "I can't believe you'd ask such a ridiculous thing."

Jo saw her mother look across the table and send an unspoken plea in her father's direction. When Daddy didn't pick up the hint, her hopes soared. "It's not ridiculous. It's . . . it's something I can do. For the war. For Johnny."

"For Johnny? Oh, please." Clarissa rolled her eyes and shook her head. "The fair citizens of Crawford and Chadron just cannot wait to put their daughters on display in hopes some soldier will marry them. Those variety shows out at the fort are little more than a . . . a . . . farm sale. It's disgusting, and I won't have you participating."

"Where's the harm in smiling and trying to cheer up a homesick soldier? You already let me go once. Some of them are from New York City. They've got to think they came to the ends of the earth when they came way out here. I bet they don't know which end of a horse eats and which end —"

"Don't be crass, Josephine," Clarissa said.

"I'm sorry. But I want to go." She turned to her father. "Aren't you the one who's saying we should all do our part?"

"You planted the garden," Clarissa said. "And you've participated in every drive we've had. You are doing your part."

"You pray for President Roosevelt," Ben added. "You write to John and keep his spirits up."

"I want to do more," Jo said.

"Maybe once you've graduated," Clarissa answered. "If there's a war still on, God forbid."

"Next year — it's always next year," Jo muttered. "When are you ever going to let me grow up?!"

"If growing up means you rebel and tell your parents they don't know what's best for you, I hope you never grow up."

Jo pressed her lips together firmly. "I'm eighteen years old. I'm going."

"I happen to know," Clarissa said, "that Mrs. Blair requires parental permission when she collects young women for the events at the fort. And you do not have parental permission. So you will not be going."

Slamming her hands down on the table, Jo opened her mouth to protest.

"Josephine," her father said. " 'Be angry, but do not sin. Children, obey your parents in the Lord, for this is right.' "

" 'Fathers, provoke not your children to wrath!' " Jo blurted out and, jumping up, she charged out the back door, down the porch steps, across the yard, and through the gate. Plopping in the damp spring grass and leaning her back against the garage wall, she let the angry tears come.

"Hey, Jo," said a familiar voice.

"Oh . . . hi, Mia."

"What's wrong?"

Jo shook her head. "Nothing too serious."

"You're crying," Mia said. She extended her index finger and touched a tear.

"Yes," Jo said, and forced a smile. "But not anymore. You cheered me up! What are you doing out here in the alley, anyway?"

Mia looked back over her shoulder toward her own house. "Waiting for Mother to come home."

"Want to wait with me?"

Mia grinned. "Can I have a horse story?"

"You bet," Jo said, and patted the ground beside her.

Four

As we have therefore opportunity,
let us do good unto all men,
especially unto them who are
of the household of the faith.

GALATIANS 6:10

Clara Joy

The third Sunday after Will left, Ben Hale asked me to meet with him in his office after the Sunday service. Now that made me nervous. I couldn't remember a time when Ben had treated me like I was a regular member of his congregation, and I didn't hear much of his sermon after he asked for that meeting, which was disappointing because I had driven into Crawford hoping for some comfort, what with Will deserting me in my time of need and all. It didn't help calm my nerves to see that Jo and her mother were upset, too. Clarissa missed more than one note when she played the offertory that morning, and I could tell by the way Jo sat turning pages that my niece was none too pleased with her mother.

I headed for Ben's office right after the service, but it took a while for Ben to arrive, since he and Clarissa always stand at the back of the sanctuary to shake hands as people leave the church. The longer I sat in front of that blasted brass desk plate with *Reverend Benjamin T. Hale* engraved on the front, the more fidgety I got. I never did understand why on earth my sister had that thing made. As if everyone in Crawford didn't already know who Ben was. It got more annoying by the minute, so finally I got up and went over to the window, which Ben had opened, I assume, to let in the spring morning air.

Now Ben's office window is just to one side of the front steps, but I did not eaves-drop on one conversation. I did notice Mrs. Frey send Mia on ahead while she paused to talk to old Mrs. Koch, who is the oldest member of our congregation and a war widow — from the Great War. It was the first time I really thought on the fact that I hadn't seen Hank Frey since he came home. I pondered that for a while, but by the time Ben came in I was back in the "inquisition chair" just about to twist the handle off my purse with my fidgeting.

"I'm about to ask you a favor," Ben said, settling behind his desk. He folded his hands over his ink blotter and smiled. "And I don't want Clarissa to know it was my idea."

I relaxed a little. If Ben was up to something that would make Clarissa mad, chances were it would be something I'd like. "Ask away," I said.

Ben cleared his throat. "Well, Clarissa is dead set against Jo going to the ranch this summer," he said. "That business with using PW labor has her riled."

I opened my mouth to say something snazzy, like maybe Clarissa would like to drive the tractor fourteen hours a day to help me out. But before I could, Ben said, "Now don't get your hackles up yet, CJ. I'm on Jo's side — and yours — and Jo will be coming. Although the fact that Will's moved out of the cabin isn't going to help matters much."

"Who told you about Will?"

"Deacon Hanson. He's been doing a lot of work at the fort lately."

"For the remount?" I snapped — mostly because I hate gossip, and the last thing I wanted was for the fools and liars of Dawes County to pull my own pastor into another round of "the plain truth" about Will

Bishop and CJ Jackson. Of course I knew Tom Hanson was a good carpenter, and it was no surprise he was working out at the fort — along with a lot of other folks from Crawford. But Fort Robinson is really three different places — a PW camp for the German prisoners of war, a K-9 division for training war dogs, and the U.S. Army Remount Service Headquarters, which is what everyone just calls "the remount." I knew enough about the way things worked over at Fort Rob to know that the three divisions were mostly kept separate, even if they did all coexist on the flat prairie between the White River to the south and the long string of rocky buttes to the north. And I also knew Tom had been hired to help build the PW camp.

"As a matter of fact," Ben said, real calm — and I will admit that Ben Hale's voice is probably one of the reasons my sister fell in love with him — "even though he works at the PW camp most of the time, Tom put in some extra hours on Saturday helping the remount get ready for the next horse sale. Something about refitting the arena to make things go more smoothly. Anyway, Tom said that Bill Harker was going on about how great it was to have someone with Will's experience helping condition and test the new arrivals."

I kept my mouth shut. When Will decided to come to his senses and come home I didn't want him thinking I was talking behind his back.

"Anyway," Ben said, and leaned back in his chair, "I expect Clarissa will get wind of Will's departure soon enough, and when she does, there will be yet another stir. But —" he smiled at me — "I can handle Clarissa. In the end, she'll realize that Jo needs the ranch like a fish needs water."

Now that helped me relax even more. Even if he is your brother-in-law, you don't want to be in trouble with your pastor. That just isn't a good feeling no matter how you cut it. But apparently I wasn't in trouble. "And the ranch needs Jo," I said as quick as I could. "She'll be a big help with gentling the yearlings. And I appreciate your standing up to Clarissa. You know I'd die before I'd put Jo in harm's way. Now let me explain how it'll work with the PWs. When —"

Ben raised his hand. "There's no need," he said. "I trust you, CJ. That's not what this little meeting is about at all."

"It isn't?"

He shook his head. "Nope. Actually, I

was wondering if you'd be able to take on more than just Jo this summer."

I sat back and adjusted my church hat. "Who?"

"Mia Frey," Ben said.

Now, while it is true that most of my maternal instincts have been spent on four-legged babies, I am still a woman, and even Clarissa, who is about as far from a soft touch as a woman can be, has affection for Mia. I had prayed for Hank Frey — just like I did Johnny and the other boys in Crawford who were in uniform — and I had just been wondering about him, so while Ben was saying things like he realized Jo would have to agree to keep track of Mia and it was asking a lot, I blurted out, "We'll take her," so abruptly I surprised myself. And then I said, "As long as it's all right with her parents. And they have to know about my plans to hire labor from the fort."

Ben nodded.

"Doesn't Mrs. Frey work out there?"

"She does. She's one of the secretaries at the prison camp headquarters."

"What about Hank? Will he agree to it?"

Ben was quiet for a minute while he studied the back of his hands. "Hank is . . ." He paused. It was one of the few times in my life I'd seen Ben Hale at a loss for words.

91

". . . struggling. He's badly scarred from what I hear."

"You haven't been to visit?" This was not like Ben Hale, who took his job as a shepherd so seriously he once cancelled a family vacation so he could take old Fred Davenport to see a heart specialist in Lincoln.

Ben shook his head. "I haven't wanted to cause a stir. Hank's been reclusive." He sighed and looked out the window. "To tell the truth, CJ, about all I know is what Mia hints at. I think her mother has told her not to talk about it." He looked up at me. "And Mrs. Frey has been avoiding me. I'm going on what Mia has said and the rumors that started way back when Hank first got home." He grimaced. "At first I thought it was a good idea to give him some time to adjust. But I've let it go too long. It's something I intend to spend some time on. After Mia is gone."

Sometimes what a person doesn't say is more profound than what they say. I may be old, but I like to think I'm still quick mentally, and I could see what Ben was getting at. He wanted Mia happily tucked away while he tried to help her parents.

"We'll make it seem like camp for her," I said. "She can learn to ride. Ned will be perfect for her. He's twenty-six years old and swaybacked and he wouldn't hurt a fly. The old boy's bulletproof." I stopped. "What? What are you smiling at?"

"You, CJ. For all your bluster and attempts to appear to the contrary, you really are a very caring woman."

If there is one thing I hate, it is sentimental talk. So I made a face and told Ben Hale to hush. Which, I suppose, is evidence enough I was no longer intimidated by the desk or the pastor's office or the brass plate. Fact is, I plumb forgot about all of that. It was just Ben and me talking about how to help out a little girl who needed some time away while her parents figured out how to cope with what the war had dealt them.

"Think you can get Mia and her mama to join us for lunch today?" I asked. "If you think Clarissa can handle two more for Sunday dinner without blowing a gasket, I'll take it from there."

Ben laughed. "I'll take care of it."

And he did. But I never suspected he would avoid getting Clarissa upset over unexpected guests for Sunday dinner by making her mad about something else.

My sister doesn't have false teeth, but if she did, her upper plate would have landed in her cherry pie when Ben asked Mrs. Frey her opinion about his holding a chapel service for the prisoners. Clarissa's mouth dropped open and she — a pastor's wife who is usually very aware of her duty to remain quiet and support her husband — well, she just blurted it out. "You *cannot* be serious!" It got quiet real fast around that table. "The Lutherans and the Catholics already have services out there. That's enough."

Ben patted the back of Clarissa's hand, which was his signal to her to behave herself. He turned to Mrs. Frey. "Tom Hanson tells me some of the prisoners are employed in your office. What do you think? Would they be interested in a chapel service led by a Baptist?"

"Well, I-I don't know. You'd have to clear it with Captain Donovan," Mrs. Frey said.

"Of course. And I will," Ben reassured her. "I'm just curious as to your insights about the prisoners themselves. I've talked to my deacon about it, but I'd like to take advantage of your woman's intuition. Have you observed any evidence of a spiritual awareness?"

When Ben glanced Clarissa's way I understood what he was doing. His wanting to sow the gospel in the mission field beyond the barbed wire was sincere, but he had additional reasons for bringing it up over Sunday dinner. I have to say I didn't realize Ben Hale had it in him. I mean, with one lunch he was trying to win Clarissa's support to start a new ministry, stop her protests about Jo coming to the ranch by getting Mrs. Frey's assurances that the PWs weren't dangerous, and prepare the way for his talking to Hank Frey without Mia being around for whatever might happen. Clearly, there was way more to Ben Hale than I had ever given him credit for. Pondering all the complexities of my brother-in-law's mind took my own thoughts away from the dinner table for a while, and when I came back Mrs. Frey was talking about the PWs working in her office.

"The two in the office right now are new. I don't know about what you are calling spiritual awareness. I don't think either of them has gone to the other services. But that doesn't mean they won't. The younger one seems especially vulnerable — almost like a schoolboy who's shocked to find himself in this situation."

"Schoolboy?" I interrupted. "How old is he?"

"Fifteen, according to his *soldbuch*," Mrs. Frey said.

95

"His what?" Clarissa asked.

Jo spoke up. "It's a book they all carry. Like an identity card. Except it tells all about them — birthplace, parents, medical history, military training . . . all kinds of things."

"That's right," Mrs. Frey said, nodding.

"And how do you know about these . . . these . . ."

"*Soldbuchs*," Jo repeated. She looked around the table. "Johnny wrote me about it. One of the men in his unit had one he was keeping as a war souvenir. Something he'd found in a ground campaign. Johnny was wondering about the man who lost it. . . ." Her voice gentled. She looked down at her hands and almost whispered, "Whether he's alive. Or dead." She sighed. "Johnny said it made the war — the things he's doing — more . . . personal. It bothered him to read about Helmut."

"Helmut?" Clarissa said.

"That was his name. The German soldier." Jo looked at Mrs. Frey. "He was really young, too."

"What kind of monster drafts children to fight a war?" Clarissa said.

"Private Bauer's entire class from school was forced into the service and trained to ram tanks with bangalore torpedoes," Mrs.

Frey said. "Apparently not many survived for long. He seems grateful to have been captured."

The quiet around the table was more than a little uncomfortable. There we all were, praying for our boys to be successful . . . and suddenly it seemed strange because maybe what we had prayed for would mean boys like Private Bauer — and Helmut Whoever — were getting killed. The more a person thinks about things like that, the more confusing it can get. I was beginning to wish I could have kept the war "over there" while I kept my nose to the grindstone out on my ranch.

Mrs. Frey tried to make things less serious. "One thing about Private Bauer is he's eager to please. I expected to miss the PW he replaced — he wanted to work in the K-9 area — but since Private Bauer arrived, you could eat off the floor in our office." She chuckled. "I think his mother must have had something of a general inside her. When I compliment him, he ducks his head and blushes just like a schoolboy — which, I suppose, he still is in some ways." She looked almost apologetic. "All the PWs who have worked in our office have challenged my idea of what a German soldier is like." She shook her head. "I haven't wanted to like them, but it's been hard not to — with one or two exceptions."

And there we were again, sitting around the table with an awkward silence. For myself, I was realizing that praying for victory over the enemy gets a little strange when you realize you are asking God to help the boys you love kill the boys someone else loves. The generic enemy is easy to hate. But who wants to hate the fifteen-year-old who empties your wastebasket?

"You said you have two prisoners working in your office," Clarissa said. "What about the other one?"

I looked at my sister and wondered if she was just being polite or if she was looking for evidence to shore up her case against the PWs.

Mrs. Frey looked down at her plate. "Dieter Brock," she said. She picked up her knife and started to butter the biscuit on her plate while she talked. I could sense there was something different about the way she felt about this prisoner.

"Well?" Clarissa prodded. "What's he like?"

"Different from Bauer," Mrs. Frey said. "A little older. More reserved." She rubbed her forearms like she was cold and asked for more coffee — which I did not understand because from the color of her cheeks it looked to me like she was plenty warm. "He's asked me to help him get transferred to a remount work detail. He doesn't like office work much," Mrs. Frey said. "Apparently his father was quite the equestrian. He's very frustrated to have landed in a place where there are thousands of horses and not be able to work with them." She looked around the table and gave an odd little laugh, "I've tried to explain to him that the remount horses are a far cry from what his father rode, but —"

"Not all of them are," I said. "Jenny Camp is a world-class jumper."

"And Dakota," Jo chimed in.

"If Dieter knew about them, he'd be even more frustrated cooped up in the office," Mrs. Frey said. "But Captain Donovan insists that Sergeant Brock is needed to interpret for new arrivals."

"He speaks English?" I was getting more interested in this Dieter Brock person all the time.

Mrs. Frey nodded. "And four other languages, according to his file."

I wanted to know more, but Mrs. Frey claimed she didn't know much more, which didn't make any sense when she'd just spouted off all that information, but then

99

Ben interrupted. "Do you think he'd interpret my sermons?"

"He certainly *could,*" Mrs. Frey nodded. "His English is flawless." She was looking down at her plate like she wanted more food, but when Clarissa offered it, she said no thanks.

I decided there was something funny about Mrs. Frey's reluctance to talk about Dieter Brock, but I also decided not to pursue it at the dinner table. Maybe I'd check in with Tom Hanson before leaving Crawford. Maybe he'd know more about Brock's interest in horses. I was going to be using more horsepower than gas during haying, and if there was a PW who knew horses and was motivated to work around them, I was intrigued.

Ben changed the subject then by patting Jo's arm and saying, "Your aunt CJ is looking forward to having you on the place this summer. She told me this morning she wanted to talk to us about it."

That was my cue to speak up about Mia, but it was an awkward segue, and I wasn't prepared. I did notice that the minute Ben mentioned Jo leaving Crawford, Mia Frey's little cherub mouth puckered up and she ducked her head.

When I didn't speak up, Ben charged

100

ahead. "I can't believe summer's almost here," he said and winked at Mia. "No more school for you soon, Sprite. Freedom!"

Mia sighed. Her mother tousled her hair. "Mia's going to visit her grandmother in Omaha this summer," she said.

I could tell from the expression in Ben's eyes, he hadn't expected that.

"Sounds like fun," I said. "I always wished I'd had a grandma to spoil me."

"My mother isn't exactly the spoiling kind of grandma," Mrs. Frey said, laughing — a little too loudly, I thought. "But I have to work, and Mia's daddy just isn't well enough to watch over her all day every day."

I was sitting next to Mia, and I could see her little hands balled up into two fists in her lap. I could almost feel the air around her fill up with dread.

"Too bad you don't like horses," I said quickly. "I've got an old nag that could use some attention. I don't have the time for him."

"Ned?" Jo asked. Bless her, I think she was catching onto the plot.

"Ned," I said. I spoke to Mia, although she didn't look up at me. "Yep. He's a swaybacked old cow horse. Just stands around looking sad all the time, thinking about the good old days when there was

101

somebody riding him every day."

"I could do that," a voice barely above a whisper said. Then Mia repeated it a little louder. "I could. I could do that." She looked up at her mother. I couldn't see her face, but I didn't have to. One little hand was reaching up to touch her mama's arm.

"Don't be silly, Mia," Mrs. Frey said. "You don't know how to ride a horse."

"I could learn," Mia said. "I like horses. Really. I do. I draw 'em a lot," she said, and turned and looked at me. Her face was shining with excitement and her pale blue eyes were pleading.

"Well now," I said, "I used to do that, too. My bedroom was covered with drawings of horses. Wasn't it, Clarissa?"

"Horses on the walls. Bugs in jars. Snakes in cages." Clarissa shuddered. "Never knew *what* you were going to find in CJ's room."

Mia giggled. Mrs. Frey smiled.

"Well, my little artist," I said to Mia, "what do you say? Would you like to spend some time helping an old lady with an old horse?" I looked at Mrs. Frey. "Do you think her grandmother would mind so much if she came to the Four Pines for a while?"

"Please, Mrs. Frey," Jo chimed in. "Say yes."

I noticed Clarissa looking very strangely at Ben. I think she knew something was going on, but she couldn't guess what. "But the Germans," she said, turning to Mrs. Frey. "CJ has filed the paper work to have *prisoners* working on the place."

Mrs. Frey smiled. "I know when the first trainload arrived back in '43, everyone was a little nervous about the whole idea. I had my own doubts — especially when the commander said he was going to hire a couple of them to clean the offices. But honestly, after having several different men rotate through our office to help out, I think most worries are unfounded."

"If the German army is made up of fun-loving linguists," Clarissa said dryly, "I don't understand why there's still a war going on."

Mrs. Frey didn't get riled. "Well, of course not all the prisoners are like Private Bauer and Sergeant Brock," she said. "Some of them — especially the first arrivals — were hard-core. But most of the more uncooperative ones have been transferred down to the camp in Oklahoma. And only the most trustworthy would be assigned to work details off the military reservation — if it's allowed at all. I think there's a question about having enough guards to allow it —

and they won't take any chances with that."
She tried to reassure Clarissa. "Really, Mrs.
Hale. You needn't worry in the least if PW
crews end up working on your sister's
ranch."

At that moment I really wished Will
Bishop was sitting at the table. I wouldn't
have *said* "I told you so," but I would have
thought it.

"Well, that's fine, then," I said.

Mrs. Frey looked down at Mia. "But we
will have to ask your daddy."

It was probably my imagination, but I
could have sworn little Mia actually *shivered.*

Clarissa got up from the table. I probably
should have helped her with something out
in the kitchen, but the truth is I didn't want
to listen to her rant. She was upset about the
PWs, and now she would be upset that Mrs.
Frey had called the Four Pines *my* ranch
when, in fact, Clarissa was part owner. She
had happily relinquished the running of the
place to me, but every once in a while she
liked to remind me that our daddy had left
the place to the both of us. And to have Mrs.
Frey assume otherwise was likely to be an irritation. It might, in fact, just result in
Clarissa's trying to force her will into the
PW issue. So I didn't give her the chance to
start ranting. There's no rant in the world

like a Clarissa Jackson rant. How Ben Hale has stood it all these years, I don't know. Then again, maybe he's found a way to charm even that out of her.

"Did I hear right? Did Daddy just tell me that Uncle Will has moved off the ranch?" Jo had followed me to the car.

"He's working at the remount," I said. "Leastways that's where he was headed when he drove out."

"But . . . ?"

I shook my head — my way of warning Jo not to pry. I forced a laugh. "Don't worry yourself over it. We had a disagreement. Will doesn't want the Germans. I need them. It'll blow over. He'll come home."

"He'd better," Jo said. "Johnny would have a fit if he thought you two were on the outs."

"And don't you be the one to write and tell him," I said. "We don't want Johnny worrying over things at home. Remember what they told us about that. Only good news from home. No complaining."

"I won't say a word," Jo promised.

I hitched up my dress and slid behind the wheel of my truck. Jo's hand was on the door and I patted it. "Glad you fell in line with the plan at lunch today, hon. It'll be fun to have another blondie on the place."

Jo grinned. "Wait until you see the real Mia Frey," she said.

"The real Mia?"

"You'll see," Jo said.

"I expect I will," I replied, and started the truck. It coughed and sputtered a minute.

"You should have Daddy look under the hood for you," Jo commented.

"Not on Sunday, Jo. Can't have the preacher working on the Sabbath, now, can we?"

Jo laughed. "Guess not." She leaned into the truck and kissed me on the cheek. "I love you, Aunt CJ," she said.

"Pshaw," I said, and swiped my cheek. "What's got into you, child?!"

Jo grinned. "You don't fool me one bit, you old softie."

I put the truck in reverse. "See to it you keep that to yourself," I said, then let out the clutch and headed toward home. As I drove by the Frey place, Mia was standing at the front gate. She waved and blew me a kiss. It did my heart good to think about Mia and Jo occupying the two empty bedrooms at the Four Pines. And old Will Bishop could stay at Fort Robinson for as long as he wanted for all I cared.

Of course, I did. Care. But I wasn't about to let Will or anyone else know.

Five

Rebuke a wise man, and he will love thee.

PROVERBS 9:8b

Will Bishop hadn't been at Fort Robinson for a week before he admitted to himself that he was miserable. It was, of course, completely the fault of one CJ Jackson. The woman turned up everywhere he went. Not in person, but since Will and CJ had grown up together in and around Fort Robinson, just about everywhere he looked he encountered a memory. As the weeks passed he tried not to think of her, but what could a man do? If he watched the sun rise, he was looking toward the old parade ground and the officers' quarters where he and his mother had come to live after his father died. While he lived in that house, he and CJ had played more pranks than a grown Will Bishop would ever own up to.

In the evenings, when the sun set over the bluffs in the distance, he was reminded of his and CJ's adventure up in those bluffs —

107

and the fall that nearly ended his life. When he reported to the animal superintendent at the remount service, he walked past the very building where his own grandfather had performed the surgery that saved his life. And even though the fort had grown many times over from the days when Will and CJ were children here, the place was still one big memory album for the aging wrangler.

It wasn't just his childhood memories of the fort that bothered Will. Every morning when he got up and headed to the mess hall for breakfast, he couldn't help but think about CJ drinking coffee all alone in the Four Pines kitchen. He wondered if she missed him at all.

Every day, as he went about the business of trimming manes and filing hooves, of mucking out stalls and evaluating horses, something inevitably happened that made him wonder about one horse or another on the Four Pines. He knew those horses as well as a parent knew their own children, and it bothered him, not being the one who fed and watered and monitored their well-being. The idea of another wrangler handling "his" herd was something like what Will imagined it would be for a man to have his children answer to another daddy. He hadn't expected to worry over them so much.

Every night, when he bedded down on a cot outside a row of stalls so he could keep an eye on the horses, Will looked up at the roof above him and wished it was the familiar ceiling at home. He would never think of anyplace in the same way he did the Four Pines. The path between the Four Pines owned by Laina and Caleb Jackson and the Rocking B Ranch owned by Nathan and Charlotte Boone was so well-worn by the time CJ and Will were teenagers that people in the area began to call it the Jackson-Boone Trail.

Will had ridden that trail by moonlight to be with CJ the night her mother died. CJ flew up the trail bareback to get to the Rocking B when Jack Greyfoot brought the news that Will's parents had been killed in a train accident back east. He and CJ had gone east together to bring the bodies of Nathan and Charlotte Boone back home. They had stood side-by-side when Jack Greyfoot's body was lowered into the grave beside Rachel's. Every Decoration Day they made sure Jack got his due as hero of the Great War even as their fathers were remembered for their service in the Civil War. And while he would never admit it to anyone but himself, Will knew that none of those family ties or memories were what made the Four Pines home. No, Will realized, the Four Pines Ranch was home because CJ Jackson was there, and he missed her — so much that the first Sunday after he left, he darned near went to church just so he could sit in the back pew and see that scruffy black straw hat of hers up near the front.

Thinking about the straw hat set Will to grinning — it being something of a private joke between him and CJ ever since Clarissa Hale tried to banish it from her sister's wardrobe.

"Say it straight out, Clarissa," CJ had snapped the Sunday Clarissa hinted at CJ's need to "keep up appearances" since she was part of the reverend's own family. "You know I don't like it when you hint."

"That hat," Clarissa had said, pointing to the hook by the back door where CJ kept her Sunday-go-to-meetin' hat, "is a disgrace."

"Really?" CJ said, glancing in Will's direction.

Will had to turn away to hide his smile, because he could see in the old gal's blue eyes that CJ Jackson had just decided that she would probably wear the black straw hat until the day she died.

"Yes," Clarissa said. "It's out of style by about fifteen years."

"Really?" CJ repeated.

Will wondered at Clarissa's oblivious perseverance when she offered to help CJ shop for something more stylish. Then he renamed oblivious perseverance "stupidity" when Clarissa went on to say, "And while we're at it, we really should get you a decent pair of shoes. Ben wouldn't say it, but it just isn't fair for his own family to be the laughingstock of the congregation."

Will saw CJ's cheeks grow red. Ordinarily he would have hightailed it out to the barn at that moment, but since he wasn't the cause of CJ's impending temper tantrum, he lingered.

"Laughingstock," CJ repeated. "I didn't know."

"Well, of course not," Clarissa said, practically falling over herself to be kind. "I know you'd never deliberately embarrass Ben. But really, CJ . . . cowboy boots with a dress?" She snorted. "And the same hat every Sunday, winter and summer . . . for years?"

CJ went to the back door. "Ben Hale," she called. When Ben peeked out from beneath the hood of his Nash, CJ waved him up to the house.

"Clarissa says I'm the laughingstock of the congregation. She says I've embarrassed you by wearing my boots and my straw hat

111

to church." CJ pointed to the hat. "Is that true, Ben Hale? Do I embarrass you?"

Will had never seen the Reverend Hale at a loss for words until that moment when the preacher raised his eyebrows and looked in disbelief at his wife. When he finally spoke it was to order his wife to help with the car outside.

For a moment, Will wished he could have wielded the kind of power over Mamie Parsons that Ben Hale apparently held over Clarissa, for at her husband's command the woman meekly ducked her head and scooted out the back door. Will couldn't resist going to the window over the kitchen sink and watching to see what would happen next. Once at the car, Clarissa slid into the passenger seat while Ben leaned against the driver's side and spoke to her through the open driver's side window. Will had never seen the reverend so animated. His entire upper body shook with the force of what he was telling his wife.

Will chuckled, but just when he turned to describe the scene to CJ, he was astonished to see that, while she was sweeping the kitchen floor, she was also crying.

He cleared his throat. CJ swept faster. "Come on, old girl," he said. "Don't you give her the satisfaction of seeing she's made you cry. She'll take those tears for a personal victory."

"I never meant to embarrass Ben," CJ muttered. She allowed Will to put his arms around her, but she didn't let go of the broom.

"And you never have," Will patted her on the shoulder. "You know how men are. They don't even notice such things."

"That's nice of you to say, Will. But it's a bald-faced lie."

"Is not," Will repeated.

"Is too," CJ insisted. "Just ask Mamie Parsons."

Will couldn't help his reaction to that name. He tensed up. CJ pulled away. He put one hand on each of the old girl's shoulders and looked her square in the eye. "You listen to me, CJ Jackson. Reverend Ben Hale is a real man — not a fool like I was when I was a young pup. And he wouldn't care if you wore your flannel shirt and your ten-gallon hat to church. And if you'll just take a look outside you'll know I'm telling you the truth." He gave her a little push, and she went to the kitchen window. Her tears stopped flowing as she watched Ben lecturing his wife.

Presently, Clarissa and Ben came to the door.

"I'm sorry," Clarissa said.

Will thought it sounded almost sincere.

"I wouldn't know what to do if that black straw hat wasn't in the third pew on the right every Sunday," Ben said.

Will knew that was sincere.

"I can only wish that half my congregation had a heart as good as yours, CJ," Ben said. He looked at his wife. "Go down to the barn and fetch Jo," he said. Clarissa went.

As soon as she was out of earshot, Ben said, "CJ —"

Will was never prouder of CJ Jackson than at that moment, because instead of dwelling on the hurt, the old girl rose to the occasion. "You know what, Ben," she interrupted. "The first time Clarissa brought you out to the Four Pines, I thought she'd corralled herself a real looker. Guess it's about time I told you that I'm very grateful for the fact that she also got herself a real man." She brushed the last of the tears off her cheeks — or maybe it was a fresh batch. Will couldn't be sure. Either way, she brushed them away and smiled up at Ben Hale, and while no more was said aloud, Will knew that volumes had been spoken.

It was memories like those — memories of CJ — that made him regret that Fort Robinson had been chosen as a site for a PW camp. If the Germans hadn't come . . . he'd still be at home. Pondering that thought, Will looked up from his chores and off toward the northwest, halfway thinking that if he could figure a way to salvage his pride . . .

"Mr. Bishop."

The voice at his side came so unexpectedly it made Will start. "What?" He sounded grumpy — which, he realized, was how he felt most of the time these days.

"Bill Harker wants you to meet him at the stud barn."

Will set the empty feed bucket in his hand on the ground and headed off in the direction of the barn where the stars of the remount's breeding program were housed. As he walked along, he passed a half-dead cottonwood tree. He remembered the first time it had been struck by lightning. It was the first time he had allowed himself to be coaxed outside after his accident. It had taken a lot of effort for Will to once again be able to stand up straight, and even longer to make his legs work well enough to make it out the front door and into his grandpa's rocking chair to watch the incoming storm clouds.

Just when CJ had gone inside to get Will a pillow to prop up his weak side, lightning had struck the ancient tree. There was a magnificent flash of light, and a *pop* that echoed all the way to the bluffs behind the house and back. When CJ charged back out to the porch, Will was so excited he forgot to be ashamed of his faltering speech. "You sh-sh-shoulda seen it, CJ!" he blurted out.

Walking by the once-towering tree that still showed the damage from that long-ago night, Will thought back to all the hours CJ had spent helping him recover, encouraging him to walk, patiently waiting while he learned to talk again. She'd even stuck by him when he had that "spell of stupid" with Mamie Parsons. It made it hard not to have the old gal around. Real hard.

"He's a great steeplechaser and has incredible bloodlines," Bill Harker said as he and Will made their way along the row of box stalls in the stud barn. "But he's a regular prince of darkness to handle and most of the boys around here won't go near him after their first encounter. I'm glad you decided to come on board. If anybody can figure out a way to humor him, I expect it'll be you."

Will followed Harker down the row of stalls to the last one on the left where the alleged prince of darkness had resided since being kicked while servicing a mare. While the effects of the injury were no longer visible, the animal was obviously disinclined to reacquaint himself with any other living flesh. Will had heard the creature snorting and stomping at the sound of their approach. Now, as the two men stood outside the stall, the horse bared his teeth and charged the stall door. Then he wheeled away and gave it a solid kick with both hind feet punctuated by a shrill whinny that Will could only describe as a scream.

"Whoa." Will backed away, almost stumbling over his bad foot. He leaned against the empty stall on the opposite side of the walkway and stood watching the stallion, who had plastered his rump against the back side of his own stall and stood there, rolling his eyes and alternately pawing the straw and tossing his head.

"We let him out twice a day — alone, of course — just long enough to muck out the stall, give him fresh water and oats, that sort of thing. You can see from the condition of his coat that he hasn't been brushed in a long time. And he isn't getting any calmer as the days go by."

Will tilted his head as he studied the animal. Without turning his gaze from the horse, he asked, "You got plans for that stall next to him?"

"We need it, but we can't use it. I thought maybe all he wanted was a stablemate, but that was a disaster. He nearly tore himself up trying to tear the wall down last time we put another horse in there. You should see him when we let him out in the corral." He paused. "I tried to get Bob Hanover to take him over to his place. He was thinking it over when he got word about his boy Ron getting killed. I'm not going to bother him with remount troubles right now."

Just the mention of Ron Hanover's death on Iwo Jima put a knot in Will's stomach. He hadn't had a letter from Johnny in a week. Or had he? Maybe CJ was being bull-headed about that, too.

"The truth is, Will, I would have asked you first, but this is definitely a hands-on project and I just never dreamed you'd be open to coming on here."

Will shrugged. "Times change." He studied the horse. "I'll just stand here a bit and see what I can see. If you don't mind, that is."

"You do whatever you think will help," Harker said. "I probably should have put him down weeks ago. He's just not the kind of animal we need around here. But . . . look at him. He's one of the most gorgeous pieces of horseflesh I've had the privilege to try to handle. And he's smart. If we can find a way to work the cussedness out of him, we'll put him up at the sale and hope for the best."

"You know how I work," Will said. "I'm not gonna hog-tie him. It's going to have to be his decision whether he trusts people or not. And that could take a while."

As the men spoke, the stallion began to move again, tossing his head and snorting. He kicked the side of his stall. Harker jumped. "I've never been afraid of a horse before, but I'm close to it with that son of a gun."

Will nodded. "He's got the evil eye, that's for sure." After a minute he added, "Can you keep the other boys out of this end of the barn for . . . oh, say, an hour or so?"

"I'm shorthanded as it is. They'll be more than happy to let you have him to yourself for as long as you want it." He sidled along the stall opposite the stallion's. Only when he was out of the horse's sight did he step to the center of the walkway. At the far end of the barn he turned and said, "Glad to have you, Bishop. Hope you stay on."

Will slowly raised his left hand to acknowledge the comment. When he did so, the stallion let out another scream and half-reared, flashing his front hooves. "Ah, shucks," Will said in a monotone. "Stop that nonsense, you big galoot. You aren't scaring me, and you're just making yourself ugly."

The horse screamed again and pawed the straw.

"Uh-huh, uh-huh. Keep being stupid. See if you don't end up dogmeat for the K-9 corps."

The horse snorted and tossed his head. He stared at Will.

Will stared back. After several minutes, the horse looked away and then back at Will, who watched the animal's ears flicking about. *You just keep listening,* Will thought, but he didn't say it aloud. Instead, he leaned back against the empty stall behind him and, hooking his thumbs through the belt loops of his jeans, kept watching the horse.

For the greater part of the next three days, Will did little more than stand opposite the stallion's stall watching his every move. When the "Prince of Darkness" was let out into the corral and the stall door closed to keep him out, it was Will who mucked out the stall. While he worked, he ran his hands along the iron bars forming the top half of the stall walls. He handled the water bucket and, after he poured oats into the horse's feed bucket, sifted the grain through his hands until everything the animal came in contact with bore Will Bishop's scent. At first it drove the animal into a frenzy. But by the third day, when the horse charged back inside his stall and lowered his head, he walked from place to place, snuffling.

"Yeah, that's right, Buster," Will said from his observation post — which, by now, was a kind of couch formed from bales of hay stacked out in the walkway. "You learn that scent, Buster Boy. That smell is connected to every good thing you get. Water. Oats. Fresh straw. There's nothing good coming your way without that smell on it. And this voice. You learn this voice, too. Your life depends on it, Buster."

"Uncle Will?"

Will lifted the shovel full of horse manure and turned around just in time to see Jo appear in the walkway outside Buster's empty stall.

"Well, well," Will said, "what brings you to the fort on a Wednesday afternoon?" His heart thumped. "Something wrong out at the ranch?"

"Daddy's talking to Captain Donovan about doing a chapel service for the PWs," Jo said. "And yes, there is something wrong at the ranch." Jo put her hands on her hips. "You moved out."

Will shrugged. "Oh, that." He reached for Buster's water bucket and headed up the walkway toward the water spigot.

"How could you, Uncle Will? How could you leave *now?* When she's already short-handed?"

"She won't be shorthanded for long," Will said. "She's got herself a fine plan to take care of that."

"The PWs," Jo said. "I know. She told me. Us. Mama's having a fit over me going out there."

Will nodded. "I'm not surprised."

"Mrs. Frey set them straight, though." At Will's questioning look, Jo explained. "She's been working here at the prison headquarters as a secretary. They have a couple of the PWs working for them, and Mrs. Frey doesn't think there's anything to worry over. In fact, she's letting little Mia come out for a visit, too." Jo frowned. "Things aren't going very well for them right now."

"Hank still not back to work?" Will asked.

Jo shook her head. Quickly, she told Will

all she knew about Hank Frey's home-coming.

"That's a shame," Will said. "A real shame." He hung the water bucket back in the stall and went for oats. On the opposite side of the back stall wall, Buster landed a thump on the door and snorted. "You just calm down, you big galoot," Will called.

Jo headed across the stall and put her hand on the door. "I'll —"

"No!" Will lurched across the stall to stop her. When Jo snatched her hand back and looked at him, Will explained. "I've got myself a real holy terror to try to handle. Nobody around here wants a thing to do with him. If I can't gentle him — at least make him manageable — he's gonna be dog food."

"Can I at least see him?" Jo said.

It was then that Will noticed the door was actually open a crack. Through the crack he could see a dark bay coat. Buster was standing quietly. If Will hadn't known better, he would have thought the horse was actually listening to their conversation.

"Say something," Will said, pointing to the crack in the door.

Jo followed his gaze. "Hi there, boy," she said gently. "What's all the fuss about, anyway? Are you so bad?"

From the other side of the door Buster snorted and stomped. But he stayed near the door.

Will pursed his lips and watched. He looked at Jo. "Come with me." Leading her out of the stall, he closed the door and latched it. At the water spigot he said, "You wait here. I'm gonna let him back inside. But don't you move until I tell you."

While Jo watched, Will went into the stall next to Buster's where he pulled on the rope he had rigged up to operate the sliding door at the back of Buster's stall so that anyone could let the horse in and out without getting near him. As soon as the door slid open far enough, Buster charged into his stall and to the door. He kicked the wall and snorted, going through the now-familiar routine of snuffling around for Will's scent on everything, tossing his head, and generally causing a ruckus. Will retreated to the walkway just outside the stall and took his seat on the hay-bale sofa.

"Now, Jo," he said, without looking her way, "tell me again what's new with you."

Jo swallowed. "All right," she said, her voice a low-pitched monotone. "I said you've got to come back to the Four Pines. For me."

At Jo's first words, Buster snorted and

tossed his head. Both his ears pointed in the direction of her voice.

"Keep talking," Will said.

"It just won't be the same without you. Aunt CJ doesn't say anything, but she misses you. I can tell."

"Keep talking," Will said as Buster stepped to the corner of the stall, obviously trying to see the owner of the female voice.

"And what would Johnny say if he knew you two were fighting like this?"

Will held up his hand. Without taking his eyes off Buster, he motioned her toward him. "Walk this way. Real slow. You've got this monster curious. Let's see what he thinks when he can take a look at you. But you stay on the far side of the walkway, and if he puts up a fuss you hightail it right back out of sight, you hear? He can't hurt you, but I don't want him hurting himself banging around in there, either. Now keep talking as you come this way."

"You once told me that Aunt CJ stuck by you through what you called your 'spell of stupid,' and I understand how you wouldn't want to be around German PWs, but honestly, Uncle Will, don't you think you could stick with Aunt CJ through what you think is *her* 'spell of stupid'?" Jo was standing next to Will by now. She came to a halt and stopped talking. "Wow," she said abruptly. "He's . . . wow."

Will nodded. "I'd say 'wow' about says it." He chuckled softly. "All this time trying to gentle him and all I had to do was introduce a female. Seems he's partial to the ladies."

"That just might be the most beautiful horse I've ever seen," Jo said.

Will nodded. "I tend to agree with you."

"Imagine what he'd look like if a person could only groom him."

"Not a chance of that . . . yet," Will said. "He's earned the name Prince of Darkness from everyone around here, although I'm partial to calling him Buster."

"Buster," Jo said, and stepped toward the stall.

Buster tossed his head, and, whirling around, presented his hindquarters and smacked the stall wall with both feet.

Jo jumped back, laughing nervously.

Buster snorted and tossed his head again, then plunged his muzzle into the bucket of oats hanging in the corner of his stall, and began to eat.

"He's big on letting humans know he's a tough guy," Will said, smiling.

"Just like you," Jo quipped.

Will frowned. "What?"

"Oh . . . you know what I mean. You make a point and then drive it home." She motioned to the barn. "We already knew you're a tough guy, Uncle Will. You can come on home now."

Six

*Wives, submit yourselves unto your
own husbands, as unto the Lord.*

EPHESIANS 5:22

Jo Hale was beginning to believe that her
father had some unusual form of the gift of
healing. It sure did seem to her that miracles
happened when Daddy "laid on hands"
under the hood of the 1935 Nash Aeroform
sedan he had been driving for as long as Jo
could remember. There just had to be a su-
pernatural component to the way the old rust
bucket simply would not die, something
beyond the known fact that the Reverend
Benjamin Hale was an anomaly — a preacher
with mechanical skills. As a child, Jo had
been present more than once when Hank
Frey's predecessor at the garage on Main
Street had fiddled and wiggled and shook his
head and told the preacher that "this was it,"
and he had better be looking for another car.

"Well," Daddy would say, as he put his
hands on his hips, "I guess it had to happen

sooner or later." And he would close the hood. But later Jo would peek in the garage window at home and there Daddy would be, tinkering and trying, and sure as the sunrise, the next morning Daddy would announce at breakfast that the Lord had decided to revive the old Nash yet again.

But on the Sunday afternoon when the Nash seemed to balk at the idea of taking the family out to Fort Robinson for the first PW service, Jo almost wished the car's guardian angels were on vacation. For the first time in her memory, Daddy had not been able to cajole Mother into having a good attitude about something against her will, and as Clarissa climbed silently into the front seat of the car with icy compliance, Jo's stomach did a flip-flop.

Just because Mother hadn't made a big fuss over last week's Sunday dinner — probably because Mrs. Frey was there — didn't mean she was going to give up, and she had taken more than one opportunity in the past week to protest. Even when everyone was in shock over the sudden death of President Roosevelt, Mother was not distracted from her goal. "Our beloved president is dead, Ben. It's the worst time imaginable to appear to be soft toward the enemy. The neighbors will shun us," she said.

When that did not sway Daddy, she tried another tack. "What about poor Hank Frey? How do you suppose he'll feel, knowing his own *pastor* —"

"Forgave the enemy the way the Bible says we should?" Daddy interrupted.

Mother pursed her lips and shook her head. "We can't be expected to obey every single jot and tittle. Not at a time like this."

"I suspect God knew about World War II when He wrote His book, Clarissa. And of course we are expected to obey. *Especially* at a time like this." Jo's dad tilted his head and looked at his wife. "I've tried to ignore the still, small voice inside telling me to do this. I can't ignore it anymore."

"Well, I'm not going," Mother said firmly.

Jo had seen very little of what her father had sometimes referred to as a "tendency to bullheadedness in my youth," but she got a glimpse of it then. "You are going," Daddy said quietly. "I'll need you to play the piano." Then he turned and looked at Jo. "Both of you are going. It will send a more positive message, both to the community and to the prisoners." He looked steadily across the table at his wife.

As her two parents warred across the dinner table, Jo watched, expecting her mother's chin to tremble and her eyes to fill with tears. Mother cried when she was angry. When no tears materialized, Jo's midsection tightened. It was a serious fight when Mother didn't try to wheedle and Daddy didn't joke. His face was gentle, but his usually clear blue eyes were stern as he stared down his wife. It seemed like hours before Mother swallowed, cleared her throat, and said, "All right, Ben. If that's what you want."

Daddy gave a little nod. "Good." He stood up and went to the door. "I'm going to go across to my study and work on my sermon," he said, then turned back. "It's not about what *I* want, Clarissa. It's the Lord who wants it." He glanced at Jo. "From all of us. The Lord's compassions are new every morning. He extends them to *all* men. We can do no less."

Jo rose to help her mother with supper dishes, but Mother waved her away. "Does that long black skirt still fit you?" she asked.

Jo frowned. "What?"

"The long black skirt you wore to Mr. Koch's funeral last year. Do you still have it?"

"I suppose so. Somewhere."

"Well, dig it out." Mother looked at her. "And I'll be getting you up early in the morning to tame that mane of yours. I won't have those —" She swallowed hard, then drew herself up. "We'll be dressing very conservatively," she said.

Jo retreated to her room, where she dug out the despised black skirt. The tension in her mother's voice was spilling over into her own mood, but when she thought about it, she realized that part of the tension was a tiny thrill of danger and adventure. She was going *inside* the prisoner compound. She was sick of hearing about Michelle Brighton from Whitney and how she'd volunteered for service. She'd just read an article in the local newspaper touting the "local girl serving her country," and there was Michelle's face plastered on the front page. Now Delores said she was going to be a WAAC, too. Well, Jo thought, let Michelle and Delores go off to Fort Des Moines, so what. Neither of them would get so much as a glimpse of the enemy in Iowa. When they came home on leave it would be Josephine Hale who'd seen the Nazis, not Michelle Brighton or Delores Black.

What, Jo wondered, perching on the foot of her bed, would it be like? Would they goose-step in? Would they have hateful stares when Daddy got up to preach? A lot of people in Crawford had opinions and ideas about the Germans, but Daddy kept saying it was all based on rumor and not to be believed. Mrs. Black said they didn't know what Jell-O was. A guard at the fort had told her the German cooks mixed Jell-O in hot water and drank it. Jo pictured the round-faced PW on the train drinking Jell-O. What, she wondered, did they think about Nebraska? What kind of people were the Germans, anyway?

The only thing Jo knew for sure about the German prisoners was what Mrs. Frey said about the two working in her office. And the only real "old-country German" Jo had ever known was Mrs. Koch, who was about as far from a square-jawed Nazi as a person could imagine. Mrs. Koch was more like everyone's favorite grandma. Her special cookies had become an expected part of every Christmas Eve celebration at the church, and she was always crocheting a baby blanket or knitting slippers for someone.

For the first time since the war began, Jo wondered if Mrs. Koch, who spoke English with a thick German accent, had relatives back in Germany. Had someone she knew lived in Dresden? Had they been hurt in the air raids? Johnny had been part of the mission back in February that destroyed three-fourths of that city. Jo didn't like the feeling

133

it gave her to think about Germans as something other than "the ones who are trying to kill Johnny." And after tomorrow she was going to have more than just the muddled impressions from the train car. She was curious and excited and a little bit afraid.

Grabbing the black skirt and a blouse of her own choosing, Jo headed out to the kitchen to set up the ironing board. "Is this blouse all right, Mother?" she asked as she plugged in the iron and sprinkled the skirt with water. She added before her mother answered, "And can I wear a hat?"

"Of course you should wear a hat," Mother snapped.

"Are you . . . afraid, Mama?" Jo asked.

"Of course I'm not afraid!"

Jo knew her Mother was not only afraid, but also more angry at Daddy than Jo had ever seen. As Jo pressed the wrinkles out of the black skirt she'd declared "hopelessly frumpy" a year earlier, she pondered the idea of a God who told Daddy to go to the prison camp and preach. She didn't doubt that Daddy was sincere. He really believed he was doing God's will. What she didn't understand was why, if God spoke so clearly to Daddy, He didn't take a minute to give Mother the same message.

And now here they were, loaded into the

car, and Jo wasn't sure if she wanted it to start or not. Maybe, Jo thought, Daddy had misunderstood the message from God. While Daddy rolled up his sleeves and jiggled parts under the hood, Mother and Jo retreated to the kitchen. For nearly half an hour Mother sat drinking tea and thumping the tabletop with her fingers in a nervous rhythm.

Footsteps sounded on the back porch. "Josephine," Daddy called, "Come out and help me!"

Jo climbed behind the steering wheel and followed her father's instructions and finally, with a backfire that sounded like a gunshot, the car rumbled to life. Daddy's blue eyes sparkled with joy as he closed the hood and winked at her. "Praise the Lord!" he said, and headed inside to wash his hands. Jo slid into the backseat, almost grateful for the unfashionable length of the black skirt that would hide most of her bare legs. Aunt CJ's ration notwithstanding, a girl had to be careful with nylons, and Jo was not about to waste a good pair of nylons on a bunch of prisoners who probably smelled of sauerkraut.

The ride westward to Fort Robinson passed in unnatural quiet. Mother was

135

taking pains to let Daddy know exactly what she thought of his idea. She sat with her head turned so she could see out the side window. She seemed to be studying every detail of the bluffs that formed a ridge looming above Highway 20 as if she'd never seen them before. As the Nash turned off the highway that divided Fort Robinson into "new" to the north and "old" to the south and wound its way past the old fort parade ground and toward the prison compound erected not far from where old Red Cloud himself had made camp and traded with the white men invading his ancestral home, Jo's pulse quickened.

When they came to a gate Jo relaxed a little. None other than Deacon Tom Hanson was waiting outside the guardhouse to greet them. When he leaned down and tipped his hat to Mother, you would never have known she was anything but excited about serving the Lord among the German prisoners of war.

"You got a beautiful spring day for your drive out, Mrs. Hale," Deacon Hanson said.

"Indeed we did," Mother replied. She even nodded inside the fence. "I didn't expect to see spring flowers planted here."

"There's a lot that's unexpected about

these men," Deacon Hanson said. "You could have quite a choir depending on who shows up. There are some true musicians inside this fence. Back in '43 we had the entire 47th Infantry Regiment Band, but they were transferred out. Still, just last Christmas Eve the band that plays for their variety shows lined up just over there and serenaded their guards. I wasn't here, but Sergeant Isaacson said it was quite beautiful."

"Now you're making me nervous," Mother said, laughing as if she didn't have a care in the world. "I'm just here to plunk out the four parts written in the hymnal."

"I'm sure they will appreciate it," Deacon Hanson said warmly. He looked past Mother at Daddy. "Captain Donovan said to park over there by headquarters." He gestured toward the building, and Jo recognized the deacon's car. "I'll wait for you here."

"You didn't tell me Tom was going to join us," Mother said as Daddy parked the Nash.

"I wasn't sure if he would be able to come."

"We should have given him a ride."

"I offered. He said he'd rather drive out on his own."

Jo was relieved when Mother waited for Daddy to get out and walk around to her door. Things were thawing.

Daddy held out his hand. Mother took it, and he wrapped it through his arm. "Josephine," Daddy said, "carry the hymnal for your mother."

Jo felt a shiver go up her spine at the thought of walking right through the prison compound, then a pang of regret when Deacon Hanson motioned them toward the chapel just a short distance away. It wasn't much of a walk. Still, they were inside the fence, and all around them were guard towers. It was at once comforting and unnerving.

"What did I tell you?" Daddy said to Mother, patting her hand. "There's nothing to be afraid of."

"I'm not afraid," Mother snapped. "I'm mad. What on earth a man could be thinking to bring his wife and daughter into this —"

"Look over there," Daddy said and nodded toward a trio of WAACs making their way toward the K-9 compound. "They have their own two-story barracks, a mess hall — even their own beauty shop — all right across the road behind the new officers' quarters."

"What woman in her right mind would want to be a WAAC?" Mother mumbled.

"Delores does," Jo spoke up.

"Exactly my point," Mother snapped.

"I think it would be fascinating," Jo said.

"Well, I don't know how fascinating it is," Daddy replied, "but they perform all kinds of important jobs. Secretarial, motor pool, all kinds of things."

"Join the army and drive a truck," Mother said. "Just what every mother dreams for her little girl. Unless, of course, she can be housed within a mile of a thousand or more Nazi prisoners. That's even *more* special."

"Tom said one of the responsibilities of the WAACs is driving the trucks that take the prisoners back and forth to their jobs over at the remount depot. You know the men can't be dangerous or that would never be allowed."

"Well, thank you, Reverend Hale," Mother said with exaggerated sweetness. "I feel so very much better." She looked at Jo. "We'll sign you right up, honey, soon as we get back to town. Who needs a college education when they can *pump gas* for the *motor pool?!*"

Things were quiet as the three headed up the steps and went inside the chapel. Deacon Hanson followed them up the

139

center aisle. "It's hard to imagine that not so long ago some of the PWs were worshiping in Lutheran churches in beautiful neighborhoods."

Jo was surprised when Mother grumbled again at Daddy — this time within Deacon Hanson's hearing, "Let's just get this over with and get home."

Seven

The way of a fool is right
in his own eyes. . . .

PROVERBS 12:15

Relax, man. Just relax. Inwardly, Private Franco Romani crossed himself and begged the Blessed Virgin to keep his voice from shaking when he made his announcement to the mess hall filled with hungry PWs. He scanned the room, watching the prisoners while he reviewed all the reasons not to be nervous.

You expected that Private Bauer to come at you with his fists the first time you talked to him. Did it happen? No.

Romani remembered the incident as if it had happened this morning instead of weeks ago. A burly sergeant had sent him to stop a prisoner from rummaging through a barrel of items they had been ordered to hand over. When the prisoner stood up with a shaving kit in his hand, he towered over Romani. The prisoner started to babble and

141

gesture, and a voice said, "He's trying to explain," and there was an Aryan poster boy looking at Romani with clear blue eyes and an unreadable expression. Feeling surrounded by the enemy, Romani barely managed to stifle the urge to step back as he barked, "Orders are to leave personal items in the barrels."

The boy began to babble again. Romani could hear the pleading tone even through what he considered to be the almost animalistic sounds of the German language.

"He asks you to take pity," the blond poster boy said. "He begs you to let him keep the shaving kit. It was a gift from his sister. She died just before the war."

The giant looked from Romani to the poster boy and nodded. It was getting embarrassing. The kid was almost in tears. "Give it here," Romani blurted out, and snatched the shaving kit away. He opened it. Looking over his shoulder, he saw the sergeant who had ordered him to handle the situation striding toward a much more threatening-looking collection of prisoners on the other side of the holding room. "Here," he said, and thrust the kit toward the kid. "But get moving." He gestured toward the poster boy. "Both of you. Over there."

"Danke, danke, danke," the kid said, bobbing up and down, and bowing as he lumbered to where Romani directed him. To keep from being called to help with a group of prisoners that looked hardened enough to have been Hitler's own staff, Romani pretended to shuttle the kid and his friend to the opposite side of the room.

And now here they were, a train ride, a delousing, and two weeks of imprisonment later, having caused no trouble at all. So why, Romani wondered, couldn't he get rid of the knot in his gut?

Not even Gunnar Stroh, who looked like he would relish the idea of eliminating Franco Romani from the earth, had caused any trouble. He grumbled in German once in a while behind a guard's back, but that was all. However, Romani was certain that one of the homemade weapons found in last month's sweep of the prison compound belonged to Stroh. The man still bore watching.

While Romani congratulated himself on getting "his" prisoners to Nebraska without incident, he pressed his back against the mess hall door and clenched his hands. He was certain his military bearing was part of the reason he'd had no trouble. He had determined to be gruff and unapproachable ever since he escorted the men through the delousing process in New York and then past the doctor who plunged a very long needle into their backsides with relish. As long as he could keep them thinking he was a no-nonsense kind of guard, maybe he'd make it through. As he stood looking out over the mess hall, he could feel sweat trickling down his back between his shoulder blades. The men must never know how poorly Franco Romani had done in basic training.

Nothing happened on the train, he reminded himself. *Nothing has happened here in Nebraska, either — unless you count the dead cow lying across the tracks when we went through town.* Romani almost sighed audibly. His image of life in the army had never included living in a place where the biggest news of the day might be a cow getting struck by lightning and stopping a train for a few minutes. Although talking to those two girls had definitely been a good thing. If those two were any indication, they grew them pretty out west.

The quiet in the mess hall brought him back to the moment. He was supposed to make an announcement. How long had he been daydreaming by the door? He cleared

144

his throat and barked out, "Attention! Those who wish to attend the afternoon church service should be ready to fall out at exactly fourteen hundred hours. I will escort you to the chapel. As we have announced, the service will be conducted by the Baptist minister from Crawford."

Darn. He had forgotten to ask Dieter Brock to translate. But without even a nod from Romani, Brock stood up and shouted German. Romani could only assume it must be the announcement about the new chapel service. Being in a room full of babbling prisoners got on a man's nerves after a while. Tiring quickly of standing still, Romani sauntered down the row of tables while the men finished eating. As he walked, conversations stopped, then started up again after he had passed. Nothing bothered him more than when they mumbled behind his back. Well, he thought, as he walked the perimeter of the room, that wasn't exactly true. Army food bothered him. And the boredom. And, he thought, as he walked past the Aryan poster boy . . . the fact that Angelina hadn't written. Not once. He could not suppress the fear that in spite of her promise to him, Angelina had kept going to the club for servicemen just around the corner from the apartment she shared with four other girls back home in Brooklyn. He was writing her every day — and Franco Romani was not a man who wrote letters. He was not, for that matter, a man to wear his feelings on his sleeve. But thinking of Angelina was one of the few things that kept him sane. Angelina thought he was brave. Angelina was proud of him.

Beloved Angelina, he had written only the night before.

Imagine nothingness and still you cannot imagine the place to which I have been sent. This part of Nebraska is called the Sandhills, but from what I have seen there is much more sand than hills. The view from the train was very discouraging, although there is a ridge of bluffs not far from the military reservation with some interesting Indian legends attached to them. I will save those for another letter.

It is very hard to look at the mounds of food on these prisoners' plates and think of how you must count stamps in a ration book. They have German cooks and no rationing. Sausage and sauerkraut and rye bread and those little cookies called pfefferneusse. (Remember that old couple who ran the bakery around the corner? They made piles of those things at Christmas). And plenty of butter and sugar and whatever else they want. Well, not everything — but still.

How I miss my girl! The citizens of the nearby town have tried to make a Servicemen's Club, and while it is well intentioned, it is not much to a boy from Brooklyn who is used to dancing his weekends away with the prettiest girl in town. And besides, if I have asked you not to go to the club in New York, the least I can do is stay away from the female company in Crawford.

I could tell you many stories of the train ride out here, but the most amusing was when one of the men accused us of running the trains in circles. He couldn't believe America was so big. I must admit I almost agree with him. I didn't think it would take us so long to get out here. Nor did I think things would be so desolate. Why anyone would choose to live in Nebraska, I cannot say. Honestly, one expects Indians to come charging across the prairie at any moment. Do not worry. I have not seen a single Indian yet, although Sergeant Isaacson says there are some Sioux employed as wranglers over on the remount part of the post.

The Germans are interested in the western legends. One day when a very spirited debate was going on, my translator said they were talking about a German writer named Karl May who wrote about the American West. He is the favorite writer of some of these men, and they seem to actually be excited about being out here. "It would be wonderful to ride a stallion across the prairie," one of them said. Of course they are thinking of riding to freedom, although after being a Nazi they don't know what freedom is. But they don't know that they don't know. The materials in their reading room are designed to introduce them to the idea. And there are classes on American government and democracy. I am surprised at how many of them attend both these classes and the church services. Yes. Church. There was a weekly Lutheran service and a weekly mass already in place when I arrived with my prisoners, and now the Baptist minister from Crawford is coming on Sunday afternoons. Never fear, America — the Nazis are getting overdoses of religion during their stay in our fair country.

Fort Robinson is actually three different places with separate military headquarters and organizations to run each one. In addition to the prisoner of war camp, there is the remount service and the K-9 corps. Remount takes in all the cavalry horses from the army and sees that they are "remounted" by civilians. There are thousands of horses just across the road. They arrive by the train-load and horse sales take place every few weeks. Some of the men want to learn to ride while they are here, but I am not one of them.

In addition to horses, we have dogs, dogs, and more dogs. Over a thousand are being trained as sentries, scouts, or messengers. The K-9 has separate bar-racks and mess halls from us, so I don't have much to do with them. But I hear them. Every night — barking and yapping and baying at the moon. When I think I have it bad being assigned to guard Nazi prisoners, I realize I could be slaugh-tering horses to feed the dogs or shov-eling manure by the ton. If only you could convince your parents to let you take the train to visit me, I would have nothing to complain about.

The Germans aren't too bad. Of the men in my compound I am only con-cerned about one or two who have hung

Nazi flags over their beds and seem to be waiting for America to be invaded by the German navy. The other day one of the men was taking the eagle off his uniform to barter for something, and a hardcase named Gunnar Stroh told him he'd better keep it, that he would need it for the occupation. I only know this because it came out after we broke up the fight that ensued. Don't worry. Stroh is in the minority. Others are almost friendly, although I am keeping my eye on my translator. Sometimes I think that beneath his blond hair is a mind plotting escape.

While his mind wandered, Private Franco Romani was the center of attention for one table of prisoners in the mess hall where he was supposed to keep order. Seated at a table with five other men who, if not friends, were at least a loose association of men who had walked through the prison experience together, Gunnar Stroh nodded his almost bald graying head toward the daydreaming guard and muttered, "He's gone again." He shook his head. "If I would have spent as much time as that idiot does in another place, I'd have died in the first week of battle."

"He's never been in a battle," Dieter

150

Brock offered. "You should have been in our car on the train. He held his rifle like we used to hold sticks when we were children playing at war."

Across from Brock, Rolf Shrader twisted around and peered toward the door, then leaned forward and whispered to the table of six men, "Ten American cents says five minutes."

Stroh shook his head. "Too easy," he said. "They'll be calling us all to line up and fall out soon. He'll have to stop daydreaming."

"All right," Rolf said, sighing. "*Ten* minutes. But you have to bet twice as much." He looked around the table. "And you ALL have to bet."

Bruno Bauer's eyes grew wide, and the young giant shook his head. "Not me," he said. "I need my money."

"What for?" Rolf said. "It isn't real money, anyway. It's not like you can take it home."

Bruno shrugged. "Maybe not, but I can buy soap at the canteen and take *that* home to Mama. And all my cousins."

Stroh looked at the younger man with disdain. "Taking soap home to Mama, are you? What a good little boy you are." He reached over and pinched Bruno's earlobe.

"Hey!" Bauer pulled away.

When Stroh reached for the other ear, his hand was stopped in midair by Dieter Brock's palm. "Leave him alone," Dieter said.

Stroh stared at Brock for a moment. When the other man didn't back down, he rattled off a few choice names for both Bruno — whom he called a weakling among other things — and Dieter.

Brock stared at Stroh, unmoved by the man's string of profanities. "Leave him alone," he repeated. "Just because you don't have a mother in Germany waiting for you to come home doesn't give you a reason to make fun of Bruno." He paused and then said diplomatically, "And you will agree that Germany will need its mothers and sons to rebuild."

"Right," Shrader chimed in. "And the mothers and sons will need soap or . . ." He made a comical face and held his nose.

"You," Stroh said with a disgusted grimace. "Always joking."

"That's me," Shrader said, and bobbled his head from side to side, "your favorite comedian." He peered at Stroh out of the corner of his eyes and worked his eyebrows up and down.

Bruno burst out laughing.

"You there!"

At the sound of Romani's voice, the men at the table glanced at the clock at the front of the mess hall.

"Three minutes," Stroh said and held out his hand toward Shrader. "You lost the bet. Pay me."

Romani's voice, thick with its own accent from the land of Mussolini, sounded across the room. "I repeat . . . those attending chapel must form up outside their barracks at fourteen hundred hours."

While the men didn't need an interpreter to know what was said, everyone pretended not to understand. Gunnar Stroh looked around his table in smug satisfaction as the young Italian guard's face flushed with the realization that he had failed — again — to ask Dieter to translate for him.

Dieter stood up. He repeated the order and grabbed his tray. "Come on," he said to Rolf Shrader. "We can get in a game of table tennis before the service starts."

Gunnar Stroh frowned. "You? Church?!"

Dieter shrugged. "It's better than sitting around the reading room all afternoon learning about this battle and that battle and surrender."

"It will change," Gunnar insisted, looking around him. "You will all need your uniforms again one day."

"Yes," Rolf said. "I personally am planning to sell mine to the first American soldier who wants a souvenir."

Stroh looked ready to explode.

Dieter maneuvered his lunch tray between them. "I take it you aren't going to church?" he said to Stroh, who shook his head. "Then let us by. And as for the guard, we'd all better hope he never figures out what we're talking about when we bet on his lapses. I don't think he would find that amusing."

"Quiet!" Romani shouted. "*Mach schnell,* ladies." He looked at Dieter and smirked. "You won't need to translate *that.*" He laughed at his own joke. No one joined in.

Eight

*A broken and a contrite heart, O God,
thou wilt not despise.*

PSALM 51:17

Having the courage to die had never been a
problem. But whether or not he had the
courage to live had been eating away at
Dieter Brock since the day his unit surren-
dered in the desert. When Hitler changed his
orders from "fight to the last man" to "fight
to the last shell," men all around Dieter had
begun breaking their shells. Dieter was so en-
raged he almost grabbed a rifle and shot them
all. Instead, he made a speech about the fatherland and glory. But this time, his musical
voice had no effect on the men. This time,
they stared at him like lifeless dolls, un-
swayed by his patriotism.

"Look down there," Unteroffizier Von
Runkle said, nodding toward where they
could see the British swarming the estate
where, only hours ago, the very men on the
hillside had been living in luxury. "Do you

think our resistance has any point at all? Africa is lost. Rommel is gone. You will have to find glory on another battlefield, Brock."

"We could escape," Dieter insisted. "I told you how."

"Oh, yes," Von Runkle snorted. "I heard you. Right into the belly of the enemy. Convince the British we are Russians. The Americans we are Dutch." He shook his head. "It's over."

Someone else spoke up. "My father was treated well by the Americans in the last war. It's only reasonable to expect the same this time."

"You aren't being captured by Americans," Brock snarled. "And we've dropped enough bombs on England to destroy most of the country. I don't think you should be expecting satin pillows and plates piled high with plum pudding. And if they give us to the French —"

"If they give us to the French, you'll be doing the same thing you've been doing since the war started," Von Runkle said. "You speak French, too, so you'll be valuable to them. You have nothing to fear."

"I'm not afraid!" Brock snarled.

"And no one said you are." Von Runkle leaned close. "Listen to me. You have the scars and the medals to prove you are one of our best. But it is *over* for us." He gripped Dieter's forearm. "Now it is time to turn our minds toward the future. To waiting until we have the opportunity to help rebuild our beloved fatherland." He nodded toward the British down below. "Once they are finished with us, we will be needed at home. And you, *Herr* Brock, will be among the best of the best. Listen to me. Do not fall in love with your hatred. I know it has given you strength in the past. More than once it kept you silent under interrogation. But this time you are *not* going to escape. Face it." He paused. "You have had the courage to die. Now you muster another kind of courage. The courage to live. Obey their orders. Eat what you are given. Preserve your strength. Germany will need you again. When she does, be ready."

All across the Atlantic, when he had been too seasick to do anything but lie in his berth and vomit into a biscuit tin, Dieter Brock had pondered Von Runkle's words. Von Runkle was gone, dead of an illness that swept the mud-soaked prison camp long before the prisoners boarded the ship that would take them to America. But his words echoed in Dieter's mind. They continued to sustain him off the ship, onto the ferry, and then to the train — which was not a cattle car, after all, but rather a first-class Pullman — and all across the vast expanse of America to the desert called the Nebraska Sandhills. He had learned about the American West by watching Tom Mix movies. But he had never heard of Nebraska. When he stepped off the train and looked around him, his heart sank. Except for a low ridge barely visible against the distant gray sky, the land was flat. Except for thick, tall grass and an occasional small tree, the land was barren.

They were treated surprisingly well. Dieter had expected to be nearly starved, but on the train and since the arrival in Nebraska, they had been fed mountains of food. He had expected they might end up living in tents — Rolf Shrader, who admired Karl May, said it would be fun to live in tepees like the American Indians — but instead they were escorted into clean new barracks. They had their own showers. Hot water. Soap. Even mirrors. Dieter had expected the guards to be surly and hateful. But with one or two exceptions, they treated their charges well. A few like Private Romani seemed to relish the chance to prove themselves "tough" with the prisoners. But men like Sergeant Isaacson, who had actually seen battle, treated them with the honor code understood by true warriors.

And now here Dieter was, twenty-one years old and still hoping that what Von Runkle said was true, that he would have the opportunity to serve his country again. More than a personal code of honor fueled his determination. He would never tell another living soul, but every time he was tempted to despair — and he had considered ways to end his own life — every time, the face of his little mother stopped him. *"You will be my first thought in the morning and my last thought at night, mein schatz,"* she had said the morning he left to enlist. *"And with each thought,"* Mama said, *"will be a thousand prayers."*

Prayers. Personally, Dieter didn't see the point. But Mama did. That was what was important. If praying for her son made his leaving bearable, then Dieter hoped his little mother "prayed without ceasing," as her Bible told her to do. At night, when the dogs barked and the coyotes howled and he could not sleep, Dieter lay in his cot looking up at the ceiling as he pictured his little mother clinging to the letter he had written her. They had been told what to write the first time:

I have been taken prisoner, and I am well. My new address is Fort Robinson, Nebraska, Box 20, New York.

There was room for Mama to answer on the very same card. But no reply had come.

He had written again, this time using the code they had devised so she would know where he was. If she didn't trust the Red Cross card, she would know from his letter it told the truth. The first letter of every sentence in the letter spelled his location in America. N-E-B-R-A-S-K-A. Still, no reply came.

As he made his way up the steps to the compound chapel, Dieter thought again of his mother. He imagined her gray head bowed over a scrap of paper as she scratched out a letter to her brother Konrad, who lived in Chicago. She would be wishing she and her only boy had come to America when Uncle Konrad invited them after Papa died. She would be blaming herself for Dieter's predicament.

As he filed up the center aisle of the prison compound chapel, Dieter wished there were some way for Mama to know that her boy was in church today. She would be pleased. Was there any more beautiful smile in the world than the smile a mother gave

160

the son she loved? As he sat down between Bruno Bauer and Rolf Shrader, his eyes began to water.

"Thank you for agreeing to translate for me," a voice said. "My grandparents were German, but I didn't learn to speak the language."

Dieter looked up. The American pastor was extending his hand and introducing himself as Ben Hale — not even using the title Reverend or Pastor. That was strange. Dieter stood up and shook the man's hand. He had a firm grip and looked Dieter in the eye.

"We'll sing a hymn first," the preacher said. "Would you come and stand beside me after that? I'll say a short prayer and then a message." He smiled. "It won't be a long sermon."

Dieter thought the pastor seemed a bit nervous. But he was sincere. Not condescending.

"As you wish," Dieter said.

"This is my wife," the preacher said, motioning toward an attractive woman sitting at the piano. "And my daughter," he said.

Nod, but don't look at their faces. While he wasn't above using his broad shoulders and square jaw to get what he wanted, Brock had learned the hard way that being

161

what Gunnar Stroh called a "poster boy" had its problems. People tended to assume things about the most innocent of gestures or remarks. Even now, Dieter could feel Romani watching him. It wouldn't take very much for the overzealous guard to decide he had done something inappropriate. Romani might depend on Brock to translate for him, but he also loved excuses to write him up for discipline.

Dieter looked at the floor and barely nodded in response to the pastor's introduction — until the hymn started. Once the wife was playing the piano, and Romani moved to the back of the chapel, Dieter looked up.

Jo stared out the rear window of the Nash until she could no longer see the prison compound gate. "Are we coming back next Sunday?" she asked.

"Your mother and I will," Daddy said.

Jo saw her mother inspecting her in the rearview mirror.

"I liked helping," Jo said, hoping she looked pious. "It made me feel good — like I'm doing something important." She looked out the window so her mother couldn't see her face. "Was it . . . odd . . . to have to wait for the interpreter to put your

162

words into German?"

Daddy grinned. "Not so much odd as disquieting. I kept wondering if he was really translating what I said, or if he was making some kind of morale speech for the Fuehrer. He certainly had the voice for it."

"Do you think — Do you think he . . . or any of them . . . believe like we do?"

"I don't know. I imagine most are Lutheran, if they are anything at all."

"So why'd they come to a Baptist service?"

"Boredom," Daddy said. "Entertainment. A chance to see Americans. I suppose there were as many reasons as there were men."

"I didn't want to appear to be staring at them," Mother said, "so I didn't get a count, but Tom said he guessed about thirty came."

"Maybe we'll have more next week," Jo said.

"Maybe," Daddy nodded. "Lord willing." He paused before adding, "But I don't think we'll have you come again."

"Why not?"

"Aunt CJ needs you more at the ranch than we need you for the chapel service," Mother chimed in. "I'm going to call her when we get home and tell her to plan on you coming out to visit after church next Sunday morning. With Mia. You can introduce Mia to Ned, and then your father and I will drive out and pick you up after the service at the fort."

"But —" Jo started to protest.

"You heard your mother," Daddy said. "The subject is closed."

Jo fumed. She was glad Mother wasn't angry anymore, but now her parents had that "united front" thing going again.

Daddy slid his hand across the front seat and squeezed Mother's.

Mother looked at Daddy with *that* smile.

Jo sighed. The subject was definitely closed.

"So," Ben said once they were upstairs in their room changing out of their church clothes. "Was it so bad?"

"It was fine," Clarissa said. She sat at the foot of the bed and slipped her shoes off.

"They certainly liked your piano playing."

"Thank goodness Tom knew to suggest 'A Mighty Fortress Is Our God,'" Clarissa said. She smiled. "I certainly never expected to find myself hearing that grand old hymn sung in German — loudly, and off-key in some cases."

"Except for the translator," Ben said. "He has a nice singing voice."

"Yes," Clarissa murmured. "He is quite the . . . exception."

"I think they were all trying to show their appreciation for our coming," Ben said.

"Even after hearing Mrs. Frey describe the PWs who work in her office, I never expected them to be so . . . human." She sighed. "The one standing beside Brock during the singing had such a boyish grin. He seemed so eager to be nice. I don't know what I expected . . ." she said, her voice trailing off. "But that wasn't it."

Ben slid his tie off, hung it up on a nail inside the closet, and began to unbutton his shirt.

"Your sermon was wonderful," Clarissa said.

Ben nodded. "Thank you kindly. I'm surprised you listened."

"I have come to bring to you the Word of God in your troubled existence," Clarissa recited. *"Jesus Christ did not differentiate between people. You are here as prisoners of this terrible war, but all men are prisoners on this earth until the Lord makes them free. Do not give up your hope in God. He has not forgotten you here. The new life that is springing up all around us on this*

beautiful spring day is proof. It may be hard for some of you to believe in God because of what has happened to you. But he who believes in God will be free, even though he may be surrounded by barbed wire, and those who do not believe are prisoners wherever they may live. 'If the Son therefore makes you free, ye shall be free indeed.'"

"What's this?" Ben said, going to his wife and swiping a tear off her cheek.

Clarissa swallowed hard and sniffed. "The tall one with the sweet face. I know we can't see the heart, but — his face beamed when he was singing. Like he was somehow oblivious to the circumstances. It made me think of Johnny, and Ron Hanover, and all the others who haven't come back yet . . . or never will." She looked down at her hands and touched her wedding ring. "And of our neighbor."

"Hank?"

Clarissa nodded. "He's *home* — free to go to work every day, free to hold his wife, free to play with his child, to talk to his neighbors, and yet —"

"He's in a prison of hatred and bitterness," Ben said.

Clarissa sighed. "It's so sad." She stood up and headed for the closet, then turned around. "I'm proud of you, Ben. I didn't want to go today. I hated the idea. I hated *them.* But then . . ." She smiled and shrugged.

"Does this mean you'll play the piano for me again next week?" Ben said.

"Just try to keep me away," Clarissa smiled, but added quickly, "but please keep saying no if Jo hounds you about 'helping.' "

Ben nodded. "Not to worry, Mother Hale." He winked. "I saw it, too. She was quite taken with our translator. Which probably means nothing more than she is a normal girl. But I also saw something you didn't. The guard at the back of the room couldn't take his eyes off her."

Clarissa sighed. "I can't believe I'm saying this, but I am glad she is going to the ranch for the summer."

"Me too, although she would be following her mother's lead concerning men in uniform if she were to be attracted to Private Romani," Ben teased as he wrapped his arms around her.

"Just because it worked for you and me doesn't mean it's right for our daughter."

"Of course not," Ben said, and nuzzled her cheek.

"And she already has a man in uniform in

her life. His name is John Boone Bishop."

"You're right," Ben said, tracing the lines of her face and neck.

"She should have an education."

"Absolutely," Ben said, and nibbled at her earlobe.

Clarissa struggled. "I need to get changed."

"Let me help," Ben said.

"So?" Delores's face was alight with excitement as she opened the screen door to admit Jo.

Jo stepped across the worn threshold and leaned over, peering into the kitchen.

"Mom's at work," Delores said.

"On *Sunday?*"

"On any day when she can earn a buck. I think there's trouble with the bank," she said. "Chase Young's been sniffing around lately. Mom's stressed."

"I'm sorry," Jo said.

"Me too. But . . . hey!" Delores pulled Jo down beside her on the worn gray couch. "We can talk about that later. Tell me about it. What was it like? Did you see any dreamy boys? How many came? Were you really inside the barbed wire?"

Jo tilted her head. "If you'll be quiet for a minute, I'll tell you."

"Oh . . . sorry." Delores sat back and primly folded her hands in her lap.

"First, when we drove up to the gate . . ."

Half an hour later, the girls had poured themselves iced tea and were sitting on the front porch swing. "So," Delores said as she turned sideways to face Jo. "Let's hear it."

"Hear what? I told you everything."

Delores sighed. "This is *me,* Josephine. Delores. Remember her? Your best friend? The one you tell everything?"

Jo could feel the color rising up the back of her neck. No matter what she did, it would creep around her collar and up to her cheeks. She closed her eyes. She shook her head. "I can't," she said. She sighed. "It doesn't matter, anyway. I'm never going back there."

"So . . . what does he look like?"

"Who?"

"*Him* — who. Him who you didn't talk about. Him who isn't the guard. Him who you noticed but won't talk about."

Jo held up her index finger and waggled it back and forth. "Exactly. What you said."

"What did I say?"

"Won't talk about. But I've got other news. I think maybe Mother will change her mind and let me help out at the Servicemen's Club here in town once in a while. Maybe."

169

There were some days, Dieter realized as he lay in his cot Sunday night, in which he did experience moments when he thought life might be worth living after all. No one suspected that he had ever questioned the value of his life, of course. Everyone looked at his pleasing exterior and made assumptions. Because they looked up *at* him physically, they tended to look up *to* him emotionally. He kept quiet, and they thought he had some kind of hidden wisdom. He defended Bruno Bauer, and they thought him courageous. He stood up to Gunnar Stroh, and they took that as a sign of strength. He wondered if he would have any friends at all if they knew the truth.

He kept quiet because these days he wasn't sure what he believed. He'd been reading some of the materials left in the reading room about democracy and other subjects, and it was beginning to make sense. But the idea that he had nearly died for a false ideal filled him with self-loathing. Could he have been so stupid?

He defended Bauer because the American guard Romani was a weakling and it was easy. Anyone could have done it. With his big ears and wide grin, Bruno had reminded Dieter more of a faithful German shepherd dog than a soldier of the Third Reich. If he'd had a brother, Dieter reasoned he could have done worse than Bruno Bauer. And so he'd fabricated the story about the dead sister and the shaving kit. It had nothing to do with courage. It was more about having a small victory over the American who was bullying Bauer.

He stood up to Gunnar Stroh because he wanted to prod Stroh to expound on his beliefs. He wanted to understand the man. Part of him respected Stroh, who hung a Nazi flag above his cot and gave the salute whenever he could. Part of him pitied the old soldier, who was so blinded by his loyalty to the Fuehrer that he would not believe the American news reports. It bordered on being pathetic. But it was intriguing. You had to admire someone who was so sure of what they believed. Gunnar's faith in the Fuehrer was just as strong as the American pastor's faith in God.

But there was an edge of cruelty to Gunnar Stroh that Dieter couldn't stand. He took obvious delight in giving the Nazi salute — especially in Sergeant Isaacson's presence. Once, when Dieter apologized for it, Isaacson told him not to. "He's just following the orders of his high command as should you," he said. Which made Dieter think less of Stroh . . . and more of Isaacson. The irony of that was almost funny.

And now there was this Pastor Hale, who seemed to have a sincere belief in God that Dieter had not seen since he was living at home. Apparently the Baptist minister would be returning every Sunday to conduct chapel services. The idea that he could look at a beautiful girl and hear a speech on religion at the same time was attractive to him.

No one knew how close to despair Dieter Brock had been in recent months. Things had continued to spiral downward for him until, just recently, with everything in Germany being destroyed and the future so uncertain, he had come to realize that if it were not for his little mother, he would have found a way to stop thinking. Permanently.

Twice a month he was allowed to write home. And while he had not heard from his mother, he knew he must not give up on her. And so he wrote, *The Americans are treating us well. I am using my time as a prisoner to learn. I am safe, eating well, and attending chapel services every Sunday.*

Mama would be pleased.

He did not mention the pastor's beautiful daughter.

Nine

What man of you,
having an hundred sheep,
if he lose one of them, doth not leave
the ninety and nine in the wilderness, and
go after that which is lost, until he find it?

LUKE 15:4

In twenty years of marriage, the Reverend
Benjamin Hale had never strayed from his
devotion to Clarissa. Not that he hadn't had
opportunity. Their marriage had had its moments. But Ben was a man who kept his
word, and when he promised his bride "for
better or for worse," he meant it. However,
Reverend Benjamin Hale was not blind, and
as he stood at his church office window on
Monday morning watching Helen Frey walk
down from her front porch and slide into the
backseat of Deacon Tom Hanson's Pontiac
next to Stella Black, he noted that Helen
Frey was a lovely woman — albeit under a
great deal of stress.

The talk in Crawford about the Frey

173

family was more about Hank's unfortunate war experience than anything else. People were curious about when Hank was going to open up his auto repair shop again. They gossiped about the extent of his wounds. Ben and Clarissa had practically been nominated for sainthood for taking an interest in Mia. No one seemed all that worried about Helen, who had a smile for everyone who asked about Hank. She was cheerful and positive and, unless a person was her pastor or old Mrs. Koch, they might not recognize the signs of trouble behind Helen's sunny disposition. But Reverend Hale had a gift of mercy that enabled him to see right through Helen Frey's smile to the slight stoop in her posture and the sadness in her eyes that had never been there before.

Today, Ben thought, there was more than a little hesitancy in the way Mrs. Frey turned back to wave at the house before getting in the car. Once in the car, she leaned forward and, as the Pontiac rolled away, looked up at the house. Following her line of sight, Ben was convinced at least one rumor about Hank was true. Helen Frey was waving at the attic window.

As the Freys' pastor, Ben had waited in vain for Hank Frey to feel "well enough" to come back to church. As a family friend, he had watched little Mia change until rarely did the sprite in her personality appear. The final impetus for what Ben was about to do had happened just yesterday, when old Mrs. Koch knocked on his office door.

"I come to you with a concern," she said. She didn't come all the way into the pastor's office. She declined Ben's invitation to sit down. Instead, she stood with her back to the door and her hand on the knob.

Ben leaned forward. "What is it, Mrs. Koch?"

"Henry Frey," she said.

"Yes," Ben replied, "I've been concerned, too."

"You will go see him, then?" When Ben hesitated to answer, Mrs. Koch nodded. "I know. It is awkward. You won't know what to say." She shrugged. "Maybe there is nothing. But you must try, Pastor. For the wife and the child, you must try."

Looking into the aged saint's watery eyes, Ben was ashamed that he hadn't already visited Hank. It was the first time in all his years as a leader of this congregation that old Mrs. Koch had even come close to "suggesting" that the pastor do something.

"You're right, Mrs. Koch," Ben said. "As soon as Mrs. Frey leaves for work tomorrow I'll go over to their house."

Mrs. Koch nodded. "Good." She smiled at Ben. "I will pray for you, Pastor."

As the door closed behind Mrs. Koch, Ben had cross-examined himself. Why, he wondered, had he been so willing to lead a chapel service for the Germans . . . and so lax about shepherding his own flock? Even Clarissa, who made no claim to any gift of mercy, had shed a tear over Hank Frey's situation. Why hadn't he done something?

I'm afraid, he realized. Scripture came to mind. *"There is no fear in love; but perfect love casteth out fear."*

I don't know what to say, he thought. *What if it's completely wrong? I could make things worse. I don't know the first thing about what Hank's going through.* Once again, Scripture came to mind. *"If any of you lack wisdom, let him ask of God, that giveth to all men liberally . . ."*

I'm ashamed, he confessed. *Here I sit in my comfortable little community with my family intact . . . when all the boys in our town are going through hell on earth.* A verse from his recent study in the book of Romans came to mind. *"Shall the thing formed say to him that formed it, Why hast thou made me thus?"* Ben bowed his head and prayed.

And here he was on Monday morning,

with sweat collecting on his brow as he anticipated walking toward the front porch steps of the little whitewashed bungalow where Hank and Helen Frey had started their married life.

The Pontiac turned right at the end of the block and disappeared from sight.

"Well, Lord," Ben whispered. "Here I go. You said I could pray for wisdom. I have. I still am." Rumors had transformed Hank Frey from a local boy who knew the cars in Crawford as well as most men knew their children, into a deformed monster who lurked in his attic and slunk along the back alleys of town after dark, half-crazed with hatred for the Germans who were responsible for his destroyed life. Ben knew the rumors were just that, but it didn't keep his heart from pounding.

Ben didn't know exactly what he expected, but whatever he thought might happen, it wasn't the booming "GO AWAY!" that answered his knock. The words were so forceful Ben stepped away from the door.

Mrs. Koch's words came to mind. *I will pray for you, Pastor.* The idea that the widow of a Purple Heart recipient was praying for him brought comfort. And accountability. Ben had no doubt that Mrs. Koch would soon knock on his office door again and ask if he had visited Henry Frey. He must be able to say yes. If he couldn't say yes, when she asked, that would bring an entirely new level of shame — one he wasn't willing to endure.

He stepped back to the door and peered through the locked screen door.

"Hank! It's Ben Hale."

After a long silence, footsteps sounded on the stairs, just visible off to the left of the door. A pair of rugged work boots and then two legs clad in what looked like overalls came into view. "Helen's already left for work," Hank said, stopping on the stairs. "Mia left for school a little while ago. Is something wrong?"

Good. The edge in Hank's voice meant his bitterness hadn't smothered his protective instincts when it came to family. "Nothing's wrong with Mia or Helen," Ben said quickly. "I came to see you."

"Trust me, Preacher. You don't want to *see* me."

Not knowing how to answer, Ben said nothing.

"You've done your duty," Hank said. "You've made your call. Now you can go."

Through the screen, Ben could see Hank start to turn around. He was heading back upstairs.

"It's my car, Hank. The old Nash." *Now where did that come from?* Ben wondered.

"Take it to Jack or Bill," Hank said without turning around. "It's not like there aren't any other mechanics in town."

"Jack means well, but he's in over his head when it comes to the Nash. And Bill retired while you were gone." Ben cleared his throat. "The thing is, Jo and Mia are supposed to go to the Four Pines with CJ after church on Sunday. Then Clarissa and I are supposed to bring them home in the evening. Will Bishop is working at the remount now or I'd ask him to bring them home. I just hate to disappoint them, but I'm not comfortable with the Nash the way it's running these days. Can't you take a look at it for me?"

"I've got no right arm."

Ben hesitated, despairing when the words that first came to mind amounted to little more than what he'd come to call a "comfort cliché." *What do I do now, Lord? What do I say?*

"Hank, you know as well as I do that you've forgotten more about Nash Ramblers than Jack ever knew. You used to say you could fix any car better than Jack could with one hand tied behind your back. But you don't have to prove that. You've got a hook. Right?"

"So?"

Ben blurted out. "I'll . . . I'll . . . leave my garage unlocked and you can come up tonight. After we're all in bed. Please, Hank. I need your help." Ben looked away from the door. A flash of movement caught his attention. He glanced at the next house where a climbing rosebush on a trellis obscured most of the front porch. He looked back inside the Frey house. Hank's lower half was still visible. He had turned back around. That was something.

"Well, you think about it," Ben said. As he watched, the toe of Hank's right boot seemed to inch forward, almost as if he were thinking of coming down. Ben held his breath. But then Hank turned around and, without a word, headed back up the stairs.

At the foot of the Frey porch, Ben looked toward the neighbor's house. "Good morning, Mrs. Bohling," he called out to the trellis. "Hope you have a nice day."

As he walked down the sidewalk, across the street, and back to his office at the First Baptist Church, Ben prayed.

Please help Hank Frey . . . because it doesn't look like I can.

★ ★ ★

"Ben . . . Ben!" Clarissa shook him awake. "Wake up, Ben! Someone's trying to steal the car!"

"Wh-what?" Ben grunted and opened his eyes.

"Someone's broken into the garage. Listen." Clarissa pressed herself against his back. "Is the back door locked?" She was waiting, breathless, her mouth poised about an inch from his ear.

Ben listened, then relaxed into his pillow. "It's all right. I asked Hank to work on the car."

"But you just brought it back from Jack's," Clarissa protested.

"It still needs a thing or two."

"That we can't afford," Clarissa replied. "And those are your very words, Reverend Hale." She rolled away from him and lay on her back staring up at the ceiling. "You never mentioned talking to Hank."

Ben sat up and shoved his feet into his slippers. "Think I'll go on out there and see if he needs any help." He pulled on his bath-robe. Just as he was about to open the bed-room door, Clarissa called his name.

"Yes?" Ben turned back toward where his wife lay on her side, her left arm bent, her head cradled in her open palm.

181

"Would you like it if I put a thermos of hot coffee and some cookies out on the back porch? Just in case you and Hank get hungry?"

Ben smiled in the darkness. "That'd be real nice, honey," he said. He opened the door.

"Ben?"

"Yes?"

"I love you."

"And I love you, baby girl."

Ben paused just inside the screened back porch and looked at the yellow spot on the backyard lawn where light was spilling through the garage window onto the grass. *I don't know what I am doing.* It was a good thing the garage door opened toward the alley. It wouldn't do for Hank to look up and see his own pastor hesitating like a coward.

Finally, after he had asked the Lord for help a dozen times, Ben heard Clarissa's footsteps behind him in the kitchen. He ducked his head back in the kitchen.

"Just leave it on the top step and go on back to bed," he whispered. "Don't want to scare him off."

Clarissa nodded. "I'll go right back up to bed," she said, "soon as I set it out."

Ben went back out to the screened porch. Still, as he contemplated walking down the path alongside the garage, he didn't know if he should open the single door right at the front corner near the house or not. Finally, he opened the porch door, stepped outside, and closed it behind him. Again, he paused, listening to the crickets chirping, looking up at the stars, and sending silent messages toward heaven. Taking a deep breath, Ben walked to the window and peeked in.

Hank had opened the hood and was intent on working something loose with the hook that was supposed to serve as his right hand. As Ben watched, he jiggled something, reached for it with his left hand, then went back to working with the hook. Finally, he held it up to the light — and Ben saw the ravaged face. He inhaled sharply and closed his eyes. Then he adjusted his approach so that, when he came around the corner and leaned against the doorframe, it would be the uninjured part of Hank's face that he saw.

"I appreciate this, Hank," Ben said. Hank's reaction brought tears to his eyes. The man started, raised his hand, palm out, as if to ward Ben off, and stepped back away from the car. Ben hoped his voice sounded calming when he said, "Now don't run off just because I came out here to make sure it was you and not someone stealing my car. I'm very relieved. Anybody trying to steal the Nash would have to be crazy as a loon."

Hank pulled his hat down over his eyes and stepped back into the shadows. But he bantered back. "Well, I can't promise I'm not crazy, but I'm mostly harmless except for the fact that I scare my own daughter," he said.

Ben ignored the comment. "Got any idea why it's misfiring?"

"Not yet. Got some things I can check" — he held up the hook — "but I'm clumsy. Everything takes twice as long. Some things I can't do at all."

Ben shrugged. "Take all the time you need. I imagine it's just like preaching."

"What?"

"My first few sermons were awful — and that's being kind. I still have no idea why they hired me." He grimaced. "But, with practice, I like to think I've gotten to where I actually form complete sentences and make sense — most of the time." He nodded toward the hook. "I imagine learning to use that will be the same. At times you'll think it doesn't make any sense at all. But as long as you keep trying . . . it'll come to you."

The gasket Hank was holding slipped

from the hook's grip and went rolling under the car. Hank swore and slammed the artificial forearm on the top of the car's fender.

"I'll get it," Ben said, and walked toward the car.

"No!" Hank raised his hand.

Ben stopped. "Clarissa was the one who heard you out here first. When I told her I was pretty sure it was our mechanic, she made a thermos of coffee — along with some of those oatmeal cookies everyone raves about. Said she'd leave it on the top step."

"She didn't have to do that."

"Well," Ben said, "that's exactly what I told her. But she insisted. And I've learned — since that first horrible sermon and my first mostly horrible year of marriage — that when Clarissa has it in her mind to do something, it's best to let her have her way and get to it." As Hank continued to stand where the metal shade on the overhead bulb cast a shadow across his face, Ben felt a tug toward the house. *It's a good start. Don't push it. Say good-night.* He cleared his throat. "You help yourself to some cookies and coffee," Ben said. "Let me know what you think about the old girl." He nodded toward the car, then shook his head. "What is it, do you suppose, that makes a man think of a car as a woman?" Without waiting for an answer, he turned to go.

"Pastor Hale," Hank said.

"Yes?"

"You come up to the house tomorrow after Helen's gone to work and I'll tell you what I find out here tonight. I'll let you know if I think she can run any smoother. I'm fairly certain it'll be fine to drive 'er out to the ranch, but I'll let you know for sure."

"I appreciate that," Ben said. "Good night, now."

Ben heard the grunt as Hank bent down to retrieve the gasket from beneath the old Nash. As he passed the garage window, he resisted the temptation to look in.

"You have a nice talk with Hank last night?" Clarissa asked as she came in from the back porch, thermos and empty plate in hand.

Ben sat down and opened the paper. "Just said hello and thanks and came back to bed. Glad to see he took a break."

"What did he say about the car?"

"Said to stop by this morning after Helen goes to work. He'll tell me what he thinks."

"Did he . . . did you . . ."

"You still have that material you wanted to use to make a window curtain last year?"

Clarissa paused. "Why?"

"Well, after talking to Hank last night it came back to me. How I made fun of you for wanting to make curtains for a garage." He ducked behind the paper, pretending to pay more attention to his reading than to the conversation. "Didn't mean to hurt your feelings, Clarissa. Sorry if I did. Fact is, a curtain at that window might be nice."

It was quiet in the kitchen for a while. Ben glanced up a time or two, but his wife was busy cooking breakfast. When she set the plate of bacon and eggs in front of him, she kissed him on the cheek. "I'll take care of it this morning," she said, and squeezed his shoulder. "And you tell Hank I'll make him some of my Boston brown bread and leave it out there for him tonight. In case he takes a mind to work on the car again. He always liked my brown bread."

Ten

And I will restore to you the years
that the locust hath eaten. . . .

JOEL 2:25

"What in blazes did they do to you, boy?"

The voice from the direction of the dark alley caught Hank by surprise. He started, raised up, clunked his head on the hood of Ben Hale's car, and did his own share of swearing as he backed into the shadows.

"Now don't bolt," the voice said. Vernon Clark stepped into the light. "I just came to . . ." His voice wavered. He shoved his hands in his pockets and gulped. "Just came to see . . ." He sighed. His voice trembled. "I didn't understand why you weren't at Delmer's funeral. You were one of his best friends, Hank. Didn't understand why you weren't there."

"I expect you got your answer just now," Hank said.

"I'm sorry. Really, I am." Vernon lingered in the doorway, alternately clenching

188

and unclenching his hands. Finally, he nodded toward the car. "Getting back into the business?"

"Just paying a debt," Hank said. "Preacher's been good to my family." He cleared his throat. "Sorry about Delmer, Mr. Clark."

As Hank watched, Vernon's face contorted. The man shuddered. "I always thought there'd be a Double C Ranch for at least a couple of generations." He choked the words out, then swallowed and seemed to get control of his grief by uttering a string of epithets against the general who, according to Vernon, sent Delmer into a "death trap," against God, who could have kept the boy safe, and most vociferously against the Germans.

Hank shrugged. "There's nothing to be done." He slowly stepped forward and went back to work, all the while being careful to keep his head turned so as to hide the worst from Mr. Clark.

"Well, I'm not sure you're right about that, friend," Vernon said. He stepped into the garage and perched atop a barrel next to the door. "Say . . . you're pretty handy with that hook."

Hank paused. He stared at the hook, almost as if he hadn't looked at it in a while.

"Now that you mention it, I guess I am getting better at it." He put the tool he was holding into his flesh-and-blood hand. "It's getting to where I'm better with the hook on my right side than the real hand on the left."

"Well, you were right-handed before. Weren't you?" Vernon asked.

"Yeah," Hank said.

"Guess your brain didn't forget."

"The doctors said that. I didn't believe them. Been knocking stuff over with it for so long I didn't expect it to change."

"Glad it has," Vernon said.

Hank stopped what he was doing and straightened up. Without looking at Vernon, he said quietly, "Hard not to feel like somebody made a mistake sending me back — like this — and losing track of Delmer that way."

"There's no sense to who lives and who dies," Vernon said. "It's all a game. Like poker. Some win, some lose. No rhyme or reason." He reached into his pocket. "Mind if I smoke?"

"Help yourself," Hank said.

Vernon lit a cigarette and took a long draw. His exhale was a great sigh. "Guess there's some comfort in that your family doesn't have to figure how to get on without you. At least Marge and me don't have a

190

daughter-in-law and grandchildren to worry over." He swallowed and his voice wavered again as he said, "It's just the two of us missing Delmer and trying to make sense of it all. Marge's gone back home to visit for a while."

"It's not just the two of you missing Delmer," Hank said quickly. "I miss him. All those months I was in the hospital I spent a lot of time thinking about the good times at home. Delmer was part of a lot of them. So don't think you and Mrs. Clark are the only ones missing him. You aren't."

Vernon looked off into the dark. "Thank you, Hank. I appreciate that." He flicked the cigarette into the dirt and stomped on it. "It's been hard seeing how quick folks are to forget about what they done to Delmer." He swore again.

"I'm not sure I know what you mean," Hank said.

"You haven't heard? Folks around here are standing in line for the opportunity to welcome the Nazis to America."

"What are you talking about?"

"Prison labor. The preacher's own family was some of the first to sign up."

"Sign up?"

Vernon nodded. "That's right. CJ Jackson put in for an entire crew of the

191

Krauts." He shook his head. "Can you imagine it? Nazis swarming all over the fields at the Four Pines while Johnny Bishop fights for his life overseas." He paused. "Rumor has it Will Bishop up and quit the ranch when he couldn't talk sense into her. He's working over at the remount now. And good for him, is all I can say. I told him I'd burn my place down before I'd let one of 'em set foot on the property." He jumped up and began to pace. "I just can't believe the way folks around here forget their loyalties. All for the sake of the almighty dollar." He gestured wildly, "Let the hay stand in the field if it has to. Let the whole darned crop rot. That's a darned sight better than hiring the Nazis to do what our own children ought to be doing!" He stopped pacing abruptly. "Sorry, Hank. I get carried away when I think about it." He reached in his pocket, pulled out a silver flask and took a sip. "Want some?" He held the flask out for Hank as he said, "You don't have to hide from me, son. I saw it all in the first one. Mustard gas, arms and legs flying around, burned flesh. I saw it all."

"I appreciate your stopping by, Mr. Clark," Hank said, pretending not to notice the flask. He reached up and pulled the chain dangling over his head, turning the light out. "I'm finished for tonight. Need a part from up at the shop."

"Mind if I walk with you?" Clark asked. "Can't seem to sleep much these days."

"Suit yourself," Hank replied. He lowered the preacher's garage door.

The two men headed up the alley toward Hank's auto repair shop. As they walked along, Vernon reached up and patted Hank on the back. "It's good to have you home, Delmer," he said, "good to have you home."

It was an honest mistake, Hank thought. Wanting to avoid embarrassing Delmer's dad, he didn't correct the old man. He let him ramble on . . . about townspeople . . . and the preacher's daughter . . . and . . . Mia. His own little Mia.

"I am telling you, sir, these Bolsheviks really have discipline. The barracks is so clean, even my mother would find nothing wrong!"

Helen smiled to herself as she heard Private Franco Romani and Sergeant Isaacson come into the office on Wednesday morning. She had grown accustomed to Romani's attempts to camouflage his personal insecurity with a cover of bluster and high volume combined with posturing that sometimes had her and Stella turning away to hide their smiles.

Today, the younger man's hand trembled as Helen handed him the stack of transport documents she had been typing. "I just wish they would do a little less Heil-Hitlering," Romani said. "We'd be a lot less nervous about transporting them off the post."

"Any of our men who are nervous about transporting work teams can request to be reassigned," Sergeant Isaacson said. "There's plenty of work to do right here on the post. The remount is begging for help."

"Well, sir," Romani said, "I know that's true. But some of the men are more nervous about horses than Hitler."

Helen turned toward Stella's desk to hide her smile. She made another paper/carbon/paper sandwich and fed it into her typewriter.

Isaacson nodded. "Would you be one of those men?"

"What?"

"One of the men more nervous about horses than the Heil-Hitlering prisoners."

Romani shrugged. "Maybe."

"As you know, Private, these aren't goose-stepping, polished-boot Nazis. They are captured men anxious to see their families again. I realize there are exceptions, but if you report any troublemakers, we can see about having them transferred."

"Brock," Romani blurted out.

Helen got up and crossed the room. With her back to the men, she opened a file drawer.

"Who?" Isaacson asked.

"Dieter Brock. Compound A. Wants to be transferred. And I'd feel better without him around."

Isaacson frowned and looked down at the papers on his desk. "Brock is quiet, but I don't think he'd cause trouble."

True to form, Helen noticed that Romani was eager to agree with his superior. She filed a document.

"Oh no, sir. I agree, sir. I didn't mean we should worry about Brock," Romani shook his head back and forth. "What I meant was, he'd be happier and less likely to cause trouble if we gave him the work assignment he wants."

"And just what would that be?"

Now apparently eager to display his knowledge of "his" prisoners, Romani rattled on. "Well, sir I've been watching them all real close, just like you said I should. The other day when they were huddled up together in the reading room, I made Brock tell me what was so interesting in the paper.

195

Turns out they were talking horses. Brock was bragging about his father. Seems he was in the Olympics in his day. Anyway, Brock seems to hanker for mucking out stalls and clipping manes instead of helping process new arrivals." Romani shook his head. "Imagine."

"So why doesn't he ask?"

"Doesn't want to draw attention to himself."

Helen heard Isaacson's chair creak. That meant he would be leaning back, with his hands folded across his belt as he stared out the window.

"Do you know of any problems with Brock? Has he instigated any trouble?"

Helen watched Romani out of the corner of her eye. He shook his head, then waxed long about his charges. "Just the opposite. The other day Gunnar Stroh said something behind my back. I didn't know what it was, but coming from Stroh — and the way he said it — I figured it wasn't anything too friendly. I know it's against regulations, sir, but I let my temper fly. Told the man exactly what I thought about Hitler and his German army and where he could put that flag pinned over his cot. I was so mad . . . and it all just flew out of me. In my mother tongue, of course." Romani smiled and shrugged. "So no harm done, right? Stroh didn't even know what I said."

"But Brock did," Isaacson said.

Of course he did, Helen thought.

"Of course," Romani agreed. "And later he comes over to me, says he is personally sorry about the war and 'any inconvenience' it might have caused me. Imagine that!"

"So . . . if most of these guys are so amicable, why are you so nervous about transporting them to work on a ranch?"

Helen exchanged silent smirks with Stella before closing the file drawer and returning to her desk. She saw Romani shrug.

"Filthy Bolsheviks."

"Nazis, Private," Isaacson said, "Not Bolsheviks. And I'll thank you to control your tongue in the presence of the ladies." He nodded toward Helen and Stella, who both nodded back and looked down at the work on their desks.

Did he know she wasn't doing anything productive? Helen wondered. *Could he read her as well as he obviously read Private Romani? Dear Lord, she hoped not.*

"Bolsheviks, Nazis . . . all the same."

Isaacson shook his head. "Not the same at all, Private." He launched into a lecture on European history.

Helen could tell that Romani was trying

197

to pay attention, but she could also see his eyes glaze over. Isaacson must have sensed it too. Helen could see him eyeing Romani as he concluded, ". . . and that's why most of the prisoners are really nihilistic Lutherans instead of lying Baptists."

Romani blanched and blurted out, "Lying? I'm no liar, Sergeant. Every word I said about Stroh and Brock is the truth. You told me to keep an eye on them, and I'm keeping an eye on them."

"Forget it, Private," Isaacson said, sighing. "I was just pulling your leg."

"Pulling the leg?"

Isaacson glanced at Helen, but she quickly covered her mouth with her hand and turned away.

"Do they even *speak* English in your part of the world, Private?"

"Some," Romani shrugged. "Not much, though."

"So," Sergeant Isaacson said after Private Romani left the office, "do you have anything to say, Mrs. Frey? Mrs. Black?"

"About what?" the women replied in unison.

"Private Brock. You've had opportunity to observe him closely for a while now. Has he been satisfactory in the office?"

Stella spoke first. "He's smart. Respectful. And gorgeous. I like having him around, and I don't care if he's a Bolshevik or a Nazi — although I doubt he's either. I think he's divine." She pretended to swoon. "But if he's unhappy being around two dolls like Helen and me, then I'd say send him on his way. Get us someone who appreciates us."

Isaacson laughed. "Mrs. Frey? Do you have anything to add?"

Helen could feel herself blush as she cleared her throat. "I agree with Stella," she said, hoping it sounded normal. "You know what the captain says . . . *'A working prisoner is a happy prisoner . . .'* and it can only be better if they are working at something they enjoy."

Stella and Helen exited headquarters and walked toward the canteen. From across the compound of tar-papered buildings came a chorus of shrill wolf whistles. Helen ducked her head. Stella waved.

"Don't encourage them," Helen said.

"Why not, honey? It's harmless fun, and I'm going to be getting precious little of that in the near future. I've got to do some serious belt tightening if I want to keep my house." She laughed and batted her eyelashes, "And it just wouldn't do to give up Tara. If it weren't for the gossips in town, I'd rent Delores's room when she leaves for Des Moines to one of these guys." She gestured toward the parade ground swarming with new soldiers. "The longer this war goes on, the more money I realize I've missed out on by being so *upstanding*."

Not knowing what to say, Helen was quiet.

"It's all right, honey. You don't have to show any righteous indignation or anything. I know I shouldn't have a male tenant. But honestly, these boys are young enough to be —" she giggled — "well, my little brother, at least. Take Romani. He's darling and completely harmless. Why couldn't I just adopt him?" She led the way to the lunch counter.

"Because then you couldn't charge him rent," Helen joked.

"Actually," Stella said, "when it comes to Romani, the army would owe me a big thanks if I gave the boy a home and he settled down."

"What are you talking about?"

Stella put a finger to her lips. Once the women were seated where no one could eavesdrop, she said, "I overheard a call he made the other day. To Brooklyn."

"On the post phone?"

Stella nodded. "I know. Strictly against regulations."

"He could get put in the stockade for something like that."

"Yeah," Stella said. "He was almost frantic. It seems his best girl hasn't answered any of his letters. He was threatening to jump aboard the first train home."

"You overheard someone threatening to go AWOL?" Helen frowned. "That should be reported."

"Not a chance." Stella took a bite out of her sandwich, then gulped it down. "I'd have to admit I was eavesdropping, and I'd lose my job." She hesitated. "But I do have an idea. . . ."

Helen shook her head. "You leave me out of whatever it is you're plotting."

"Just listen," Stella said, leaning forward. "If the problem is he's homesick, then he'd probably welcome a little taste of home, wouldn't he? I bet a lot of our boys would love to have somewhere to go besides the Servicemen's Club for a change. I could offer a home-cooked meal for, say, fifty cents. How many of the boys do you think would go for that? 'Sunday Dinner at Stella's.' What d'ya think?"

"I think," Helen said, "that you are out of

201

your mind. And that you already work hard enough." She glanced down at her watch. "And we need to get back to the office."

Outside the mess hall, Stella pulled out a pack of cigarettes and lit up, smoking as they made their way back to work. "You can't tell me you are rolling in the dough now that your hubby's back. Maybe you could help me out. We can split the profits fifty-fifty. Wouldn't your old man be impressed with that!"

At the mention of Hank, Helen blinked tears out of her eyes.

"Oh, honey . . . I'm sorry. I didn't mean to make you cry." Stella waved her cigarette in the air, tossed it on the ground, and stomped it out. "Hey, I was just kidding before. But honest, why don't you help me once Mia's gone to the ranch?" She raised both eyebrows and winked. "You'd be protecting my reputation. Come on. . . ."

"I don't know." Helen shook her head.

"Think about it."

"All right," Helen said. "But don't say anything to anyone yet."

The only person Stella mentioned Sunday Dinner at Stella's to was Private Romani . . . who mentioned it to someone . . . who mentioned it to someone. . . . And by the end of the day, the first Sunday

202

Dinner at Stella's was promised to six homesick soldiers.

Stella beamed.

Helen sighed. She would have to tell Hank. As soon as she told him about Mia going to the ranch for the summer. As if he would care.

Eleven

Say not thou, I will recompense evil;
but wait on the Lord,
and he shall save thee.

PROVERBS 20:22

Helen Frey had just fallen asleep on Wednesday night when Hank threw open the bedroom door.

"Is it true?" he asked, his voice deadly quiet.

"Wh-wh-what?" Half asleep, Helen clutched the blankets to her chest as she sat up.

"Delmer Clark's dad stopped over at the Hales' last night while I was working on the reverend's car," Hank said. "And he tells me CJ Jackson is hiring Germans to work the Four Pines. And I also heard from him that my own daughter is going to visit the ranch with Jo Hale on Sunday — and maybe stay for the whole summer. Tell me you didn't know about the Germans. And when were you going to tell me about my own

204

daughter's summer plans, anyway?"

"I . . . I . . ." Helen ran her hand through her hair.

With a glance up the hall toward Mia's room, Hank stepped into the bedroom and closed the door behind him. "You knew about the Germans!" he said. "I can hear it in your voice. You *knew!*"

"Th-there are rules. Strict rules. Guards. And no fraternization. CJ wouldn't let . . . Jo wouldn't . . . Mia won't go anywhere near —"

"I don't want her there," Hank said.

"But I've already promised —"

"Well *un*promise!" Hank ordered. "I won't have my daughter —"

"No." Helen could hardly believe the sound of her own voice. "I won't disappoint her."

"What did you say?"

Helen took a deep breath. "I said . . . no. There's nothing to worry about. The Grants over on the White River ranch have a work team of prisoners and —"

"I know all about the Grants and their little lunches with the Nazis," Hank said. He spat out the word. "Vernon Clark has just the word for them. Traitors."

"They are no such thing," Helen said. She gained courage. "And whatever you are thinking about the German boys who have been sent to Nebraska — it's wrong. We've had a couple working in our office. They are educated. Respectful. Honestly, Hank, they are so *relieved* to be out of the fight. So *thankful* to be in America."

Hank stepped back as if he'd been hit. "I can't believe my own wife has forgotten —"

"Don't you say that. Don't you *dare* say that to me!" Helen barely managed not to yell at him. "I haven't forgotten *anything*. I remember . . ." She choked the words out, "I remember all the way back to the night before you left . . . and the whispers."

"Stop," Hank said. He raised his hand to his scarred face.

Helen couldn't stop. "I remember your promises . . . and the way your hand stroked my neck . . . and then . . ." She was sobbing, blubbering, out of control. "I remember my wonderful husband. . . . Where is he? What happened to him?" She looked up at him through the tears, oblivious to the scars. On her knees, she reached for him, clutched the front of his shirt. "Sometimes I think he must be in there — beneath the scars — somewhere." She jerked on his shirt. "And if I can only be patient . . . maybe, just maybe my Hank will come back to me."

Hank grabbed her hands. Forcing her to

let go of him, he backed away.

"Don't you dare run up those attic stairs!" Helen screeched. She slid to the edge of the bed. "Who *are* you? Where's my Hank? Where did he go?"

He turned his back on her and put his hand on the doorknob. Speaking over his shoulder he said calmly, "I don't want my daughter at the Four Pines."

"She's going," Helen said. "Think about what you're saying, Hank. Think about what you're asking. Do you remember her laugh? When she talks about the ranch, her face lights up with joy. You can't want to take that away." Swallowing hard, Helen said, "You can do whatever you want to *me,* Hank. I'm your wife, and I'll keep my wedding vows. I'll take it. But I won't make Mia stay in this house. I won't."

Hank leaned his forehead against the doorframe. "Wh-what do you think I'm going to do to you, Helen?"

"I . . . I don't know." She gulped and whispered, "I don't know you anymore. I never see you. You never let me —"

"You want to see me? Is that what you want?" He whirled around, flipped on the bedroom light, and pulled off his hat. "There," he said, thrusting the scarred side of his face toward her. "Is this what you want? Take a look. Take a real good look." He pressed closer and closer to her, until Helen's back was against the wall, her hands above her head. With Hank's hot breath and barely controlled rage roaring around her, she put her hands over her ears. "Stop," she begged. "Please, Hank. You'll wake Mia. Please stop."

"NO!" He reached across the bed and pulled her hands away from her ears. "I won't stop. You want to see your loving husband? Well, here he is, in all his glory! Take a good look, Helen. Tell me what you see. Do you see your loving husband? Here he is, honey. Back from the war!"

The warmth of his hot breath on her cheek and the smell of whiskey and motor oil and sweat was overwhelming. She could defend Mia with all the ferocity of a she-bear, but when the attack shifted and she was the target of Hank's rage, all of Helen's courage melted. She cowered against the wall, weeping, while he raged on and on about fire and peeling skin, about pain and kind nurses, about stepping over smoking bodies and lifting a man's head to comfort him and finding it was no longer attached to a body. Horrors and more horrors, made even worse because they were uttered in an eerie stage whisper. When she could bear no more, Helen balled up her hands into two fists. She intended to hit the scarred face. Instead, she fainted.

Helen's first thought when she woke early the next morning was that she had had a nightmare. Only when she sat up in bed and saw the grease stains on the once crisp white sheet did she have to face the truth. *Not a nightmare. Reality.* Closing her eyes, she remembered every harsh and ugly word, every whispered threat. She could feel Hank's breath on her cheek and smell the whiskey. And the scars. She saw the scars as they had been — dark red because he was so angry.

She slid out of bed. Clasping her hand over her mouth, she tore out of the room, down the hall, and to the bathroom where she leaned over the sink, retching. Once finished, she rinsed out her mouth with cold water and stood, grasping the cold edge of the sink with both hands, peering at her pale face in the mirror. She couldn't leave Hank. Not now. But she felt she had to go. For a while. For Mia. With trembling hands, she washed up, then retreated to her bedroom. It took only a few minutes to throw her own clothing into a suitcase. She woke Mia.

"We're going to visit Stella," she said,

opening Mia's drawers and throwing her clothes into the suitcase with her own. "Get up and get dressed. We can talk about it later, but right now I want you to hurry. And be quiet."

Mia obeyed, her eyes wide with uncertainty. She clung to Helen's hand as they went downstairs. As they passed the kitchen, Helen put the note she had agonized over since dawn at the bottom of the stairs where Hank would see it.

Helen was calm until her friend's front door opened. Stella took one look at the suitcase and pulled them both inside. Her kindness overcame Helen's resolve to be calm for Mia. She put her head on Stella's shoulder and let the tears come.

Clarissa waited until Helen and Mia crossed the street and were inside Stella Black's house before she stood up. She'd been stooped down trying to retrieve Ben's morning newspaper from where it landed nine mornings out of ten — beneath the spirea bush.

Before the sun came up on Thursday morning, Hank had crept down the attic stairs in the night and stood outside what used to be their bedroom door, wanting to knock, longing to beg for forgiveness. When he put his hand to the doorknob, it was cold against the skin of his left hand. He looked down at his right hook. He leaned his head against the doorframe. If she said even one nice thing . . . he pictured sweeping her into his arms . . . and the hook . . . and her expression of revulsion. Hank headed back to the attic and lay awake, staring at the beams supporting the roof. He'd have to pick the right one. And strong rope. He was a big man. It wouldn't do to pick the wrong beam.

When Hank woke again, Mia had left for school and Helen had gone to work. His stomach was rumbling. He couldn't remember everything he'd said the night before, but from the way his head was pounding, it probably hadn't been good. Helen always left his breakfast on the counter. If he had to make his own breakfast today, it would serve him right.

At the bottom of the stairs he saw the note:

When Stella Black first offered to let Mia and me stay with her for a while, I preached her a sermon. I still believe everything I said, but I have to think of Mia.

211

She didn't even sign it. Hank read the note over and over again. He carried it with him to the living room, where he sat down and stared out the window that faced Stella Black's house. Things were beginning to green up. Funny he hadn't really noticed. The pots where Helen usually planted pansies were still on the wicker table in front of the window. Empty.

He got up and went into the kitchen where a small mirror hung over the row of coat hooks beside the back door. Maybe if he raised his collar. Maybe if he — Who was he kidding? For the next few minutes, he paced around the kitchen, alternating between grief and anger, guilt and blame. Helen would probably go to the preacher, he finally thought. She would tell him all about last night. About how Hank had acted. Shameful. Frightening her. And the preacher with the perfect skin and the perfect family and the perfect life would take her side. As would everyone else in this town.

Someone knocked at the back door. When he saw who it was, Hank crumpled the note into a tight ball and shoved it in his pocket. If that was the way she wanted it, so be it. He would be the villain, so she could be the saint. Maybe that would be better for everyone, anyway. It sure would make things easier for Spridget.

Hank opened the back door. Vernon Clark had a plan. A way they could do a little payback on behalf of Delmer and the men like Hank whose lives had been ruined by the Nazis.

Hank listened.

Twelve

An hypocrite with his mouth destroyeth his neighbor.

PROVERBS 11:9

"Give it a while longer," Will said, trying to downplay Buster's most recent fit. "He's bound to come around. I've got a few tricks up my sleeve yet."

"I've got to be honest with you," Bill Harker said. "I'm running out of patience, time and — more important — budget money for a stallion that's too unmanageable to stand at stud."

"That's why you hired me," Will said with a smile. "I've got the patience and the time to get Buster to contribute to the budget instead of draining it."

"Are you sure it's worth it?"

Will nodded toward the horse. "Look at him, Doc."

"All right," Harker agreed. He headed off toward Barn 3. "Keep me posted."

Will nodded. "You bet."

Harker was at the end of the row of stalls before he turned around and said, almost as if he were apologizing, "You do know, Will, if I was running my own ranch, I'd do whatever it took. He's from the Imperial Prussian stud, for goodness' sake. But the remount isn't a ranch. We just don't have the luxury of catering to problem animals."

"I understand," Will said. "I can't take forever." He smiled his slow, easy smile. "But I can take a while longer, right?"

Harker nodded. "I'm trusting you to prove my instincts right about this one."

As Harker exited the barn, Will turned around and began a conversation with Buster. While the horse had nothing to say, he did listen, his dark eyes locked on Will, his small, perfectly shaped ears alert.

"Now, you," Will said, "better behave yourself or you *are* gonna be dogmeat. I bought you some more time, my friend." He stepped toward Buster's stall. "But —" The horse half-reared, snorted, and landed a kick on the side of his stall. Again. Scratching the back of his neck, Will backed off and sat down on the hay bales across from the stall.

He'd said he still had a few tricks up his sleeve. It wasn't exactly a lie. There must be a trick up one sleeve or the other . . . if only he could think of one. Sighing, Will slapped his knees. Buster jumped. "Oh, settle down," Will said. "I'm just going to feed some of the more well-mannered critters around here." He got up and walked into the stall next to Buster's. "And while I do, you see if you can't trot some of the meanness out of those flashy legs of yours." Knowing what was about to happen, Buster walked expectantly toward the sliding door at the rear of his stall. Will let him out, closing the door behind him.

Mucking out stalls had never bothered Will before. It was part of the business of horses, and he loved the mix of aromas in a barn — even when manure was part of the mix. But the work here at Fort Robinson was becoming increasingly tedious. The fact was, Will admitted to himself, he was tired. Bone-tired. Weary. Homesick, even. The endless series of remount chores were mindless stuff for an old wrangler. Trimming manes, trimming hooves, feeding, watering . . . and rising again to trim more manes, clean more feet, muck out more stalls. Thousands of horses and mules needed the same thing, and there was precious little about the work that was interesting, except for Buster.

Will was at the end of his rope with the

horse. For the first time in his life, it looked like he was not going to be able to solve the mystery of a hard-to-handle horse. While the prospect of Buster's demise was depressing, that wasn't the main thing making him grumpy. He missed CJ. Blast it. He did.

"Hey, wrangler. There's a wild horse in the stud barn that needs your attention."

Will had been slower than usual making his rounds. Between the cloudy sky and thinking about the Four Pines, he was feeling low. The sound of Jo's voice was music to his old ears.

"Hey, cowgirl," he bantered back. "Who let you loose today?"

Jo threw her arms around Will and hugged hard.

"Whoa." He pretended to be smothering and pushed back, looking around him to see who might have seen Jo's display. He tugged on the brim of Jo's cowgirl hat. "You can't just hug a man in plain sight like that. You'll have these wranglers thinking I'm a soft touch."

"Like they don't already know," Jo said.

"Know what? That I'm touched?" Together they laughed.

"Daddy's over at the PW camp making plans for a weeknight Bible study," she said.

"If you can imagine that. Apparently some of the prisoners have expressed an interest."

"I'll just bet they have," Will said and turned away to grab another forkful of hay.

"I know, Uncle Will. It's probably not from real interest," Jo said. "Daddy already said that. But he also said that if the Lord can use a talking mule to accomplish His purposes, He can probably use boredom." She linked her arm through her uncle's. "So how's Buster the wonder horse?"

"No 'wonder' to that lame-brained critter," Will grumbled.

"Can I see him?"

Will shrugged. "Sure."

As they crossed the parade ground and headed between a row of barracks toward the stud barn, Jo told her Uncle Will that she and Mia would be leaving earlier than expected for the Four Pines. When Will expressed surprise, Jo told him about the Freys. "Daddy and Mother just think it's best for Mia to have something good in her life right now." She smiled. "And the Four Pines is it."

"You gonna miss graduation?" Will said.

Jo shrugged. "Probably. But I don't really care. Delores will be gone before that. It's just a walk across a stage and a piece of paper. Daddy went over and talked to the principal, and I'm going to keep up the schoolwork on my own, and they'll mail me my diploma. Honestly, with the war and everything, no one's much in a mood to celebrate, anyway."

Will patted her on the back and told her he was proud of her. Together they entered the stud barn.

"Buster's out in his corral behind the barn. Come on through with me, and we'll pick up some sugar. He likes you. Who knows, maybe he'll even get within three feet if you have a treat for him. He's probably pacing back and forth at the door right now, giving it a good kick now and then, wondering when he's going to get back in."

But Buster wasn't kicking the door. He wasn't even *at* the door. With Uncle Will behind her, Jo pried the door open just enough to see Buster poised in the middle of his small exercise pen staring at someone standing at the fence. She motioned for her uncle to come. Buster tossed his head. Will opened his mouth to warn the intruder, but stopped short when Buster shook his head from side to side and whickered . . . and then took a step forward toward . . . the PW.

"I know him," Jo whispered. "He's the one who translated Daddy's sermon last Sunday. And I'm pretty sure he'll be doing it again tomorrow. Buster seems to like him," Jo said.

Will said nothing.

"Yes . . . you. Beautiful. *Liebling*." He sang a line of a lullaby before saying, "So you like German music . . . ? Maybe that is why you have been so much trouble — no German music. You remind me of my father's horse. Almost I think you have some of those bloodlines. How about it? Are you demisang like Renzo? Would you jump to the skies, if only they would let you . . . ? Is that what you are trying to tell them — that you want to jump . . . ?"

His heart pounding, Dieter held out his hand, amazed when the infamous stallion from the stud barn didn't come charging at him. He'd heard about the creature from some of the men in Compound A who had volunteered to work over in the remount. When their romantic Karl May–fueled images of stables and cowboys and Indians were smothered by rancid hay and manure, most philosophized that at least the days passed by quickly. They kept at it, happy to embellish their work for the ears of anyone who would listen.

"Jenny Camp?" Dieter said one evening in disbelief. "You must check again. Jenny

220

Camp cannot be in this place." But she was. The famous Olympic mare was stabled just across the road. Brock grew even more impatient with office work. But today Rolf Shrader was sick, and Isaacson had appointed Dieter to substitute for him. He had not yet seen Jenny Camp with his own eyes, but here he was watching a magnificent stallion dancing around a too-small corral. He was feeling almost content. Earlier in the day, Isaacson had asked him about working with the horses.

"Your education merits a better job, but Romani told me that you'd like to work over at the remount. If that's true, there are a lot of the stable crew on furlough right now, and they are screaming for help."

"I have never wanted anything more than to live and work around horses," Dieter said.

"Romani mentioned your background." Isaacson frowned. "But there's nothing in your file about a knowledge of horses."

Dieter shrugged. "Perhaps Private Romani has not yet filed my requests."

"Requests? What requests?" Isaacson thrust his chin forward as he spoke — a sure sign he was concentrating on something besides what he was saying.

"I have asked many times to work in the

remount," Dieter said. "Private Romani said that you said I am needed in the office."

Isaacson's gray eyes narrowed. The fine muscles around his mouth pulled the corners of his mouth downward. "I see," he said.

"I . . . I don't mean to speak ill of the private from New York," Dieter said. "Please, I do not want any trouble."

"There won't be any trouble," Isaacson said. "At least none that can be traced back to you."

Once again, Isaacson understood — a fact that both surprised and confused Dieter. During the long journey to America, he and his comrades had wondered what would happen once they were delivered, body and soul, into the hands of their enemies. That would be bad enough. No one imagined they might be at the mercy of a member of the most hated race in the fatherland. When they first arrived at Fort Robinson and Isaacson introduced himself, the hair on the back of Dieter's neck stood up. Surely this was the essence of being without protection in the land of the victors. But, like many things in America, Sergeant Isaacson was not as expected. He reprimanded another guard who was unnecessarily rough with the prisoners. "It is not a crime to be German," he said. "May I remind you that America is heavily populated with Germans. Did you know that even our great President Lincoln had a German on his cabinet?" Even the prisoners like Gunnar Stroh, who didn't trust Isaacson because he was Jewish, eventually came to view him with grudging respect. Other, less prejudiced prisoners, soon came to seek him out when they had a request, knowing that Isaacson was less inclined to say no.

An intelligent Jew, who was both generous and kind, was confusing to the boy who had never owned any creed deep in his soul. Standing alongside his little mother in church, Dieter was a good Lutheran boy. In the Afrika Korps, he was a Nazi. Now he was in America, and everything he had experienced reminded him that Dieter Brock had no idea what he really believed. His parents had taught him to be truthful and to fear God. In the Hitler Youth he was taught to love the Fuehrer and fatherland. But here, in a prison camp in America, where Jews deserved respect and newspapers were allowed to criticize the government, things were becoming increasingly unsettled in his mind. Everything in the world was upside down.

Rolf Shrader had teased him about his

impatience with office work. "Wouldn't you miss this?" He motioned with his hands down his body, adding curves in the air and batting his eyelashes.

"Being around females is —"

"Delicious?"

Dieter shook his head. "Disturbing."

Gunnar Stroh snickered. "What's the matter, Brock? Not used to being in the candy store and not being able to have all you want?"

For all his crudeness, Stroh had hit on a truth. Being around the American secretaries was beginning to fray on Dieter's nerves. It was only natural for a man to be attracted to beauty, but his attraction to any American woman could only lead to catastrophe. He was used to holding out his hand and having what he wanted fall into it.

Now, as he looked at the beautiful horse before him, his heart soared. Here, too, was beauty. And just like a painting or a piece of sculpture, this was beauty that could be openly admired. Others might think it a small thing, but to a man coming from battlefields to prison, even a small window of beauty was a gift to be treasured. To have a creature such as the one before him come to him of its own free will would be something of a triumph.

Dieter knew the animal's reputation. Even the professional cowboy who worked in the stud barn was having difficulty with Buster.

"If only they spoke German," he said to the horse. "That is the key, *ja?*" While he talked, he reached into his pocket and retrieved a small, square biscuit and put it in his open palm. Instead of reaching out toward Buster, though, he rested his hand on the top railing of the corral and waited.

Buster's nostrils flared.

Dieter could almost see the horse thinking. "Sure. You smell that? That was the favorite treat of my father's horse. You think that smells good?"

Buster shook his head and took one step forward.

"Sure. You smell me, but you smell that, too. You can't have that delicious treat unless you trust the man holding it." As the horse watched him, Dieter began to sing quietly. Buster took another step forward. Dieter sang. Another step. Dieter kept singing. "You should come ahead," he sang, abandoning the lullaby's words and conversing instead with the horse. "Because soon it is time I must go back to my barracks."

The stallion tossed his head.

Two blasts on the post horn announced

the end of the workday and summoned the PWs to their truck. Dieter stopped singing. "All right, you," Dieter said in German. He put the *pfefferneusse* back up on the fence post. "That's good enough for today, then. You don't kick, and you don't charge me . . . so you get the treat." As Dieter walked away, Buster whirled around and whinnied a protest. He pranced toward the fence, snatched up the small cookie and stood watching Dieter retreat, pawing the earth and whinnying.

From their vantage point just inside the barn, Jo and Will looked at one another in disbelief.

"I've never seen anything like that," Jo said. "It was like they were actually talking to each other."

Will nodded. "And Buster just told him to come back," he said, as Buster danced along the far edge of the corral watching the German walking away and trumpeting loudly. The German didn't stop and look back. Instead, he jogged away in the direction of the parade ground.

The minute the German was out of sight, Buster whirled about, shook his head, and, trotting to the sliding stall door, gave it a quick kick.

Jo jumped back. "Well," she said, laughing nervously. "The old Buster's back." She headed out of the stall with Will, and together they rolled back the door to admit Buster.

"Give him some sugar," Uncle Will said. "See if his sweet mood comes back."

Jo spoke to the horse while she perched a sugar cube atop the side railing of his stall and stepped back. Buster minced forward, inhaled, snorted, and pushed the sugar cube off the railing.

"You brat!" Jo said, shaking her finger at the horse and laughing. She turned to Uncle Will. "Apparently he only speaks German."

"You're kidding, right?"

Will thought Bill Harker could at least try to hide his amazement. "No, sir. I saw it with my own eyes. My niece says he translated the sermon last Sunday afternoon. Could you find out if he'd want to work in the stud barn?"

"Isn't *avoiding* the German PWs what brought you to Fort Robinson in the first place? Because I've had to be pretty creative to keep them out of your area."

Will shrugged. "I appreciate that. Really, I do. But you asked me to take special care of Buster. I'd be cheating you *and* the horse if I didn't say — or do — something about what I saw yesterday."

"But, Bishop, if you're going to work with PWs, you might as well have —"

"Yeah. I know. I might as well have stayed on the Four Pines." Will took his hat off and pretended it needed shaping. He looked up. "I told you I had a trick or two up my sleeve. I guess I'm the one being tricked." He chuckled softly. "By a dadgummed *horse,* of all things."

Harker slapped his knee and began to laugh. "I can't believe it. A stallion that speaks German."

"And likes whatever it is that guy had in his pocket," Will added. "Don't forget that."

Harker stopped laughing. "Are you sure you want him working in the barn with you?"

Will shrugged. "You asked me to try and save the horse, and I think the horse is worth saving." He stood up. At the door of the vet's office he turned around. "Just make sure this guy understands that my boy's in the air corps. If he's got any brains at all, he'll know I'm not exactly predisposed to make friends. And he'd better not give me any trouble."

No one in Crawford, Nebraska — least of

all Helen Frey — would have imagined Clarissa Hale as their angel of mercy. Helen's prewar opinion of Clarissa had been forged in the fires of the women's sewing circle that met twice a week in the fellowship hall of First Baptist Church. And it was perfectly clear to anyone attending, that from the day she married Ben Hale, Clarissa Jackson had demonstrated a peculiar talent for annoying the women at First Baptist Church.

Helen could recite — although she never did — an impressive list of reasons why the women spoke about their pastor's wife with raised eyebrows. Mrs. Hale had the blue ribbons to prove she was a good cook, but she never volunteered to make a meat loaf for the church supper. Mrs. Hale could stitch circles around any woman in the church sewing circle, but she avoided the weekly meetings in favor of "important" projects like making curtains for her *garage* of all things. Once her own child was raised — and she had only one, which was a shame, the women said, given the fact that Ben Hale was such a wonderful man — Mrs. Hale quit volunteering to work in the nursery on Sundays and gave up helping with vacation Bible school. No, the women agreed, Clarissa Hale was nothing like what a congregation had a right to expect. It was widely agreed — and often discussed — that if Pastor Hale weren't such an exceptional man, the deacons would likely have formed a search committee and sent the Hales packing long ago.

Which was why, once she had been forced to stop attending the sewing circle and go to work at Fort Robinson, Helen Frey was amazed when Clarissa Hale had become her angel of mercy. The first time Helen retrieved Mia from the Hales' backyard, the child was working alongside Jo in the garden, manhandling a hoe twice her height and chattering away about mama's job at the fort.

"I hope she wasn't a bother," Helen said.

"A bother?" Jo replied. "She's a hard worker." Jo patted Mia on the head. "Mia's welcome as often as she wants to come. I always wanted a little sister."

And now, as the days went by and Helen didn't move back home, she got a taste of what it was like to be the main topic of discussion among the women of her town. It was a subtle thing — the change that Helen came to view as her fall from grace. There were strange silences when she shopped around town. Meaningful glances. Cold shoulders. It was hurtful. But it led to

Helen's conclusion that when the chips were down, she could trust exactly two women in town: Clarissa Hale and Stella Black. At least she had been able to trust them so far. Helen didn't know what they would think when — and if — she told them the complete truth about herself and Hank. Wondering about it kept her awake. Doubting kept her quiet. And hope kept her sane.

"Thank you for seeing me, Mrs. Hale," Harriet Bohling said.

Clarissa, who had been dreading this moment since Hettie's phone call right after lunch on Saturday, opened her front door and stepped outside. How she wished she had gone with Jo and Ben out to Fort Robinson.

"Let's just chat here on the front porch, shall we?" she said when Hettie arrived. There was no way she was going to get trapped in her own home. "It's so pleasant out here, don't you think?" She guided Hettie to one of two lattice-backed rockers. "That's the reverend's favorite chair, and I'm sure you'll see why. Isn't it comfortable?"

Yes, the chair was comfortable, Hettie agreed, perching on the edge of the seat like a nervous bird. Yes, it was nice to be able to finally enjoy the porch again now that spring was here, but you never knew when a late snowstorm would ruin it all. "You know how it is out here in the Sandhills," Hettie said. "We've only got the two seasons — winter and July."

Clarissa smiled politely and waited for the real reason for the visit. It wasn't long in coming. People, Hettie began, were concerned for Henry Frey.

"So are we," Clarissa said, rushing to defend her husband from the implication that the pastor was somehow not doing enough. "Ben is doing what he can."

As usual, Hettie was more interested in what she had come to say than what Mrs. Hale could contribute. Why, did Mrs. Hale know that Mrs. Frey was going to have to keep her job out at Fort Robinson?

"It would be a hardship on her fellow workers if she left right now," Clarissa said. "Mrs. Frey says they are almost drowning in paper work. Did you know there are something like fifteen forms to be completed for every PW?"

Did Mrs. Hale know that little Mia was afraid of her own father?

"Mia is a delightful child."

It was wonderful, of course, that young

Josephine was good with children and that Mia had a place to go. And it was certainly an answer to everyone's prayers that Mr. Frey had taken to working again, but didn't Mrs. Hale agree it could not be good for the family for Hank to be "in there" at night with all the shades drawn. And Vernon Clark — who everyone knew had simply not accepted Delmer's death and had taken to drinking — was hanging around Hank's garage.

"I wonder," Clarissa said, "if it's ever possible to *accept* the death of a child. I just don't think the English language has words for what's going on in our world right now."

Hettie plunged ahead without commenting on Clarissa's comment. As far as anyone knew, she continued, Vernon Clark was the only one in Crawford who had actually *seen* Hank Frey. And that couldn't be good for Hank. What if he took to drink, too? He was already acting strange. And people had heard the two of them ranting about the Germans.

No one was blaming Mrs. Frey, of course, but Hettie had heard that "just the other day the poor woman was seen crossing the street, suitcase in hand, and taking refuge —" Hettie leaned forward and lowered her voice before almost hissing — "at Stella

Black's. And we all know what that will lead to!"

"I-I'm afraid I don't know what you're talking about, Mrs. Bohling." Clarissa felt as though she were swimming through mud. Hettie had come up for air, but Clarissa didn't know how to break the surface of all the dirt that had been slung in the last few minutes.

"Sarah Fosdick told all of us at circle. She was sweeping the front walk and she saw it for herself. Helen Frey came out her front door with a suitcase, walked across the street, and went into Stella Black's house. Then the two of them came out a little later and got into the back of Deacon Hanson's Pontiac just like always and headed off. And then, when they got back from work, Sarah just happened to be out on the front porch doing a little mending, and she saw them go inside together, and Mrs. Frey never came out. So don't you see? She's left her husband. I can't imagine what's to become of Mia."

Hettie leaned forward a little farther. Clarissa found herself wishing the woman would just slip right off the edge of Ben's rocker.

"I knew you'd want to know," Hettie said. "So the reverend can finally *do* something about the Freys."

It was the word *finally* that gave Clarissa the courage to interrupt Hettie. *Finally?* What did she mean *finally?* As if Ben had been ignoring the pain in his flock? Who did the old hen think she was, anyway? Clarissa stood up. "Mia will be staying with us for a few days. In fact, she and Jo are going to enjoy an early summer break. My sister is delighted to have them at the ranch, and my husband has arranged it with the school."

"Good for him," Hettie said. "We've been concerned."

"I beg your pardon?"

"Now relax, Mrs. Hale. . . ."

I would if you'd get your claws out of my back.

"No one is criticizing the reverend. . . ."

Of course, no one *is . . . but about a half dozen of you just can't help yourselves, can you?*

"Josephine is an adult, after all. She can certainly look after herself, but are you quite sure your sister is equipped to handle a child by herself? I hear Mr. Bishop is no longer —"

With supreme effort, Clarissa resisted the urge to go inside and slam the door in Harriet Bohling's face. Instead, she sat back down. "I'm afraid I don't understand," she said, "what you are talking about."

"The *Germans,* Mrs. Hale. The *Germans.*" Hettie's eyes grew large and she nodded with what Clarissa could only take as an unsuccessful attempt to look like a sage. "Everyone knows your sister has requested workers. Which is, of course, her prerogative. It's not like she's the only one. But —"

My husband . . . my daughter . . . the Freys . . . and now . . . CJ? Clarissa snapped. She stood up.

"Of course, your sister has always been eccentric, but —"

"I-I believe I hear my phone. Excuse me." Clarissa let the door slam behind her. She did not know how long Hettie waited on the front porch, but by the time Clarissa had finished crying and assured herself her eyes were no longer bloodshot, her husband's rocking chair was vacant. And then the phone really did ring.

The way CJ shouted into a telephone had always irritated her. But today, Clarissa smiled as she listened to her sister's enthusiastic plans for Jo and Mia.

"Sis?" Clarissa finally interrupted.

"Yes?"

"I love you."

Thirteen

Be ye therefore merciful as
your Father also is merciful.

LUKE 6:36

Knocking on Stella Black's front door was
one of the hardest things Clarissa had done in
years. She was shaking all over when Helen
Frey pulled back the window curtain to see
who was there.

"What . . . what's wrong? What's happened? Is it Mia? Is she hurt?" Helen's face
had gone white and she was clutching
Clarissa's arm.

"No, Mia's fine. Ben took her and Jo
downtown for a treat. The girls are all
packed, and Mia was about to implode from
excitement. I just —" Clarissa put her hand
on Helen's shoulder. "Helen. Calm down.
Really. Everything's fine."

Helen's dark eyelashes fluttered away the
tears of relief while Clarissa talked.

"I just talked to CJ, and she has all kinds
of plans for the girls. She was asking me if

237

Mia liked this or that, and what her favorite foods are — all kinds of questions. She is so excited about having her. I wanted you to know." She paused. "It's going to be all right, Helen."

Helen took a deep breath and let it out. She brushed her forehead with her open palm. Then she forced a smile. "Maybe you could let Mrs. Bohling know."

Clarissa feigned innocence. "What?"

Stella appeared at the doorway to the kitchen. "Are you kidding, honey?" She flourished the wooden spoon in her hand. "There's a big old *nasty* grapevine that crawls all over this town. Helen landed on my doorstep at 7:30 Thursday morning, and I can pretty much guarantee that by 7:45 most of Crawford knew."

Helen ducked her head.

Clarissa sighed audibly. "I know. I'm sorry. I was hoping maybe the grapevine would have died back — just a little."

Stella snorted. "Dream on. Mrs. Fosdick up the street almost broke her neck trying to watch when Helen and I got home from work yesterday." She strode to the front door and out onto the porch. Clarissa and Helen exchanged horrified glances as they heard Stella holler, "You go on in and cook supper, Mrs. Fosdick. The preacher's wife is on the case. Helen's staying here for a few days. And say hello to Mrs. Bohling when you talk to her!"

Stella marched back inside. She paused at the kitchen door. "You're welcome to share my mostly beans chili, if you want to hang around," she said to Clarissa.

"Thank you, but, actually —"

"What was I *thinking?*" Stella brought the back of her hand up to her forehead in mock horror. "The Baptist minister's wife can't be caught dining with a 'mackerel snapper.' " She retreated, laughing, into the red and yellow kitchen.

Clarissa, who had always wanted a red and yellow kitchen, called after her. "Actually, I came over here to invite both of you to come with us to the ranch tomorrow evening." She looked at Helen. "I'm thinking you'd like to see just where your little cowgirl will be."

"Is this an invitation to the ranch or an invitation to the ranch with church strings attached?" Stella reappeared at the kitchen door.

Clarissa smiled. "It's an invitation to the ranch. No strings."

"All I have to do Sunday is go to mass," Stella said. She winked at Clarissa. "With all the flirting I do out at the fort, I have to get my regular dose of forgiveness. But then you've probably heard all about that from your husband's deacon."

Clarissa didn't know where the next thing she said came from. The only thing she had prayed for before walking across to Stella's house was that Mrs. Fosdick would tell Mrs. Bohling that Pastor Hale's wife had done her duty and visited Mrs. Frey . . . and then leave Ben off the gossip tree for a while. But what came out of her mouth seemed to be inspired by someone other than herself. "The grapevine spares no one," she said. "Not even the preacher's wife." She looked past Stella into the red and yellow kitchen and then back at Stella. "So we'll expect you to join us, Mrs. Black?"

"Stella."

"All right. Stella. As long as you call me Clarissa. Now tell me about Delores. How does she like it in Des Moines? When the paper ran that picture of this year's Easter bonnets and included the women's military hats, I was trying to picture her in her new uniform. Do you have a photo yet?"

As Stella tipped her head sideways and looked at her, Clarissa had the unwelcome feeling of being measured and weighed. Judged. Again.

"Why don't you come back here and have

a cup of tea while I finish this pathetic chili?" Stella laughed. "I think I've already worn Helen's ears off bragging on my daughter. And yes, I have a picture. She's far too pretty in that uniform, by the way."

In the kitchen, Stella put a water-spotted teakettle on to heat. And friendship climbed out of the primeval ooze of tea leaves, hot water, and lemon.

Clara Joy

The woman who climbed out of Ben Hale's Nash earlier this evening looked like Clarissa, but she didn't sound a thing like her. She seemed almost proud of the Four Pines. "You'll have to ask CJ," she said when Stella Black asked a question. "She's the rancher in the family. I'd be good at feeding the wranglers, but I don't know the first thing about horses or haying."

"CJ had that built," she said, pointing out the new barn down by the spring. "Of course, in the old days when our papa had to be able to get to the barn in a blizzard, he wanted the barn close to the house. But when we outgrew the old barn, CJ decided to put a new one closer to the bunkhouse so it would be easier for the men to do chores." Clarissa laughed, "They still have to be able to get to the barn in a blizzard, but CJ always thinks of her wranglers when she improves the place. That's how she keeps hands for so long."

Now, all of what Clarissa said today is true, but she's never let on like she cared about a bit of it. Shoot, in the '30s when the oats didn't head up and the high meadow spring went dry, Clarissa did everything she could to make me sell the place.

"Half of it's mine," she yelled one night, "and half of a worthless ranch is just that: *worthless*. Sell it now and get what you can and be *done* with it!"

"So that's it," I snapped. "It's the money." And I really let her have it. Of course, I was scared to death about losing the place and I really wasn't myself or I wouldn't have said everything I did. I called her a coward and a goody-two-shoes. I accused her of not caring about Mama and Papa's dream and all they'd done to give us a home. It was a terrible row. We didn't speak for nearly a year.

Finally the weather broke. I was feeling pretty smug when I got the hay contract down at Fort Robinson. In fact, I actually joined the line of people shaking the preacher's hand one Sunday just so I could hand Clarissa her profit-sharing check in a semipublic way. I thought it would feel real good to do it, too. But it didn't. God sort of nudged me about how prideful that was. I hung around to apologize and, while the rest of the congregation passed by, God really got my attention. I once heard someone say that "crow is a tough old bird," and they were right. I've eaten my share. But one of the biggest helpings I ever ate was that day when I apologized to Clarissa for being so prideful.

Since then, we've managed what I like to think of as a peaceful coexistence. She doesn't give unsolicited advice about how I should run the ranch, and I come to church. Oh. And Jo comes to live with me every summer. Between the obvious fact that living with Ben Hale all these years has mellowed Clarissa and the years living alone have mellowed me, we get along all right. Now and then when there is a glitch in our sisterly relations — like that thing about me wearing boots with my Sunday dresses and the same hat for all those years — we work it out. Or Ben does. Once in a while, Will Bishop even has a hand in keeping the peace between Clarissa and me. Although I guess that won't be happening anymore.

Now there I go again. It just seems like, lately, no matter what I'm thinking about, it always ends up turning to Will Bishop. I've gotta stop that.

"Watch me, Mama, *watch* me!" Mia screeched with delight as she bounced along astride the swaybacked old gelding CJ Jackson called Ned.

"I'm watching, baby!" Helen called back.

"Giddy*up,* Ned," Mia said, rattling her reins and flopping her legs. "Giddy*up!*"

At Helen's side, CJ chortled. "Ned lost the 'giddy' in his 'up' about five years ago."

Helen smiled. "He doesn't seem to be minding all the commotion in the least," she said.

"Ned never did mind commotion. He's one of those old cow horses that has more sense than most of the cowboys who ever rode him. He'll be perfect for your little blondie. They'll be best friends in no time."

Helen leaned against the corral pole and watched her daughter. Jo Hale was standing in the middle of the corral with a long lead attached to Ned's bridle. The old horse grunted in protest when Jo said, "trot," but he obeyed. When Mia lost her hold on the saddle horn and started to slip to one side, Ned stopped.

"Is he actually waiting for Mia to right herself?" Helen asked in disbelief.

"I think he is," CJ said. "Ned's always had a sense about things. Even as a two-year-old he had a talent for adjusting his behavior to his rider. Of course, back then 'adjusting' sometimes meant taking advantage of an inexperienced rider. All horses will test a rider now and then. But Ned's past that. You don't have to worry. I wouldn't let Mia near any animal I didn't know was safe."

"I'm not worried," Helen said. When Mia climbed down, she stood beside the old gelding, patting his neck and talking to him. When the horse lowered its head and nibbled the top of the little girl's head, Mia pulled away.

"Hey," she said, then laughed and said, "I'm not *hay!*"

Her daughter's laughter brought tears to Helen's eyes. "I don't know how to thank you," she said to CJ. "For letting Mia come."

CJ shook her head. "No thanks needed. Blondie's welcome to stay as long as she wants." She paused. "Do you want her back home before the labor crew from the fort starts here?"

"I've got enough to worry about without adding imaginary problems to my life," Helen said. "I guess it's lucky I've been working in the PW headquarters. I know there's nothing to worry about with that. And I don't know when —" Helen swallowed, and thought *or if . . .* "I don't know when we'll be ready to bring her home."

"I'm sorry," CJ said, "about Hank's . . . difficulties." She cleared her throat. "After Johnny got that worthless old car of his, he used to haul Hank out to the ranch to work on it. Used to irritate me, sometimes, the way Hank could always see the silver side of a cloud."

Mia grabbed Ned's reins and walked over, playacting the cowgirl.

CJ kept talking. "Will was wishing Johnny would just let him haul the old thing out to the junk pile in the canyon, but Hank always had something else to try . . . and he always found a way to make it run again."

At the mention of her father, Mia lost her smile. She looked sideways up at her mother. "I don't want to go back home."

Helen blinked back the tears that were all too close to the surface these days. "I thought you were going to show me how much you know about taking care of horses," she said abruptly. "I don't know a lot, but I know there's a lot more to it than just jangling reins and yelling 'giddyup.' And if Miss Jackson is going to let you stay out here, you have to be ready to help."

On the opposite side of the corral, Jo was opening the gate.

"Come on, Ned," Mia said, leading the old horse to the barn. She called back to her mother, "I'll help. I'll work *hard.*"

Helen took a step toward the barn.

"She can stay as long as you need her to," CJ said, just loud enough for Helen to hear. "And I mean it."

Helen nodded, swiped at her eyes, and headed after her daughter.

As Reverend Hale drove his old car over the winding road that led from the Four Pines Ranch, up the ridge, and back down into the valley where Fort Robinson and the city of Crawford nestled beside the White River, Helen stared out the passenger-side rear window of the old car, purposely tuning out the conversation around her and the concerned stares being exchanged between Clarissa and Stella. When Pastor Hale pulled the Nash over to the curb in front of Stella's house and let the ladies out, Helen thanked him, hoping that Mrs. Bohling and Mrs. Fosdick were watching. They would likely be upset at the idea of Pastor Hale and his wife supporting her new abode, but it still gave Helen a warm feeling when Pastor

Hale even opened the gate that led up the sidewalk to Stella's front porch, and he and Clarissa lingered to talk.

"Thank you," she said. "I feel so much better knowing Mia is happy." She looked across the street. "I know Hank and I have to . . . do . . . something. But I don't know what. Having Mia gone is best for now."

"You don't have to know what you're going to do, honey," Stella said and slipped her arm around Helen's waist.

"I agree," Pastor Hale said. "Take some time. Watch and pray. I might have an idea . . . but I'm not sure. . . ." He smiled at Stella. "Be thankful for friends. And keep busy."

Stella nodded. "There's a dance at the Servicemen's Club tomorrow night. I promised Mrs. Blair I'd help chaperone." She turned toward Helen. "You should come with me," she said. "It'd do you good to get out."

"Oh, no," Helen said. "I couldn't."

"Of course you could," Clarissa spoke up, then looked at her husband. "Couldn't she?"

"Why don't all three of you go," Reverend Hale said. He smiled down at his wife. "I could use the time to get an early start on next week's sermon."

Just inside the back door Clarissa emoted. "Do you *want* to get fired?"

"What are you talking about?"

"I can't go to a dance at the Servicemen's Club."

"You aren't going to a dance," Ben said. "You know Mrs. Blair will shuttle you into the kitchen the minute you show your face. No one can possibly take issue with you doing your part to help the men from the fort have a wholesome evening instead of frequenting the bars." He kissed her cheek. "Clarissa Hale is the best cook in Dawes County, and everyone knows it. Those boys from Fort Robinson have no idea what a treat they are in for. If you like, I'll even walk the three of you to the club," he offered.

"That's all right, honey. You said you wanted to get started on next week's sermon."

"And I will. But . . . I was thinking I could just happen by Hank's garage on my way home."

Fourteen

*My little children, let us not love in word,
neither in tongue; but in deed and in truth.*

1 JOHN 3:18

Clara Joy

When the phone rang Monday morning, I
could not believe my ears.

"You coming to the dispersal sale next
week?"

"Wh-what?"

"I said," Will repeated, "are you coming to
the sale next week? Here. At Fort Robinson."

"Wasn't planning on it,"

"Think you should," Will said.

My old heart thumped at the idea the old
fool might actually be missing me. He'd
only been gone for a little over a month, but
it seemed like a year, and I was hoping he
felt the same way.

"There's a horse you should see.
Demisang. Gorgeous head. Good bloodlines."

The old fool wasn't missing me. He was talking horses. I let him hear the irritation in my voice. "If he's so perfect, why's he going on the sale? Bill Harker's always been willing to make room for new blood — at least for a season or two."

"Too much fire. Needs special handling."

"All men do," I snapped, "and most aren't worth the trouble."

Will cleared his throat. "Buster is."

"Buster?"

"The stallion I want you to see."

"See? Or buy?" There was no reason for me to drive to the dispersal sale just to look at a horse.

"Buy," Will admitted.

"With a name like that I'll be expecting a plow horse."

"There's not a drop of plow horse in Buster. You come to the sale, and you'll see what I mean."

What was he thinking? "Will, things have changed since you left, and the very last thing I need at the Four Pines right now is a hard-to-handle stallion. Jo and Mia are already here."

"I know," Will said. "Jo told me about it. Sad about the Frey family."

"Well, if you know about it, you know I've got my hands full, and I don't need any more challenges at the moment. No more wranglers have sprouted from the rocks since you left." He was quiet for so long I thought the line might have gone dead. "Will? Hello? Are you there?"

"I'm here," Will said.

He was talking very slowly, which meant he was about to say something real important. I am not a patient woman, but once in a while I give Will Bishop the benefit of the doubt. So I hung on and waited to hear what he would say.

"If you come to the sale . . . and you want the horse . . ." Will cleared his throat. "I'd be willing to take him on as a special project." More silence. Then, "He's w-worth it, CJ."

"My work request was approved, Will. I'm getting fifteen PWs to help out around here. And I'm not waiting until July. I've been talking to the Walkers. Margaret says that other than the fact they don't like sweet potatoes and prefer rye bread to white, there hasn't been one thing happen that's anything but great. In short, my work crew is coming before haying season, and if they are any good at all, I'll keep them coming for as long as I can get them."

"Ask for one named Dieter Brock."

"What?"

"I said," Will repeated, "ask for Dieter Brock. He's got a way with horses. Especially Buster." Will swallowed. "You need me to spell his name for you?"

It was my turn to hunt for words. "Am I hearing you right?" I finally said. "You want me to come to the sale and risk . . . I don't know, probably a hundred dollars on an unknown horse named Buster —"

"It might take more," Will said. "Vic Dearborn was watching the German work with him the other day. Seemed pretty impressed. I think he's coming to the sale."

I couldn't resist being just a little sarcastic. "So I should pay serious money at a sale that usually brings about fifty dollars a head. . . . And if I do, you'll move back on the place . . . and you want help, but not just any help — you want *Nazi* help?"

"He's not really a Nazi," Will said.

"Really? I seem to recall you saying they all are." Of course, I knew more about Dieter Brock than I was letting on. The minute Will said the name, I remembered Helen Frey talking about him over lunch at Clarissa's. But I wasn't in the mood to make things easy on Will. Not yet.

"Well, I was wrong," Will said. "Brock is . . . I don't know. He doesn't act like a Nazi, anyway. I haven't really asked him about it."

"I expect not, unless you've been studying German." I am ashamed to admit that I carried things this far with Will. Helen Frey had made a point to tell us all that Dieter Brock spoke English real well, and of course I knew he was translating for Ben's services. But I was taking a sinful kind of pleasure in making Will squirm. I am not proud of that, and I have repented. But I'm also telling it straight, and that is what I did.

"He . . . he speaks English. You get him on the crew," Will said, "you won't have anything to worry about. He talks better than me. 'Course that's not s-saying m-much." He paused before saying, "I-I'm sorry, Ceeg. I was wrong."

Will hadn't called me *Ceeg* — pronounced like *siege* — in years. But my stubbornness wasn't about to fold yet. "Did I just hear you say you're sorry?"

"You did."

That did it. "Come on home, Will. I've missed you."

On Monday night, when Hank let himself into his auto repair shop via the alley door in the back, he kicked what proved to be a set of keys across the floor. Someone had used the key drop. Again. It had started happening soon after he'd worked on the preacher's car.

He used his flashlight to find the keys, then, checking to make certain the front door was locked and all the blinds were drawn on the windows up front, he settled on a stool behind the front counter to read the note from Bob Hanover.

Need Ron's old Buick running good before we sell her. Call before you do the work. Don't have much cash.

After staring at the note for a few minutes, Hank made his way to the back door, opened it, and peered out into the dark alley. Assured there was no one lurking there, he raised the garage door, went to Ron's old car, started it up, and pulled it into the first of two bays.

As soon as he raised the hood, a knock sounded at the back door. Hank ignored it.

"It's me," a now-familiar voice yelled. Hank sighed and went to unlock the door.

Once inside the shop, Vernon perched on a metal stool to watch Hank at work. On occasion, he retrieved a wrench or a belt.

"You're getting good with the hook," he said at one point.

Hank shrugged. "They told me not to give up with it. Said before long it would be second nature. Almost like a hand."

"Looks to me like you're there," Vernon offered. "You could open up again. The way you keep getting night visits, it's pretty obvious folks are glad you're back."

Hank said nothing.

"A man needs to know he's worth something," Vernon said. "That he can provide for his family."

"I've got no family," Hank said. "Not one that wants me, anyway. Helen took Mia and moved out."

"I heard," Vernon said. "Never figured her to quit on you like that."

Hank propelled himself out from under the car. "She didn't quit," he snapped. "She did what any woman would. Mia's afraid of me. And who can blame Helen if she can't stand to look at me. It's not her fault."

"Calm down, man," Vernon said. "I'm on your side, remember? 'Course it's not her fault. Pretty little gal sends her high school sweetheart off . . . and look what happens." He spun off center again into a colorful litany of now-familiar curses against the Italians and Mussolini, Hitler and the Krauts.

Hank scooted himself back under the car. When Vern offered him a drink, he turned it down. As the minutes passed, Vern drank the little silver flask dry.

"It's not enough anymore," he said, holding the flask upside down, then bringing it to his mouth to lick away the last drops. He stood up. "Got to get some more."

"G'night, Vernon," Hank said without sliding out. "You be careful walking home now, y'hear? Maybe go home and get some sleep."

"Sleep," Vernon said. "Wouldn't that be something? To actually sleep."

From beneath the car, Hank listened for the *click* that meant Vernon had locked the door behind him. When it didn't come, he slid from beneath Ron's car . . . just in time to see Reverend Hale come in.

"Evening, Hank," Ben said.

"E-evening," Hank said, pushing himself quickly back under the car. His heart was thumping. The preacher had looked straight at him. He hadn't even flinched, and Hank didn't know what to make of it.

"Just came by to let you know we drove out to the ranch yesterday," the preacher said. "Thought you'd like to know Mia likes it out there. Jo is teaching her to ride one of the old horses on the place."

Hank lowered his arms from the car's exhaust system and tried to picture Mia on horseback. "She used to draw horses all the time. Made me read *Black Beauty* to her until I was sick of it." After a minute he said, "I imagine she can read it for herself by now."

"I don't know about that," the preacher said. "Maybe you should ask her."

"That would be a little difficult, seeing as how she screams and runs away every time I come near her. And then there is the fact that she's out at your wife's ranch getting to know the Germans up close and personal." He went back to banging on the rusted muffler. His stump was beginning to ache from the impact. He paused, waiting for the preacher to defend his wife.

"I don't imagine you care to hear my thoughts on that," the preacher said, cool as could be. "But I can tell you that CJ Jackson would never do anything to risk Mia or Jo's safety." He paused. "If you like, I'll drive you out to the Four Pines myself. You can check it out."

"Maybe I'll take you up on that," Hank said. "Just as soon as hell freezes over."

The preacher cleared his throat. "If you change your mind, you let me know. In the meantime, I stopped by to tell you I walked Clarissa and Stella Black and your wife to the Servicemen's Club tonight. Helen's going to help Clarissa in the kitchen once in a while. I wanted you to know it was my idea. In case the town gossip burned your ears with another version."

The rusted muffler finally gave way. Rust flew into Hanks eyes. He shot out from under the car and ran for the lavatory. With his back to the preacher he rinsed out his eyes and dried his face. "I know you mean well, Preacher. But . . . why don't you just up and say why you really stopped by?"

"Why do you think I stopped by, Hank?"

Hank leaned against the doorframe with his good side facing the preacher. "Don't tell me you haven't been working on a speech. Everyone has a speech. Helen has her 'I love you and it doesn't matter' speech. Vernon Clark has his 'the sons-a-blanks destroyed your life and you should take revenge' speech. Don't you have a Romans 8:28 speech?"

"There'd be no reason to give that one," the preacher said. "You already know the verse. And I can't answer the question."

"Which question is that?"

"The one about how good is going to come from your situation." The preacher pointed to the stool recently vacated by Vernon Clark. "Mind if I take a seat?"

"Suit yourself," Hank said.

259

The preacher sat down. "Bob told me they were going to sell Ron's old car."

"So you *are* the reason I keep finding cars behind the shop." Hank grabbed a new muffler and headed back toward the car. "Thanks for that."

"You've got the wrong one," Ben said.

"What?"

"The wrong muffler. It *is* for a Buick, but Ron retrofitted his exhaust system before he went overseas. Put a Plymouth muffler on it."

Hank looked at the muffler in his hand. He shook his head. "Forgot about that." He looked toward the shelves where a pitiful array of car parts had waited for the garage owner's return from the war. "Darn," he said.

"Jack'll have one." The preacher rushed to add, "I could stop up there in the morning before I go into the office for you. Pick one up. If that would help."

"It would," Hank said. "And thanks." He reached into his pocket and withdrew a roll of bills with his hook.

The preacher stood up. "Forget it. Wait 'til we know for sure Jack has the one you need. Prices have been crazy since you left. You can pay me back when I deliver a new one."

"Whatever you say." Hank shoved the roll of bills back into his pocket.

The preacher rose to go. "Want me to lock the door behind me?" he asked. "Or is Vernon coming back? I saw him leave just as I rounded the corner at the other end of the alley. He didn't seem to be feeling well."

Hank shrugged. "He's probably at home sleeping it off." He hesitated, then added, "To tell you the truth, I don't think he would welcome a visit from you, Preacher."

The preacher sighed. "Which is an indication that that may be exactly what he needs." He shook his head. "That's the hardest part of my job. And the part I like the least."

"What part is that?" Hank asked.

"Chasing after folks who not only don't want to hear what I have to say . . . but are openly hostile about it."

"Don't take it personally," Hank said. "As far as I can tell, Vernon's openly hostile to just about everybody these days." He lifted the hood of the old Buick. "I never gave much thought to the idea of a preacher not liking his job."

"It's no different from any other job. Parts you love. Parts you don't. I love studying God's Word," the preacher said.

"And I like the idea that maybe once in a while something I say from the pulpit does somebody some good. Hospital visits are all right, too."

"You wouldn't have liked visiting the hospital I was in," Hank said.

"Why do you say that?"

"Every last one of us burned, and no one knowing much to do about it beyond putting on bandages and waiting for the scars to heal it over."

The preacher was quiet.

"It's a strange thing to be on fire," Hank said. He looked past the preacher as his mind retreated into the past. He told the preacher more than he ever planned to tell anyone, but the man listened without any hint of revulsion. "Anyway," he concluded, "I ended up in a hospital outside London. Mostly Royal Air Force. They took me there because the burns were so bad. Said to get me to some doctor they called 'The Maestro.' " Hank grimaced and pointed to his face. "This was the best he could do. And believe it or not, this is pretty good, given what he had to work with." He tried to laugh. "Some of the guinea pigs needed what they called 'total reconstruction.' At least I have half a face left."

"I can't begin to imagine what you've been through, Hank. I don't even know what to say."

That was different. A preacher who didn't know what to say — who wasn't spouting clichés.

"You know," Hank went on, "we were forced out into the village every chance we got. Doctor said it was part of our therapy. Soon as we could. They called it 'the town that didn't stare.' Folks were used to seeing burned soldiers. Then I came home." He looked down at the floor. "And all I get is stares."

"People can be cruel," the preacher said. "I wish I could change that." He stood up. "When should I bring you the muffler? To-morrow morning?"

"Night," Hank corrected him. "I'm a creature of the night now."

When the preacher had gone, Hank went to the front of the shop. Pulling a shade away from one of the windows just enough to peer out, he looked up the street toward the Servicemen's Club. He waited for a long time. Finally, Helen came out arm in arm with Stella. Two men walked alongside them. One of them was Deacon Tom Hanson. The other one was in uniform. Young. Handsome.

★ ★ ★

After the preacher delivered the muffler for Ron's car, word seemed to travel even faster about the rather unique reopening of Hank's Garage. The next few nights several cars appeared in the back alley. And the notes people left with their keys weren't just about what needed fixing. They were personal notes to Hank:

> *Glad to have you back.*
> *Sure missed you.*
> *Finally — a mechanic who knows*
> *   what to do with a Hudson!*
> *We prayed for you every day you*
> *   were gone.*
> *Crawford is proud of you.*
> *Welcome home, hero.*

He folded each one in half and tucked it in his pocket, and when he went home — always before dawn — and climbed the steps to the attic past the closed door to Helen's empty bedroom, he would take out the note and tape it to the wall along with the others.

He kept his garage doors locked and the shades drawn. He put cash in an envelope for Helen and left it on Stella Black's back stoop, weighted down with a rock. Mr.

264

Clark stopped in nearly every night to perch on a barrel in the corner. Some nights he was quiet, others talkative. His talk centered around the Germans at Fort Robinson — although he had much more colorful terms to describe the prisoners of war. Did Hank know Jim Grant's wife invited them into their ranch house and served them like members of the family?

Hank did not. And, no, he did not think that a good idea.

Did Hank know that CJ Jackson was going to have them cut hay for her?

Hank knew.

"Did you know they're over there in the prison eating steak while most of us are still counting ration stamps?" he grumbled. "Somebody ought to do something."

On Thursday night when Vern entered the shop, he gripped Hank's shoulders, and said, "You know what I think? I think people need to see what the Krauts did to you. Maybe a few of 'em would wake up."

"It wouldn't make any difference," Hank said. But it made him think. The doctor in England had had them wear their uniforms when they went out — and he had insisted they go out. He believed civilians should see the price being paid for their freedom.

After Vernon left the shop that night, Hank went into the little washroom tucked into the back corner of his shop and turned on the switch. A hundred-watt naked bulb washed his face with bright and unkind light. Hank lifted his chin, turned from side to side. "Face it," he murmured. When he realized the play on words, he smiled — with only half his mouth. The other half barely moved. He reached up with his index finger and lifted his upper lip. The scar tissue was numb.

He remembered when it hadn't been numb. He remembered the screams of the crew pinned inside the wreckage. . . . *Welcome home, hero.* Staring in the mirror, he whispered the words aloud as he reached up and covered the scarred part of his image with his hand, so that all he could see was the good side . . . the side washed with tears. He wasn't a hero. All he'd done was run for his life . . . and roll on the ground to put the flames out before he passed out. If the people who had written that note knew what followed in the hospital — how he screamed with every bandage change, how he begged not to be immersed in the saline bath — they wouldn't call him a hero.

And after all the suffering, still no one wanted to look at him. Even if he did put on his uniform and stroll through town, people wouldn't be encouraged to hope their husbands and sons might come home, too. They might manage to smile — in time — but at home, late at night, they would get on their knees and beg God. He knew the prayer, because he'd prayed it himself. "Let them die."

Hank turned out the light. He'd finish working on Stinson's Buick tomorrow.

Before stepping into the alley, he looked both ways. It was growing light. With his heart pounding, Hank ran for home.

Fifteen

A righteous man
regardeth the life of his beast.

PROVERBS 12:10

"Will we see lots and lots of horses at the sale?" Mia asked Jo on Friday afternoon as she bounced up and down on the front seat of Aunt CJ's pickup.

"Hold still," Jo laughed. "You'll kick Sadie out of gear."

"Huh?"

"Sadie," Jo said, tapping the dashboard of her aunt's old pickup.

Mia looked up at Jo. "I wish I had a hat like yours."

"Your mother might not approve. Mine hates it when I wear flannel shirts and denim jeans."

"My mama doesn't care," Mia said. "I'm asking for a cowgirl hat for my birthday."

"When is your birthday, Blondie?" Aunt CJ asked.

"August 18," Mia said, frowning slightly.

268

"What's the matter?" Jo asked.

"Nothing."

Aunt CJ patted Mia's leg. "Nothing is something. So tell us what's the matter."

"Will you come to my birthday?" Mia said. "No matter what?"

CJ and Jo looked at each other. "Of course we will," Jo said. "In fact, I bet my mama would bake your favorite cake if I ask her. What kind do you like the very best in the world?"

"Angel food," Mia said.

"Well, you are in luck, because my mama won a blue ribbon last year at the fair for her angel food cake."

"I know," Mia said.

"Really?"

"Uh-huh. Mrs. Bohling that lives next door to us got the red ribbon. She was *mad.*" Mia went on to describe Hettie Bohling coming home with her red-ribbon cake in such a way that both CJ and Jo were red-faced trying to stifle their laughter.

"Well," Jo said, "you can count on it, Mia. Angel food cake for your birthday in August. Anything else you want?"

"To have my party at the ranch."

After a long pause, Jo changed the subject. "You're gonna see more horses than you can count today, Mia."

"How many are we gonna *buy?*"

"Only one," Aunt CJ answered. "And I'm not even sure about that one. But Will says he is one of the prettiest you'll ever see."

Mia pretended to hold a horse's reins. "I wanna ride him!"

"You won't be riding this one," Jo said.

"Why not?"

"Well," Jo replied, "because Ned would get jealous. You don't want to make Ned sad, do you?"

Mia shook her head. She looked up at Jo. "Are *you* gonna ride the new horse?"

"No." It was Aunt CJ's turn to speak up. "If we get him, he won't be for riding."

"What's he for?"

"Making baby horses."

"That's *all?*"

Aunt CJ nodded.

Mia fumed. "Can I at least *pet* him?"

"We'll see."

Mia sighed loudly.

"What's the matter?" Jo asked.

"When grown-ups say 'we'll see' . . . it always means 'no.' "

As they walked toward the holding pens where hundreds of sale horses milled about, Mia wrinkled up her nose. "Phew," she said.

Jo laughed and tugged on the child's ponytail. "If you're gonna be a cowgirl, you've got to get used to that."

Mia made a face, then pointed to a horse in the pen nearest them. "What do you call the gold ones?"

"That's a buckskin," Jo said.

"I thought gold ones were palominnows."

"Palo-*mee*-no," Jo corrected her. "See the dark legs and the dark stripe down his back? That's a buckskin." She scanned the horses milling around in the pen. "I don't see a palomino. We probably won't. Aunt CJ told me once that the army usually preferred dark colors — and solids."

"Why?"

"So they didn't draw attention in battle."

"Why?"

Jo sighed. Aunt CJ had gone to find Uncle Will and to see Buster close up . . . and she had made a lame excuse as to why Jo and Mia couldn't come along. But Jo knew the real reason. Dieter Brock was likely to be the one handling Buster, and Aunt CJ had promised to keep both she and Mia as far away from the Germans as possible. It wasn't fair. And it was silly. She had watched Brock's face when he translated Daddy's sermon. She had seen how gentle he could be when he talked to Buster. She had heard him sing a lullaby. Whatever he might be, Jo was convinced that Dieter Brock posed no threat to anyone in Nebraska, least of all anyone Will Bishop cared about.

"Look! That one looks like Black Beauty!" Mia pointed to a horse in the far holding pen.

"That *is* a pretty one," Jo said, tugging on Mia's hand and leading her away. "We'd better get Aunt CJ's seat saved for her."

"I wanna sit up high," Mia said as they climbed the grandstand, and Jo led the way into a row halfway up.

Jo shook her head. "Aunt CJ will expect to find us here. She likes to sit in the same place."

"Why?"

"Well," Jo said, taking a deep breath and forcing herself to stop scanning the holding pens for a tall, blond PW, "the auctioneer knows her, and he'll look her way when a horse comes up he knows she might like."

"How's he know what she likes?"

"Aunt CJ is pretty well known around here. And I think she and the auctioneer went to school together."

Mia frowned. "I never thought of Aunt CJ going to school."

"Of course she went to school," Jo said.

She pointed into the distance, "In fact, her school was right over there in a log house by the old parade ground. But the building's gone now."

"Did Aunt CJ like school?" Mia wanted to know.

"I don't think so. Not very much."

"I don't like school, either," Mia said. She grinned. "I'm glad we got to quit early this year. Aren't you?"

"Uh-huh," Jo said.

"You aren't listening," Mia said, tugging on Jo's sleeve.

"Sure I am," Jo said. "I just want to watch for Aunt CJ and make sure she can find us."

"You said she always sits here," Mia replied.

Jo sighed. "You're right." She forced herself to stop looking for Dieter Brock and smiled down at Mia. "So . . . what should we call the gray one in the first pen?"

"Sneezy." Mia giggled as the horse in question let out a wheeze.

Jo laughed. "That's a good name. Do you see one we could call Dopey?"

Mia nodded and pointed to a dun mare with her head down. They had named horses for all seven dwarves and several other fairy-tale characters before Aunt CJ finally arrived.

"Will stayed over in the barn with Buster," she said.

"Well? What do you think?" Jo prodded her.

"I think he's a looker and a trouble-maker."

"So . . . you don't want him?"

Aunt CJ sighed. "What I want is for Will Bishop to come home."

Jo looked sideways at her aunt.

CJ looked back. "What?"

"You old softie," Jo said, and nudged her shoulder.

For the next two hours, except for two brief breaks, Jo and CJ and Mia watched horses sold at the rate of three per minute.

"I bet Uncle Will is tired of trimming hooves," Jo said.

"And manes and tails," Aunt CJ muttered. "He should have known his old back wouldn't take it." She looked at Jo. "But don't you tell him I said that."

"Don't worry," Jo said, "I learned to stay out of your squabbles with Uncle Will when I was in fourth grade."

"Is that so?" Aunt CJ said, feigning irritation.

Jo nodded. "It is. I was really upset when the two of you were fighting over where to build the new barn."

Aunt CJ looked down at the sale bill. "I didn't realize you knew anything about those disagreements."

"It's all right," Jo said. "I learned something about you and Uncle Will."

"Really?"

"Well, not then. But since then."

"I cannot wait to hear this," Aunt CJ said. As she spoke, she reached up and jerked on her hat brim.

"I see you, Miz Jackson," the auctioneer said, "and you're in for five."

Aunt CJ's eyes got big. She looked down at the sale ring. "Oh no!" She muttered, "Just what I need. A charity case."

"Way to go, CJ," a voice sounded from above them.

Looking back over her shoulder, Jo saw Vic Dearborn sitting a few rows above them. "Oh, brother," she whispered.

"What's wrong?" Mia wanted to know.

Jo shook her head.

"Sold!" the auctioneer said.

"And a bargain at five dollars," Dearborn teased.

"Did we buy that horse?" Mia said.

"Suppose you tell me what you learned about Will and me?" Aunt CJ said.

"Well, Mama said that love looks different to different people. That it's a lot more than a feeling you feel when you feel like you're going to feel a feeling you haven't felt before. And that between you and Uncle Will, sometimes love looks like a spat. But it's still love and it's still strong. And then she said, 'It's the same way with your aunt CJ and me. She is stubborn and so am I, and we have had more than our share of words, but don't you ever doubt that we love each other. We may not be soul mates but we are sisters, and that's a bond no man can break. And it's the same between your aunt CJ and uncle Will. They have had their share of words over the barn, but don't ever doubt that they love each other.' "

"Your mother said that?" Aunt CJ asked.

Jo nodded.

"Well, let's go get some lunch," and with that, Aunt CJ stood up and headed off in the direction of the pickup.

Clara Joy

I spent the entire walk to the truck alternately fuming over being tricked into buying the dun mare the girls had named Dopey and Vic Dearborn's rubbing it in. I never have liked that man. He was in school with Will and me, and as a boy he always took an evil kind of joy in teasing Will about his slow speech and his bad leg. And when Will lost the ranch, Vic was right there at the sale, lowballing the bid and winning it. Thanks to his daddy's money he waltzed into a good deal, and he struts around Dawes County like he's the biggest shot in the Sandhills. I cannot stand him. So when he intercepted the girls and me on our way to get our picnic lunch out of the truck, it didn't take much to get my goat.

"You starting a new business out at the Four Pines?" he said, and gave me that grin that he thinks makes him looks handsome.

"Why?"

"That last purchase. Thought maybe you were building a glue factory."

"Ha. Ha. Ha. Ha." I said the words with a space in between. He got the point.

"Heard I'll be up against you for the bay stallion," he said.

"What bay stallion?"

"The one Will couldn't handle. The one that's partial to Nazis."

If I have ever wanted to throttle a man it was then. I am not exactly a petite woman, and honestly, I think maybe I *could* have, I was that mad. But I cry when I get mad, and I could feel the tears threatening as he stood there bad-mouthing one of the best men that ever lived. But Jo interrupted.

"Dieter Brock is no Nazi," she said. And there was fire in her blue eyes.

"Is that so? And what would you be knowing about it?"

Thank goodness I had the presence of mind to notice Will headed our way. "We've got a letter from Johnny in the pickup for Will," I said real quick. "He asked to be transferred to the Pacific. We're hoping it will say where he ended up. Marion didn't ask to be transferred, did he?" My reference to his little prissy son pretty much got rid of Vic Dearborn.

As it turned out, Johnny's letter was old news, but assuming that Jo was always eager for news from John Bishop, Will did the kind thing. He read the letter aloud.

Every time Jo was mentioned — which was often — I'd glance up at her. Most of the time she was listening, but once or twice she was looking over toward the holding pens. I figured she might be watching for Buster, but Will had already told her that he was going to be handled a different way and that Dieter Brock would be walking him from the barn, hoping that maybe that would keep him calmed down.

When Will read Johnny's reaction to

President Roosevelt's death, I felt like we ought to have a moment of silence out of respect, it was that moving.

I cannot tell you how many times hearing his voice on the radio or encountering his personality on the newsreels rallied my confidence and reminded me why I am fighting. Losing him is almost like losing a member of my own family. We were counting on him to help us shape a new peace after our work over here is done. Now that he is gone, I wonder who will step into those great shoes.

"I do believe that boy could have written the president's eulogy," I said, and looked over at Jo, figuring she would be sharing in my moment of pride in our boy. But she wasn't. She was daydreaming about that horse again.

"Well," Uncle Will said, folding up Johnny's letter and tucking it into his shirt pocket. "Best be going. Time to convince Buster to put on a halter."

"Mr. Brock doesn't even have him halterbroke yet?" Jo asked.

"Well, of course he does. Sort of. He puts

the *pfefferneusse* in his fist, and when Buster puts his nose through the halter, he gets the treat."

"I don't have time for baking pfeffer-whatevers," grumbled Aunt CJ.

"We'll do it," Jo offered. "Mia and me." She turned toward her uncle Will. "Where do *you* get them?"

"The PW kitchen," he said.

"Do you think Mr. Brock can give you enough to get him into his new stall?"

"I reckon," Will said. "Buster's coming up right away in this next group," he said, looking at Aunt CJ. "Don't be late."

"He sure is vocal," Jo said, leaning across Mia to whisper in her aunt's ear while Dieter led Buster into the sale ring.

Aunt CJ nodded. "Vocal. And gorgeous."

Jo agreed mentally — about both males in the sale ring. She scolded herself and scanned the crowd. Vic Dearborn was no longer sitting behind them. Now he was positioned on the opposite side of the grandstand in about the third row.

"Are we going to buy him?" Mia asked.

"We're going to try," Aunt CJ said.

The bidding began at fifty dollars. At a sale where most horses sold for thirty, it was a lot.

"Don't forget the horse comes with Uncle Will," Jo said. She could have sworn Aunt CJ blushed. The thought that maybe the horse would come with a certain PW made *her* blush. *What is* wrong *with you? Didn't Uncle Will just read you a letter from Johnny?*

Aunt CJ raised her hand and took the bid up to one hundred and twenty-five dollars.

Jo looked across the arena as the bidding continued. "It's Vic Dearborn," she hissed. "Don't let him win, Aunt CJ."

"Don't worry," CJ said between clenched teeth. She nodded again.

"One hundred and seventy-five dollars. Do I hear one-eighty?" The auctioneer was looking toward Dearborn, who had apparently motioned that he wanted to take a closer look.

Dieter tried to signal the rancher to stop, but Dearborn kept moving in on Buster. Uncle Will stepped up to the edge of the sale ring and spoke to Dearborn. He didn't listen.

"Why won't he listen to Uncle Will?" Jo muttered.

"Vic Dearborn's never had any use for any of us, and his ego sure isn't gonna get any smaller in front of all his cronies," Aunt CJ said.

Buster tossed his head, sidestepped, and snorted. When Dearborn stepped over the fence into the arena, Dieter barked, "Stop!" Dearborn ignored him. The closer he got, the more Buster danced. When Dearborn tried to take the lead rope out of Dieter's hands, Buster let loose, ripping the rope out of Dieter's hands, spinning around, and letting fly with both rear hooves. As the men ducked, Buster spun back around and launched himself across the dirt toward Dearborn with bared teeth. He skidded to a halt at the edge of the sale ring just as Dearborn flew over the fence to safety, but even with Dearborn gone, Buster wasn't finished. He reared and pawed the air while Uncle Will stood on one side and Dieter on the other, their arms at their sides.

Dieter began talking loudly — reciting something, Jo thought, something rhythmical — a poem? Whatever it was, it got Buster's attention. He came to a halt in the center of the sale ring, his head lowered, his front legs splayed, his velvety ears at attention. He was ready to lunge away at any moment, but he was listening to Dieter. He pawed the dirt nervously, but he listened. When Dieter finally took a step forward Buster didn't move.

"Has he got *magic?*" Mia whispered.

"I'm beginning to think so," Aunt CJ answered.

Absolutely, Jo thought, as the gorgeous man reached out a huge hand toward the gorgeous horse. Finally, Buster stretched out his beautiful head, his dark muzzle quivering with anticipation. Dieter slowly reached into his pocket. When he held up what Jo knew was a small square cookie, the horse whickered and loped toward him.

"What about it, Vic?" the auctioneer said quietly. "One-eighty?"

"I wouldn't give one dollar and eighty cents for that monster," was the answer.

"You still in, Miss Jackson?"

Jo looked at her aunt, who seemed to take forever to nod.

"Sold!"

Aunt CJ looked at Jo. "I hope we aren't going to have to tranquilize him to get him into the trailer. You take Blondie here in search of 'the facilities' and meet us at the truck," she said. "I'll hook up with Will and the German. I want Will to be sure that man is part of my work crew. I love the way he handles a horse."

As if to prove Aunt CJ right, "the German" got Buster loaded without a hitch. While they watched him work his magic, which amounted to a combination of gentle prodding and bribery with *pfefferneusse,* Aunt CJ turned around and winked at Jo. "Maybe I should'a tried that on your Uncle Will a few years back," she said.

Jo laughed and took Mia's hand. Dieter Brock was going to be working on the Four Pines. She finally had something interesting to write Delores about.

"Not me," Rolf said, shaking his head back and forth. "Not in a million years."

"Me, either," Bruno Bauer agreed. "I'm afraid of horses."

"Come on," Dieter argued. "Don't you want to see what Karl May was writing about? Don't you want to get outside the barbed wire?"

"I've already been outside the wire," Rolf said, "and I saw what May was writing about from the train. I'll get off this place as soon as the war is over and we can go home. Which may not be long, from what we are reading. The Allies approach from the west, the Russians from the east, and . . ." Shrader marched his hands toward each other through the air and clapped. "Bam! Germany is split in two! The fatherland is being battered into fragments. Soon it will be over."

"And so you are happy shoveling manure

in the stables?" Dieter said.

"What's the difference where I shovel manure?" Rolf wanted to know. "At Fort Robinson or on some ranch. It's all still manure and it all stinks."

Bauer nodded agreement.

Rolf closed the magazine he had been reading and leaned forward. "And just because they want you on that work crew doesn't mean they will take us, anyway. Look, Dieter, you go ahead. I understand. Really, I do. They want you, and you want to work with the horse. But I don't know the first thing about — "

"It doesn't matter," Dieter said. "Miss Jackson suggested I might know who would be better workers from our compound." Dieter looked from Rolf to Bruno. "And you are two of the hardest workers I have ever known. And you said you thought the prairie was beautiful."

Rolf sighed. "I didn't mean it. I was just trying to annoy Gunnar Stroh. It always made him angry when we said anything nice about America."

"Look," Dieter said, "It's all kinds of work. Cutting hay. Working in the field. I don't know what else. But I do know that Company D comes back every night talking about the huge meals the rancher's wife

285

cooks for them and —"

"That's against the rules," Rolf said.

Dieter looked toward Bauer. "Piles of potatoes. Pie. Beef. And they even had orange soda."

Bruno Bauer smiled and patted his belly. "I'm convinced," he said. "I'll go if you can get permission."

Dieter nodded, "That's good." He turned to Rolf. "Come on, Rolf. We've been together all along. Why change it now?"

"I'll protect you from the runaways," Bruno joked.

"Oh, all right," Rolf said. He threw his magazine at Dieter. "I guess it will be better than crawling around in the dirt planting flowers with the theatrical troupe."

"There they come!" Mia said, and pointed to a plume of dust rising toward the sky.

"Good eye, Sprite," Jo said. She peered toward the horizon through the dormer window of Aunt CJ's nearly empty loft.

Jo put her arm around the child. "We'll go out and saddle Ned as soon as the truck goes by," she said.

"There she is. There's Sadie!" Mia said just as the cab of the old red pickup came into view.

It looked like a guard was seated next to Uncle Will. In the back of the pickup was the cage he had built so he could haul a few calves to the railroad depot or a sale without hitching up the big trailer. The cage was now packed with denim-clad PWs. Jo squinted, but the truck flew past too fast for her to see if the one Buster liked was among them or not.

Jo stood at the far end of the barn doing her best not to show any kind of uncertainty as she stared into Buster's brown eyes. She swallowed. "Mia," she said quietly. "You back out — slowly — and run get Aunt CJ."

"She's gone out to the fields to see about the prisoners," she said, as she backed away from the horse that had somehow gotten out of his stall.

Shoot. I knew that. "Oh, right," Jo said quietly. "Well then, walk slowly toward the back door and just go on up to the house and wait for me."

"What are you gonna do?"

"I'm going to get Buster back into his stall."

"That's too dangerous," Mia said. "He kicks. And bites. Unless you've got *feffer-noses*."

"It'll be fine," Jo replied. "But you go on

up to the house. Just move slow." She didn't take her eyes off Buster as Mia slipped away.

"So," she said as calmly as possible. "Care to tell me how you got out of your stall?"

Buster snorted and tossed his head.

"Don't you laugh at me," Jo said, pleased when Buster didn't seem inclined to rush her. "We had no idea you were an escape artist."

Buster seemed to lose interest in the conversation and turned toward Ned's stall.

"That's Ned," Jo said. "He's old and harmless. No challenge to you at all. Be nice to him. He's Mia's horse for the summer."

Buster pawed the earth outside Ned's stall, then lifted his head and touched noses with the aged gelding. Jo watched as they snuffled and whickered and nipped, just as if they were having a private conversation. While Buster's attention was on Ned, Jo inched her way along the wall of stalls. Her heart pounding, she opened the door to one stall and then the one across from it, hoping Buster would not rush the opening between the doors where she stood. To her amazement, Buster not only didn't rush her, but when she opened the stall next to Ned, he walked in. As Jo stepped carefully to close the door, Buster waited quietly. When the door clicked, his ears came forward, and he nodded his head.

"You old meany, you," Jo teased. "Is that all it takes to calm you down?" She rested her arms on the top of the stall door. "Who would have guessed that all you needed was a baby-sitter named Ned?"

She waited for a long time watching Buster and Ned. When she heard hoofbeats coming up the road, she hurried outside just in time to see Aunt CJ dismounting over at the house where Mia was jumping up and down on the porch, gesturing toward the barn.

"It's all right," Jo called. She trotted across the road.

"Did he really get out of that stall?" Aunt CJ asked.

"He did," Jo said. "But he had a reason."

"Which is?"

"He wanted a pet," Jo said, laughing.

Clara Joy

I have known a lot of horses in my time, but not a single one like this Buster. Sometimes I am tempted to check for evidence that he really is a stallion, because now that he has a stablemate he acts like a big baby half the time. When Jo saddles Ned so Mia can take a ride, Buster throws a fit because he doesn't want to be left behind. And that is how we got Buster really and truly halterbroke. Ned took Mia for a ride, and Buster practically pushed Will over to get trussed up and taken for a walk. Actually, it was more Buster taking Will for a walk. Straight out of the barn and straight to the corral where our little Blondie was riding. It was comical. Buster screamed at Ned. Ned answered. And that was that. Buster gave a big old sigh and lowered his head and practically went to sleep. Ever since then, whenever we turn Buster into the corral we let Ned out, too. The two are like a couple of old soldiers telling war stories.

If Vic Dearborn gets wind of what a big baby Buster has turned out to be, he is going to think the whole thing at Fort Robinson was staged between Will and me and Dieter Brock. Which would be a violation of the "Instructions for Persons Using Prisoner of War Labor in Your County." And everyone who knows CJ Jackson knows she is a stickler for following rules.

That is a joke, by the way.

Sixteen

Be ye angry, and sin not.

EPHESIANS 4:26

It had become almost a ritual. On Saturday nights, Clarissa brought over cinnamon rolls and helped Helen and Stella prepare the little bungalow for Sunday Dinner at Stella's. This night, Stella grabbed the cinnamon rolls from Clarissa and motioned her onto the porch swing beside Helen. "I've got news," she said. "Now you both wait right there while I get us some tea." She grinned. "I am taking a sinful amount of pleasure in noting that Mrs. Bohling keeps finding excuses to come out onto her front porch — and I want her to see that the Mrs. Reverend Hale herself is gracing my porch swing." With a little laugh, she disappeared inside.

"Do you have any idea what on earth she is talking about?" Clarissa said.

"Just look," Helen replied, motioning with only her eyes toward Mrs. Bohling's house.

"Not that," Clarissa said. "I mean the news."

"Not a clue," Helen said, and settled back to wait.

Stella reappeared with a tray of cookies and three iced teas. "To Chase Young," she said, raising her own glass in a toast.

"The banker?" Helen said. "You're toasting the banker?"

"You bet I am," Stella said, laughing. "That poor boy is going to swallow his tie on Monday." She pointed at Clarissa. "You had better be saying a prayer for him. He just may have a heart attack."

"What on earth are you talking about?" Clarissa asked.

"On Monday morning, May 7, 1945, Stella Black is going to sashay into the Farmers Bank in Crawford, Nebraska, and make her house payment in *cash money*." She hooted with joy, raised her arms in the air, and danced a jig.

"Praise the Lord!" Clarissa said.

"Amen!" Helen agreed before adding, "So . . . maybe you won't need to have a soldier rent a room here after all?"

"I've got a roomer all lined up, and the wolf is still at the door," Stella said quickly. "But he's gonna have to make tracks if Stella's little boardinghouse keeps it up."

She sat down and lit a cigarette. "Look, honey," she said to Helen, "the hens in this town have been serving me up for dessert ever since Charlie flew the coop when Delores was a baby. Whether I do or don't or will or won't doesn't really matter. I think it's my mission in life to provide fodder for the feeding frenzy. I cared when Delores was little — for her sake — but she's all grown up now and I don't care anymore." She punctuated her defense with smoke rings. "If you don't want to see it through, I understand. You're a married woman with a child to consider."

"You can stay with us," Clarissa said to Helen from her chair beside the trellis. "You can have Jo's room." She looked at Stella. "And I don't mean that as judging you. Really, I don't. It's just another option for Helen."

"I understand," Stella said.

"And it frees up another room for you," Clarissa added. "If two dollars a week is a big help, four dollars a week would be even better. Am I right?"

"Mrs. Hale!" Stella said, putting her hand to her throat in mock horror. "Can you possibly be suggesting what I think you are suggesting?"

"What?" Clarissa said. "That you actually

293

make *two* house payments *in a row* . . . without being rescued by a man?"

"Talk like that will get you in trouble with your husband," Stella said.

"Talk like that got me a husband," Clarissa shot back. "Ben never was one to be attracted to a shrinking violet."

"Good for him," Stella replied. She lifted her iced tea glass again. "Here's to strong Baptist men. Long may they reign."

Helen could hear Stella singing the minute she woke up the next morning. "Uncle Sam ain't a woman, but he sure can take your man."

Slipping out of bed, she dressed quickly, made her bed, and headed for the kitchen. Unaware of Helen's presence, Stella continued singing at the top of her lungs while she added to the mountain of pancakes already in the warming drawer that made up the right half of her old gas stove.

"You let me sleep too late to be of much help," Helen said.

Stella whirled around, "Oh, honey, I'm sorry. I didn't know you were standing there." She apologized. "That's just a dumb old song I used to sing after Charlie —"

"It's all right," Helen said. She forced a smile. "There's a lot of truth in it."

Stella tipped her head and looked past Helen into the living room.

"Is that what I think it is by the front door?"

Following Stella's gaze to where her suitcase stood by the front door, Helen nodded.

Stella frowned. "I was hoping you'd stay."

"It's past time for me to go," Helen said.

"I told you I'd understand," Stella said. "And I do. You've got a reputation at stake. Mine's already —"

"No. It's got nothing to do with your decision about boarders — except that it maybe nudged me in the right direction sooner than I would have gone on my own." She sighed. "I'm not making any sense, am I?" She took a deep breath. Her voice wobbled as she sang, "Uncle Sam ain't a woman and he's *not* gonna take my man. . . ." Her voice gave out and she blinked back tears. "At least I'm going to try to see to it." She swiped the tears from her eyes and cleared her throat. "I have to go home. I can't raise two children on my own. I just can't."

Stella's eyes opened wide and tilted her head. "Two? Oh, honey." Pulling her skillet off the fire and turning down the burner on the sausage, she went to Helen, took her hand, tried to lead her to the kitchen table.

"Come and tell me all about it."

Helen pulled away. "Not now. I can't. I just didn't want you to think it was anything you'd done that sent me out the door." She looked behind her at the suitcase. "But I've got to go — before I lose the courage. I've got to try to get my family — my life — back." She put her hand over her abdomen.

Stella hugged her. Hard. "You know where to come if you need . . . anything," she said before asking, "Does Clarissa know?"

"No one knows. Except Doc Whitlow. And now you." She bit her lip. "I don't want anyone knowing. Not even Hank. Not yet."

"Not even Hank?"

Helen shook her head. "We have to fix . . . us first. If we can't be fixed, then I don't want —" Her voice cracked. "I don't think I can raise two children on my own, but if I can't have my Hank back because of *love* . . . I couldn't bear to have him back out of *duty.*"

Stella nodded. "All right, honey. Whatever you say. Does Clarissa know you're going home this morning?"

Helen shook her head. "She and Pastor Hale will have walked across for church by now. I don't want to upset their morning."

Stella put her hands on Helen's shoul-

296

ders. "Are you sure about this?"

"I'm not sure about anything. Except, if I don't try I'll spend the rest of my life wondering."

"Wondering what, honey?"

"If I did everything I could. If the Hank I fell in love with was in there all the time . . . and I just didn't fight hard enough to bring him back to me. To give my children a daddy."

Stella stood looking into her friend's blue eyes for a long minute. She squeezed her shoulders. "I won't say a word. And I'll light a candle for you at mass this morning." She laughed self-consciously. "I know you don't think that means anything —"

"It means you care."

The women hugged and Helen went to the front door. She picked up her suitcase and then turned around and called Stella's name.

"Yes, honey?"

"Light a dozen candles."

"Consider it done."

How long was it going to be before he stopped having these dreams? Helen having a baby, Helen cleaning house, Helen swimming in their favorite swimming hole, Helen . . . frying bacon? Hank opened his eyes and inhaled. He listened. Someone was clattering around the kitchen. He had to put a stop to Mr. Clark's treating the place like he lived here. It was good to have someone to talk to, but he didn't need a roommate, and some of the old guy's talk lately had been a little too crazy for Hank's taste. He almost wondered if he should say something to Pastor Hale.

Coffee. Vernon Clark didn't even like coffee. Is this what it had come to? Hank Frey and Vernon Clark living like two old bachelors? The idea gave Hank the creeps. He sat up on the edge of the cot and grabbed his work pants, oblivious to the grease stains from the long night of work in the garage. At the base of the attic stairs he paused and called out, "Mr. Clark? Is that you?" before continuing down to the first floor where he closed his eyes and inhaled again, this time catching the lightest scent of . . . perfume?

"No, it isn't Vern," Helen said. "It's your wife." She didn't turn around as she said, "Now go back upstairs and make yourself presentable. Breakfast will be ready in about ten minutes. I'm waiting for the biscuits."

He turned to go.

"Hank," she said.

"What?"

"I'm sorry." Her voice was trembling.

"What?"

"I said, I'm sorry." She turned around and looked at him.

He held his hand up to hide the bad half of his face. "I don't want your pity." He turned away.

"I'm not offering you pity," she said. "I'm apologizing."

He looked back at her with his good eye. "What do you have to apologize for?"

"I didn't get mad enough soon enough."

"I'd say you got plenty mad," Hank said. "You moved out." He dropped his hand, but turned so that what she could see was scarless — mostly.

"I wasn't mad when I moved out, Hank. I was frightened."

He shrugged. "Can't blame you for that. Between the way I look and the way I acted that night —"

"Well, I'm past being frightened and back to being mad." Her voice had a new tremor behind it — of strength.

"So why'd you come back if you're still mad?"

"Because I'm not mad at you. I'm mad at the whole world. The whole blasted bunch of people who are so sinful and so selfish and so lost that they let things like this

299

happen. Wars and rumors of wars that destroy men's lives and tear up everything important. But you know what? I've decided something. The enemy and the Allies and the good guys and the bad guys can take everything I own and everything I hold dear, but as long as there is one breath left in this body they are *not* taking my family.

"People are overseas fighting for freedom and democracy and all those high-sounding words. I can't understand it all, and I never will. How is it that *German* can mean something as harmless and lovable as old Mrs. Koch to us and then become something awful and hideous like Hitler? How is it that one minute children can be playing in the street and the next minute be dead because someone looked at a map and said to drop bombs there? How is it that one minute I can send the only man I've ever loved off to fight for everything I care about and the next . . . Well . . . that's where it ends. I can't stop the bombs. I can't fight the battles. But there's one battle I can fight, Henry Frey, and that's this one.

"I sent a beautiful man off to war and I got back a scarred man who's anything but beautiful to look at. But I am here to give notice to the enemy: I DON'T CARE! I AM GOING TO FIGHT, AND YOU AREN'T

GOING TO WIN. You don't have to look at me and you don't have to visit our bed, Hank Frey. But I'm not leaving and I'm not giving up. I'm going to cook breakfast in *my* kitchen and hang out laundry in *my* backyard and clean *my* house.

"That's who I am, Hank. I am Helen Frey, your wife and Mia's mother. It's the only job I ever wanted. And I'm going to do it, and there's not a single Nazi in this world who is going to tell me I have to stop. So you go upstairs and wash that face of yours, and come back down here and sit across the table from me and drink your coffee. If you want to cover up the scars, then figure out a way to do it. But you will get your behind in that chair and treat me like a human being. This is *my* war we are fighting now and I am *not* going to lose it."

She had begun to cry in the middle of the speech, and now, with tears streaming down her face, Helen whirled around and retreated to the kitchen sink while Hank retreated upstairs. With shaking hands, he washed his face and put on clean clothes. When he came back downstairs and sat at the table, she was waiting to pour him coffee. Her hands were shaking so badly she sloshed it all over the table. How he longed to reach out and hold those hands in his.

But he dared not. He sat so she couldn't see most of the scars.

She handed him the morning paper. "Here. Clarissa says Ben hides behind the sports page every morning. What's good enough for the preacher is good enough for you."

Seventeen

Be ye therefore merciful,
as your Father also is merciful.

LUKE 6:36

The afternoon sun poured through the panes of the dormer window in Aunt CJ's loft, warming Jo to the point of drowsiness and making her golden hair glow with soft light. Aunt CJ had been worried when Jo declined a ride to visit her parents while she and Uncle Will attended a meeting in Crawford — until Jo mentioned a new letter from Johnny. Then, with a knowing smile and a pat on the shoulder, Aunt CJ collected Mia and was gone.

Jo puttered around the house most of the morning, baking enough *pfefferneusse* to fill two half-gallon canning jars, putting a load of kitchen towels and feed-sack aprons through the old wringer washer and hanging them on the line to dry, and all the while leaving Johnny's letter unopened on the kitchen table.

She went to the barn right before lunch and spent a full two hours with Buster, brushing him down, cleaning his already clean feet, handling him for the pure joy of running her hands over his gleaming coat.

"Uncle Will told me that Dieter says you are built for jumping," she whispered in the horse's ear. Buster turned his head and nibbled at her sleeve. "I'd like to know how it feels to sail over a jump with you."

Ned thrust his head across the top of his stall and grunted.

"Sorry, old man," Jo said, and reached out for him. "You want equal time, eh? Uncle Will said that Dieter thinks you're like a tranquilizer for this guy." She patted Buster's neck and then went back to scratch behind Ned's ears.

She sighed. Dieter Brock was in her thoughts a lot these days, and she didn't like it. It wasn't like the man had ever said a word to her. Of course, even if he wanted to, he wouldn't dare, not with Private Romani watching like a hawk to make certain the "Rules for Those Employing Prisoner of War Labor" were followed. Which was funny, because plenty of those rules had been broken in the first few days the PWs were on the place. In fact, when Aunt CJ posted the rules on the kitchen wall beside the back door, she had made it a grand joke.

"Listen up," she had said to whoever might be listening, "because these are things we need to know. Things we would not have thought of on our own," and in a tone of mock seriousness she read, " 'Do not help a prisoner of war escape.' "

She turned around and shook a finger at Uncle Will. "So you stop making plans right now, Will. It's against the rules."

"Now don't be that way," Will said. "It's a serious subject."

Aunt CJ looked at the list again. " 'Do not accept any written communication from a prisoner of war.' " She grinned at Jo. "So you'd just better throw away all those love letters."

When Aunt CJ said that, Jo was grateful she was able to quickly turn back to washing dishes so that no one saw her cheeks grow red. Why she was blushing she didn't know — or at least didn't want to admit.

Uncle Will was not amused. "There has to be rules, CJ. You think you can do better, maybe you should be working for the government."

"I already am," Aunt CJ said. "I'm raising hay for half the remount and employing their prisoners to keep them out of trouble."

"Then you better be following the rules," Uncle Will said.

The rules were making Jo crazy. Even now, as she grabbed a rake and began mucking out stalls, she was reminded how like her Aunt CJ she was. Rules and regulations drove her to distraction.

Do not give a prisoner of war anything. As if, having discovered the key to Buster's antics they were going to stop supplying Dieter Brock with *pfefferneusse.* As if they were going to expect the men to work on the paltry lunch they were provided by the PW kitchen.

"Now you listen to me," Aunt CJ had said when Private Romani first objected to the family-style lunches Aunt CJ and Jo served under the cottonwood trees near the back door of Aunt CJ's house. "If these men are good enough to sweat for me, they are good enough to eat my food. You may call a hunk of rye bread and a piece of meat a decent meal, but I do not. So you just have yourself another pile of mashed potatoes and hush."

Romani hushed. The young private from Brooklyn who didn't know a horse from a house was no match for Aunt CJ. Thinking back on it, Jo wished she knew what it was that gave Aunt CJ such power over people. If she knew, maybe she would be able to get a certain male to break a rule or two and at least acknowledge her existence. Why that was important, she didn't understand, but the fact that Dieter Brock was working with Buster every day and knew the horse better than anyone, just drove her crazy. She wanted to understand what he knew. What secret understanding enabled him to charm Buster into doing those amazing gaits she had observed from the dormer window? It was more than *pfefferneusse*. Of that, Jo was certain.

Coming out of the barn, Jo shaded her hand from the sun and looked up the hill. Being alone on the ranch had always been some of Jo's favorite times, a time to day-dream about the day when maybe, just maybe, she would be Aunt CJ's right-hand "man." Today, she was restless, alternately listening for the pickup and watching the horizon.

The letter on the kitchen table called to her. Sighing, Jo walked across the road. Inside the house, she grabbed the letter and climbed the ladder to the loft. Tucked into her usual spot beside one of the double-hung windows, she picked at the flap of the envelope. Beside her was the fabric-covered box her mother had given her.

"I saved all your daddy's letters in a box just like this one," Mama had said when she presented it to Jo.

"Thanks," Jo had said . . . and hoped she sounded sincere, although what she was really feeling was that tightening of her midsection. The sensation had become familiar. Everyone who knew John Bishop and Jo Hale assumed that once the war was over and "Johnny came marching home," Jo would give up her silly ideas of independence and become the rancher's wife she was born to be. And the closer the world moved to that day, the more often Jo's stomach hurt.

Sighing, she took the newest letter out of its envelope and looked down at Johnny's familiar scrawl.

Air power — that's me, Jo — has destroyed a lot of their transportation system and the war industry. We've put the oil refiners out of business . . . we are only suffering a one percent loss now . . . the tide has turned.

She knew Johnny was right. She had been pouring the PW named Bruno Bauer a glass of milk when a car roared in and Sergeant Isaacson walked over and read the announcement. That had been on Monday, May 7.

> *"The war in Europe has ended. The German Army has surrendered unconditionally. The German Reich has ceased to exist. The German army is no longer bound by the oath of loyalty to the Third Reich. From this point on the wearing of the German uniform is forbidden. The same goes for the wearing of all emblems, insignia, and medals of the German National Socialist Regime. Conduct against these directives will be met with severe punishment. The German prisoners of war in the United States of North America will be returned as soon as necessary transports are available."*

The men had barely recovered from the news that Hitler had committed suicide at the end of April. Of course, they must have known things were ending, but still, Jo would never forget the quiet around the lunch table after Sergeant Isaacson told the men. She could hear the buzzing of a horsefly as it hovered over the table. Bruno Bauer let the tears flow. Rolf Shrader, the clown in the group who could make even

Dieter Brock laugh, sat with his head bowed. Sergeant Isaacson encouraged the men to "look toward the future, continue your good work for these good people, and keep your faith strong."

Aunt CJ grabbed Mia's hand and together, along with Jo and Uncle Will, they left the men to themselves for a while. When Aunt CJ went out and told them she would understand if they didn't want to work anymore, Dieter Brock said they would take Sergeant Isaacson's advice. It would help no one for them to sit idly in their quarters.

It was Saturday now, and as she sat in the dormer alone, Jo wondered what the PWs were doing. Would more of them come to Daddy's service tomorrow seeking answers from God, or would they be angry with Him and leave Daddy to preach to an empty room? She hoped not. She should pray that Daddy would know what to say, but she had not really prayed for a long time. Since Delores left for Fort Des Moines she hadn't even thought much about God. Maybe that was part of her problem.

She looked down at the letter again. Of course she wanted Johnny and all her friends back home. She wanted them safe. She wanted the war to be over and life to get back to normal. Except she wasn't sure what normal was anymore. The war was changing everything. Thinking back over the past few weeks, Jo realized the effects of the war had sent tentacles into just about every area of life in her part of the world. Because of the war, the Frey family would never be the same. Because of the war, Jo's best friend had left Crawford. Because of the war, most of the boys she knew were gone — two were dead. Because of the war, Mama was coming out of her shell and helping down at the Servicemen's Club. She was even friends with Stella Black across the street, which was nothing short of a miracle. Because of the war, Uncle Will had almost left the Four Pines for good. And, because of the war . . . Jo Hale was confused.

Being around Bruno Bauer and the others had changed the way she read Johnny's letters. When he wrote *victory,* Jo saw a destroyed city and wondered about the PWs' families. Dieter Brock was from Dresden. He had confided in Uncle Will that he had not heard from his only living relative since February, when wave after wave of night raids reduced Dresden to a fiery inferno. Bruno Bauer was from Berlin. Johnny said the center was gutted. Rolf Shrader was from Essen. She had seen newsreels at the picture show of the damage. Eventually, she began to dread reading Johnny's letters. She didn't want to know about more German cities reduced to rubble.

Over the past few weeks, the PWs had worked hard and Dieter Brock grew tan beneath the prairie sun, Jo began to long for the end of the war for new reasons. And to dread it, too. Johnny would be *coming* home. The PWs would be *going* home.

As the afternoon sun spilled into the dormer window, Jo leaned her head back against the wall and closed her eyes. Her daydream involved a soldier climbing down off the train and coming toward her with outstretched arms and a beautiful smile. She opened her eyes and looked toward the empty corral. She called herself a fool. The soldier in her dream was not John Bishop.

Clara Joy

I did not like the idea of leaving Jo alone on the ranch all day Saturday, and I did not believe for a minute that she wanted to be alone to pore over Johnny's letter. Jo is like me and she does not *pore* — she *scans.* But whatever it was that made her want to be alone was something I decided to respect for the moment and investigate later, and so

Will and I met Helen Frey at Clarissa's and left Mia there before heading to the school auditorium for a meeting with other ranchers interested in using PW labor. Of course the meeting was after the fact for Will and me, but Captain Donovan had rung me up and asked if we would come to help "allay any fears" in the community. At first I didn't think there would be any fears left. I mean, other work crews have been out and about for a while now, and there hadn't been any trouble. I figured folks would have calmed down. Was I ever wrong.

"I do not know for the life of me what all the fuss is about," I said, after the third person got up and protested. "First of all, Crawford is thriving, thanks to all the soldiers swarming into town for rooms and entertainment. And as for the PWs themselves, if the ten men they sent me are any indication, people have nothing at all to worry about and a lot to be thankful for. They haven't been a minute of trouble, and they've been a lot of help. They've mended fences and begun to build a new corral, and they seem to be grateful for whatever they get."

"If they're so grateful, why won't they eat our corn?" someone called out from the back of the room.

"They think it's for pigs," I said. "Found that out the hard way." I sat down. Of course, that caused some stir when they realized that if I knew the PWs don't eat corn that meant I'd been feeding them. But Deacon Tom was running the meeting and he helped get me out of that spot by changing the subject to reading the pamphlet of rules. Of course, I break those rules just about every day in one way or another.

For example, Dieter Brock has been helping Will with Buster. Will isn't as spry as he once was and Jo seems to have a notion that she'd like to ride Buster — at least once. There are all kinds of competitions and exhibitions in the panhandle every year, and Jo seems to have her heart set on showing off on Buster. I don't think that will work out, but the more sensible Buster is the more valuable he will be to me, so I agreed to the idea of seeing how far Buster would like to go in developing his skills. Getting Brock involved makes sense because the horse likes him. The first couple of days I told Jo that she and Mia would have to stay up at the house for the hour or so that Dieter was in the corral with Buster. I even posted the rules by the back door. But the girl is a lot like me, and posting the rules just seemed to encourage her to find a way to bend 'em. And just a few days later, Jo and Blondie were standing by my side at the corral watching Will watch Brock and Buster. I am old, but I am not dead, and there are few sights more beautiful to behold than a beautiful man and a beautiful horse getting along.

It's more than that, though. I did not want to let myself care about them, but some of these prisoners are likeable. We serve them lunch under the cottonwood trees out back. They are respectful and seem sincerely grateful for the home-cooked food. Bruno Bauer can eat more than any human being I have ever known. He doesn't care what we feed him, he loves it. Rolf Shrader likes fried chicken. Dieter Brock is partial to cherry pie.

Private Romani had a problem at first with Dieter breaking off from the crew and going with Will to handle the horse, but that worked itself out when Jo sweet-talked him into letting Dieter help with *her* horse. I didn't put her up to it. She's got her heart set on showing Buster, so she figured out a way to get Romani to let Brock help with the training. Of course, if Romani knew that Jo and I watch the sessions, that would probably all fall apart.

As for Dieter Brock, he is quiet, but now

315

that I have been around him some, I don't see it as ominous at all. I think he is just careful, especially around women. He doesn't even look at Jo. He will talk to me, if I speak to him. But get him to working the horse — or talking to little Mia — and that handsome face of his lights up. He has a beautiful smile.

Dieter's got Buster behaving on a longeing rein like he was born doing it — the horse, not the man. I almost think maybe Jo wasn't crazy when she mentioned riding Buster last week. But there is no way I will tell her that. I'm not about to risk losing Jo's summers at the ranch by letting her do something crazy. And if Clarissa ever got wind of me letting Jo within earshot of one of the PWs, that's exactly what would happen.

The rule about using German labor that makes me laugh the hardest is the one that says *Do not, under any circumstances, allow women into any field where there are prisoners of war.* I'm real careful about it with Jo and, of course, with little Blondie, but honestly, it's my ranch and no one can tell me not to have anything to do with the men working for me.

In the end, most of the ranchers at the meeting down at the school had good, honest questions. I think the air has cleared and things are going to be all right. The only one I'm not sure about is Vernon Clark. The man just gives me a bad feeling. At today's meeting I had a little speech all prepared, and I finished it with this: "So here's the deal about the Four Pines: I know we are at war. I love John Bishop like he was my own son, and he's over there right now. Hiring these men to work our places isn't anything like 'fraternizing with the enemy.' At worst, it's a necessary evil. At best, it's an answer to our prayers for help until our own boys come home. Don't let your personal feelings interfere with your neighbor's right to run their place the way they see fit. If you are German, the fact is that their fatherland and yours is the same country. And remember that, when it's all said and done, the PWs are somebody's sons and husbands, too. And those mothers and wives love them just as much as we love ours."

Vern Clark wasn't impressed. When he got up it was plain as day that he'd been drinking. "Any of you here seen Hank Frey since he's been back?" he asked. Of course no one had. "Didn't think so." He belched. Didn't even excuse himself. "Well, I have. And I can tell you straight up, if you'd seen

what I have, you wouldn't be coddling the
—" I can't repeat the rest of what he said in
polite company.

Vern Clark worries me.

Eighteen

Now we exhort you, brethren,
warn them that are unruly,
comfort the feebleminded, support the
weak, be patient toward all men.

1 THESSALONIANS 5:14

Lord give me strength. Hank grabbed the newspaper off the kitchen table on Monday morning and opened it wide. If only Helen had known what she was saying a week ago when she handed him the paper and said that if Pastor Hale could hide behind the sports page, so could he. What Helen didn't know was that while Pastor Hale might use the newspaper as a shield against his wife's moods — which were no secret to the citizens of Crawford — Hank needed to shield himself from temptation. Didn't she realize it drove him crazy when she put her hair up like that? He could see the blond streak that grew just at the nape of her neck. And all those little curls. Didn't she know what the scent of her perfume did to him? When she turned

319

around with the platter full of breakfast and headed toward the table, Hank raised the newspaper high.

"Stella and I have to work a little overtime tonight," she said. "Tom Hanson has to stay, too. Something about repairs to a roof that leaked the last time it rained. He said he'd drive us home."

Deacon Tom. Hank pressed his lips together. Who would have suspected?

"They decided they need *two* originals for all those work requests," Helen sighed. "As if we don't have enough to do. Is it all right with you if I go out to the ranch Saturday afternoon? CJ's invited us."

Us. Like they wanted him to grace the table. "Go ahead."

"Are you going to work that night?" she asked. "I could come over after I get back. Let you know how Mia's doing."

"Sure. Fine." Maybe it would be easier to be around her at the shop. Especially if Mr. Clark was there when she came.

"Are you feeling all right?"

"I'm fine," Hank said. He put the paper down and began to eat.

"Because there's a bad flu going around. Can't imagine it this time of year."

"I'm fine."

A horn honked. "There's my ride," Helen

said. She got up and untied the apron.

Hank could not take his eyes off her waist.

She bent to kiss him on the cheek — the scarred side.

He heard the screen door slam shut. Heard the deacon call a greeting. Heard the car door shut . . . the engine rev . . . the departure. He sat at the kitchen table with his good hand curled into a fist.

"Honey, you can't keep this up," Stella said, opening her purse and passing a handkerchief to Helen, who sat crying in the backseat of Tom Hanson's car.

Helen thanked her and dabbed at her nose. "I have to," she said. "I can't think of any other way."

"It's tearing you up." She leaned closer and whispered, "You've got to tell him."

Helen shook her head. "This is what God wants me to do," she insisted. "I know it." She looked out the window, fighting back another round of tears. "If only I can do it." She looked toward Tom Hanson for support. "What's that verse about being strong when we're weak?"

"When we are weak, then He is strong," Tom quoted, glancing at her in the rearview mirror.

"That's it," Helen said. She looked at

Stella. "The Lord will be strong for me. He already has been."

"Sure He has," Stella said, looking out her window. "That's why you blubber all the way to work every day."

"Not every day," Helen said. She inhaled sharply. "Let's talk about something else. How are things at Stella's Boardinghouse?"

"Great," Stella said. "Private Romani is very neat, he doesn't mind helping out once in a while, and he's completely respectful." She glanced at Tom Hanson. "It drives me crazy."

Helen laughed.

"I mean it, honey. He treats me like I'm his *mother*. Even cried on my shoulder the other night when he got a 'Dear John' from some little number named Angelina." She grunted. "I'm not *that* much older than him!"

Helen arched one eyebrow.

"Oh, all right," Stella waved at her. "I am old enough to be his mother. Still, a girl doesn't like to be reminded."

Tom Hanson opened Helen's door first, then went around to Stella. Helen heard him clear his throat before he said, "I was wondering . . . would you . . . could you . . . ? Any chance you'd go to a movie with me?

Matinee on Saturday? It's *Arsenic and Old Lace*. I think I remember you like Cary Grant?"

"Honey, every woman in America that ain't six feet under loves Cary Grant." Stella looked toward Helen, then back up at Tom. "You're blushing," she said. "That's adorable. Completely." She patted his shoulder. "Sure. I'd love to go."

"You . . . uh . . . won't have too much work to do for the Sunday-thing?"

"You trying to back out now that I said yes?"

Tom shook his head. "Of course not. I could . . . help. If you . . . wanted me to, that is."

"I'm frying chicken," Stella said. "Sort of a one-woman job."

"And I'm making the biscuits," Helen said.

"What about trout? Or walleye?"

"What *about* them?"

"Think they'd like some? With the chicken? On the side? I'm going fishing with the preacher early Saturday morning."

"Tom's a great fisherman," Helen said.

"Really?" Stella smiled. "Well" — she looked up at her suitor — "as long as you clean 'em *before* you bring 'em to the house." She held her nose and exaggerated a nasal voice. "Stella doesn't like fish guts by the back door. It bothers the customers." She looked toward Helen. "Ain't that right, honey?"

"Right," Helen agreed.

Tom laughed. "I'll do better than that." He followed the women inside headquarters. "I'll filet 'em."

"You do that, honey. And I'll give you your own little skillet."

As the deacon went out the door, Helen said, "You'll likely have fish filets coming out your ears, Stella. Those men know how to fish."

"Like Deacon Tom is really going to show up," Stella said as she plopped down at her desk.

"What do you mean? Why wouldn't he?"

"Think about it, Helen — a Baptist deacon and a nominal Catholic, if she's anything? And he's going to be with the preacher Saturday morning? If Ben Hale catches wind of this, he will have a fit."

"Don't be so sure," Helen said. "Although you can probably count on a call from the preacher next week."

"Great," Stella said. "Just great. Maybe I'll invite Father Jennings over and the two of them can duke it out for my soul." She balled up her fists and boxed the air.

★ ★ ★

The nights were the worst. Hank left at sundown for the garage. He always went up the alley. Helen always watched him from the kitchen window, hating the way he moved — almost like a thief skulking between the neighbors' garages, hoping not to be seen.

She wasn't afraid to be alone, but she still spent long hours lying awake, listening to the house, hoping to hear footsteps on the back porch stairs . . . the creak of the screen door . . . the now-familiar sounds that would say Hank had come home early.

As light began to glow in the east, she slept lighter, almost as if her closed eyes could see the change in the sky. She always heard the click of the alley fence gate. Her heart would start pounding as she heard him come up the stairs. Sometimes he went to the kitchen first. She'd hear him open the icebox door. Sometimes he sat at the table to eat the cold supper she left every night before going to bed, sometimes he carried a plate upstairs with him. Whether he stopped in the kitchen or not, she would lie listening as he mounted the stairs and passed by her door.

Please, she would think. *Please.*

But he never turned the knob. Sometimes

he paused. If it weren't for that, she wouldn't have any hint that he even missed being married. What they had now was not marriage. It might *look* like marriage to the community. But it was little more than a pitiful ruse. And the strain was beginning to show. Like the crying jag in the car this morning on the way to work. Stella said Helen couldn't go on like this. She was beginning to think Stella might be right.

Helen had been so sure she was doing what God wanted her to do. Not long ago Reverend Hale had preached a sermon on the Israelites leaving Egypt. He described the terror all the Israelites felt on the shore of the Red Sea when they realized Pharaoh was coming after them. Reverend Hale had made the congregation laugh when he held up both his arms and paraphrased God's words to Moses. " *'Who told you to park it?' God asked. 'I said* go. *So* go.' " Helen had taken that sermon to heart. She'd thought God was using Reverend Hale to tell her to go home. So, instead of "parking it" at Stella's, she moved forward into her own Red Sea of raging waters. She came home. But God wasn't parting any waters, and more often than not, Helen felt like she was drowning.

Sure, Hank came to the table and ate with

her, but he still held her at arms' length. He almost cringed when she kissed him on the cheek. He never initiated a conversation. Other than bringing her the money from the shop, he had nothing to do with homelife at all. A particular hurt was that he didn't even ask about Mia. Didn't he miss her?

Mia was still afraid to come home. Helen could see it whenever she went out to the ranch with the Hales. Everything was strained until she heard Helen say, "Daddy said to say hello and he loves you and you can stay at the ranch as long as you are a good helper to Miss Jackson — as long as you come home in time for the beginning of school." Only when Mia knew she didn't have to go home did the smile spread from her mouth to her eyes. Sometimes Helen could literally feel the little girl relax in her arms.

"They that wait upon the Lord shall renew their strength; they shall mount up with wings like eagles; they shall run and not be weary, they shall walk and not faint." Helen was clinging to that promise for all she was worth. There were days when she claimed it every few minutes. There were nights when she felt the baby's featherlight movements and she lay in the dark, her hand on her abdomen, tears rolling down her cheeks. If

something didn't happen soon, she was going to faint because she was weary. Oh, how weary.

She began to leave the bedroom door open. Maybe that would send the message. Maybe then he would respond. Every morning at dawn, she awoke when Hank's tread sounded on the bottom step. In the glimmering shadows of dawn, she hoped. And night after night, Hank paused . . . and climbed the attic stairs.

Hank had barely gotten started on Chase Young's Cadillac when someone banged on the garage door. Hank ignored it. They banged again. Wiggled the doorknob on the locked door. Banged again.

"You want me to get that?" Vern Clark offered from his perch on a stool beside Hank's tool bench.

"Let 'em be," Hank said. "I've got too much to do as it is. And if they don't know how I operate these days, I'm sure not gonna enlighten 'em at ten o'clock on a Friday night."

"Come on," Vern said. "You're under a car. Who's gonna see? Who's gonna care?"

"All right," Hank said. "See who it is. Tell 'em I've got everything I can handle until next Wednesday. Tell 'em to leave the car in

328

the alley and drop a note through the key hole in the door Tuesday night. And get rid of 'em."

When Vern opened the back door, Hank heard an aged female voice exclaim "Eez goot" with a thick German accent. "Praise to God," Mrs. Koch said. "He has brought your business back."

Hank called a greeting from beneath the car. "I am booked solid, Mrs. Koch. At least through Tuesday." He reached for a bracket before saying, "Didn't think you were still driving."

"Twenty years ago they said I was too old. Probably, they were right."

From beneath the Cadillac, Hank heard the old woman tell Vern to get out of the shop. "I have business with Hank that is not yours. You will please go!"

Part of him thought he should do something to stop her from treating poor Vern that way. But part of him could barely keep from laughing at the vision of bullheaded Vern Clark being shooed off his stool by an elderly woman. Hank was tired of Vern, who was too seldom sober and too often ranting — if not against the Germans, then against God. The irony of Vern's being turned out of the shop by a German who was undeniably close to God was too rich.

Hank didn't interfere. Amidst protests, Vern apparently obeyed, because Hank heard the door close and the latch catch. Outside, Vern was hollering something unintelligible.

Mrs. Koch shouted back. "You leave whiskey flask here! Maybe Hank will pound it flat. Go home. Sleep. Pray to God!" In a moment, she said, "Slide out from beneath the car, Henry. I wish to talk to you."

"I can hear you just fine," Hank said. Suddenly the old woman's domineering attitude wasn't so funny. And she was calling him Henry. Just like his mother used to when he was in trouble. He could see her shoes and the tip of her cane from beneath the car. Her ankles were so puffed up they literally flowed over the tops of her shoes. She tapped the side of his leg with her cane.

"I will look into your eyes when I speak."

When Hank didn't move, the shoes stepped away. The cane tapped its way toward Vern's usual perch.

After a minute of silence, Mrs. Koch said sternly, "You cannot outwait me, Henry Frey." She paused. "Come," her voice gentled. "Don't be afraid."

"I'm not afraid," Hank snapped.

"Good," Mrs. Koch said. "Because it makes no sense to fear being seen by an old

330

woman whose husband's face was burned in the *first* war. Before they knew their Tannafex only made things worse."

"I may have only been about five when he died," Hank replied, "but I remember your first husband. He didn't have any scars on his face."

"You speak of Adolph," the old woman replied, "and you would be right. He had beautiful skin. But he was *second.* I am speaking now of Jakob — the first." She chuckled softly. "*Ja. Tree* times I have been married. Is surprising, I know. But I am an *amazing* cook."

Hank smiled in spite of himself.

"My Jakob," Mrs. Koch went on, "oh . . . what a handsome man. Until the test flight when he crashed. Then he was no longer handsome. No ears. No nose. Of course, *you* know what he endured. What you do not know, is what the wife endured."

"I can imagine," Hank said.

"No," Mrs. Koch said quietly. "I think that you cannot. And that, dear Henry Frey, is why I am here."

Hank heard her grunt as she stood up. Once again the shoes appeared in his line of sight. This time, she bent down and grasped the edge of the creeper and pulled.

"Come out, now. If you have a nose, I

have seen much worse. So come."

Was he really going to make a scene and struggle with a woman who was probably ninety years old? And what did it matter, anyway? He did have a nose and ears. Apparently she *had* seen worse. He slid out from beneath the car.

Mrs. Koch didn't pay any attention to his face. Instead, she reached for him. "Give me your arm. Do you see my ankles? Humor an old woman."

Hank stood up and offered her his arm. Together they walked toward the front of the shop where Mrs. Koch sank onto the old gray sofa with a sigh. "Sit," she said to him, patting the spot next to her. Even though the blinds were down, when the streetlight just outside the shop door came on, the room was brighter than what he liked. Instinctively, he raised his hand to his face.

Mrs. Koch caught his hand in hers. "Ah, my dear," she said, "it's all right." She patted the back of his hand. "From me you do not hide."

Still avoiding her gaze, Hank let her hold his hand.

"My dear," she said, "My poor, poor dear." She cupped his scarred cheek in her free hand. "Look at me, Henry. Don't be afraid."

Annoyed, growing angry, defensive . . . Hank glared at the old woman. The list of reactions he had come to expect was long. It included things like horror, fear, pity, repugnance, and one he thought of as "pretend." That was the one where they couldn't stop staring at the scars even while they attempted to carry on a normal conversation.

None of these things shone in Mrs. Koch's gray eyes as she held his face in her hands and said, "I am so sorry for the price you have paid, my dear Henry . . . but oh, how I bless you for it." She let go of his face, and kissed the back of both his hands. "Because of you and others like you, I can worship my God where I please. Because of you and others like you, I am safe today." Tears flowed from her eyes. "You must stop hiding, Henry." She dabbed at her eyes with a handkerchief. "Let people stare. When they see you, they see the price that has been paid for their freedom. Yes, some will *say* stupid things. So you explain you were burned in the war. Yes, some will *do* stupid things. So you walk away. Or you make a joke." She smiled gently. "You say, 'Don't worry. Is not contagion.' "

"You mean contagious," Hank said.

She shrugged. "Whatever. You are smart

333

boy. You will find better words. But you see what I am saying." She smiled at him. "Dear Henry, for every *one* that does or says these stupid things, a *thousand* would get down on their knees and bless you . . . if only they had the courage." She put her hand on her heart. "They feel it here. They don't say it, but you are still the hero."

Hank shook his head. "Don't," he said. "That's not — I'm not — I wouldn't —"

Mrs. Koch finished his thought. "You are not feeling so much like the hero. I know. But you *are*. Don't hide. Let us thank you." When she spoke again, her voice was gentle, the voice of a grandmother advising a child. "You listen to me, now. *Listen.* There are people right here in Crawford who care about you — who want to help. But even better than friends, Henry, is the wife who loves you."

Hank shook his head. "I can't face her." His voice broke. "I love her . . . but . . . LOOK at me!" Hiding his face in his open hands he began to sob.

Mrs. Koch put her arms around him. "There, there, little one," she crooned, "you cry now, *ja*. There . . . there." She waited for him to calm down before speaking again. "Think, Henry — think. If you lose your family and your life, then for

334

what did you suffer?" She nodded. "Take them back, Henry." She held out her hands before her, palm down and made two fists and jerked them toward her as she spoke. "Take them *back*." She patted his knee. "Your Helen was gone for a while. But she is home again. She came back to you. Now it is for you to come back to *her*."

"You don't understand," Hank said.

"But I do. I know she waits for you because she told me. 'I went home,' she said. 'And I will wait for him.' She offers you the gift of her love. Open it, Henry. Take your family back."

"Is that what Jakob did?"

Mrs. Koch sighed. She shook her head.

"Sometimes I think Helen and Mia would be better off if I had died, too."

Mrs. Koch frowned. "You misunderstand. Jakob did not die in the crash. He came home. But he refused to see anyone. He slept in the attic." She paused. Her voice trembled as she said, "And that is where I found him."

"Found him?"

"Dead. Hanging." Mrs. Koch dabbed at her eyes. "Of course, he was dead long before he did that to himself. But as you can see, Henry, all these years later and after two happy marriages, I am still wondering

what could I have done . . . what did I not do
. . . was it my fault?" She waggled a finger at
him. "You have a good woman, Henry.
Love her. Let her help you. Let her keep the
promise she made to God when she married
you."

Hank shook his head. "Even if Helen
would have me back . . . Mia. She's afraid of
me."

"I don't know about Mia," Mrs. Koch
said. "God did not bless me with motherhood." She pointed toward the sky. "But
you can ask Him." She reached out and
patted him on the head as if he were a little
boy. "So much pain, Henry. So much pain.
Make it matter for *something*. Don't give
those —" She paused, seemed to consider,
then used a swear word to label the enemy
before going on. "We are winning the war.
Everyone knows it. But what does that
matter to you if you lose the battle you must
now fight to get your life back?"

Hank was so shocked that sweet old Mrs.
Koch had said a swear word, he just sat on
the couch while she unlocked the front door
and left. He leaned forward and rested his
elbows on his knees, his head in his open
hands. He closed his eyes and ran his finger-
tips over the scars. After a few minutes, he
got up and opened the front door. Up the

street someone had opened the windows at the Servicemen's Club. He could hear laughter and music. He wondered if Helen was working up there tonight. She hadn't said anything about it. But she wouldn't. They hadn't had a real conversation in — how long? He couldn't remember. The thought of her just up the street, laughing — of someone else seeing the dimple appear in her left cheek . . . He closed his eyes against the idea and weariness washed over him. He should go back to work on the Cadillac, but he stretched out on the couch and fell asleep.

He woke at dawn. His first thoughts were of Helen. Mia. His family. And what Mrs. Koch had said. If he lost them . . . then the enemy had won. Slowly, he got up and went to the door. His hand shook as he set the cardboard clock to tell people he would open at 9:00 a.m. on Monday. With his hook, he rolled up the window shades to let in the early morning light.

Nineteen

The steps of a good man are ordered by the Lord: and he delighteth in his way. Though he fall, he shall not be utterly cast down: for the Lord upholdeth him with his hand.

PSALM 37:23–24

Helen sat at the kitchen table trying not to panic. She'd been there since dawn, her ragged emotions alternating between anger at Hank for not coming home and fear that there had been an accident at the garage. She would wait ten more minutes and then — She yelped at the jangle of the phone. More fear. Something *had* happened. She glanced at the clock.

"I fell asleep on the couch in the shop," Hank said. "In case you wondered."

His voice was different somehow. Less defensive, Helen thought. She swallowed the anger. "I was worried."

"I'm sorry. I'll . . . I'll be home in a little while."

"I'll scramble some eggs," she said, preparing to hang up.

"Helen . . ."

She put the phone back to her ear. "Yes?"

Silence. She waited.

He cleared his throat. "I-I'll be home soon."

Helen hung up the phone and tried to calm herself down. She told herself she was reading too much into a phone call. Too much into his voice. He would come home, eat breakfast, and head upstairs to sleep on the cot in the attic. He would hardly look at her. She had to expect that, because she might not be able to stand much more hope. She should just stay in her bathrobe and leave her hair a mess. What did it matter, anyway?

Helen told herself these things all the way up the stairs. She preached to herself as she brushed her teeth . . . combed her hair . . . slipped into the housedress that he used to say made her skin look like peaches and cream . . . and dabbed cologne behind her ears. It wouldn't matter. It wouldn't make any difference at all.

Her hands trembled as she buttoned the dress.

It was 9 a.m. and Hank felt sick. There

was no way he was going to be able to eat breakfast at home. He had a good plan, but as he slunk up the side of the building toward the sidewalk that led to the store's front door, his courage was failing fast. He paused at the sidewalk and looked around the corner of the building. Up the street, a cluster of ranchers was headed into the donut shop for their Saturday morning round of coffee. Sweat gathered on the part of his forehead that wasn't scar tissue as he hurried up the sidewalk half a block and put his hand on the doorknob of the western store. He swallowed. *Lord give me strength.* He opened the door and went in. *Whew.* The store was empty.

"Can I help you?" A female voice rang out from the back. He didn't know whether to be glad or not that he recognized Mrs. Jarvis's voice. "Isn't this a beautiful spring morning?"

"Sure is," Hank replied, feeling awkward. A normal conversation was not something he was used to. "I'm looking for a hat. For my daughter." He went to the wall of hats and stood with his back to the shopkeeper.

"How old?"

"Six. No . . . eight." He shook his head. "I've been gone. Guess I didn't think she'd grow while I was . . . gone." He forced a laugh.

The silence behind him made him uncomfortable. What was it Mrs. Koch had said . . . ? Something about making a joke to put people at ease, even though you were the one who was terrified. "Guess you've heard plenty about me," he said, "but don't worry" — he turned to face Mrs. Jarvis — "it's not contagious."

"Hank?" She looked at him — really *looked*. Her eyes filled with the tears. She came to him and gave him a hug. "Welcome home. It's so *good* to see you." She smiled. "We've lost so many. It's good to get one back."

Hank held up his hook, "Well, part of one, anyway." He shrugged.

The woman patted his shoulder. "If you're getting a cowgirl hat, I presume Mia must be liking life out at the Four Pines."

At his look of surprise, she smiled, "I help out over at the Servicemen's Club on Tuesdays. With Helen." She nodded. "She's so proud of you and Mia. We've heard all about the little cowgirl's adventures."

As the woman reached for a small straw cowgirl hat, Hank frowned. Had he heard right? Did she say Helen was proud of *him?*

"How's this?" Mrs. Jarvis asked, holding up a straw hat with a red strap.

Hank nodded. "I should think that will be just fine."

He had paid his money and was waiting for the package when the door at the front of the shop opened. Two girls came in, stopped, stared. Whispered.

"Good morning, girls," Mrs. Jarvis called out. "Is something the matter?"

One of the girls shook her head. The other could not seem to take her eyes off Hank's face.

When Mrs. Jarvis handed him the sack holding Mia's cowgirl hat, Hank reached for it with his hook. He could see the girls take another step back from him. As he walked by them, he nodded. "Don't worry," he said. "It's not contagious. Unless of course you know how to fly a B-17. Then you might catch it."

The girls looked away.

He left the shop, but paused just outside the door to collect himself. Behind him, he could hear Mrs. Jarvis's voice. Lecturing. He was shaking all over. Looking down at the sack in his hook, he realized that while it had taken guts, it had also taken love. He had both. He just hadn't had them both at the same time in a while. Surviving the injury and all the operations had taken more guts than it had taken to man the B-17. And it was going to take even more courage to re-claim his life. Funny how he hadn't thought about that. He'd had the courage to die. Now the question was did he have the courage to live? He looked down at the sack in his hook again. He had love. If he hadn't completely stamped it out. And he didn't think he had. Helen was, after all, still leaving the bedroom door open. He looked up the street. Even though it was still quiet at this hour, he ducked up the alley and headed for home. As he walked along, he wondered exactly how long it would take for word about Hank Frey's new face to get around town. He jogged home, hoping Mrs. Jarvis hadn't called Helen yet.

"Why would Mrs. Jarvis call me?" Helen asked as she ground coffee for breakfast.

"She said she works with you at the Ser-vicemen's Club. I figure she knows all about —"

"I don't talk about you behind your back, Hank." From the way she said it, Hank could tell she was miffed. This was not the way he had hoped their first almost-normal conversation would go. "Well, I take it back. I do talk about you. I make up all kinds of wonderful things about the two of us." She paused. "It makes things easier."

"I wasn't trying to pick a fight," he said. "I just thought she might want to be the first to tell you."

"Tell me what?" She turned around and looked at him.

He held up the sack.

"I don't understand," Helen said, setting the empty coffeepot down on the counter.

He cleared his throat. "I . . . uh . . . stopped by her store on my way home." He held out the sack. "Take it. I know how to let go."

Helen reached for the sack. Hank released the hook.

"Does that . . . uh . . . is that . . . weird?"

"What?" Helen looked at him. All he could see was confusion in the beautiful brown eyes before she glanced down at the sack.

He inhaled. "Taking something out of a hook like that. I'd think it would be . . . weird. Maybe kind of repulsive."

Helen shrugged. "Actually, I've been wondering how it works."

He showed her. Then he said, "Now take a look. In the bag."

Helen pulled the hat out.

"It's for Spridget. Do you think it's the right size? Mrs. Jarvis thought it would be about right."

"I think so. She'll love it when you give it to her."

He shook his head. "*You* give it to her."

"But —"

He shook his head. "Not yet. I . . ." He sighed. "I want to talk to her. But, I've got to figure out how to explain this." He pointed to his face. "So she won't be afraid."

"She's over that," Helen said, putting the hat back in the bag. "Of course, it would help if she could actually *see* you."

"She deserves to know what happened. How. And . . . that the way I look isn't going to improve much, but that I'm still here — underneath it."

Helen was looking at the floor, her brow furrowed. She swiped at her cheeks. Cleared her throat. "*Are* you?" She looked up at him again with those eyes — those amazing brown eyes.

"Am I what?" His voice was hoarse.

"Still . . . here?" She put her hand over her mouth and looked away, trying — unsuccessfully — to control her emotions.

"Oh, baby . . . I am. But —"

"What'd I do?" She sniffed and reached into her apron pocket for a handkerchief.

"What do you mean, what did *you* do?"

"Wrong. What did I do wrong? To make

345

you so angry. To make you hide — to not want —" She shook her head and gestured around the room. "This . . . us. . . ."

"Is that what you think?" Hank said. He remembered Mrs. Koch's words. Even to this day, the old woman still wondered what she could have done differently. Exactly what Helen was saying now. "Oh, baby. It's not you. It's never been you. It's me. This . . ." He turned away from her. "No woman in her right mind could love or want a man who looks like this."

He felt her come up behind him, press herself against him, wrap her arms around his waist, lay her cheek against his back. He raised his flesh-and-blood hand and laid it over her arm. He wanted to caress her skin, but he didn't dare. He wouldn't be able to stand it if she pulled away.

But she didn't pull away. She held on tighter. "Then," she said, "call me crazy." She stood on her tiptoes and barely managed to reach high enough to kiss the back of his neck just above his collar. "I asked for God's help to know you were still in there. To see the butterfly . . . not the cocoon. Oh, Hank . . . I love you so."

She let go of him and ducked under his arm. She pulled his arms open and tucked herself up next to him with her cheek on his chest and her hands around his neck. She didn't look up at him. His heart quickened. He started to tell himself that she probably couldn't bear to look up. But then he realized this was just the way Helen had always snuggled up against him — her cheek on his chest. He had always had to lift her chin to get her to kiss him. His heart was pounding as he lifted his hand and touched her chin . . . and lifted it. Again, she didn't resist him.

"Let me see you, Hank. Really see you."

His entire body tensed. What an end to an almost-moment. Everything in him screamed no. But he followed her to the kitchen table, sat down opposite her, took off his hat, and let her look. He could not, however, bear to watch. He still had those memories of the tenderness in those dark eyes. He wouldn't trade those for what he knew he would see now.

She began to cry softly as she ran her finger from the tip of his nose, between his eyes, across the bridge of the eyebrow, along the cheekbone, into his hair . . . down the jawline.

"It doesn't hurt," he said. "It's numb mostly. Burns that deep take the nerves, too."

"Shh," Helen said. "Shh."

While he sat, waiting, he thought about

old Mrs. Koch and wondered if this is what she had wanted to do. He was trying. He was frightened. And he was back to the subject of guts and love. When Helen started to cry, he knew he couldn't handle it any longer. The scent of her cologne and the memory of the hug would have to be enough. He raised his hand to brush her away, but she caught it, and then she was climbing into his lap, kissing the scars, crying harder, and finally . . . kissing his mouth. His arms went around her. He jabbed her with the hook and she jumped.

"Ouch!"

"Sorry." He felt so clumsy.

But then she laughed. She wrapped her arms around his neck. And kissed him and laid her head on his shoulder and sighed. "I love you, Henry Frey," she said.

"I love you, too. But —"

"But?" She sat up.

"There are still so many things to figure out."

"I know," Helen said. "And I don't know or pretend to know the answers."

"Mia," Hank said.

Helen shook her head. "I don't know. I think we should ask Ben and Clarissa. Maybe . . . there is someone we can talk to who's . . . Doesn't the army have someone we can talk to? Who's been through this?"

"We'll ask," Hank said.

"We'll figure it out," Helen said.

The phone rang. Helen hopped up and answered it. "Yes," she said, smiling at him as she talked. "Thanks, Mrs. Jarvis. I'll tell him." She had just finished telling him that Mrs. Jarvis wanted to make sure he knew Mia could exchange the hat if it didn't fit when the phone rang again. "Really? Well, if the sign says Monday morning, then it's Monday morning. Yes. Much better. I'll tell him you're bringing in the Buick."

She came back to his lap. "News is out." She kissed his cheek.

"That a monster is roaming the streets of Crawford?" Hank said.

Helen made a face. "That Hank Frey bought his daughter a cowgirl hat — and that he'll be open normal business hours on Monday." She wrapped her arms around his neck. "What happened?"

He sighed. "Mrs. Koch happened." He told her about Mrs. Koch's visit, concluding, "She was right. About everything. After she left, I realized I was turning into Vern Clark. All he does is spout hatred and resentment, and that just makes me sink deeper. I've thought I lost everything for so long. Mia ran away to the Four Pines. You

349

went to Stella's. For a long time, it seemed like Vern was right. The Nazis took everything I had, and people around here were feeding them steak. But then . . . you came back. And you left that door open." He pointed up the stairs.

"But you never came in."

"I couldn't, honey. I wanted to —"

"Do you still?"

"Do I still . . . ?" He read the message in her eyes.

"You don't have to prove anything," Hank said. He looked away.

"Don't tell me what to do, Henry Frey," his wife said. She untied her apron.

Helen skipped Sunday School on Sunday morning.

"You have to go to church," Hank said, nuzzling her cheek and then pulling back the blankets. "I gave this town enough to talk about yesterday just by going into Jarvis's for Mia's hat."

When Helen opened her mouth to ask him to come, too, he put his finger over her lips and tapped gently. "No," he said. "Not yet. Someday. But not yet." He stretched. "But I *will* make breakfast for you before you go."

At church, Clarissa Hale was waiting just

inside the door. She slipped her arm around Helen's waist and lowered her voice. "Thought maybe you'd want to sit with me this morning." Helen looked toward the sanctuary, suddenly aware of the eyes watching her. Apparently the phone lines of Crawford had been buzzing. She smiled at her friend. "God bless you," she said.

Sunday Dinner at Stella's began with a hug and a laugh as Stella said, "All I can say, honey, is thank you for taking some of the heat off me. No one seems to care if I'm housing soldiers or not. Mrs. Bohling hasn't spoken to me since Private Romani moved in. But she flagged me down right after you left for church this morning to ask if I knew Hank had been shopping downtown."

As the days went by, Helen was increasingly thankful for her two girl friends, because things were not easy. People were still stupid, and Hank didn't always tell her about it right away. When he tried to bear it alone, he inevitably withdrew from her, and although she tried to be patient, it hurt her feelings. He resisted the idea of visiting Mia. "It's too soon," he said. But they talked. In the morning, before work, Hank descended to the kitchen and made coffee. He took it back upstairs and they talked. In the evenings, they lingered at the supper table to talk. And each night, lying in one another's arms, they talked some more.

For Helen, it was like getting to know her husband all over again. There were things inside him now that hadn't been there before — negative things, like bitterness and fear. But as they fell in love again, Helen discovered that everything new about Hank wasn't bad. He seemed to cherish her more than ever — and he told her. He savored his food more slowly, took time to inhale the aroma of his morning coffee, and noticed when she filled the planters on the front porch with pansies. He was, Helen decided, a man trying to celebrate life even while he bore the scars of death.

Friday night, one week after Mrs. Koch had invited herself into Hank's garage, the Freys invited her for dinner. "Three steps you take forward," she said, "two you take back. But you don't give up. Two out of three husbands taught me this, and we were happy."

On Saturday, Hank called up Pastor Hale and asked him to stop in whenever he had time. "I know you're busy today . . . but maybe one evening next week?"

But Pastor Hale knocked on the front

door half an hour later, Bible in hand. Helen thought she would burst with love for Hank as he sat on the living room sofa holding her hand, and said, "I want my life back, Preacher. But I can't do it by myself. So I'm listening."

"I will tell you right up front," Pastor Hale replied, "that I don't have any experience counseling wounded veterans. But I've got plenty of experience looking for comfort for myself." He paused, looked at Hank, cleared his throat. "I don't have any visible scars, Hank, but I was in the other one." Helen realized she had forgotten that. Ben Hale was a veteran himself — of what they had called The War to End All Wars. How sad that it wasn't. She saw something pass between the two men. The preacher cleared his throat. He looked down and pulled a piece of paper out of his Bible. "These are the things that helped me. After a while. After a long, long while."

Hank took the piece of paper.

The preacher said, "I promise to pray with you and for you. And I want you to know that I feel very humble right now, that you'd even listen to me after what you've been through."

Helen noticed the preacher's eyes get red as he swallowed and drew in a breath. He cleared his throat. "I'll likely say some stupid things and do some stupid things, but when I do, I'd appreciate your letting me know, and I'll try to do better. I guess that's all I can promise. Humans fail each other all the time. But God never fails." Pastor Hale spread his open hand over the Bible. " 'The grass withers and the flowers fall, but the word of our God stands forever.' That's not just a Bible verse, Hank. It's the truth. The true truth."

Hank nodded. And he asked the preacher to pray for them.

It was early June before Hank would sit out on the front porch with his wife, but when he finally did, the people of Crawford began a parade by the house. They didn't come up the walk, but they made it a point to call a greeting and wave hello. At first, Hank said it made him feel like he was in a zoo. Helen worried that he would withdraw again. But he didn't. Stella came over a couple of evenings. It took her about three minutes to make Hank laugh . . . and Helen cry, because she had forgotten what Hank's laugh sounded like. She loved Stella even more.

Hank said maybe, just maybe, he would go to church soon. "I like a man who doesn't pretend he knows all the answers," he said about Pastor Hale, "but is really convinced that God does." He looked at Helen and smiled. "I think we're going to make it. And . . . I think I may have a way to reach Mia." They were sitting on the front porch. He got up and went inside. When he came back, he handed Helen a handmade book. "Tell me what you think."

When Helen had finished the book, she leaned back in her chair and closed her eyes, clutching it to her chest. "It's wonderful," she murmured. "Perfect." The baby fluttered. She opened her eyes. "Mia can read it to her little brother — or sister — when the time is right."

Hank's mouth fell open.

Helen nodded.

He slid to his knees in front of her.

Trembling, she took his hand and spread it over her abdomen.

"Are you sure?" he croaked.

"I'm sure."

"When?"

"In the fall." She tilted her head. "Is it . . . is it, all right?"

"It's . . . miraculously wonderful," he whispered, and pulled her into his arms. Right there. On the front porch. In front of Mrs. Bohling and anyone else who might be watching.

★ ★ ★

Mia burrowed into the corner of Ned's stall and sighed happily. She loved the way the barn smelled. She didn't even mind the manure smell, which was never all that strong because she and Jo worked hard to keep all the stalls in the old barn clean. Buster and Ned and the other horses had it good. And they seemed to know it. They were happy. Mia could tell. Even now, Ned and Buster were out in the corral, nose-to-tail, heads down, dozing in the sun, lazily brushing flies away from each other's heads the way horses always did.

"How'd they learn to do that?" Mia had asked once when she first came onto the ranch.

"God taught 'em," Aunt CJ said.

Now Mia looked down at the book in her lap. Daddy had written on the cover, *God Teaches Henry*.

Mommy had brought the book out a few days ago. Around the dinner table, no one said very much about Daddy, which was nothing new. Except that something about the way they *didn't* talk about Daddy made Mia think they had things to discuss she wasn't supposed to know about. It wasn't like before, when they didn't talk about Daddy because it made everyone sad. Now it was as if they didn't talk about Daddy because they all had a happy secret. Mia knew one thing was for sure . . . Mommy was smiling more.

Another thing that was different was that Mommy had stopped trying to talk Mia into coming home for a visit. That made Mia wonder what was going on, too. And then, right before she left, Mommy had pulled a big envelope out of her purse and handed it to Mia. "This is from Daddy," she said.

At first Mia was disappointed. She'd liked the cowgirl hat and the boots and the candy and the bracelet. Daddy was good at picking out presents. But when she opened the book and saw it was something Daddy had *made,* Mia couldn't help but pout a little.

Mommy didn't seem to notice. She just kissed Mia good-bye and got in the car with the Hales and drove away. Mia ran into her room right away and read the book. Then she read it again. And again. In less than a week she had it memorized. But she still liked to look at it. She'd brought it out to the barn and put it behind the loose board in old Ned's stall, and in the afternoons, when Jo was talking on the phone or writing letters and Aunt CJ took her nap, Mia liked to come out to Ned's stall and read her book.

Once there was a man named Henry. He

had a wife and a little daughter and he loved them very much. There was a drawing of a woman and a girl and a daddy.

He loved his country, too. An American flag.

Far, far away, a man named Adolph Hitler decided he wanted everyone to do things his way. A Nazi flag.

Henry was afraid. He didn't want to leave his family to fight Hitler. But when his country asked him to, Henry went. He didn't want Hitler to take away people's freedom. A family in jail.

When Henry joined the army, they said he should help with the airplanes. Henry was excited! He liked flying and he felt proud to be helping his country. An airplane with Henry waving out the window.

But one day when Henry was flying, his plane caught on fire. The plane with flames all around where Henry is sitting.

Henry parachuted out of the airplane, but his face and his hands hurt very bad. Henry and a parachute floating toward the ground. Henry's face and hands are black.

In the hospital, a doctor tried to make Henry better. But his skin couldn't go back to the way it was. Ever. Henry felt very sad. Henry's face with a frown and tears.

Henry went home. But Henry is ugly now.

People stare at him. They make him feel very sad. Henry wonders if anyone loves him anymore. Sometimes people are afraid of him just because his face is ugly. This makes Henry feel sad, too. Don't they know he is still Henry inside? He wants to tell them. But he is afraid they will only laugh and say, "Get away from us! You are ugly!"

So Henry hides. A picture of Henry looking out the attic window of his house.

Henry wants to tell his little girl that he loves her very much. He is ugly, but he still wants to swing her on the tire swing. He wants to see her ride horses. He would like to hug her, but he doesn't want to scare her.

So Henry wrote a story to tell his little girl what happened, so that maybe she won't be afraid anymore.

Daddy had drawn a heart at the end of the book. Inside the heart it said, "Daddy loves Mia."

Sitting in Ned's stall, Mia pored over the book. She spent a long time looking at the page with the plane on fire.

Twenty

The sacrifices of God are a broken spirit:
a broken and a contrite heart,
O God, thou wilt not despise.

PSALM 51:17

Dieter was in a nightmare and he could not climb out, so he closed his eyes and waited for it to go away. But it didn't go away. Every time he opened his eyes they were there — the skeletal bodies, the shrunken heads, the barely human forms — some smiling, some weeping . . . alive and yet appearing dead. There were dead ones, too. Piles of them. Open mass graves with bodies lined up waiting for the earth to cover them. He wished the earth would fall on him. Then he wouldn't have to find a way to live with this nightmare.

He didn't know. They wouldn't believe it . . . but he didn't know. Bruno Bauer was sitting next to him in this nightmare in the dark with the flashing lights on the screen at the front of the room. Dieter could hear him breathing, barely controlling the sobs that

racked his body. Rolf Shrader was here, too
. . . and every other German PW held at
Fort Robinson. It was a nightmare, but one
the men must endure while awake. They
had been crowded into the room and told
they were going to see a film . . . so that they
would know what the Reich had done.

Dieter didn't want to know. Not about
this. He hadn't been completely ignorant,
of course. He knew people who disagreed
with Hitler were taken away somewhere. To
labor camps. He knew about the Jews. In
labor camps. But . . . dear God in heaven,
would anyone ever believe he didn't know
. . . about this? Not this. He ducked his
head. Waited for the nightmare to end.
Wondered if he would ever again be able to
look Sergeant Isaacson in the face.

Twenty minutes of nightmare ended. The
film was over. The Allies had freed them all.
Places Dieter had heard of . . . and forgotten. They had been only names.
Auschwitz. Buchenwald. Only names. But
not anymore. Now they were nightmares.
He would have them forever. He deserved
it, he supposed. He had worn that same uniform. What would he have done if he had
known? The questions and the horror and
the shame swirled in his mind as Romani
flipped on the light and the German PWs

were left to sit and think. *This is your army. This is your Third Reich. This is you.*

No, Dieter thought. This is not me. I would never — And then he thought of his little mother. What would he have done, he wondered, if they had threatened to put her in such a place because the son resisted the call to fight for the Reich? What would he have done if they had decided the residents of Dresden were the undesirable elements of German society, not fit to be part of the new order?

The room was silent. He could almost hear the men breathing. Thinking. Trying to absorb such a hideous truth. At Dieter's side, Bruno Bauer was scrubbing the tears off his face while he stared blankly down at the floor. Around him men sat in stunned silence. They were ordered to form up. The sounds of chairs scraping the concrete floor were harsh. Still, no one spoke. No one looked up.

Later, after lights were out in the barracks and he lay looking up at the ceiling, Bruno Bauer called his name in a stage whisper.

"What is it?" Dieter growled.

"What can we do?" the young prisoner asked.

"About what?"

"About . . . that."

Dieter took in a deep breath. "I don't know."

"I feel so ashamed," Bruno whispered.

The words caught in the boy's throat, and Dieter could tell he was trying not to cry. Again. "Go to sleep, Bruno."

"Can God forgive even that?" the boy whispered.

It was too much. "Am I your confessor?" Dieter said. "Go to sleep. If you want to talk about God, ask the minister on Sunday. But for now, go to sleep and leave me alone." Bruno didn't ask any more questions. And Dieter lay on his cot, staring up toward the ceiling, ashamed to be a member of the human race.

On Sunday afternoon, three times the usual number of men filled the pews in the chapel. The pastor spoke of things Dieter had known all his life, only now he drank in the words like a man dying of thirst. *Forgiveness. Mercy. Steadfast love. Never ending. New. Every morning. New.* While his human mind said such good news could not be true in light of the newsreels . . . his broken heart prayed it was.

Jo heard the yells long before she saw the man. It had been a long, hard day for the PWs. Given the chance to work longer than

363

usual and help with a new fence in the west pastureland, the men elected to stay, working madly beneath the broiling sun with relentless purpose. Aunt CJ took them water, filling two old crockery coolers from the well and driving Sadie up and down the fence line while the men toiled. The work was appreciated, Jo knew, but she also knew that Aunt CJ was concerned. The men were quiet. Not sullen, just quiet.

"You'd be quiet, too," Private Romani had said a few days ago, "if you'd just been shown what your army did to the Jews."

For the first time in Jo's life, that she could remember, Aunt CJ had nothing to say. Jo shuddered. The news was just now coming out . . . news that was so horrible her own mind couldn't quite believe it. How, she wondered, could this same sun that shone on the peaceful ranchland she loved so much, also shine on men who did such things? She tried not to think about it. But every morning, when the PWs arrived, it came to mind. *It wasn't you,* she wanted to believe. *You were far away from that. You didn't know. Did you?*

Daddy said his chapel services had doubled in size. The men were quiet there, too. He said he was keeping things simple. Good news about Jesus and assurance that forgiveness was offered freely by the Lord who loved them. He didn't know if any of them had accepted that forgiveness, but Daddy said he had done his best to be kind — and to forgive in his own heart.

And now, someone was shouting. The sun was low in the sky, and Uncle Will's pickup full of silent PWs had driven by the house and disappeared over the first hill half an hour earlier. Aunt CJ had driven into town with Mia to deliver a letter the child had written to her daddy. And so Jo stood at the kitchen sink washing dishes, enjoying the scent of fresh earth and the June breeze, trying not to think about the news, when she heard shouting — in German.

A running man came into view, and she sidestepped away from the sink to where she would be hidden behind the lower half of Aunt CJ's feed-sack cafe curtains. Her heart thumping, she stood with her head down, listening. When the shouting subsided she peered around the curtain just in time to see Dieter Brock snatch the cap off his head and stomp on it. He stood for a minute looking around, then headed for the old well where he hauled up a bucket of water, plunged both his hands into the icy water, and splashed it over his face. He ran his hands through his blond hair and began to pace. Jo could almost see his mind working as he looked down the road, paced, paused, looked up the road, paused. When he started across the road toward the house, Jo's hand went to her throat. The thing she feared — and yet longed for — was about to happen, and she was alternately thrilled and terrified. When Brock hesitated in the middle of the road, Jo glanced toward the door.

She looked at the phone, then through the window at Brock, who clearly did not know what to do. Back at the phone. How could this possibly have happened? Romani counted everyone several times a day. Had he been daydreaming again and mis-counted? Even if that was what happened, why didn't Rolf Shrader or Bruno or one of the other PWs say something? For a second, Jo contemplated the possibility they were all part of an escape plot. Isn't that what the authorities had warned? *Do not think a PW likes you. He does not. Do not think a PW will not try to escape. He will.* But if Brock were trying to escape, he wouldn't be standing in the road right now trying to decide what to do. He'd have quietly sad-dled a horse and ridden away.

Romani. Jo had heard him call Dieter "pretty boy" behind his back. Romani made sure Dieter got the hardest jobs — the least savory. For his part, Dieter always shouldered whatever it was without complaint and without comment. Romani had been especially hateful these past few days since that newsreel had come to the fort. Aunt CJ had even threatened to report him for shoving one or two of the men when they were unloading in the morning or when they didn't do something as quickly as he thought they should. "You should follow your sergeant's example, young man," Aunt CJ had said to Romani. "You were there the same as me when Bruno Bauer tried to talk about that newsreel. You saw how Sergeant Isaacson put his hand on that boy's shoulder and said revenge was God's business and not his."

Romani had seemed to get the point, but Jo never had liked him, and now . . . Had he somehow engineered this to look like an escape attempt . . . just out of spite? She wondered what was done to prisoners who tried to escape. Would anyone believe Dieter Brock over the word of an American soldier?

She looked back toward the phone and the wall next to it where Aunt CJ had posted the "Instructions for Persons Using Prisoner of War Labor in Your County."

367

Number three was clear. *Do not talk about the prisoners of war over the phone.*

Once again, she looked through the window. Brock had put his hat back on. He was walking up the road after the truck. As she watched, he broke into a jog. Fearing that if she thought about it a minute longer she would talk herself out of it, Jo shrugged out of her apron and hurried outside.

"Herr Brock!" she shouted. He didn't seem to hear, so she hurried to the front of the house and cupped her hands around her mouth. "Herr Brock!" When he stopped and turned around, her heart thumped again. After all her daydreaming and all her wondering, the impossible had happened. Here he was. Here she was. And no one to stop them from talking. No one to stop them from anything.

This could not be, Dieter thought as he looked down the hill toward the house. Logic told him he had better run away and fast. But something else tempted him to wait and see if she came closer. If she came closer, he would have a chance to really see her — to really listen to her voice without wondering who was watching and what they would think. He had daydreamed about this happening. Sometimes, as he lay awake in his cot at night, thoughts of her came uninvited. Even now. Especially now. Thoughts of a lovely girl were a welcome diversion from the nightmare. He had told himself a thousand times that thinking about women was pointless and only made him restless. But thinking about this young woman seemed to be something he could not control. And now, here she was, calling after him, with no one to see and no one to object. He was . . . terrified.

As she hurried up the hill toward him, his heart began to pound a rhythm that was unrelated to his short run. Perhaps, he thought, it was fear. For surely he should be afraid. She could say anything and she would be believed. She could ruin him. Nothing positive could possibly come from this moment. He should run. He should. But his feet seemed to have grown roots into the sandy soil. He could not move. Was she walking or floating? Either way, she was moving toward him, that glorious fringe of golden hair shining in the evening sun. . . . *Evening!* He had to get back. He had to do something.

"Stop!" he said, more harshly than he intended, but at the sound of his voice the girl hesitated. "Don't — come — here." He waved her toward the house. "Call . . .

someone. Tell them what has happened. That I am coming."

She kept walking toward him. "Exactly what *has* happened?"

He gestured after the truck. "I don't know. I don't understand. Private Romani sent me into the barn." He waved toward the new barn down by the spring. "He said Herr Bishop needed help up in the . . . where the hay . . . ?"

"In the loft." She supplied the word.

"Yes." He nodded. "In the loft. But when I climbed up there, I heard the truck start, so I jumped down and . . ." He clenched his jaw to keep himself from swearing.

He allowed himself to look into her eyes. For a moment he said nothing, so acutely aware was he of the miracle of the moment as a beautiful American girl stared at him with no emotion other than concern. There was no hint of dislike, no fear . . . only . . . Dare he think Josephine was able to look past the PW painted on his work clothes and see only a man?

"Romani!" she said in a tone that hinted of less than respect. She shook her head, then looked back at the barn.

"You must go back in the house," Dieter said. "Please."

"But you're going to be in terrible

trouble," the girl protested. "And I'm not afraid."

"I know you aren't afraid," he said. "You are, I think, like your aunt — and more likely to load a rifle than run away when you face something you fear. But you are right that I am in trouble. It is I who am afraid." He turned up the road. "If you could please call and —"

"I can't," Jo blurted out. "It's against the rules."

"Rules?"

She nodded. "I know. You haven't read them. One of the rules is we can't let you read the rules. But anyway, we aren't allowed to talk about problems with PWs over the phone." She seemed to be thinking about it anyway, but then she said, "and it's a party line, so I don't dare break the rule. There'd be a full-scale mobilization."

"Party line?" He was trying to picture what a gathering of Americans at a celebration had to do with Josephine calling the fort about his predicament.

She held one hand before her mouth and with the other she appeared to be holding something to her ear. "The phone," she said. "Anyone can pick it up at any ranch sharing the same line." She pointed to where a wire went from the house to a pole

. . . and another pole . . . and on across the hills of sand into the distance. "If I call about you, everyone will know."

"That's bad," Dieter said.

"Yes," Josephine answered. "Very."

"If someone calls *you* . . ."

Jo shook her head. "It's the same. Anyone could listen."

He was wasting time. He had to get moving. "Thank you," he said. "I will go now."

"You can't run all the way to Fort Robinson," she said. "It'll be long after dark before you get there."

"Someone will come," he said. "I must be trying to get back. Maybe there is a chance they would believe me."

"Of course they'll believe you," she said. Her lovely voice had taken on a crispness that, if it was on his behalf, he liked. "I'll tell them exactly what happened. And they'll believe us. Please, wait. I-I've wanted to talk to you. To know about you. Can't you wait? Can't we just . . ."

The nightmare returned. The sadness descended. "Ask me," he said. "Whatever you want." He steeled himself for the questions about the Jews. It would be miniscule penance, but he willed himself to accept it, just as he had willed himself to beg Sergeant

Isaacson's forgiveness a few days earlier. He could only hope this beautiful young woman would be half as kind.

"How did you know Buster was a good horse?" she blurted out. "I saw you that first day at Fort Robinson. By the corral. And you knew. I could see it in the way you approached him. You sensed . . . But how?"

He was dumbfounded. She wanted to talk about horses. Only horses. Thank God — *horses.* He tried to smile. "If only we had met in another place. In another time," he said. "Then I would gladly share with you all that my father taught me."

"Your father?"

"He was the great horseman in our family. From him I learned everything. Because of him I knew to be amazed at Jenny Camp and Dakota, even though when I first saw them at the fort they had been rolling in the mud. They looked nothing like when I saw them back in 1936."

"You *saw* Jenny Camp win that medal?"

He nodded. "My father was there. Riding for the German team."

"How? Where?"

"He died right after that. A riding accident," Dieter explained.

"I'm sorry," Jo almost whispered. She had moved closer to him while he talked, and now, she was standing almost close enough that they could be having a normal conversation anywhere. Almost. She smiled up at him. "Do you have other family?"

"Only my mother." He looked away from her toward the horizon and shook his head. "I don't know if she is . . . alive. I write. She does not answer."

"I'm sorry," Jo said. "Really." She sighed. "War confuses . . . everything." She looked down at the ground. "I hope she's all right."

"Thank you," he said. "And I hope your John Bishop returns home."

Jo jerked her head up and looked at him with a little frown.

His smile was gentle and warm. "Mr. Bishop told about his son at our first meeting. He let me know his own feelings about the war." He took in a deep breath. "And since this news, he has been . . . so kind. I cannot believe that he is so kind."

Jo sighed. "Uncle Will has strong opinions. But he's a good man at heart." She paused and bit her lower lip before adding, "I don't know what to say about that . . . other."

Dieter nodded. He looked back up the road and then toward Jo. "Thank you."

"For what?"

"For these minutes." He looked down

and pointed to the white PW painted on his shirt. "For these minutes when you looked past this."

"I've wished —"

Jo stopped. Her heart was pounding again. He reached out and with the tip of one index finger he touched one blond curl just above her left eyebrow. She closed her eyes. She could just barely feel the curl move beneath his gentle touch. Before she opened her eyes again he was gone, running . . . running . . . up the road, his footprints leading him away from her and toward the sunset horizon.

Vern Clark could not believe his good luck. He'd been watching the Four Pines for days now, formulating his plan, and now the golden boy of all the PWs on the place was about to be delivered right into his hands. He had to clamp his hand over his mouth to keep from shouting with joy. He'd have to hurry. The German was young, and Vern wasn't spry as he used to be. Sliding away from the ridge where he'd been watching and planning, he headed for the pickup he had driven across the hills and parked in a gulley about a quarter of a mile from CJ Jackson's barns.

Vern arrived at his truck with burning

lungs. As he bent over and tried to suck in enough air to catch his breath, he pondered how lucky it was he never went anywhere without his rifle. A person just never knew when he'd have a chance to clip a coyote or two. As he climbed into his truck, Vern grabbed the rifle out of the truck bed and laid it across the dashboard.

"An eye for an eye, a tooth for a tooth," he said aloud.

Dieter swiped at the sweat on his forehead with the back of his hand. Bending over, he tried to catch his breath. His stomach was growling, and he was thirsty. But even through the discomfort, he had to smile a little. From the top of the hill where he stood, the Four Pines Ranch was little more than a dot in the distance. Josephine would be back in the house by now. Her reaction to him had lifted the clouds of shame a little more. Dieter imagined he could see a tendril of smoke climbing into the sky from just about where the ranch house would be. He pictured her in the kitchen. Maybe she was baking *pfefferneusse*. Or maybe she had gone across to the road to tend the horses. She was pretty. Spirited. Lively. Like the heroine in a Wagner opera. *Idiot. What good does it do to think about women?*

Think about your predicament. What are you going to do?

He broke into a lope, discouraged by how quickly it was growing dark. *More running, less thinking.*

There was nowhere to go and nowhere to hide. And someone was coming. On horseback. The moon had risen. Once, Dieter thought he heard a pickup truck, but it made no sense because, according to what Will Bishop had said, the ranches in this part of America occupied vast tracts of land and there were no other roads for miles. Dieter didn't think there was a road in the direction from which he thought he heard the truck. The Sandhills, he concluded, must play tricks on a man's hearing. That had to be the explanation for what he thought sounded like the hoofbeats of more than one horse on the road behind him.

Clara Joy

Will has been telling me for years that I have a lead foot when I drive and that someday it was going to get me into trouble. Of course me being the gentle and easygoing thing I am, I have been telling him for years to mind his own darned business. But that night in early June of nineteen and forty-five, I almost made Will's prophecy come true. Almost. Thank God that Dieter Brock is the horseman he is and that Buster is the horse he is — because I came flying up over a hill and had no time whatsoever to react to the unexpected sight of my niece and Dieter Brock riding horses in the direction of Fort Robinson. And bareback at that.

Of course *they* had heard me coming and had seen the headlights, so it wasn't all that much of a close call. Except for me. By the time I got Sadie slowed down and onto the side of the road, I was shaking all over. Mia, who had been asleep beside me, was sitting up asking what was wrong, and when I couldn't answer her right away — the cat really did have my tongue, I guess — she got scared. So I was busy calming Mia down and didn't even hear Jo and Dieter Brock ride up until they were right at the side of the pickup.

"What in tarnation is going on?!" I boomed.

"Romani tricked Dieter into getting left behind at the Four Pines," Jo said.

"I was walking back," Dieter said. "Since you are not allowed the use of the phones and the celebration line to call for trouble."

"He means we aren't allowed to use, the *party* line to call for *help,*" Jo said quickly.

I was more than a little surprised to see that Buster was tolerating a night out on the prairie with no saddle between him and his rider, but apparently that unseen communication between Buster and Dieter Brock was real, because the reins were loose, and Dieter was relaxed — about the horse, anyway. He was absolutely bonkers about everything else.

As I have said before, I am good in a crisis, so in about two shakes I had Mia behind Jo on her gelding, and Jo and Mia leading Buster back to the house, while Dieter climbed into the truck beside me, and away we went toward Fort Robinson. Dieter Brock was quiet, and I let him be. When Sadie backfired, I nearly jumped out of my skin. I really do need to get Hank Frey to look her over. One of these days, when I really need a truck, she's gonna give out on me, and then I will be sorry.

Twenty-One

Be not hasty in thy spirit to be angry:
for anger resteth in the bosom of fools.

ECCLESIASTES 7:9

They were laughing. It made him sick. Healthy young men driving machinery, bundling, picking up bales and tossing them on the truck, stacking and creating mountains of hay. They had no right to be healthy. No right to be here. Someone had to make a point of it, wake people up — make them see the wrongness of it all. Just watching them made Vern cry for Delmer.

Delmer should be driving that tractor while Johnny Bishop threw bale after bale aboard the flatbed trailer and Ron Hanover stacked them high. Those boys always worked together, and where were they now? Ron buried up on Walnut Hill, Delmer buried only God knew where in Europe, and Johnny . . . Well, who knew where Johnny was? The Pacific, Will Bishop said. He was fine, Will insisted. But Vern knew better.

The world was messed up, and that was all there was to it. The good boys dead or in prison camps while the very enemy that had done it all strode tall and healthy beneath a blue Nebraska sky, baling hay for CJ Jackson.

He'd missed his big chance that night when the golden boy got left behind. He'd been watching the Four Pines, waiting for a chance, and he thought that was it. But then things got too complicated. The preacher's daughter provided the horse, and then CJ herself drove up — and then he missed. He never was a very good shot. It was just as well, though. Now he knew why God let that happen. There was a better way. A bigger way to send a message than killing only one. Thanks to those newsreels about the concentration camps, he wasn't the only one who knew what they were really like.

Of course, people like CJ Jackson and that preacher in town were already talking about forgiveness. Saying that the PWs in Nebraska had nothing to do with that — didn't know about it. Felt awful. Well, Vern thought, maybe they had been quieter than normal for a few days . . . but now they were right back to their old selves as far as he could see.

He'd had to be so patient, waiting for the

sun to do its work first and dry things out. Letting God prepare the fields for harvest so Vern Clark could do his part. Right after the German surrender, the PWs were put on half rations. Vern rejoiced when he heard that some of them had lost a lot of weight. Served them right. But then Hank told him that CJ Jackson said it was wrong for their rations to be cut, and she began feeding them even more, trying to make up for what she called "bad treatment."

It was just one more thing to convince Vern he was right to make an example of the PWs on the Four Pines. Make an example and send every last PW working out on the ranches back inside the barbed wire where they belonged. Hank Frey was the only one Vern had ever been able to get to listen to him, and lately even he wasn't listening too good.

He couldn't blame Hank, though. He had enough troubles as it was. No one could blame him if he said he was done with the Krauts and didn't want to fight anymore. One look at that face and you knew he'd done his share.

It was time, though, for someone to step up and show them. Make them pay. Send the message. The day was perfect for it. He never would have thought he could be thankful for the heat and lack of rain, but all through July, when it didn't rain and the fields got dry and the heat kept on, Vern was glad. And now, sitting here on the hillside watching the Krauts in the field below him, he was ready. And he knew God was on his side.

He wiped the sweat from his brow and took another drink from the silver flask. He waited. The heat and the liquor made him sleepy. That was all right, though. He had time. They had to be gone for lunch before he could do the first thing.

When he first heard how good CJ Jackson treated them, it made him so mad. But now her craziness helped his plan. The PWs were in the habit of old Will Bishop picking them up in the field and bringing them back to the house so they could eat in the shade of the cottonwood tree. At the very picnic tables where the boys used to take their lunch breaks in better times. The Krauts weren't worthy to sit in the dust beside those tables. He laughed to himself. Old CJ Jackson wouldn't be treating them to lunch after today. Nodding happily, he closed his eyes. He had time. Time to wait.

"Hey, Dad."

Looking into the sun, Vernon couldn't quite see the face. "Delmer? That you,

Delmer? Where you been son? They told me . . . told me you were dead."

"I'm gone, Dad . . . but you aren't. You can do it for me. . . . You are doing it. Thanks, Dad."

In the last couple of days, Vern had had trouble telling what was real and what wasn't. Delmer was dead. Delmer couldn't talk to him. But every once in a while, when he nodded off, it seemed like Delmer had things to say. Vern couldn't be sure, but he thought Delmer was the one who came up with this idea. Maybe. Maybe not. Either way, Delmer was pleased with the way things were going. That made him feel good.

Vern started at the sound of a gunshot. The sound terrified him as he wondered if the Krauts were after him . . . or Will Bishop, who had somehow gone from knowing what was right to moving back to the Four Pines. Rolling over on his stomach, Vern separated the tall grass and peered toward the work crew. The old blue pickup must have backfired as she hauled them out of the field. There they went, out of sight. Gone to get lunch. Gone. Gone. Gone.

Vern stood up. His legs were stiff. He stretched and looked around, marking where the baler was parked. Where they were stacking. He nodded while he stood on the hill surveying. With a grunt, he bent down and grasped the handle of the can. He had a long way to walk. A long way to walk and just a little while to walk it. He hurried down the hill. At a certain spot, he unscrewed the lid. He began to sprinkle the dry grass.

Lightly. Lightly. Make it last. Make it last . . . a better blast . . . make it last. He walked along, smiling as he worked. *Smell it, boys? Smell it? That's death. See how you like that. See how it feels to be on fire. What you did to Hank Frey and my Delmer . . . to all the boys. . . . See how it feels.*

By the time the can was almost empty, he was jogging, laughing wildly, pouring generously. When the last drop came out it was exactly as he had prayed. He could lay flat out in the dip in the earth, and they would never see him . . . never see the match . . . never know . . . never guess. The only thing that could be more perfect would be if God let the wind come up. That would transform his creation into a true thing of beauty . . . a perfect masterpiece from a sincere patriot.

When Rolf Shrader slipped off his seat at

the lunch table and fell to the ground, moaning and clutching his head in his hands, Dieter dropped his spoon. "Poison! They poison us!"

Next to Dieter, Bruno Bauer's face went white as a sheet. He bent over and spat his ice cream onto the ground.

Rolf sat up and made a face. He rubbed his head with his hands. "Never mind," he said. "I only ate too fast. Too much cold on a hot day . . . makes the brain . . . freeze!" He popped up off the ground and held out his bowl to Miss Jackson, batting his eyelashes and pleading for more.

Laughter echoed around the picnic tables beneath the cottonwood trees as first one, then another of the PWs who formed the work crew at the Four Pines pantomimed the joke on Bruno Bauer.

When Bruno looked at Dieter, and Dieter shrugged and took another bite of ice cream, his face went from white to red. For a moment, the laughter subsided while the men waited to see if Bruno's red face meant rage or embarrassment. Rage could be a problem in a man the size of Bruno Bauer.

With Bauer leering at him, Rolf shinnied up the cottonwood tree. He was perched high in the tree when Sergeant Isaacson came driving in. "Here comes the infantry," Rolf quipped. "And Isaacson likes me, so you don't dare hurt me."

"I don't want to hurt you," Bruno said good-naturedly. He grabbed Rolf's bowl. "But I do want your ice cream."

Isaacson strode up to the table where the men were seated. Dieter noticed the serious look in the sergeant's eyes.

"I know, I know," Miss Jackson said. "It's all against regulation. But it's hot, and they work hard." She grabbed a bowl. "Sit down, and I'll dish some up for you."

Isaacson shook his head. "It is over," he said, looking around the table with a grave face.

Rolf dropped out of the tree. The men all sat staring at the guard they had grown to trust and respect. Isaacson continued. "I am informed that the Japanese have agreed to unconditional surrender."

"What does that mean — for us?" Dieter spoke up.

Isaacson shook his head. "I am sorry to say it may not mean much, at least for the immediate future. They will begin compiling transport lists, but I haven't seen any. Other than the fact that certain classes are no longer optional, your daily schedule will not vary for now."

Bruno whined. "More classes? What classes?"

"They want us all to be champions of democracy before they let us go home," Rolf said. "It wouldn't do if we all go home and become communists."

"As long as the Americans don't set up some terrible regime," Bruno said, "they don't have to worry." He changed the subject. "Whoever gets home first must immediately visit the families of the others."

"What are the classes we must take?" Rolf asked.

"Knew you'd ask," Isaacson said, and reached in his pocket for a rumpled piece of paper. "We aren't supposed to know. But I sort of . . . found this . . . in the trash." The men around the table applauded. He held up the paper and read, "The Democratic Way of Life. The Constitution of the United States. Political Parties, Elections, and Parliamentary Procedures. The American Economic Scene. Why the Weimar Republic Failed. The World of Today and Germany. New Democratic Trends in the World Today."

The men shrugged. Rolf sighed. "If I promise not to be a communist — if I swear on my mother's grave — will that relieve me from all those hours in a classroom?"

"Your mother isn't dead," Bruno said. "You've been stockpiling soap to take to her. And haircombs."

"The haircombs aren't for his mother," someone else sang out and looked around the table with a grin. "Unless his mother is named Ellie and has the blond hair of our kind hostess." He nodded toward the ranch house porch where Jo had just come out and was heading toward the tables.

Dieter turned his back on her and suggested they get back to work.

Quietly, the men followed Dieter's lead, stacking their used dishes on the tray at the end of the tables and going with Will to the blue pickup truck.

Miss Jackson teased, "You're welcome to lend a hand with the haying, Sergeant."

Isaacson smiled. "I have another work crew to check on in Crawford." He gave a half-salute and headed for his jeep.

"You'll be going home," Jo's voice sounded so near to him, Dieter was startled. Before he could step away, he was looking down into her blue eyes.

She was smiling. "You must be feeling wonderful about that."

Miss Jackson moved toward the two. "You must write to us, and let us know how you are," she said. "I hope your time here

389

hasn't been too awful."

Dieter shoved his hands in his pockets. He took a couple of steps toward the pickup before turning back. "That March day when we climbed down off the train, and it was so cold, I looked at these bluffs looming above the fort, and I thought it must be the most desolate place on earth. Now, when I look at them, they remind me of the castles on the Rhine. When I think of returning to bombed cities and a countryside over which men have stretched barbed wire and barriers . . ." He shrugged and forced a smile. "My country will need good men to rebuild. To find our way out of the mess left behind. I will do my best for her." He glanced at Jo. "But I will never forget you." He nodded toward the old barn and the pasture where Buster was rolling in the dirt. "I thought I might be able to take him over a jump someday soon." He sighed. "The world is turned upside down when the prisoner dreads being free."

Will honked the horn. The men shouted for him.

"Thank you for being so good to us," he said. "Knowing people like you still live in this world helps me realize it is worth trying to rebuild a better one."

Will honked again.

Dieter turned on his heel and ran to catch up with the field hands. Maybe, just maybe the nightmare was over.

Finally, they were coming back. If only there was more wind . . . but the gasoline should help things along. Vern struck the match, smiling as a beautiful little orange flame licked at the first blade of grass, consumed it, advanced, and — *Swhoooosh!*

He backpedaled out of the way so quickly he fell on his backside. He lay on his back looking up at the wall of flame. He could have sworn he saw Delmer in the flames. The boy was smiling.

Dieter had his back to the row of men and was tossing a bale of hay up into the wagon when he heard a loud pop and felt a rush of hot air. He whirled around just in time to see a stream of fire erupt, almost as if it were following a prescribed trail along the ridge looming just above the field.

"Fire!" Someone screamed. For a moment, everyone hesitated.

Dieter was the first to move. Running to the team of draft horses, he grasped their halters and began to turn them away from the advancing fire.

Bruno stood transfixed, watching the fire

391

advance like a soldier paralyzed by fear in the face of an oncoming enemy.

"Go to the truck!" Dieter screamed at him, barely managing to keep on his feet as the horses caught the scent of smoke.

Will had lowered the tailgate and was yelling for the men to climb into the back.

Dieter flung himself up on the wagon and, grabbing the reins, headed the team away from the fire. He heard the truck come to life. It barreled past him as he lashed at the team, driving them out of the field. Up the hill in the distance, he could see the truck skid to a stop at the house. Miss Jackson came out, looked toward the field, then charged for the old barn just across the road from where the truck had stopped. As the team tore into the yard, Dieter caught sight of Jo headed inside the ranch house with Mia on her heels. Throwing his entire body weight against the reins, he barely managed to stop the horses from charging right past the old barn where the PWs were already at work, some hauling empty barrels out and lining them up in the bed of the pickup while others turned on a spigot and began filling the barrels with water.

"Are there more barrels?" Dieter called out.

"Water tanks," Miss Jackson called, motioning back the way Dieter had come with the team. "Down in the new barn."

Dieter yelled for Rolf and Bruno, instructing them to jump into the back of the wagon while he turned the team around. Miss Jackson climbed up beside Dieter, and he lashed at the team and charged back down the hill. Under her direction, they loaded a water tank in the back of the wagon and collected burlap sacks.

When they saw Will heading back their way with the pickup, Miss Jackson shouted to Dieter, "Just do what Will says. Tell him I'm gonna plow a firebreak," she said, and ran for the old tractor.

"Will it start?" Dieter called out.

"God only knows," she answered, then looked up at the sky. "Please!"

Will's pickup shot past, with PWs clinging to the running boards, PWs seated beside Will, as he drove them toward the flames.

"Hello?"

"Mrs. Hale?"

"Yes. This is Mrs. Hale."

"Thought you'd want to know," the operator said. "There's been a fire call. For the Four Pines."

Clarissa set the phone down and wiped

393

her trembling hands on her apron. She stared for a moment at the rows of cinnamon rolls Helen Frey was frosting for Stella's Sunday dinner.

"What is it?" Helen wanted to know.

The women tore off their aprons and ran for the garage, where Hank and Ben had been all afternoon, trying to once again resurrect the Nash.

Dieter and Bruno were climbing into the wagon, preparing to follow the truck into the burning fields, when Jo and Mia ran down the hill.

"Where's Aunt CJ?" Jo yelled.

"Trying to start the tractor," Dieter answered. "Do you know why?"

"She'll plow up the dirt around the house . . . to save it from the fire."

Rolf grabbed Dieter's arm and nodded toward the horizon.

"It'll be here. Soon," Jo said, looking around her helplessly.

"Take Mia back to the house," Dieter said. Just as Jo headed off, he heard the old tractor come to life. It came into view and headed up the hill, stalling halfway to the house. But it was only partway up the hill. Behind them they could see flames licking at the horizon now. Miss Jackson had climbed down off the tractor and was standing beside it, frantically wiggling its parts. Dieter yelled at Bruno to drive the wagon after Will and help fight the fire. "You don't have to know anything," he said. "Just do this." He demonstrated slapping the team's rears with the reins. Bruno nodded. Rolf let out an authentic cowboy "yee-hah!" and the horses took off.

Dieter ran to the tractor.

"Climb aboard," Miss Jackson shouted. "When I say go, see if you can start it. Just pretend it's a truck."

It seemed to take a maddening amount of time for the thing to sputter back to life. When it did, Miss Jackson shouted for Dieter to get the horses out of the new barn. "Just get them out and turn them loose," she said, nodding toward the horizon where the flames seemed to have skirted the firefighters. "I'll get them back."

Will's truck appeared at the top of a hill in the distance, men clinging to the running boards and the back. As Dieter watched, Will Bishop swung the truck around and headed east. Behind him, Miss Jackson threw the tractor into gear and sputtered toward the house.

He tore down the hill and to the corral. Flinging open the gate, he charged into the milling horses, waving his hat, slapping rumps, running about wildly until the last skittish horse, a white yearling, finally darted away. The horses made for the south en masse. Heading into the new barn, Dieter opened the stalls, sending every horse out the wide door in the same direction as the herd.

He ran uphill toward the house where Jo stood on the porch, gesturing wildly up the road. "Help is coming!"

Looking over his shoulder, Dieter realized that help might be too late. It looked like the rest of the men might be surrounded by flames. Miss Jackson drove the tractor into view. She had just completed the last turn around the house. A wide swath of earth ringed the house, but as she headed across the road toward the old barn, the tractor sputtered again and died, right in the middle of the road. Once again, Dieter climbed aboard, and once again, Miss Jackson wiggled this and waggled that. But this time, try as they would, they could not get the tractor started.

The flames marched toward them.

"There's still a chance it'll turn," Miss Jackson said. As she spoke, the truck appeared in the distance, this time driving ahead of the wall of fire, picking men up as it drove in a crazy pattern across the earth. From a distance they could see someone trip and fall . . . two others help him up . . . and another running for his life with tongues of fire in pursuit. The flames reached the edge of the old corral, consuming the aged wood instantly and then beginning to lick at one corner of the old barn.

As Jo screamed Buster's name, a car roared over the hill, drove across the plowed earth and skidded to a stop right next to the house. Four people jumped out. Dieter recognized the pastor and his wife. The other man he had never seen. His mind registered scars . . . and terror on the face of the woman beside him. He turned back toward the barn just in time to see . . . the little blond-haired Mia . . . disappear inside.

The women screamed. The men yelled. Suddenly nothing in the world existed for Dieter Brock but the barn door. He raced through it, into the darkness, toward the screams of Ned and Buster, into the hot breath of death. Flames climbed the walls. Above him, they licked at the shingled roof, then at the first of the massive beams supporting it. Thinking Mia would go to Ned, Dieter headed for that stall. The door was open. He thought he saw Ned's bony rump up ahead . . . but where was the child? He bellowed her name. He begged her to come to him. There was no answer.

Buster was whirling, screaming, banging the walls and door of his stall. Dieter ignored him until the stall door opened. There was a flash of golden hair — and Buster shoved the door aside. He slipped, his hindquarters landing full against the stall door. Dieter ran forward, grabbed the horse's halter, and dragged him toward the wide door, aware that as Buster followed him and the stall door swung wide, Mia's still form crumpled to the earth.

The beams began to fall. One landed between Dieter and Mia. He shoved Buster away, bringing his hands down on the animal's rump with all his might and screaming for the horse to "Go-go-go!" Everything swirled about him. He staggered, then regained his footing and leaped across the burning beam and scooped up the unconscious child. The roof was going — everything happening slowly. Flames and smoke . . . and quiet. Unbelievable, peaceful quiet. He was aware of the roof falling behind him . . . or was it ahead . . . ? Which way to run . . . which way . . . ? He propelled himself forward, not certain if he was running into the flames or away. . . . But there it was . . . a patch of sun . . . light . . . the roof falling . . . blazing beams. . . . With all his might he threw the burden in his arms toward the light.

Twenty~Two

Trust in the Lord with all thine heart;
and lean not unto thine own understanding.

PROVERBS 3:5

Jo clung to the porch railing and watched what was taking place around her as if in a dream. Helen Frey was at the edge of the burning barn, screaming and alternately fighting and clinging to Hank. She would hide her face against his chest and then push away and look at the smoldering remains, all the while babbling "Oh, God, no . . . oh, God, no. . . ."

While those two tried to absorb or avoid what they were facing, Uncle Will drove up with a truck full of scorched men. As they climbed out of or off the truck, one or two stumbled. Others helped them up. They didn't seem to know what to do, and for a split second they stood, reeling, looking around uncertainly.

Aunt CJ took charge. "Here, boys," she said, taking one by the arm, "you come right on up here on the porch. Clarissa, we're gonna need water and lots of it. You all right, Will? Good. Then get some bandages. You can tear a sheet up if you need to. Ben, you help Will."

The new activity roused Jo enough that the memory-film of what she had just witnessed rewound and replayed itself, and as she looked toward the barn she began to tremble. Helen was still yelling into her husband's chest. Jo had noticed Hank before, but she hadn't really seen him, and now that she did, the horror of what might be found beneath the red-hot ruin that used to be the old barn hit her full force. She raised her hand to her mouth to stifle her own cries. In the beehive of activity around her, Bruno Bauer stood motionless, blinking as if just now awakening. His eyes were like candles on a dark night as he rubbed smoke away and began to call Dieter's name.

Aunt CJ went to him. She put her hand on his shoulder and nodded toward the barn.

As the reality of what he was being told sunk in, Bruno roared like an angry bull. He charged the barn, pacing back and forth, calling Dieter's name. Finally, he grabbed the uncharred end of a blackened beam and, roaring with emotion, staggered backward. The effort threw him off balance and he landed on his backside in the dust. He put his head in his hands and began to sob.

Rolf Shrader went to him.

Jo's feet found wings. She ran to the two men, knelt in the dust, wrapped her arms around them, wept, overwhelmed by the awfulness of this moment, the sense of loss. She could not bear to think of Mia . . . could not stop thinking of Dieter.

At some point, Daddy arrived. He wrapped her in his arms. She could not look up at him, but she could feel his body quaking. He was crying, too. She had never loved him more than at that moment . . . when she thought she might have lost her own love.

When the preacher ran out to comfort his daughter, Hank turned away. He became a soldier again, doing what had to be done, not thinking about himself, denying his own feelings in favor of duty. His little girl would never need him again. The searing pain of that reality had to be put away — for now — or he would be of no use to Helen, who was clinging to him, mewling like a stricken kitten.

"Come on, sweetheart," he whispered, turning toward the house. "You come in and lie down. I've got to help these men."

Helen followed him inside. At the doorway she faltered and he swept her into his arms, carried her down the hall and hesitated at the doorway of the room where childish drawings of horses were tacked to the log walls above the bed. Physical pain shot through his heart. He turned away.

"I'll stay with her."

It was Clarissa Hale. Hank lay Helen on the bed in the next room. Clarissa sat down next to her, took her hand. Helen was pale, almost unresponsive.

"She's in shock," Hank said. "Put her feet up on a pillow. Maybe get her to drink some water." He looked toward the hall. "Wish there was a doctor."

"My sister called for help," Clarissa said. "I imagine Doctor Whitlow is on his way. He'll check everything. I'm sure it's all right. The baby will be fine."

Hank bent to kiss Helen on the forehead. He whispered love for her and their unborn baby into her ear. By the time he stood back up he was a soldier again, leaving his charge with someone else, returning to duty.

Out on the front porch, men were coughing, moaning, sighing . . . staring at the smoldering barn. Hank moved among them, hardly aware of their stares. Their burns weren't bad. He was glad for them.

Will Bishop came up. "I don't know much about this kind of thing," he said. "But if you can tell me what to do —"

"That's not as bad as it looks," Hank said, pointing to a forearm. He forced a smile at the terrified soldier looking up at him. "I know it hurts, but it won't look like this." He pointed to his own scars and shook his head no. "You'll be fine. Doctor's coming." Whether it was his tone of voice or the actual words, the man nodded and seemed to relax a little.

Hank moved from man to man, assessing their burns. Most were only superficial. He was more worried about the lungs of the ones who were coughing. "They need the doctor worse than the ones with scorched skin," he said, frowning.

"On the way," Will said. He looked toward the horizon. "Sure wish he'd hurry."

Somehow, her daddy knew not to make her move. He sat with her in the dust and let her cry. When her tears finally subsided enough for her to think of someone besides herself again, Jo reached out and took Bruno Bauer's massive hand in both of hers. Rolf Shrader got up and stumbled back to the porch, leaving Jo and Daddy and Bruno looking at the smoldering ruin of the barn.

Jo saw her first. She dropped Bruno's hand and scrambled to her feet, rubbing her eyes, thinking it must be a dream until she heard Mia crying; Mia, stumbling into view from the back of the barn, sniffing and sobbing as she came toward them.

Jo was the first one to reach the little girl, to fall on her knees before her, to hear the sobbing account. "I wanted to get Ned. And the man . . . he . . . came . . . and he grabbed me up . . . and the barn was falling and he . . . he . . . *threw* me out. He . . . spinned around and around and he *threw* me out — and then . . ." She hid her face against Jo's shoulder.

"What," Jo pleaded. "Then what?"

"It fell," the little voice said. "It fell down."

Seconds later, Jo heard Mia whisper "Daddy?" and Hank Frey pulled her out of Jo's arms.

Bruno Bauer came back to life. He got up and ran around the back of the barn, out of sight. Jo could hear him calling Dieter's name, over and over again. Her tears returned. Shouts of joy over Mia behind her made the disaster before her seem even worse. She closed her eyes, trying not to think. It only made her think more. She looked up at the sky. *Where were you?*

405

What were you doing? You saved Mia. . . .
Why couldn't you save him, too? What
about his mother . . . Bruno . . . Rolf. . . .
They need him. Please. Help.

Bruno was bellowing something. Jo
launched herself toward the sound . . . terrified, hopeful, and — when she saw . . . when
she smelled it — terrified once again.

Ben and Clarissa arrived first. Their only
daughter was seated on the grass crying. She
had lifted Dieter Brock's head into her lap
and was leaning low, whispering to him, ca-
ressing his hair.

"Josephine." Clarissa went to her, and as
Ben watched his wife minister to their
daughter, his heart nearly burst with love.
He would never forget the smell. When
Hank strode up, he heard the man take in a
ragged breath and realized the news would
be bad.

"Is he alive?" Hank asked.

"Yes." Jo looked up at them. "I can feel
. . . his heart, feel . . . his breath." She swallowed hard.

Ben watched his little girl's tears wash a
clear path down her smutty cheeks. At Jo's
side, Clarissa knelt, one hand on Jo's
shoulder, the other on Dieter Brock.

"We need to support that leg," Hank said,

and began to peel off his shirt to be used as a sling. "Especially the foot. The beam must have landed right on it."

Ben wondered if there still was a foot beneath what looked like a blackened stump.

Hank spread his shirt out on the grass. "I'll lift his leg. You pull my shirt underneath. It'll do for a sling to get him to the house." As he bent down he swore softly. "Where's the doctor, anyway?"

Hank looked at Clarissa. "You take Jo and go on up to the house. Have a couple of the men drag a mattress out on the porch . . . to keep him more comfortable. Get some water." He waited for Jo to lower Brock's head to the earth. When Clarissa had pulled Jo to her feet and he was sure they were out of earshot, Hank looked at Ben. "Don't you drop him. No matter what happens when we pick him up, don't drop him."

"What could happen?" Ben said.

Hank swallowed. He looked up at Bruno and then back toward Ben. "Look, Preacher," he said. "I'm not sure if that foot is even going to stay *on*." He nodded toward Bruno. "Wish I could say that in German."

Ben shuddered. He tasted bile and clenched his jaw. He nodded. "All right."

Bruno knelt beside Brock's unconscious form. Hank lifted the leg. Ben slid the shirt beneath it. They did what had to be done. The foot stayed on. The charred skin did not.

Watching her daddy help Hank and Bruno carry Dieter to the porch, Jo once again retreated emotionally. She sleepwalked through the next half hour. She could not understand why they didn't bandage Dieter's leg . . . why they kept it covered and didn't try to treat it. Asking that question was the only thing she managed to say aloud. Hank Frey answered. "We're protecting it as best we can."

The military ambulance arrived. They didn't even move Dieter off the mattress the men had hauled out for him. They picked the whole thing up, put him in the ambulance, and drove away. Bruno Bauer almost self-destructed before Sergeant Isaacson intervened and Bauer was allowed to climb inside the ambulance with Dieter. A medic checked the other men. Jo didn't think he looked very interested in their condition. He waved them toward Uncle Will's pickup.

When Jo moved toward the truck, her mother tried to stop her.

"I'm going," she said.

Daddy came forward and took her arm.

He guided her toward the pickup and climbed in beside her.

"I wish —" Seated between her father and Uncle Will in the hospital corridor, Jo bit her lip.

"You wish what?" Daddy slipped his arm around her shoulders.

"I wish I spoke German," she said, laughing sadly and swiping at the tears that came and went without warning. She cleared her throat. "Bruno seems so sad. If we could talk to him. If you could . . ." Her voice became a hoarse whisper. "Maybe you could say something that would help."

Daddy pulled her close. "All I'd do is pray with him. I don't have any magic words for times like this, honey. Look at me. I don't even know how to comfort my own daughter."

"Oh, Daddy," Jo said, putting her head on his shoulder. "You're doing it."

"I didn't realize —" He cleared his throat. "I didn't know how you felt."

"Neither did I," Jo said. She lifted her chin and looked up at the ceiling. She shook her head. "It's been a muddle. Still is."

"Since when?"

"I don't know. It just kind of sneaked up on me." She looked at Uncle Will. "I'm sorry, Uncle Will. I didn't mean for it to happen. I still love Johnny, too."

Uncle Will patted her hand. "I know you do. Don't you upset yourself about that, now." He stood up slowly and stretched. "I'm gonna get some fresh air. Maybe stretch out in the truck for a rest. You take all the time you need," he said. "I'll take you back home when you're ready."

Jo watched him go, feeling more miserable than ever.

"Don't worry about Uncle Will," Daddy said. "Things will work out. They always do."

"Dieter hasn't done anything . . . wrong. I don't want you to think —"

"I don't," Daddy said. "But I also don't want my little girl to get hurt. And . . . you . . . and him . . . It's impossible, you know."

Jo nodded. She looked toward the hospital ward door, which might as well be a stone wall.

Jo woke with a start, to the sound of creaking hinges and quick steps. She pushed herself upright, off her father's shoulder.

"I didn't realize you were still here, Reverend," the doctor said.

Daddy stood up. Jo followed suit. "I've

gotten to know Brock these past few weeks. He translates my sermons on Sunday afternoons. He's been a good worker for my sister-in-law, as well. I was hoping you'd have some good news for me." He looked down at Jo and put his arm around her again. "For us."

The doctor shook his head. "Too early to know much. It's a bad injury. Broken bones in addition to the burns. We'll do all we can."

"But he's going to live," Jo said.

The doctor shrugged. "As long as we can control infection."

"Can we see him?" Daddy asked.

"That's against regulations."

While Daddy tried to invoke "pastoral privilege," Jo slipped away. She was through the ward door before the doctor could turn around. Ignoring the amazed looks that came her way from the other hospital beds, Jo hurried toward the bed in the far corner of the hospital ward — the one with screens surrounding it. Bruno Bauer sat in a chair fighting sleep. When he saw Jo, he stood up and stepped back, pressing himself against the wall, a silent sentry.

Dieter's face looked deathly pale against the crisp white pillowcase. There was a tent erected above the burned foot. He was too long for the bed. His good foot protruded through the railing. Jo curled her hands around the bedrail, watching him breathe, wondering if he was drugged, thinking he must be.

Bruno said something in a low, and surprisingly gentle, voice. When Jo looked up at him, she realized he wasn't talking to her.

"Jo," Daddy said behind her. He put his hand on her shoulder. "You can't be in here."

"I know," she said, her voice miserable. "I just wish —" Impulsively, she reached into her pocket.

The ward nurse approached with a frown. "You have to leave," she said. "Now."

Bruno stepped forward.

The nurse looked up at him. "Set yourself down, you big galoot," she said in a voice that belied her stern face. "I've spoken to the doctor and told him I need an extra pair of hands."

"So I am medic?" Bruno said in English.

Jo's mouth dropped open. "You . . . ? When did you learn English?"

Bruno's index finger went up. "In America." He nodded toward Dieter. "He is teaching. Is secret. Until now."

"It would seem," the nurse said, "that

412

Frankenstein over here has some medical training. It would also seem that we would have to shackle him to keep him out of this hospital. So we've come to an agreement. I'm the nurse. He's in charge." She chuckled softly under her breath, but then her face hardened. "And you, young lady, are sorely in need of rest. And some respect for rules."

"Come with me, Jo," Daddy said, prying her hand off the bedrail and gently pulling her away. "He's in good hands."

"Good hands," Bruno repeated, holding up his recently scrubbed paws.

"Wait," Jo said, and took something out of her pocket. She showed it to the nurse. "I think it will make him feel better. When he wakes up, I mean."

The nurse frowned. "He can't eat it."

"He won't want to," Jo said. She looked up at Bruno. "From Buster."

Bruno took the *pfefferneusse*. He inspected it with a little frown, raised it to his nose, sniffed, and then understanding lighted his eyes. Smiling, he tucked it in his shirt pocket. "He will know," he said, nodding toward Dieter.

"I hope so," Jo replied.

As they walked the length of the hospital ward and through the door, Jo swiped at her tears again. "If they can have a female nurse, why can't they have visitors?" she grumbled.

"I suspect things will continue to relax as time goes on," Daddy said. "But it's still a prison camp. And she was right. You must respect the rules."

"Do you really think he's in good hands?" Jo asked. "That nurse wasn't all that friendly, even if she did seem to like Bruno."

"I'm not talking about earthly hands," Daddy said.

Jo shook her head. "I don't know that I trust the heavenly ones, either," she said. "God could have turned the flames. He could have —"

"But He didn't," Daddy said gently.

"Why?"

"Sometimes, instead of calming the sea, He calms us."

"That's not an answer," Jo protested.

"It's the Lord's job to rule. It's mine to let Him. We can trust Him to do all things well, Jo — in light of eternity, not in light of our selfish desires."

Jo shook her head. "I can't see it."

"If you could see it, sweetheart, it wouldn't be faith."

As they approached the truck, Uncle Will

sat up. Daddy gave a quick report, and with a nod, Uncle Will started the truck. Jo was asleep before the pickup topped the first rise on the way home.

Twenty-Three

But love ye your enemies, and do good,
and lend, hoping for nothing again;
and your reward shall be great,
and ye shall be children of the Highest:
for he is kind unto the unthankful
and to the evil.

LUKE 6:35

Unteroffizier Dieter Brock tried to fight his way out of the nightmare. Voices swirled around him, yammering nonsense. Just when he thought he might swim through the murk around him, agonizing pain took his breath. He would gasp, and descend once again into an abyss. He visited the desert . . . wandered bombed cities . . . fought battles . . . was part of a throng crowded into a square . . . heard a familiar and yet hated voice screaming slogans. There were gentler dreams, too. His mother smiling over him. A giant looming large in the night, offering him water . . . begging him to eat . . . wiping his brow . . . drying the tears he could not hold back when

416

shrouded figures said they were helping but caused him such agony he screamed and fainted.

Gradually, the periods of consciousness lengthened. Memory returned. And then, one blistering hot August morning, Dieter opened his eyes and asked Bruno about Mia Frey.

Bruno reassured him. "The little *fraulein* is all fine."

Good. That was good. Now he wanted to see his foot. To know what was going to happen. When they would send him home.

"You are in such hurry," Bruno scolded. He claimed he didn't know anything.

Dieter asked the ward nurse, a middle-aged woman built like a battleship, with hair the color of steel and gray eyes that met his without blinking. "You'll have to speak to the doctor about that," was all she would say. Dieter suspected she knew more than she would say, but at that moment in his recovery, her resolve was stronger than his will to argue.

Pastor Hale visited. So did Miss Jackson. Even Will Bishop stopped in, to tell him Buster was settling back down. He reported that Jo had spent some time in town right after the fire, but she was back at the ranch now, working with Buster every day until she left for school. And they planned to build a new barn on the old site.

He dared not ask more. *She is going to school.* That would have to suffice.

So. What had never existed was over. It was time to go home. If only the foot would heal. If only he would be able to walk again.

Hank hadn't counted on all these feelings coming back. He thought he'd gotten past the worst of the memories, but the smells in the hospital room, the tent over Brock's foot . . . and what he knew must lay beneath the clean white sheet . . . brought it all back — longing for morphine . . . dreading the saline baths . . . trying not to scream . . . screaming . . . skin grafting. Hank barely managed not to shudder as he stood looking at a sleeping Dieter Brock.

When Brock opened his eyes and saw Hank, he asked a question in German, then switched to English. "Where is Bruno?"

"Just outside," Hank said. "Making sure I don't do anything wrong."

Brock sighed. "Having Bruno for a friend is not unlike having a faithful shepherd dog at one's feet." He winced. "Are you the new chaplain?"

The flawless English threw Hank. The guy didn't even have an accent. At least not

one you would recognize as German. "No
. . . I . . ." Hank swallowed. "I'm Mia's
father. I wanted to thank you." He looked
down at the bed. "But I don't really know
how."

"You just did," Brock said.

"It's not enough," Hank said. He motioned toward the foot. "Is it bad?"

Brock shrugged. "It is . . . inconvenient. It
keeps me here, while my friends make their
way home."

"Are they taking good care of you?"

Dieter shrugged. "As good as they know
how. Unlike you," he said, "they have little
knowledge of burns."

Hank nodded. He pointed at his own
face. "Hash-browned climbing out of a
wrecked B-17," he said.

"They did much damage to our cities,"
Dieter said. "Sometimes the guards taunted
us with pictures."

The two men stared at each other for a
minute. Dieter broke the silence. "But that
is past now. The duty has been done. One
side has lost, the other has won. Probably
one will be a lot better off than the other.
And the other will have to pay its dues." He
paused before forcing a smile. "I am truly
happy the little one is all right. When the
roof began to fall in . . . all I could do was say

a prayer and throw as far as I could. Toward the light."

Hank looked away. "She didn't even have a smudge on her beautiful little face."

"God is good," Dieter said.

Hank had warred with himself for many nights over this meeting. It was not at all as he had expected. In spite of what Helen had told him about the PWs, he had expected to see the enemy incarnate — a sober-faced, hard-jawed German with hatred in his eyes. Dieter Brock was a wounded young man with nothing in his eyes but pain and what Hank thought might be kindness.

The medic named Bruno came in. "He must have this," he said, wielding a syringe. Brock protested; Bruno insisted. Brock drifted off. His mouth fell open. He began to snore. "He must sleep now," the medic said, and shuttled Hank toward the door.

Hank turned around and pointed to Dieter's leg. "Is it . . . all right?"

Bruno shrugged. "What is 'all right.' I don't know. The doctor does not seem to know, as well."

"What do you mean — the doctor doesn't know?"

" 'I don't know so much about burns, but I will do what I can.' That is what he said." Bruno shrugged. "You Americans have been good to us. It will be what it will be."

"Too old," Jo said, and laid her pink sweater aside.

"Too frumpy," she said, and discarded the straight gray skirt.

"Too plain . . . too baggy . . . too short. . . ." One by one, as Delores watched, Jo deposited most of her clothing on her bed, rejecting each item as being unfit to wear to the V-J Day celebration. There would be a parade, followed by a dance, and in honor of her best friend's visit home, Jo had been given permission to attend both.

Yesterday, after asking permission and hearing the response, she had stared at her mother in disbelief. "You do know it's a dance, right?"

Her mother had nodded and said, "And you do know your father and I expect you to behave appropriately, right? Which, in this case, means no slow dancing with strangers."

"Define stranger," Jo teased. At her mother's look, she laughed nervously. "Just kidding, Mother. And . . . thanks."

"I'll be working in the kitchen at the Servicemen's Club. And Helen and Stella will be there, too. So —"

"All *right*," Jo said. "I get it. You'd think I

was about to elope or something."

It had been a truly momentous occasion for Clarissa Hale to give her daughter permission to socialize with the soldiers from Fort Robinson. But now that she had permission, Jo didn't know if she even wanted to go. She said as much to Delores.

"What's the *matter* with you?" Delores sat on Jo's bed, alternately approving or disapproving as Jo took inventory of her wardrobe. "For the first time in our lives, both our mothers are agreeing to let us go to the Servicemen's Club . . . and it's not just any old party, it's the *end of the war* celebration. Come on, girl, get with it! The Bobby *Mills* Band is playing! They're great!"

Delores leaned down and looked up at Jo's face. She patted her knee. "I know what it is. You're at loose ends. Johnny's coming home, but he isn't here yet, so you're waiting. You can't decide about school or — anything — until he's home."

Jo frowned. "I can decide anything I want. I don't need Johnny telling me what to do. 'Johnny this and Johnny that' — everyone keepings talking about it. It's like we're already married." She ran her fingers through her blond curls. "I wish people would just *shut up* and stop planning my life for me."

"Hey, kiddo, are you having second thoughts?"

"*Second* thoughts? I never really had *first* thoughts. It's always just been assumed. By everyone. Including Johnny."

"Wow." Delores leaned back against the headboard and crossed her arms. "Have you told him?"

Jo shook her head. "I wasn't about to write a 'Dear John' letter to a guy who's off defending motherhood and apple pie." She grimaced. "Sorry. That wasn't very respectful. But I don't know, Delores. I just don't know."

"Have you met someone else since I enlisted? Down at the Servicemen's Club? Or at those chapel services your daddy started? One of the guards, maybe?"

Jo jumped up and began returning clothes to her closet at a furious pace. "Why is it that everyone always assumes a woman is just naturally planning her life around a *man?* Why can't I just go to school and study and come home and run the ranch or join the Red Cross or be a WAAC or move to Germany or do whatever I want?! Aunt CJ never got married, and she seems happy enough!"

"Hey," Delores said, holding up both hands. "Don't yell at me. I'm on your side, remember? Come on, Josephine. . . . What is it? To look at you, you'd think we're going to a funeral instead of the V-J Day celebration."

Jo sighed. "Sometimes I wish I'd gone with you to Des Moines. Maybe things would be less confusing."

Delores studied her friend. "Okay, Josephine Hale. I'm just going to throw out a wild guess here, but I'm thinking this blue mood of yours doesn't have much to do with Johnny. But I'm also guessing — since you are protesting so *very* loudly — that it is about a man." She waited. When Jo said nothing, Delores tilted her head. "It's about him — the guy you didn't want to talk about before I left. Isn't it?"

Jo looked out her bedroom window toward the garden. So much had happened since she planted the rows of snow peas. They were long gone, replaced with hills of pole beans. By the time the pole beans were harvested, Jo would be in Lincoln attending classes at the university, and Dieter Brock would be . . . gone. How quickly a person's life could change. Sometimes she almost felt old.

"Is he *still* him-who-you-can't-talk-about?" Delores asked.

"I probably shouldn't," Jo sighed. "I

don't know. I just can't seem to take it all in. Ever since the fire . . ." She shook her head. "I'm confused."

"About what?"

"Everything," Jo said.

"Try to be more specific, honey," Delores said.

"You sound like your mother, *honey.*"

"Some people think I *am* my mother," Delores quipped. "Down at the Servicemen's Club last night Mrs. Fosdick called me Stella more than once. She's a hoot. All sweetness now that I'm wearing this," Delores spread her hands out like a fashion model.

"You look great in that uniform, by the way," Jo said.

"Thanks. You want to hear something funny? I *love* the army. I'm not kidding. I love it. They are going to have to drag me out of the service kicking and screaming."

"I'm glad you're happy," Jo said.

"So . . . is this an attempt to get me off the subject of your true confession?"

"For now," Jo laughed.

"Touché," Delores said. "But it's time to decide. Are you going to the parade with me or not?"

"I thought you'd be *in* the parade," Jo said.

Delores shook her head. "Nope. I'll be at the club all morning making coffee and serving up your mom's cinnamon rolls — how many hundreds has she made, anyway? — and then I'm solo for the parade. So, I repeat — are you going with me or not?"

Jo nodded. "Sure." She pulled on her pink cashmere sweater and turned around so Delores could button it up the back.

"Do try to smile, honey," Delores said. "We did win the war, you know."

Hank Frey donned his full dress uniform. He had yet to make peace with mirrors, so Helen straightened his tie.

"Calm down, sweetheart," she said. "The parade is to celebrate the victory, and you are the best trophy of victory this town has." She kissed him on the cheek. "You've won over all kinds of enemies — foreign and personal."

"I'm a trophy, all right," Hank muttered, "a trophy of fear." He put his hat on. "There. Not that it helps any."

"What's a fee-a-fear?"

Hank wheeled around to face Mia. "What'd you say, Spridget?"

"What's a fee-a-fear?"

"Fear," Hank said. "I'm nervous about the parade."

"You're scared people will stare. Like you said in your book."

Hank nodded.

"I'll hold your hand," Mia said. "I'll walk with you. Then you don't have to be afraid." She slipped her hand into his. "All right?"

"You can't be in the parade, sweetheart," Helen said.

"Why not?"

On September 2, 1945, Crawford, Nebraska, joined the nation in celebrating the victory over Japan. Flags flew all over town. Helen Frey draped their entire front porch with red, white, and blue bunting. Stella Black wrapped her porch railing with patriotic streamers. Together, Helen, Stella, Delores, and Jo made their way downtown.

They viewed the parade from in front of Hank's Garage, alongside Mrs. Koch, ensconced in a chair brought for her by Reverend Hale just for that purpose.

Mrs. Koch rose to her feet as the last surviving Civil War veteran passed by, waving from the rear seat of Virgil Harper's Model T Ford.

Egged on by her friend Stella, Mrs. Reverend Hale forgot herself and blew a kiss as Ben passed by, head and shoulders above

427

most of the other veterans of the War to End All Wars.

And Helen stood on the curb with tears streaming down her cheeks, as the town hero, Hank Frey, strode along, with his daughter in his arms and a smile lighting up his scarred face.

Twenty-Four

Trust in the Lord, and do good. . . .

PSALM 37:3

It was the apathy underlying her daughter's compliance that worried Clarissa Hale more than anything. "She just isn't herself," Clarissa said to Ben one evening.

"I know," Ben teased, "she's been far too easygoing."

"Don't joke," Clarissa said. "Something's wrong. But I can't tell what. She *seemed* to enjoy our visit to Lincoln. She *seemed* to be happy about the plan for her to stay out at the ranch through the fall to help CJ and Will recover from the fire. She helps me bake cinnamon rolls for the Servicemen's Club every week. She spends time with Mia. I know she hears from Delores because she tells me her news. But it's all so . . . completely without enthusiasm."

"Honey," Ben replied, "for most of Jo's life the two of you have been in a constant state of turmoil. So I can't help but wonder about the fact that it's *now* — when Jo is doing exactly what you ask, including cooking and sewing — that you're worried?" When his wife didn't reply but only sat on the porch looking at him, Ben frowned. "All right. You may have a point." He filled his pipe. "You want me to talk to her?"

"Well, she's not going to confide in me," Clarissa said.

"Now, honey —"

"I'm not whining. That's just the way it is. And you know it." When her husband didn't respond, Clarissa said, "She got a letter from Johnny today."

Ben puffed on his pipe before asking, "So what's the news from John?"

"I don't know," Clarissa said. "She hasn't opened it yet. It's still in there on the buffet."

Ben frowned. "I'll talk to her tonight."

"Thank you, dear," Clarissa said.

Ben stood up and stretched. "Need to run a little errand out at the fort." He bent over and kissed his wife on the cheek. "Won't be late."

Gone to have coffee with Stella. Pineapple upside-down cake in the oven. Share a piece with your father when he gets home.

430

Mother had paper-clipped the note to Johnny's letter.

"All right," Jo muttered, plopping down at the kitchen table. "I can take a hint." She ripped the letter open.

"You don't seem overly eager to get John's news."

She looked up at her father, who was standing in the doorway, car keys in hand, watching her manhandle Johnny's letter. Jo sighed. She pointed to her mother's note. "It says here I'm to share some pineapple upside-down cake with you." She stood up, went to the oven, and pulled out the cake — which Clarissa had already inverted onto a plate.

"Makes my mouth water," Daddy said. "Just look at that caramel."

"I'll cut you a piece," Jo said. "But . . . could you get it over with?"

"Get what over with?"

"Whatever the trouble is I'm in," Jo said.

"What makes you think you're in trouble?" Daddy sat down at the table.

Jo shrugged. "Mother's been like a detective looking for clues to a murder mystery for the past few days."

"We're both concerned about you. You haven't been yourself." He took a bite of cake. "Only difference between your mother and me is, I think I know what's wrong."

"I don't know what you mean."

"I think you do," Daddy insisted.

"I'm just . . . tired. I spent most of the summer entertaining Mia. Then the fire. Now I can't start school right away."

Daddy nodded. "I know. It's a confusing time to be alive for everyone."

He rattled the car keys. "Let's go for a ride."

"Now?"

"Nice night for a ride. Beautiful evening. Full moon. Fall air." He stood up. "Come on."

"It's all right, Jo," Daddy said. "It took some convincing, but Captain Donovan approved it. One time only. And we don't make it a topic of conversation in town."

Jo slid out of the front seat of the Nash and followed her father. Just inside the hospital front door, they were met by the same nurse Jo remembered from weeks ago. The woman had nearly chased her out of the hospital ward then. Now she met them with a grim smile and a nod.

"What happened to her?" Jo whispered as they followed the woman down a corridor and up a flight of stairs.

At the top of the stairs, the nurse turned around and faced them. "What happened to me," she said, "is watching your father with these men. Knowing he has a good heart. And trusting that he's not a complete fool."

Jo pressed her lips together. She could feel herself blushing. "I'm sorry. I didn't mean for you to hear that."

"It's all right," the nurse said. She led them down another hallway and outside a door. "Ten minutes," she said, looking intently at Daddy.

"We understand," Daddy said. "Thank you."

With a nod, the nurse was gone, and Jo was following Daddy into Dieter Brock's room.

He looked better than she expected. Almost better than she remembered. He was tired, but the blue eyes were smiling.

Jo smiled back. She had daydreamed about what she would say if she ever saw him again. But now those things seemed silly. Trivial.

Daddy stayed by the door. She could feel him watching her. He cleared his throat. "You two can talk, you know."

Dieter nodded. He smiled at Jo. "Buster is all right?"

Jo nodded. "I-I'm going out to the ranch

on Sunday. To stay for a few weeks. Until I go away. To the university." She bit her lip. "We're building a new barn. Where the old one was. The men — Rolf and the others — they helped clear the site."

"Rolf told me," Dieter said.

Quiet again.

"Miss Jackson and Mr. Bishop are well? And John? He comes home soon?"

"Everyone's fine," Jo said. She didn't want to talk about Johnny. Not with him.

"They are taking me to the East," Dieter said. "To another hospital. Then home."

Jo nodded. "That's good." *That's awful. I don't want you to go.* She swallowed. "It's healing, then."

"Thanks to your friend."

"My friend?"

"Mr. Frey. He made the doctors call all the way to England. He paid for the calls."

Daddy spoke up. "Hank came out to visit. Thought Dieter would benefit from a second opinion. He arranged to have the doctors here consult with a Dr. McIndoe — the doctor in England who treated Hank."

"I-I didn't know that," Jo said. *God bless Hank Frey.* "So everything will be all right. You'll be able to ride again. When you get home."

He nodded. "And finally I have heard from my mother."

"That's good."

This was awful. She thought it would be wonderful. It wasn't. It was too hard to look at him and think she'd never see him again. Too hard. Tears were pressing against her eyelids. She reached up and swiped at the corner of her eyes. She cleared her throat. "I . . . I hope —" She broke off. What could she possibly say, when all she wanted was to feel those arms around her. Just once.

"We'd better be going, Jo," Daddy said.

"Thank you," Dieter said to Daddy. "For this."

Daddy put his hand on her shoulder. "Say good-bye now, Jo."

"Good-bye." It was a whisper — all she could manage without bursting into tears.

"God be with you," Dieter said, "blessing you and keeping you always." He faltered, swallowed, then grinned at her. "Give Buster the *pfefferneusse* from Dieter."

Jo nodded. She turned to follow her father out of the room, but at the door, she turned back. Rushing to Dieter's bedside she took his hand. Leaning down, she kissed his cheek. "Come back to me," she whispered, and fled the room.

"What do you mean you are going to send a Christmas package?" Will scolded. "You don't even know if Dieter is home yet. For all you know, he's still in that hospital back east. For all you know, his mother has moved. For all you know —"

"Just hush up and find me a box," I said. So Will grumbled and complained and went and got a box. I filled it with soap and combs and all the kinds of things Tom Hanson said the men had been buying up to get ready to go home. There were only a few hundred PWs left over at Fort Robinson by Thanksgiving, which is when I got the idea to send a little Christmas spirit overseas.

I sent the package to the address Dieter had left with Ben. And even though I didn't get an answer, I sent another one a few weeks later.

Johnny came home at Christmas. With a war bride from Japan! Now how is that for a surprise? Will and I were both just plain flabbergasted, but it didn't seem to bother Jo one bit. I have finally realized that everyone's expecting that they would get married was just that — everyone else's plan, not theirs.

Johnny and Kim Su moved to Omaha so

Johnny could go to engineering school.

Jo began her studies in Lincoln at the beginning of the new year.

And in the early months of 1946 we finally heard from Dieter Brock.

My dear American friends,

Your wonderful and generous packages have arrived and with each one my mother claps her hands with joy and blesses the Americans who were so good to her son. I wish to thank you for everything you did for me that gives me a hope-filled future. Even though I have left the land that is the most free under all the sun, still I carry with me the memory of your kindness. I think that if more of my comrades had come into contact with persons like you, it would be better for all the world. You showed a high measure of tolerance for us, and you did many things to lighten our burden.

Please greet the beautiful Josephine for me. I hope that her studies are going well and that she is still making friends with Buster. I have many regrets, not the least of which is the reason I was in America, but there is also the regret that I will not see Buster through all of his training. You asked my advice, and I say yes, he has the heart to be a fine jumper. Josephine also has the heart. She only lacks the skill, which can be learned.

Your friend,
Dieter Brock

Will and I were drinking coffee on the front porch one spring morning, listening to a meadowlark make a racket. I was feeling mighty satisfied with having the new barn up and three mares in foal to Buster when, out of the blue, Will set his coffee cup down and started talking about the fire.

"I don't think I will ever be able to get the picture out of my mind of you riding that tractor and it dying on you." He shook his head. "I've had nightmares about what might have happened if the wind would have blown a different way."

I have never heard Will Bishop talk so fast. I think maybe he'd been practicing. Anyway, all of a sudden he took his hat off and said, "Just how'd you like to prove what an old fool I really am? Marry me. I love you, old gal. I should'a asked you every day for the last twenty years until you said yes. And that's the truth."

For a minute I thought of saying something snappy, like maybe he was touched in the head with spring fever. But for once in my life I zipped my lips long enough to use my head, and I realized that you do not turn a man like Will Bishop down twice in one lifetime. Not unless you are a complete fool. And I am not that. Although, I guess I do fool around now and then — when it's just Will and me.

Twenty-Five

*Wait on the Lord: be of good courage,
and he shall strengthen thine heart.*

PSALM 27:14

Summer 1947

"I just don't want to be a teacher," Jo said. She looked across the kitchen table at her mother. "I tried it your way for almost two years, Mother. Can't I *please* transfer over to the Ag College for my junior year?" She paused. When her mother said nothing, Jo added, "You can't change a zebra's spots."

"Zebras do not have spots, Josephine," Mother said.

"And I don't have what it takes to be a teacher."

Daddy spoke up from behind his newspaper. "You played right into her hands, Mrs. Hale."

Mother sighed. Finally she said, "Reverend Hale, there are monumental decisions being made in this kitchen, and I would appreciate your putting that newspaper down."

As Daddy lowered the paper, he winked at Jo. Mother spoke up, pretending to be upset. "You two have already talked about this, haven't you?" She looked from husband to daughter. "Sometimes I wonder what other secrets you've kept from me over the years." She sighed. "All right, all right. I give up. I never could do anything with either of you."

Jo jumped off her chair and did a little dance in the kitchen before bending over to kiss her mother on the cheek. She headed for the back door.

"Where are you going?"

"To tell Aunt CJ!" she said.

"You could call, you know," Mother said.

"Huh-uh," Jo shook her head. "This is too good to be shared on the phone."

Jo climbed the ladder to Aunt CJ's dormer, a fabric-covered box that had once held John Bishop's letters tucked under one arm. The box still held letters — nearly two dozen signed *Your friend, Dieter Brock* — letters Aunt CJ kept for Jo to read whenever she was at the ranch. Not once had Dieter complained, but between the lines of what he said, Jo read the truth. It was a struggle to get enough to eat. He talked of learning to eat new things and deciding that rich foods were not good for him. New clothing was almost impossible to find. He made it a joke . . . thanking God for providing through his mother's ability to remake the old and mend and make things last. He called Fort Robinson his "golden cage," because of the abundance of food and the warm barracks.

They laugh at me, but I tell them I have seen one of the finest places in the world to raise horses, with excellent grass and water, and terrain that develops great strength and substance and wind in the horses that live there. . . .

His foot had required grafting and surgeries. Some of them had been less than perfect, but he said he walked without a cane and only limped a little. He was going to church. He was doing office work again. His knowledge of other languages kept him in demand. He was managing for himself and for his mother. He was philosophical, talking about how things that men had meant for evil, he could now see God using for good. Even things like his injury, which he said ended up giving him the friendship of a wonderful American family and hope for the future.

Jo's heart thumped. Was he talking about her? Was he sending a message about the future . . . and what she had whispered to him that night in the Fort Robinson hospital?

Summer 1948

The horse beneath her lowered its head and planted its front feet, watching every move the jittery cow made. Whether they won or lost the event, it would be mostly up to Bruno — the heavy-boned quarter horse who had earned his name when Uncle Will called him a hulk, and they all ended up reminiscing about the PW named Bruno Bauer and wondering where — and how — he was. Jo held the reins, but the horse was really in charge, and they both knew it.

After a long summer of hard work with Jo in the saddle, Bruno was proving his mettle. As the cow bawled and took off in a desperate attempt to rejoin the herd, Bruno whipped around and prevented the reunion. The crowd roared its approval. Jo took off her hat and waved it toward the place where Mother and Daddy, Uncle Will and Aunt CJ, and the Freys stood applauding and cheering. *Miss Josephine Hale,* the paper

would say, *astonished the judges at the for-*
tieth annual Fort Robinson Gymkhana
today, by winning the cutting contest
astride her registered quarter horse,
Bruno. Miss Hale's victory was made more
impressive by the reputation of the assem-
bled contestants, among them some of the
best known riders in this part of the state.

January 1949

It was funny, Jo thought, how a person could work and work toward a goal and finally reach it and then . . . still feel like something was missing. She wondered if it would always be this way. She had a tendency to take on things just to prove a point, and even when the point was proven, it didn't satisfy. In her head she knew that she was supposed to trust God's plan for her future, but lately the sense that she might never be happy was beginning to haunt her.

Johnny and Kim Su Bishop were expecting their second child. Hank and Helen Frey, their third — after giving Mia a baby brother three years ago. Even Aunt CJ had a man to love her. Now that they were married, Uncle Will seemed to be trying to make up for all the years they'd been too stubborn to admit they loved each other.

Mother had written that he bought Aunt CJ a gift every time they came to town. He'd bought himself a new suit and seemed to honestly enjoy squiring her to church.

Delores's mom was engaged to Tom Hanson — and had become such a radical Baptist she had alienated half her old friends by asking them if they were saved. Jo could just hear her, "Listen, honey, I thought I was all right with Jesus, too. But you know how it is. Sometimes a girl just has to wake up and think for herself. And I've gotta say, if you're trusting anything but Jesus to get you in, you're out. And out, honey, is a hot, hot place." It would be just like Stella to single-handedly start a revival in Crawford. But while Delores's letters had expressed disdain for her mother's new-found devotion to God, Jo's mother wrote about how happy Stella was, and how de-voted Tom Hanson was to his bride-to-be. Everyone, it seemed, was doing great.

Sometimes Jo caught herself thinking "what if." It was a bad sign to be twenty-three years old and be wondering "what if" — as if your life was over. When she felt that way, she gave herself a pep talk. She told herself to work harder at school. It was going to take her an extra year to get the degree she wanted, thanks to Mother's insistence that she start as an education major. But that was all right. Jo had never been afraid of hard work. She would graduate summa cum laude. She would, once and for all, throw away the letters and put the past behind her, where it belonged.

She had no one to blame but herself. She had sent him her address in Lincoln. And Dieter had written. Seven letters just for her. Seven letters — and then no more. To her. He had continued writing to Aunt CJ, who talked about him sometimes when Jo visited home. But Aunt CJ didn't offer to let Jo read the letters anymore, and Jo didn't ask. It would hurt too much. Aunt CJ seemed to understand.

And so Jo kept her worries to herself and her goals before her: Train Bruno to be a champion cutting horse. Graduate summa cum laude. Throw away Dieter's letters.

By the summer of 1949, she had accomplished two of the three.

June 1949

When the train slowed at the Crawford station, Jo already had her cosmetic case in her hand and was waiting to jump down onto the platform.

"Where's Mom? Is everything all right?"

446

She hugged her dad with a little frown of concern.

"You know your mother," Daddy said. "Always looking for an excuse to show off. She's arranged a little graduation party for you."

"I told her she didn't have to," Jo said.

"And she didn't *have* to. She *wanted* to. Let her show you — in her own way — that she's proud of you."

"No matter *what* my degree is in?"

"No matter, honey," Daddy said, smiling. "We're just glad you aren't marrying a rancher from Wyoming and taking off for the mountains."

"Not a chance," Jo said. "He told me learning dressage was a waste of time and steeplechasing wasn't a real sport." After retrieving Jo's luggage, they made their way toward the street. Daddy stopped beside a tan Chevrolet and opened the door. "Don't tell me —"

"Yep." Daddy nodded. "The Nash finally gave up the ghost." He closed the door and walked around the car. "This was Mrs. Koch's car."

"Then it's a good one," Jo said. "I bet you got a good deal."

"Very good," Daddy said. "She gave it me." He winked at her. "The Lord provides." He patted her hand. "Welcome home, honey. Aunt CJ and Uncle Will can't wait for you to come out."

"I'm ready to get to work," Jo said. "I told Aunt CJ I'd be out after church on Sunday. If you can take me?"

"I can take you," Daddy said. "But I think we'll just go on out there tonight if it's all right with you. Your aunt CJ is very excited about you coming home."

"She isn't coming to my party?"

Daddy shook his head. "No. Something came up."

Jo tried not to be hurt. After all, Uncle Will and Aunt CJ weren't getting any younger. Soon she was surrounded by the Frey family, Stella and Tom Hanson, and what seemed like half of Crawford. Home again. Life was good.

"What do you *mean* she's hired a new foreman?!" Jo spun in the seat and looked at her father in disbelief. She sat back. "No wonder she didn't want to come to my party."

"Now, Jo," Daddy said. "Before you jump to conclusions —"

"I'm not jumping to conclusions," Jo muttered. "I completely understand Uncle Will's wanting to slow down. But they don't need anyone else. They've got me." She

448

tried to keep the tears from falling and failed. "What do they think I've been studying my brains out for?"

"It'll be all right, honey," Daddy said. "You'll see."

When they drove into the Four Pines, it was nearly dark. As always, when they came up over the last hill and looked down into the low spot where the ranch nestled between two spring-fed ponds, Jo felt something give way inside her. Finally, she could breathe. The moon was full. Jo sighed.

" 'Trust in the Lord with all your heart,' Josephine," Daddy said. " 'And lean not unto your own understanding.' "

If Daddy was quoting Scripture at her, Jo figured things were going to be challenging. As soon as he pulled up to the ranch house, she grabbed her suitcase from the car and went inside, where the scent of Uncle Will's aftershave and the joy in Aunt CJ's eyes mitigated her disappointment.

"So," Jo said, setting her suitcase down, "Daddy tells me you've hired a foreman."

CJ nodded.

"Before he starts, can I at least make a case for my —"

"He's already started, honey," Aunt CJ said. "Last week."

The tears welled up again.

"Now, before you get all upset with us," Aunt CJ intervened, "we all think you should meet him." She looked at Uncle Will. "Didn't he say he'd be checking on Buster's leg this evening?"

"Buster's leg? What happened to Buster? You didn't tell me anything about —"

"Why don't you just go on over there and see for yourself," Uncle Will said.

"Hello?" Jo called out as she entered the new barn.

Buster nickered.

"Is anyone here? Aunt CJ sent me out here to meet —"

But they had met. And she had been haunted by those blue eyes ever since.

"H-how?" Jo asked.

"An American sponsor," Dieter said. "And forms, and applications, and appeals. And a thousand prayers answered yes, to re-unite Mama with her brother in Chicago and to bring me here."

"Who?" Jo answered her own question. "Aunt CJ."

Dieter shook his head. "*Nein.* In truth, it was Mr. Bishop who signed my documents. He assured the authorities I would be a good citizen."

"You stopped writing."

"I was too much —" He stopped, put his hand on his heart. "Afraid. If everything ended with *no*."

"When you stopped writing . . . I thought about that night in the hospital . . . I thought you might be laughing at me . . . that maybe those letters were just . . ."

He stepped close. "Never." He reached up and touched the curl at her left temple. "A thousand times," he said, "my thoughts have rushed across the ocean, over the railroad tracks, and toward the prairie. A thousand times they have found their way to these hills of sand . . . and to a barn where there is the scent of fresh hay and a beautiful bay stallion with great dark eyes and an appetite for *pfefferneusse*. . . ."

"So that's it," Jo said with a nervous laugh. "It was the horse." As if on cue, Buster thrust his head over the top of his stall door and whickered. "He wants his treat," she said.

"He," Dieter whispered, "will have to wait."

Rise up, my love, my fair one,
and come away.
For, lo, the winter is past,
The rain is over and gone.
SONG OF SONGS 2:10–11

About the Author

A native of southern Illinois, **Stephanie Grace Whitson** has lived in Nebraska since 1975. She began what she calls "playing with imaginary friends" (writing fiction) when, as a result of teaching her four homeschooled children Nebraska history, she was personally encouraged and challenged by the lives of pioneer women in the West. Since her first book, *Walks the Fire*, was published in 1995, Stephanie's fiction titles have appeared on the ECPA bestseller list numerous times and been finalists for the Christy Award, the Inspirational Reader's Choice Award, and *ForeWord* Magazine's Book of the Year. Her first nonfiction work, *How to Help a Grieving Friend*, was released in 2005. In addition to serving in her local church and keeping up with two married children, two college students, and a high school junior, Stephanie enjoys motorcycle trips with her family and "Hills Angels" church friends. Her passionate interests in pioneer women's history, antique quilts, and

French, Italian, and Hawaiian language and culture provide endless storytelling possibilities. Contact Stephanie via her Web site, *www.stephaniegracewhitson.com,* or at 3800 Old Cheney Road, #101–178, Lincoln, Nebraska 68516.